HE leaned away from her as she stood up from the bed, averting her face. He sneered his disbelief. "I know not what game you play, chit, but I trust you not."

"What game is there in it? Pray, how can such an offer be yet another trick?" Cassie asked in impatience.

"Divorce is not readily available to us," said the viscount. "I have my family name to think of . . . and there are reasons that make it difficult. . . ."

"Yet I offer it freely . . . and know this: you represent the end of all I ever wanted from life. *Your wife?* 'Tis a mockery of all I have ever cherished. I hate you, with every beat of my heart, I hate you . . . and I warn you, my lord . . . never, ever will you bed me again!"

CASSANDRA

Claudette Williams

FAWCETT CREST • NEW YORK

*Dedicated with appreciation
to my editor, Barbara Dicks*

CASSANDRA

Published by Fawcett Crest Books, a unit of CBS Publications, the Consumer Publishing Division of CBS Inc.

ISBN: 0-449-23895-4

Printed in the United States of America

10   9   8   7   6   5   4   3   2   1

1

Last days of May, 1819

"Let's wind it, Starfire!" It was a command, though softly spoken, yet for the flame-tinted stallion a command all the same. He took his mistress's left lead, bounding forward into a steady canter, every muscle in perfect harmony with the rider astride his back.

Starfire was a beauty of a steed—proud and spirited as the lady who loved him. His mane flowed like a red wave, just a hint darker than her free-flowing cinnamon tresses. He brought his ears forward expectantly, preening beneath the lilt of her musical voice.

They took the open glen, riding into the cool morning breeze, smelling the scent of spring blossoms, leaving the sun at their backs, exulting in the sense of freedom. Both were creatures of nature, both with needs, yet the lady's needs had been passed over. Not so Starfire. He had been given his feed, his stable was awaiting his return, and his mistress was on his back. Starfire snorted with contentment as she slowed him to a trot, making for the narrow woodland path. The lady's full rosy lips curved at the sound of his exuberance, but her pale green eyes were lost in thought. She gazed on the surroundings of her heart, but something was missing, and the sigh that escaped her spoke volumes.

Cassandra Farrington was well liked by her tenants and neighbors. Now Farmer Hubbins looked up from his cycle and watched as she approached. He raised his hand in a greeting that was genuine. "Ho there, Miss Cassie! Fine day we been given." His deepset eyes traveled over her faded blue riding habit and he felt an inward pinch of annoyance. 'Twas a sin, he thought, the way her own blood treated her . . . and her a fine lady . . . born and bred true . . . not like that wife the present squire had foisted on them. Well, she was gone now, that one . . . and 'twas not his concern . . . he had his farm and his own family . . . but still he had loved old Squire John and his son after him . . . and knew it would break their hearts to see their beloved Cassie so ill-treated.

Cassie gave the farmer a warm smile but declined to stay and chat. She had not missed his wandering gaze and the accompanying frown. She felt her pride sustain a pinch as she thought of her guardian. With a toss of her curls, she forced her thoughts away from her shame and focused her attention on her projected excursion.

Cassandra Farrington was impulsive by nature and had escaped the house this morning to avoid her guardian and the guest he had brought home only last evening. The thought of the two men brought a nervous chill to her spine and, unconsciously, she hurried her horse over the dirt path. The cool breeze tickled her face and played with the curls above her forehead and ears, but her fine, dark brows were drawn together by the intensity of her musings. Everything was so different . . . had been so different since Farrington Grange had gone to Cousin Charles.

"Oh, Starfire, how long will it go on like this?" she asked, bending low over her horse's neck and pressing her cheek against his smooth silkiness. The stallion's ears twitched. He was enchanted by her voice. It was strangely

6

calming and exciting all at once, and he only wished she would go on speaking to him. With her shoulders well laid back and her knees hugging his flanks she looked no less magnificent than the prime blood she rode, yet her appearance at this particular stage of her life meant little to her.

As she approached another clearing she brought up her horse, sending him into a canter and giving him his head. She had to run, to banish all the unhappiness from her thoughts, somehow make them—if not vanish—at least subside for a time. "Oh, faith! How I wish I were anywhere but at Farrington Grange!"

It was startling to hear such words from her own mouth. For as far back as she could recall, this had been the home she loved. The Grange, her parents, her brother . . . they had been her all. But then, typhoid had come, leaving her to Jeremy, her older brother. And then it was 1815, Napoleon had escaped from Elba, and Jeremy went to meet him at Waterloo.

It happened so quickly. Life turned upside down, and in the midst of her heartache came the family solicitors. The Grange was no longer her own. How could it be? Her father, her brother, they would never have allowed her to end in such straits. Oh, but it was explained. Her parents had never thought that their son would die before providing for Cassandra. The Farrington Estate could not go to a female while a male Farrington was living. Cassie's father's cousin, Sir Charles Farrington, had come to claim his rights as squire of all his holdings. An ancient entailment quite overlooked in the past—yet one that stood nonetheless. At sixteen she had found herself totally helpless and under the auspices of Cousin Charles and his wife, Esperida.

The day they had arrived to take up ownership was vividly etched into Cassie's soul. Jeremy's body had been sent home for burial in the family vault, and Cassie had attended the funeral with a heavy sense of loss. He had forgotten about the title entailment to the estate, for he would never have gone off to war and left his young sister so ill provided . . . he had never thought he would not be there to see her married. But Cassie was not thinking of this as she saw him being buried. She only knew she was alone in the world, divided from all those dear to her. She returned to the quiet of the library, attempting to make sense of it all, when the doors opened and she looked up to find the new squire and his bride upon the threshold. They entered and Charles took up a chair at the Oriental desk beside the window and began thumbing through the papers prepared for his signature. His young wife cast her eyes about the room, planning the changes she would make, when her dark eyes glanced over Cassie's quiet form. Even at sixteen, she was already giving indications of great beauty. Her hair then, as now, was long and flaming bright. Her dark lashes and winged brows framed light green eyes, and her skin was creamy smooth. Esperida saw this and pouted. She was herself an attractive beauty, tall, dark, and with ambitions above her station. She disliked having such a beauty in the house.

Esperida's gaze hovered over the young girl calculatingly until her jealous eyes spied a gold heart-shaped pendant trimmed with very fine diamonds hanging from Cassie's delicate neck. She went to it and fingered it as Cassie stared in puzzlement. She noted the initials of Cassie's parents inscribed upon it before she allowed it to drop. Then quite suddenly she turned and pursed her lips thoughtfully, calling her husband's attention. "Charles . . . did you not say that all the Farrington jewels were to be mine?"

Her husband brought his hazel eyes up from the sheaf of papers and looked adoringly at his wife. He was a young man, dark and not unattractive, whose faults lay in a weakness of character. He had little moral fiber and an abundant devotion to his alluring wife. "Eh . . . jewels? Yes, of course, darling. They are all yours," he said absently, returning to the papers in hand.

"Then your ward flaunts both the dictates of the entailment and your own instructions," said his wife waspishly.

"What's this?" he asked raising his eyes once again, this time with some casual interest. He had scarcely noticed his ward since their arrival a day ago. He had cared little about his cousin, John, even less about John's son Jeremy, whom he had seen but once or twice. And he had no interest whatsoever in Cassandra.

His wife pursued insidiously. "She wears my jewelry without my leave, Charles!" She gave her short black curls a toss and stamped her foot for emphasis as Cassie's jaw dropped with open disbelief.

"Nay!" cried Cassie rising to her feet. "This is not part of the family collection," she said, holding it in her closed fist. 'Twas my mother's . . . and I wear it as a keepsake. Surely . . . it has no value to you."

"You will not address me so rudely, and I shall be the one to judge which of my gems has value or not," snapped the woman, avoiding the pain in Cassie's eyes. She turned to her husband. "Charles darling . . . she is upsetting me with all this bickering . . . after the ordeal we have been put through. You will exert your authority . . . "

He rose and joined his wife, taking her hand and putting it to his lips. "Of course, my pet, don't allow this to fret you." He turned a hardened expression to Cassandra. "Really . . . did not my late cousin teach you to respect your elders? You will give my lady the piece she speaks of—at once!"

Cassandra had always been strong-willed. This came from the indulgence of doting parents and then the protective though easy relationship she had enjoyed with her older brother. She was angry, incensed with their cruelty and blatant disregard for her sensibility. She had no intention of giving over anything she considered her own. She had given enough. Her answer came quietly and without fear. "No, Cousin Charles. This pendant was my mother's . . . it is now mine."

Sir Charles looked at her with some surprise. He had not expected any real trouble from this quarter, and he was startled as well as irritated to have his will resisted in the presence of his bride. "My dear girl, you have no choice in the matter. I am your guardian as well as your

9

cousin, and as such you will obey me or find yourself very much the worse!"

"I could not find myself in any worse straits than I already am. I shall retain what little is mine until I come of age and the small competence my father was wise enough to set aside for me comes into my hands. Your lady has the Farrington jewels, but she shall not have this piece!"

He took an angry step forward and his hand reached out, but Cassie had anticipated such a move and rushed out of range, her voice lowered in a strangely threatening pitch for a girl of her years. ". . . and if you are so unwise as to try to take this from me, I shall bring legal action against you. Mark me . . . you have inherited the Grange, but I well understand the terms and know what you may and may not take from me. If you dare to molest me in this, it will be heard throughout the county, and your lady will not be readily accepted into the World she aspires to enter!"

"You brazen doxy!" growled her guardian as he stepped forward, unhampered by her threat, and landed her a vicious blow across the cheek. He scarcely felt his wife's restraining hand, keeping him from further action until she cooed his name softly to attend her.

Esperida had already weighed the girl's words and knew they rang true. She had every intention of taking her place as the county's leading hostess. It would not do to antagonize the local gentry, for they were sure to have a ready sympathy for the orphaned girl.

"Stay, Charles . . ." she murmured quietly, bringing his eyes round to her own. "It is rather an ugly piece after all. Let the chit keep it. I should not have you bothered over such a paltry thing. Come . . . walk with me in our gardens." She assuaged his ruffled pride, for his heat was up and he was inclined to pursue the matter, if only to show the chit she could not deal so with him. But the call was in his bride's eyes and he followed.

Cassie watched them go, her cheek still smarting. She felt her first wave of despair . . . and hate. It whipped at her heart and found the emptiness left there by the loss of all her loved ones. And Cassie wept.

Remembering this now, Cassie hardened and once again spurred Starfire into a faster gait. Starfire . . . a gift from Jeremy. A Spanish stallion brought back from the wars with Boney. Esperida would have had him, had the horse allowed any but Cassandra upon his back. But he would not, and Starfire remained one of Cassie's few treasured possessions. Four years—it had been a difficult time of growing, and Cassie had never thought it could degenerate. It had though. Unexpectedly, things took on an ugly hue, bringing Cassie's world still further down.

Life with Esperida had been uncomfortable, thorny, and subtly unpleasant, but it had turned into a nightmare without her. Cassie had served as a whipping post for Esperida's moods. Then quite suddenly the squire's young wife showed signs that she was with child. Ruefully, Cassie had often thought it would be a strong whelp and even looked forward to the day, for she sensed a bit of softening in the woman. However, neither Esperida nor the babe survived childbirth.

Esperida had been gone more than a year, and her loss was keenly felt. When she lived, she had kept up appearances, allowing Cassie some of the necessities her position required, but these all vanished with Esperida's death. Sir Charles became a man demented—a creature worthy only of contempt. He turned to drink and even opium—to bring him the sensation of his wife's body in his arms; and when he was sober—which was more and more rare—he was like a man crazed with fever. Cassie's only comfort was that he chose to spend most of his days in the hells of London.

In the past year, the estate had gone badly. His drinking, his need for pipedreams, and his gambling had cost him much. His visits to the Grange were infrequent, and his guests were few. And then last night he had brought a stranger with him to Farrington Grange.

Cassie's mind wandered back to her first vision of the

tall, handsome stranger. He was powerfully built and when he doffed his top hat and inclined his head, an abundance of iridescent blue glinting in his black waves caught her eye. Then he raised his head and she met those eyes—black and piercing—and was reminded of a stalking panther. She watched Lord Kirkby Welford quietly as her guardian introduced him and caught the expression of contempt his lordship held for Sir Charles. No friend this one, she thought to herself. So . . . why is he here?

She found his black eyes appraising her beneath his thick dark brows and though naturally reticent before strangers, she felt uniquely drawn to him. Once again she met his black eyes . . . and froze beneath their hardness.

Viscount Welford had watched the lithe beauty cross the polished oak floor, her faded blue muslin swinging as she came in answer to her guardian's call. His brow arched slightly to find her light green eyes open in shy solemnity, and he marveled at the innocence he saw there. However, his gaze then shifted to her hair. It fell to her waist in a cascade of cinnamon gold, while short curls framed her piquant, heart-shaped face.

Cassie had an instinct for people. Had his gaze not hardened upon her, she would have found a liking for the stranger taking root in her breast. Instead, she felt suddenly frightened. She gave him her hand nervously, greeted him missishly and felt her guardian sneering at her side.

"Damnation, chit! We want none of your maidenly airs! His lordship and I will be in the library, and since . . ." he glanced over her derisively, ". . . you have nothing more to offer, you will see that we are left undisturbed—until such time as you are called!" He turned to Lord Welford and indicated the room across the hall with a gracious hand.

Cassie watched them go. Lord Welford turned just before he stepped over the threshold of the library. His gaze once again swept over her, and his black eyes were unfathomable! It was then that she made up her mind to it. She would avoid them both if she could. She pleaded illness at dinner and remained in her room with only Meg to bring up a tray for her. Then this morning, she had escaped before either man was about. There was only one to whom she could go and pour out her fears; and it was to Jack Rattenbury she rode.

2

He was a tall, athletic man,
Well formed to stand in battle's van;
His raven curls appear'd below
The calpac that conceal'd his brow;
And to that swarthy, sun-tanned face
Did lend a wild peculiar grace
Such is the man who plough'd the deep—
Whose eye was rarely known to weep.

Such was writ about Jack Rattenbury, known to his intimates as the highest ranking smuggler in Devonshire. Cassie had become acquainted with the fellow many years ago when she and her brother were sailing off the coast of Dorset. They had been caught in a squall and washed overboard only to be taken up by the smuggler's galley.

His thatched, white cottage stood on the crest of a hill, half hidden by the budding trees, and she felt her heart lift as she made her way towards it. He was nearly twice her age, but in his own simple way he had endeared himself to Cassie, and he had much good sense.

She reached his small garden and stabled her horse before making her way to his small front door. She burst in, a smile upon her lips to find him stretched across his cot. Her entrance brought him to semiconsciousness and his hand jerked sharply, leveling a gun at Cassie's chest. He blinked and then in spite of the lovely vision standing before him, gave out with an oath. "Lordy, woman, you gave me a queer start bumping at me like that! And besides . . . that ain't no way to come upon a cull . . . could've been in the altogether . . . and then *you'd* have yerself a toss!" She tilted her head innocently, her eyes full of inquiry, for of late Jack was forever throwing such talk at her, and she sensed it alluded to things she had no knowledge of as yet. Heedless of his rebuke, she went to him and flung her arms about his lean body, overlooking the fact that he was naked to the waist. She never stood on ceremony with Jack Rattenbury.

"Jack, don't be such a bull," she admonished gleefully. "Aren't you pleased to see me?"

Again he pulled a face, but seeing the hurt creep into her eyes, he relented, cocking his head sideways at her and allowing his hand to stray over her small, well-formed back. "Sure I am, little darlin', but ye be a sore tease, ye know . . . throwing yer pretty arms over me and then holding back with the rest. Now I give ye fair warning to let go . . . or ye'll get tossed . . . child or no!"

She laughed and stood up, allowing him to rise and go to the washstand. He threw his face into the basin of water and brought up a towel to dry his lean countenance before turning his pale brown eyes on her. "Trouble is, lass . . . ye don't 'ave a mind to think of me as a man . . . but I am, and ye be a woman full grown!"

She frowned but said nothing to this, having nothing really to answer. Sighing heavily, she changed the subject. "Jack . . . he has brought someone home with him again."

"Eh? That same young covey ye told me of?" asked

15

Jack, his mind darting to the plans he had made with his crew for the morrow's undertaking.

"No, someone quite different. His name is Lord Welford . . . and . . . oh, Jack . . . something is wrong! I know not what . . . but I just feel something dreadful is about to happen." Her tone held a whine, which was unlike her, and Jack turned, comb in hand, to gaze at her full.

"Don't fret it, darlin', nuthin' 'as 'appened yet . . . and if ye keep feeling pinched . . . ye got me to come to!"

"Oh, Jack, I know I can always depend on you, but . . ." Her voice trailed off, unable to speak her fears.

"Lookee 'ere, lass . . . ye be a lady born and not of m'kind . . . but I been wanting ye . . . though ye ain't paid me no mind. Well, ye got m'name . . . whenever ye want it . . ." he said, coming forward and lifting her chin with his finger to face his own crooked smile. It was an offer, though but halfheartedly given. He had been yearning over Cassie some time now, but he would not take the chit in her innocence; and marriage was a thing he had been avoiding as much as the revenuers.

His proposal startled her, and she cast him a look of open surprise. She had never thought of her big oafish Jack in that particular manner. He was handsome enough, and his occupation gave him the aura of romance, but he had too many years on her. And then too, she had always thought of him as a brother. She put away his offer with a musical giggle. "You're jesting, Jack. What would all the girls at the Spithead do to see you tied to such a role?"

He joined in her laughter. "Aw now, lass . . . I said nuthin' 'bout giving up m'pretties . . ."

She slapped his arm playfully but sank back against the wall, watching him shrug into his white linen shirt. She frowned once again. "But truly, Jack . . . I do feel uneasy."

He stopped and regarded her from beneath a thoughtful frown. "This 'ere lord . . . 'as 'e been bold wit ye, child?"

"Oh, no, 'tis not that. Why, he has only just arrived . . . and I have managed to stay out of his path."

"Then, lordy, Cassie, m'girl . . . what's to do? I don't ken yer meaning," he said with some show of impatience.

"It . . . was the way he looked at me. Jack, he doesn't know me, and yet I had the feeling he loathed the sight of me."

Jack laughed. "Now, lass, 'tis in yer mind! There ain't a man alive that could 'ave 'is eyes filled wit ye and not fall slobbering at yer feet! Ye jest don't understand men yet . . . and best be watchful fer I'd wager a monkey this 'ere lord 'as 'is mind up to 'ave ye!"

"Oh, Jack, I don't think so. There is something far more purposeful about him. Charles has sent the estates into deep debt . . . and Lord Welford's being here at this time . . . oh, Jack . . . I just don't know."

"Well, lordy, girl! It don't matter about the Grange . . . do it?" He proceeded to answer this himself. "It's hard, I knows . . . coz if Sir Charles managed to kill himself between his brandy and his *black drop*, the Grange would go to ye as it should, but ye got that little nest egg yer papa done put aside fer ye . . . so in truth ye ain't got to fret. Ye waited this long, child . . . it be but a year more ye got to wait!"

"But I do so love the Grange . . ." said Cassie in forlorn tones.

He put his arm about her shoulders comfortingly. "Well, darlin', ye best get used to meeting life head-on. There ain't no other way . . . and it won't all be fun. Ye got yerself . . . yer mind . . . yer soul . . . and whatever else comes along . . ."

"I suppose . . . but I wonder what Cousin Charles is up to?" said Cassie almost to herself.

Sir Charles was up to his usual. He sat upon his huge four-poster bed, his long-throated pipe in hand. The mauve hangings his wife had installed before her death concealing his movements from the daylight. A small wax candle burned beside him on the nightstand as he took his brew.

It had all started so innocently, he thought to himself. A small solution of opium in quince juice. He had needed it to forget her, and he purchased his first draught for eleven shillings. But it hadn't made him forget . . . it brought him dreams instead—dreams of her—and they were as tangible as reality and far more pleasant.

The mixture became a daily need, until the quince and lemon juices were cast aside for a full tael a day. He sucked delicately, lovingly, on his pipe and reclined upon his pillow. There . . . he could just make out Esperida's face. She was taking shape in a cloud of smoke, enchanting his senses. He felt her body beat against his own, felt her hands entwine themselves in his hair, and he sank back into a seductive dream.

A knock sounded at his door, once, twice. It pounded through his head, rocking his senses to alertness, and he called out in irritation, "For God's sake, man . . . what in blazes do you want?"

It was Harris, and he begged admittance. Sir Charles whipped at the air with his hand, attempting to conceal the smoke. He bent and laid his pipe on the far side of the bed and allowed his butler to enter.

"So sorry to intrude, Sir . . . but his lordship be wishful of knowing how ye be. Seemed to think ye took ill this morning . . ." said Harris timidly.

Sir Charles frowned, remembering the quick sense of nausea that had come over him earlier. He had needed his opium. . . . "Never mind that. Tell his lordship I am better, but resting. I look forward to seeing him tonight at dinner. In the meantime ask my ward to keep him entertained . . . go now . . . go on."

The butler was a small, frail, elderly man, but he had been in service at the Grange since his youth. He had his loyalties, and they were not with Sir Charles. He had no intention of advising him that Cassandra was not home. He bowed himself out, slightly clucking his tongue. He was saddened to see the Grange beneath the hands of such a master . . . *an opium eater!*

The viscount stood before the fire, which lit up his face, half shadowing it with talons of flame. The lines of his lean cheeks were hard drawn in thought, and his eyes told little with their blackness. His elbow rested on the mantelshelf, with his fist pressed to his thin but sensual lips, while the knuckles of his left hand rested on the buckskin cloth covering his narrow hip. He was glad for these moments alone, for he had an overwhelming disgust of his host. Thus far, his plan had gone well though, and that made up for it all. It was just a matter of time.

He had gone to Weller's Hole in Fleet Street with a purpose last week. He had gone to that hell, one he had never frequented in the past, simply to lose a bit of the ready to Sir Charles Farrington.

It had been easy, for he had not played a cautious game, though he had been at pains to display an uncommon ignorance of picquet. And it had not taken long to wangle an invitation to Farrington Grange. Sir Charles thought he had found himself an easy dupe and one with fat pockets to boot. His appetite for more, his need to add to the five hundred pounds he had already won, nearly caused him to froth at the mouth in the hope that his invitation to the Grange would be accepted. It was, and had Sir Charles been less intoxicated with the carelessness his addiction inspired, he might have thought it slightly odd that such a corinthian could be so ham-handed with the cards.

The butler entered the library, his face solemn with the news that his employer was indisposed and would not make an appearance until dinner. His lordship accepted this piece of information with knowing look, for he could wait. He detained the elderly man with an uplifted brow. "And Miss Farrington, is she also . . . indisposed?"

The butler's faded eyes flitted with some confusion. He loved his mistress well. She was the daughter of the house, and in his heart he felt her to be the rightful heir. This noble guest was a friend of Sir Charles . . . and Sir Charles, though quality, was beneath Miss Cassandra in every imaginable way. He felt it incumbent upon himself to protect her and, as it would not do for this bold viscount to know what she was about, he answered somewhat enigmatically.

"Miss Farrington is, I believe, quite well."

The viscount glanced shrewdly at the butler and wondered what he was attempting to conceal. "I am very pleased to hear that. Will you send word to her that I would be honored if she would condescend to take tea with me." It was a command, for all his cold politeness.

The butler bit his lip and faltered, "Er . . . your pardon, m'lord, but . . . Miss . . . is out riding."

Again, the black mobile brow went up quizzically. "Really? Perhaps I shall join her . . . if you will be so kind as to put me in her direction."

The harassed butler felt the earth sink about his feet. "I . . . I wouldn't be knowing that, m'lord. Miss went out early this morning."

"Unaccompanied?" cut in the viscount with a show of some surprise.

"Aye, Miss has always had free run . . . even after . . ." He caught himself up gruffly for it wasn't his place to talk so openly of his betters even in Cassie's defense. He continued in a tone far more subdued. "Well . . . the thing is, there ain't another that could keep pace when Miss rides Starfire."

The viscount smiled quietly, well aware now that the butler was Miss Farrington's man and not Sir Charles's. "I see, very well then, there is nothing for it but to await her return. See that she is informed that I await her pleasure in the library, for no doubt, she will be returning soon . . . if, as you say, she has been out since early this morn."

"Very good, sir," said the butler, relieved to be dismissed, and making good his escape.

Harris closed the library doors behind him and started across the dark oak floor only to be pulled up short by a

20

creaking sound at the large, heavy front door. Green eyes peered cautiously around the door's edge, surveying the hall, and a sigh was released from full rosy lips. She spied her butler and swiftly, deftly, moved inside, closing the door at her back and whispering to her butler to approach. He did, leaning towards her conspiratorily as he had often done when she was but a wee child. "Oh, faith, 'tis that pleased I am to find the hall empty . . . where are *they?*" breathed Cassie, dropping her gloves onto the center table.

"Yer cousin be taking a bit of a rest," said Harris, indicating with his eyes just exactly what that meant. "But the viscount . . ." he indicated with a motion of his head toward the library doors at his back, ". . . he be wanting ye to join him for tea."

"Does he? Does he indeed?" breathed Cassie suddenly taking umbrage. "No doubt, our quiet life here leaves him sorely lacking in entertainment. Am I to fill that post?"

"I had no idea you would find the notion repulsive," said the viscount suavely. He stood before the open library door, facing her.

Harris spun around and immediately retreated to a corner to await the outcome of this unexpected clash. His mistress, eyes glaring across the room, met the challenge defiantly, at the same time attempting to calm herself by assuming a cool, controlled manner. "Repulsive? Indeed, no, my lord. Merely that I find the command *tasteless!*"

He smiled, and his eyes no longer seemed hard glowing coals, but soft black magic. She was aware of his excellent form in his finely tailored buckskin jacket. Through her anger, she could see that his knit breeches of buff were molded to thighs that were hard and athletic, that his hessians glowed black to his knees, and that he was in every way a virile man. His voice came to her ears in a soft cajoling tone, and she knew not just how much it was intended to please. She only knew that it did. "Ah . . . but you mistake, Miss Farrington. I did not issue a command . . . but a plea. The prospect of your company did so fox my mind, that perhaps I did not voice

21

my wishes as I should have . . ." he cast an injured glance towards Harris, who colored.

It was a strategic move, for Miss Farrington saw and immediately relented, not wishing her servant to catch blame. He saw this in her expression and opened the door at his broad back, standing aside while he offered her his hand. "Please, Miss Farrington, take pity on a lonely man . . ."

He had won, for Cassie was not totally immune to his charm. She smiled her acquiescence and spoke lightly over her shoulder to her butler, advising him that he should bring on the tea.

As she passed by the viscount, her shoulder brushed his hard chest and she looked up, somewhat surprised by the sensation that shot through her. She found the viscount's eyes upon her, and though they were not hard, they still concealed his inmost thoughts.

She moved to the sofa and, as she took up a rather stiff position on its brown velvet plush, she noted a spot on her riding skirt that was worn and threadbare. She pleated it quickly, lest his lordship observe, and brought up her eyes to find him taking a seat before her.

However, he had seen her quick motion, and it brought a mild frown to his countenance. It was odd, how poorly she was clothed. Not at all in keeping with the assumptions he had formed before his arrival at Farrington Grange. He gave her a friendly smile.

"I take it you had an enjoyable ride?" his tone was casual, though he was curious to know where she had been.

She smiled shyly in return. The light flirtations she had had with the local youths during Esperida's control of the Grange had not prepared her for anyone so overpowering, both in appearance and experience. Her anger subsided, she was no longer at ease. "Oh . . . yes . . . the ride to Christchurch is always a most pleasant trip."

"Ah! You went shopping then?" it was more a satisfied statement than a question, and Cassie's answer brought a look of surprise into his eyes.

"Shopping? No . . . I . . . I was visiting a friend,"

she said shortly. She had no wish to lie, but she had no intention of giving him any more on the subject.

He frowned, for the girl was beginning to intrigue him with her subtle mysteries. He attempted another approach. "I happened to be in the stables yesterday evening, and my groom, Chips, pointed out your mount. He is one of the finest specimens of horseflesh I have ever seen!"

She sparkled at once. "He is that! My brother brought him home to me . . . back in '13 . . ." She strayed off into another realm, but caught herself almost immediately, shrugging it off and attempting a smile. "My family thought he was too large for me then . . . but I trained him myself . . . and as it happens Starfire will let no other on his back!"

"He has the look of Spanish blood," he said idly, hoping she would continue in the same animated fashion.

"Yes, of course, my brother fought in the Pyrenees . . . he brought Starfire back with him, you see," she said, but her voice had lost its sparkle as memories intruded.

"Really? What regiment? I was the Fifth myself," he pursued, still looking for an opening.

"You were in Spain fighting Boney?" she asked with some surprise. It added further depths to him and made him all the more exciting.

"I was, and I had the satisfaction of seeing him defeated at Waterloo!" said the viscount grimly.

She sighed. "I lost Jeremy at Waterloo . . . he was in the Eleventh Regiment . . . most of them were killed . . ."

He felt momentarily affected by the childlike sense of loss written on her face. But he had his wits about him and looked further. Tea was brought in and he watched her pour. He noted the movement of her arm, her hands, the fullness of her breasts as she bent over the tea tray. She was exquisitely sensuous, and he felt a sudden yearning in his loins, until a long strand of firelit hair fell over her shoulder. Cinnamon gold! It reminded him of his purpose. Thus, when he looked further he saw a lusty woman, preparing him with her gentle airs of innocence for the slaughter, and he had no intention of falling—*but he would play her game!*

She looked up to hand him his cup and caught the strange expression on his face. His eyes seemed to be frowning over her hair and almost without thinking she put up a hand to smooth back her locks. She wondered with a blush, if they were even more tousled than she had thought, and she said self-consciously, "I . . . I suppose . . . I should have gone up first and refreshed . . ."

His countenance relaxed immediately into a gallant smile. "Not at all . . . you look lovely just as you are. In fact, I was admiring the shine of your hair. 'Tis a wondrous shade of burnished gold. I can't recall ever before seeing a woman with your particular hair color!"

She gave him a long questioning look. His tone seemed somehow to mock his words. He found her eyes and for a moment lost himself in their depths. He drank his full of their tangy sweetness and he came up thirsting for more. She attempted a sally. "Good gracious, my lord, I know not if I should thank you . . . as your tone quite frightens me."

He laughed easily. "Thank me? You need not. *I* am not responsible for your beauty, Miss Farrington. I was but making my observations known to you."

Again, his tone seemed to hint at meanings not contained in his words, and her brows drew together delicately over her nose. Was he not from London? Was he not a member of the *haut ton* . . . and were *they* not all very oddly mannered? She shrugged and gave him the fullness of her smile. It was as pure as her innocence. He found himself lost in its sweetness and for a moment forgot the honey held a trap. But, he *was* a London gentleman, and indeed hers was not the first beauteous face he had beheld . . . and he had reasons to know her soul was less than it seemed. He regained his composure at once, and cynicism returned to protect his heart.

She sipped her tea and watched him from beneath her

24

dark curling lashes. Lud, but he was everything she had always dreamed a man should be! She saw Childe Harold walk out from his pages, the Byronic hero personified in all his cold, cynical, mysterious, and infinitely magnetic form. She was drawn to him as the babe is to bright colors. "Very well, then, my lord. Since you have seen fit to bestow your observations upon me, I shall not be backward. You are town-bred . . . a nonesuch, my brother would have said. Your clothes indicate that you come from a tailor of the first stare . . . your sophistication shouts your status . . . What then are you doing *here?*"

He shot her a penetrating look before relaxing and giving a rueful smirk. "You mean by that . . . what am I doing in the company of your guardian?"

She blushed but looked at him squarely. "If you find bluntness more serviceable . . . yes, that is exactly what I mean."

"Your guardian is wont to travel . . . about the edges of my circle, you know. It is not so odd that we should have met. I lost quite a pretty roll to him playing picquet, and he was kind enough to invite me to his home in order to give me the opportunity to have at him."

"I see . . . but why did he come home then? Why not continue your game in London?" she was frowning, for the question troubled her.

"I believe he mentioned something about having to return to his estate . . . on business," said the Viscount idly, showing little interest.

"Really?" she asked somewhat dubiously. "I find that singularly interesting."

"Why?" he asked his gaze narrowing, "What is so unusual about a squire looking after the management of his estate?"

She scanned the room in an effort to compose herself. She was ever sparked with irritation when she thought of Sir Charles's drain on the estate. But it would not do to complain of her guardian to this stranger. That was not her way. She said merely, "My guardian . . . has, of

25

late . . . been somewhat apathetic about the Grange affairs." She paused slightly. "I find it . . . odd that his interest should send him hotfoot to Farrington!"

"Perhaps his business here has nought to do with the Grange?" suggested the viscount, hoping to elicit a less guarded comment from her. Of one thing he was certain now—she loved her home.

She cast him a troubled look for indeed, Sir Charles had been involved in something . . . she knew not what, but was quite sure it had little to do with the management of his holdings. Again, she gave a noncomittal reply. "Perhaps, it is as you say." She got to her feet suddenly. "I think, my lord, that I will go up now. I dearly want a bath and a short rest before dinner."

He stood up and bowed low over her hand, touching its smooth whiteness with his warm lips. It sent a titillating shiver up her arm which in turn communicated itself to her heart. She cast the viscount a hurried glance, wondering with some concern whether or not he was aware of her reaction. His low voice caressed her and undulated with something beyond her ken as he said, "Until later, Miss Farrington."

She blushed in raw confusion for his eyes swept her and, unable to respond to such drama, she rushed from the room. As she took the hall stairs she chided herself silently. "You are an idiotic schoolgirl . . . a . . . a ninny. Whatever will he think of you? Faith . . . all he said was . . . 'until later, Miss Farington,' and you are behaving as though . . . he had taken you in his arms . . . *Stoopid!*"

3

Sir Charles picked at his strawberry crepe before pushing it aside with but slight effort to restrain his impatience. He was expecting a caller, one whose consequence was nought in the world, yet one who would bring him the payment for a job well done. He cast his bright eyes towards the mantelshelf clock, noted that the hour was already past eight, and reached for his half-empty glass of wine.

Cassie observed her guardian's movements and her dark brow went up. She had seen him act in such a manner on two other occasions, and both times had preceded the arrival of a small, dark-clad gentleman. The servants had buzzed curiously amongst themselves for days afterward, and she had picked up the tone of their comments. Watching her guardian now, she wondered whether his mood portended yet another visit from the same little man. She glanced away from him rather than meet his eye and found the viscount studying her countenance. His black eyes seemed to extract her thoughts from her, so deep was their penetration. And too, she was struck with his bold good looks. She liked the way his black hair swept across his forehead. She liked the way his brows would go into action with his thoughts . . . and if only his eyes would smile . . .

"May I compliment you on your menu, Miss Farrington. This meal has been superb," said the viscount easily, his smile warm upon her face.

"You are too kind, my lord. I am sure you found it lacking after the elaborate meals you are used to in London," she returned.

"You overrate London and underestimate yourself," he said gently.

"Heigh–ho . . . don't be filling the girl's ears with such round tales!" snapped Sir Charles bitingly. "She don't have the way of selecting a menu yet." He turned on her, "Blister it, girl, I've told you I don't care for radishes . . . and damn if there weren't half a dozen in the salad!"

Cassie put up her chin. "Were there? How dreadful for you!" Mockery was in her eye, and it was when she looked just so that her guardian felt the need to slap her.

He narrowed his eyes but she was spared his retort by Harris who appeared suddenly and placed the silver salver near the squire's hand. Sir Charles looked down at the card it held and took it up with some eagerness. "Have him wait in the study. I shall be there immediately." He turned to the viscount and gave a rueful smile. "As I must leave you now . . . and you appear to have made a conquest with my ward, I know I leave you . . . er . . . pleasurably occupied."

Cassie's jaw dropped slightly and in some confusion she objected, "But . . . Cousin Charles . . ."

He rounded on her irritably. "What do you want? Speak up, girl . . . I am in a hurry and have no time for dallying!"

"You . . . you will be back shortly, I assume?" she said on a strained note, for it was not at all the thing for her guardian to leave her alone with a gentleman for any length of time.

"No, not tonight, my dear." Again he gave a smile to

the viscount. "I am certain you, my lord, will understand . . . unavoidable business." With that he turned on his heel and left the room.

Viscount Welford and Miss Farrington watched Sir Charles's brisk departure—the former with some degree of curiosity, the latter with much embarrassment. Cassie knew not where to look. 'Twas most humiliating to be thus thrust upon a man. The viscount's eyes found her withdrawn behavior baffling. Was this not part of the game these two played? Why, then, was the chit put out . . . or was it play-acting?

He pushed his chair back and as he rose she could see him from a corner of her eye. He wore a blue superfine short-tailed coat over a white satin waistcoat. Both appeared to have been molded to his form and showed to advantage the powerfulness of his shoulders and chest. His smile lit upon her as he came round the table and offered her his arm. "Dare we order our drinks brought to the fire . . . we could talk . . . and be comfortable?" His tone assuaged her fears.

"Oh, yes, that would be . . . nice," she responded shyly.

They moved across the room and, as Harris opened the door for them, Cassie directed him to bring the port for his lordship to the library. They were crossing the central hall when their heads were brought round by the sound made by a crashing fist as it met a hardwood table, and they heard Sir Charles's shout.

"No, by damn! That was not the figure agreed upon. I delivered as promised . . . and you will tell him I want my full share!"

Cassie blushed to hear her guardian speak in such a vulgar manner within the viscount's hearing and was grateful that they had reached the library doors. The viscount led her to the brown plush sofa and saw her seated before taking up a position on the sofa's far end. The room glowed from the roaring fire in the hearth. The rich brown velvet hangings had been drawn against the night air. A branch of candles had been lighted for them, and it rested in a corner of the stainwood coffee table at their knees. Cassie gazed into the fire, trying to steady her absurd palpitations and began searching her mind for conversation with which to dazzle the experienced man beside her. He began it for her.

"What do you do in the way of amusements here in Hampshire?" asked the viscount, showing genuine interest.

She almost sighed her relief. "Do? Why . . . many things. Though I imagine they are nought compared to the entertainment offered in London. I ride, of course . . . and visit with our tenants. My mother had a knack with herbs . . . she passed on the knowledge to me, and I do what I can for those who fall ill in the village."

"That is how you pass your time?" he asked incredulously.

"And I read," she offered.

"Miss Edgeworth's novels, no doubt?" he teased.

Cassie did not like his tone. A sparkle lit her green eyes and caught his attention. "I have read Miss Edgeworth's novels and delighted in them. Does that put me beneath a man's level? I assure you, my lord, 'tis the broader palate that makes the educated mind!"

He put up his hands as though to shield himself from attack. "Ho, there, Miss Farrington, I did not mean to cast aspersions on Miss Edgeworth's novels. 'Twas expected you would have read her . . . don't all young maids?" he still bantered.

"And hasn't any man who has been in town frequented Watier's, Brooke's or White's? What does that signify but that we pick up on the recommendations of our friends! I find your observation ridiculous. You are a man. Have you not read *The Monk*? Do not all of London's fashionable gentlemen own a copy of it?"

"Indeed, yes . . . in fact . . ." he was laughing, "I happen to have the misfortune of being a particular friend of 'Monk' Lewis."

She opened wide her green eyes. "You are a friend of

Matthew Lewis? Really . . . oh, how exciting. What is he like?" her manner was almost childlike.

"Monk Lewis is a cad and a rogue. He goes about town breaking hearts with his vain, pompous airs, but he is the best of goodfellows and a rare friend!" laughed the viscount, watching her expressions. "Did you read *The Monk?*"

"Oh, yes, indeed. It was famous good fun and nearly frightened me to death!" responded the lady, twinkling.

"He jotted it off in less than ten weeks, you know. He is a wicked fellow, but you would like him thoroughly." He cast his eyes about and found the room devoid of servants. Slowly, he had been moving nearer to her. He was barely inches from her now, and his arm casually slung over the sofa back allowed his hand to fall languidly just above her shoulder. She was simply clothed in a high-necked blue muslin, yet the sight of the full roundness of her breasts beneath the thin material stimulated an ache in his loins. "You would enjoy London. You should ask your guardian to bring you with him during one of his jaunts," he said in a low voice.

She blushed as she thought how very little he understood of her situation. She looked up and found his nearness quite distracting. She was twenty and her own blood had been stirring for some time, waiting for the right man. She saw before her just the man, and the thought terrified her. She faltered as she answered, "I . . . I doubt that he would."

"He is not a happy man . . . is he, Miss Farrington?" inquired the viscount gently.

"No, no, I don't suppose he is. But happiness is a relative thing, is it not?"

"Indeed . . . perhaps one day we will pursue that; but tell me, does he often conduct his affairs in this manner?"

"What manner do you speak of?" she said softly, melting beneath his dark gaze, wanting suddenly to know the feel of his embrace.

Her tone enticed him. There was a trace of huskiness in

31

her voice, and imperceptibly his arm went still further as he brought his head lower. "I am referring to his night caller . . . do you not find it odd?"

"Indeed. But my guardian does not discuss his affairs with me."

"No? And you take no interest?"

"I do . . . I love the Grange . . . but I know very little of this new kick-up of his."

"Ah, then he *has* received such a visit before." It was a statement, more to himself than to her.

"Yes, two others . . . from the same man . . . I think. I have never seen him though I heard the servants speak about him."

"And on those other occasions . . . were you also left to entertain his guests?" His question came sharply, but his presence overwhelmed her. She felt the room swim around her as her desire grew. She wanted him to hold her. She blotted out her thoughts . . . knew only that she wanted him to kiss her. She answered hoarsely, "We . . . we had not the honor of guests on those particular evenings."

"How much wiser of your guardian, but he is quite at fault leaving you to me, you know." His arm slipped from the sofa and found her dainty shoulders while his other hand discovered the smallness of her waist. He drew her to him, pressing her body against his own as his lips took hers. His tongue explored the honey of her mouth hungrily, and Cassie felt herself introduced into a dark world lit with bright red, white, and gold lights. One skillful hand found its way to the voluptuousness of her breast and fondled its fullness through the thin material of her gown. She had been lost in his kiss, in the wonder of its power, in the passion it aroused within her, but this move shocked her!

The knowledge of what she was about hit her mind like a spear of cold ice and her head put her heart on the rack. She attempted to pull away, gasping, "Stop . . . my lord . . ."

He heeded not the words for the girl's arms were still about him, and there was a fire in his blood. His mouth silenced her, and his tongue taught her to respond. It was torture, wanting him, and knowing that prudence commanded her retreat. She had never before experienced such a kiss. She had never been fondled, and she had not been prepared for this onslaught. It left her breathless. She could feel the hard muscles beneath his coat, and they rippled against the softness of her breasts, and she needed him. But her mind did battle with her emotions. It taunted her. 'Think what you are . . . what you owe your name . . . your family . . . think, Cassie, think.' "No!" she shouted at him and pushed herself free. She found herself released at once, for in truth he had not in reality forced her into such a position. She had gone into his arms willingly, and it was a humiliating thought, for she had all the pure ideals of youth to hound at her conscience.

She jumped to her feet and ran her hand over her gown in an attempt to set things to rights. "Please, my lord . . . you will excuse me . . ." she whispered before she fled the room.

The viscount stood up and watched her go. His yearning left him frustrated, though he was in full control, for his lovemaking had been contrived. He found Cassandra Farrington a most desirable female, but he was well able to control his lust, especially to achieve his own ends . . . and he meant to achieve them. Yet the chit was a mystery. He knew her part in these blasted dealings well. He had the proof of it still on his person, and emblazoned into his memory, yet she would play the maid . . . the chaste and gentle maid . . . *but for what purpose?*

Well, he had neither traveled Europe, nor reached the age of seven and twenty without being fully cognizant of the fact that women worked in guiles rarely fathomed by men. Evidently this little pretty had notions of her own, apart from those of her guardian. Was she in fact setting her cap for him? He snorted in the quiet of the library, for the lady stood little chance.

Cassie reached for her room with a sob. She closed the door behind her and leaned against the cool white painted surface and allowed her eyelids to close. Only the flames from the small hearth gave forth light. A log fell as its support burned into ashes, and the sound brought her eyes to the grate. Her body still trembled with the violence of her emotions. She had to come to grips with herself. She had to understand the motives that drove her . . . for if she had anything in this world . . . she had herself, and her soul would be as useless as the ashes in the hearth if she did not know her way.

Very well then Cassandra Farrington, you allowed a man, a great stud to be sure, but merely a man, one whom you have scarcely met, to take you into his arms. The thought, the memory of his mouth on hers tortured her. Confound it, Cassie, what is wrong? You have never wanted a man in such a way. Could it be that I am in love? she asked herself in wonder. How could it be? Is it then . . . lust? What do I know of him? Nothing really —'tis only his face, his eyes, his body that move me . . .

Self-recriminations began. What would he think of her? She was quite sure he didn't love her . . . he couldn't love her. He was attracted to her, and she had shown herself a willing maid. Why wouldn't he attempt to make love to her? 'Twas meaningless to a man of his kidney. And how . . . how for the love of all that was holy could she ever face him again?

And it was not until later, very much later, that she slept.

The air nipped at Cassie's cheeks and blew the hood of her brown cloak away from her glossy locks, playing with the curls that framed her face. She was engrossed with the sparkling stream beneath the covered bridge and she did not hear the approaching footsteps.

The viscount stopped a moment and filled his eyes with the vision before him. For all his self-control, for all his will, he had not slept well last night. The feel of her in his arms remained ever present, haunting his dreams, arousing his desires. He gazed past her free-flowing tresses to her profile and found her face bright with youth and beauty. Her cloak blowing away from her slender figure allowed his experienced eye the measure of her provocative lines and he felt once again that stirring in his breast. It would do no harm after all, he thought, to linger awhile.

"Good-morning, Miss Farrington," he said easily, as though he had never held her in his arms, had never kissed her mouth, never sent his hand exploring . . .

She blushed and attempted a cool greeting, but her voice, barely audible, belied her emotions. "Good-day, my lord."

He smiled gently and his eyes went to the book she held in her hands. "Miss Edgeworth . . . ?" There was the hint of a tease in his voice.

She smiled suddenly and pulled a face at him. "No, my lord. 'Tis *Endymion* . . . by that young poet Keats, and it is very good."

"The *Quarterly* does not agree with you . . . but I do," he said, coming forward to take up the book and flip through the pages.

"Blast the *Quarterly*," she grinned. "They may represent gods to the poor few who aspire to pen their thoughts . . . but they are held in no such heart with me. I can read, and I can make my own judgments. I need no stranger to do that for me!"

"Bravo, my pretty! Does that mode of thought extend to life as well."

"Of course, but one can never be certain when dealing with people. A book is there . . . it has its ending. One can set it aside and think before making up one's mind. But life . . . life is far more complicated. Don't you think so, my lord?"

"Indeed I do. People are rarely what they seem." There was an undercurrent to his voice, but his smile seemed to disguise it. "Come, Miss Farrington, you must be feeling more the thing, for you look ravishing."

She colored for he was referring to her absence from breakfast. She had sent a lame excuse, claiming a headache. "Thank you, my lord. I do feel better indeed. It must be the fresh air."

"Very well then, we shall continue to allow it to soothe

your spirits. I beg a boon of thee, fair maid . . . walk with me?"

She smiled prettily. "Of course, my lord. Shall I take you to see our evergreen maze?" she asked with some animation.

"Of course!" he answered immediately. "It sounds delightful."

She had never believed it would be so easy to converse with him again—not after last night. But it was, and she was actually meeting his black eyes without the least bit of difficulty. Her night of misgivings seemed suddenly to drift away, and she felt whole, wondrously whole.

As he walked beside her, she explained as much with quick little movements of her gloved hands as with words, "The maze was a favorite place of ours . . . Jeremy's and mine. We would play there for hours when we were small . . . and each year our gardener would add another row, to throw us off . . . oh how we loved it!"

"You speak of it in the past . . . do you never revisit your haunts?"

"No," she said with a bitterness in her voice.

"Why?" he pursued the matter, curious in spite of himself.

"Because I was afraid . . . if I showed too much interest in it . . . she might have it torn down . . . replanted . . . scattered . . ."

"She?" he asked, one brow up.

"Sir Charles's wife. She enjoyed changing the house around; I liked seeing it remain as it was when I was a child," she said simply, her pale green eyes retreating from him. Then all at once they lit up and she pointed to a large patch of dark evergreens. They were cut in pyramids and tall cubicles and there were endless rows of the trees clustered closely together. She was bright as a child as an idea lit upon her face, "I have a notion, my lord. I could take you through . . . just once to the center—there are several avenues—but I shall show you the quickest route. Then we could start over, but I would give you a count of

36

ten as a lead . . . and we could race to the fountain in its middle? What say you?"

He chuckled, "Done!"

She giggled and took his hand. It was a simple action, the touching of hands, yet it sent shivers through them both. When all is forbidden, the slightest touching of flesh against flesh can do much to excite. She flushed, met his intensely black eyes, dropped her gaze and his hand on the instant, and said in a far more subdued manner, "This way, my lord." And she wondered what power it was that could so discompose her.

He followed, watching the sway of her hips, and had no difficulty finding an answer to the molten state of his blood. He wanted the chit, damn her! Even knowing what she was, what she had done . . . he wanted her . . . and he damned himself for a rutting stud! He followed her, and the fancy was born within him that he had the power to bring her down to her proper level!

They zigzagged and made their way through to the center where a stone shell had been placed as a bird bath. She turned round expectant eyes to him. "There . . . think you will be able to remember?"

He nodded, grinning widely but took her by the hand. "Only do show me how to return—just on the remote possibility that I am more a dunce than I think myself."

She hurried him back to where they had begun and laughed. "Now then . . . I must take another avenue . . . and give you a count of ten on me . . . START!"

He was gone on the instant. She reached her limit, giggled, and rushed through another aisle in some great haste. She felt young again. She felt a child again, because she desperately wanted to find a root . . .

The viscount made his way through the maze and reached the fountain in time to catch a glimpse of her skipping through the aisle at a spanking pace. He grinned and went to her avenue's opening, propping himself against the branches of a fir tree. As she raced through, his arms caught her round the waist and, he laughed, "I

believe you have lost by a length, my fair charmer . . .
'tis time to pay the piper!"

She laughed and twisted in his embrace. "Devil! How
did you manage that?"

"You underestimated your man," he said quietly.

She more than half expected him to kiss her, she more
than half wanted him to, and when he didn't, she felt a
wedge of disappointment. He released her, but eased her
pique by slipping her hand through his arm. "Come, Cassandra, we must talk."

She walked beside him quietly, sensing that his talk
would not be idle, wondering what it was that drove him.
What was his real purpose at the Grange? After they had
left the hedges well behind, he said, "I am curious . . .
you said Sir Charles has allowed the management of his
estate to slip in the past year or so . . . do you know
why?"

"He . . . he has his reasons. His young wife died in
childbirth you know . . . he was much devoted to her,"
she answered cautiously.

"So he turns to the comforts of brandy, and . . . other
poisons," he said waiting for her to comment.

"I . . . I suppose . . . they are a way to ease the
pain . . . "

"And you, pretty princess of Farrington Grange . . .
locked in your tower—how is it no man has come along
to rescue you?" he teased, but she sensed there was far
more intensity to his question than he would have her
realize. "Because, my lord, I don't live in a fairy tale . . .
nor do I believe in them. Life has been quite realistic for
me."

He put his finger beneath her chin and turned her to
him, a rueful smile upon his lips. "Cassandra . . . are
you a *cynic* . . . with years numbering just twenty?"

"A *cynic* . . . faith, no! I believe in many things you
would laugh to hear . . . but that does not make me
blind to life as it is. When my cousin's wife was alive, we
entertained, and now and then some of the local gentry

38

brought their sons. All very eligible, and some paid me court, but I discouraged them."

"Why?" he believed her. It was preposterous that he should believe a jade. But he did believe her and was suddenly in urgent need of her answer.

"I found very quickly that I was not in love with any of the beaux that sought my hand . . . and even to escape the drudgery of living with Esperida, I couldn't . . . 'tis where my realism ends and my foolish ideals begin," she said quietly.

He had nothing to say to this. He had to digest it. It was not in keeping with what he knew of her. He found her eyes and they were glorious and he allowed himself to sink into their depths. "Cassandra, have you any notion just how beautiful you are . . . or how much you stir a man's blood?" He did not wait for her answer. Instead he turned her about and said gruffly, "We had better return to the house."

Cassie walked beside him in silence, afraid to break the stillness with conversation. She was nearly terrified by the excitement that shot through her because of his presence. What was he? she would ask herself, then answering, he is but a man . . . only a man, and add, but so very different from all I have ever known.

At length it was he who broke the quiet air. "Since Esperida's death, your guardian brings no male visitors to the Grange?"

She cast him a puzzled gaze. "No, oh . . . yes . . . one about five weeks ago. A young man, Peter Eaton . . . he stayed only a short while."

"And missed his mark no doubt?" It was almost a sneer and she glanced at him quickly.

"I . . . I don't take your meaning, my lord?" she said.

"Did he not meet with your approbation?" he asked more to the point, less harshly.

"Oh, well, he was very nice, but as I said, he was here only a short while." She added after a short pause, "His business was with my guardian, not with me, and they left together after only a few days here."

"I see, and so . . . your heart remained intact." He had a habit of forever making statements rather than putting forth a question, yet she answered it all the same.

"My *heart* remained intact, my lord . . . because it was never offered!"

The house was in sight and there too stood Sir Charles in the bowed window looking out onto the lawns, turning to gaze at them. She sighed and excused herself, "I bid you good-afternoon, my lord. My horse wants a run."

He took her hand, and his lips sent a shiver through her.

"Of course, Miss Farrington."

She looked away hurriedly and hastened her steps, putting him out of her mind, thinking only . . . Starfire . . . she would ride Starfire and forget all these strange emotions.

4

Cassie's room was lit with tapers on each wall, and there were branches beside her vanity. Her maid, Meg, fussed over her, smoothing the lines of the green velvet gown she had altered that very afternoon. "An' sure, m'love, 'tis that puzzled I am why ye be so tittery. It wouldn't be that ye 'ave in mind to cast yer cap at his lordship now, is it?"

"Oh, hush, Meg . . . of course not. What is so odd in my wanting to look . . . more presentable before our guest? Faith! You would think I had gone to Bond Street in London for this gown. 'Tis years and years old."

"Your mama used it but once," said the middle-aged woman with a sigh. "Oh, but she would be that pleased to see ye in it . . . and looking so grand." She sighed again, "Mayhap it will turn out fer the best. Lord knows ye deserve the best."

"Now, Meg . . . don't get all misty on me. Here, look, do you think it will be noted that my slippers are a shade too light for this gown?"

Meg cast her eyes downward and snorted, "Lord love

ye, child! He ain't goin' to 'ave his poppers clapped on yer feet . . ."

"Meg!" admonished her mistress, twirling round before the long looking glass. Her flame-colored tresses were piled in Grecian curls at the top of her head. Her gown, though somewhat outdated, was a rich shade of lawn green, and the plush of the velvet (after some preening by Meg) looked fresh and new. Its sleeves hugged Cassie's arms to the wrist where small pearls had been embroidered, and its neckline was cut square across Cassie's high full breasts, where the pearl motif had been repeated to the waist. The gown clung tightly to Cassie's provocative lines, falling in straight to her ankles. For ornamentation she wore only the gold pendant that had belonged to her mother. She glanced at herself critically, thinking she would have to do, but not realizing the impact of her loveliness.

"Aye, lass, ye'll do . . ." said the maid, moved to speak. "Too well, I fear."

Cassie smiled happily and turned on her doting servant to crush her in a bear hug. "Never fear for me, Meg. I am well able to look after myself."

With this pronouncement she took herself off, stopping beside the bed only long enough to scoop up an ivory silk shawl she had found in the attic with the gown. She was feeling in high spirits for no reason at all and had to restrain herself from skipping down the staircase. The door to the dining room was opened for her by Harris and she stepped through quietly, expectantly.

Wax candles glittered from the chandelier and wall sconces, creating light and shadows to the high vaulted ceiling. Cherubic figures danced in plaster above the flickering flames and the crystals reflected the blue of the chamber walls. Cassie gazed at the viscount across the room and marveled at how well he fitted his surroundings . . . as though he belonged! Ah, but she was being foolish, she chided herself immediately.

The viscount came forward, for he had been waiting for her entrance. By God, he thought with some force, she is a rare piece! He smiled warmly as he reached her, bringing the color to her cheeks as his perusal journeyed down the slender column of her neck to the lusciousness of her well-shaped breasts. He bent low over her hand. "I am enchanted, Miss Farrington. You have gained your purpose well."

She tilted her head and her brows went up. "My purpose?"

"Indeed, love. You set out to bewitch me with your many charms, and bewitch me you certainly have," he said brazenly.

It was, of course, the very thing that would have sent an experienced woman into wicked mirth, such was the tone, the look, the magnetic quality of the man. However, Cassie was not an experienced flirt. Her jaw dropped and she sought words with which to slap his face. Of all the arrogant, overbearing, self-centered . . . At last she found her voice, "I think, my lord, you overrate your mark. I have done no more than dress for dinner as any gentlewoman might. If in the interim, my toilet has bewitched you, rest easy. No such cap in hand was sought, or desired. Easy conquests rarely are, you know!"

He laughed aloud, bringing Sir Charles's head round. The squire watched them with calculated interest. He had played picquet that very afternoon with the viscount, whose game—or luck—had improved. He lost the five hundred pounds he had won while in London, and he was on edge, nervous to continue the game . . . or perhaps another. He poured himself yet another glass of brandy and sipped it quietly, lost in his own thoughts.

Cassie shot her guardian a quick but penetrating glance. His clothes were even more carelessly put together than usual. He seemed lost to severe mental calculations and totally divorced from his surroundings. What a poor host he was, to be sure, thought Cassie with contempt. He happened to glance her way at that particular moment and caught the disdain in her eyes. Charles gritted his teeth and glared at her. She turned from him to face the viscount.

It is interesting how a man with his wits about him, a man considered by most of his cronies to be a "knowing fellow," could view this particular passing between cousins and believe it to mean something altogether different. The viscount observed his host, saw the glare Charles had shot Cassie, and took it to mean he wished his ward to entertain their guest. The viscount wondered suspiciously what was toward.

As he happened to hear Sir Charles order a footman to refill the glasses, the viscount next assumed *they* meant to ply him with drink in order to dupe him during the next gambling encounter. He felt a sardonic sensation, and contempt worked its way to his heart.

It is not surprising therefore, that dinner turned out to be a strained, somewhat odd passing of time. Sir Charles rarely spoke and scarcely touched his food. He was impatient to end the meal and rush his guest off to the card table. Cassie felt awkward. She noted the viscount's eyes upon her and felt disconcerted by his glance. It was a distinct relief to her when the dessert was taken away, and she was able to end the ordeal. She rose to her feet rather hurriedly. "I shall leave you gentlemen to your port, while I take up my embroidery in the library," she said politely.

"No, Miss Farrington, you can't mean to desert me now! Your guardian has every intention of fleecing me . . . stay and give me support!" bantered his lordship.

"Fleece you? Damn it, Kirkby! 'Tis you have scorched me. Took every last pound I won from you in London," returned Sir Charles mirthlessly.

"But I intend to give you every opportunity to try and win that—and more—provided, of course, that your ward remains at my side . . . for luck," said the viscount idly. He had his own reasons for wanting the chit where he could see her.

Sir Charles glanced shrewdly at them both. "Eh . . . took a fancy to her, did you? Ha! You don't stand any more chance than did young Eaton—and he was a pretty boy, I must say! Has her heart set on a common smuggler—Jack Rattenbury by name!" announced Sir Charles pugnaciously.

Cassie gasped and her cheeks burned as the viscount turned his face and his eyes swept her countenance. She ignored him and rounded on her cousin. *"How dare you!"*

"Thought I didn't know where you ride off to?" he smirked. "Esperida made it her business to find out . . . told me all about you and that unlawful thug!"

"Don't you speak of Jack that way. He is ten times the man you claim to be," she snapped, forgetting herself.

"This . . ." interrupted the viscount—there was an edge to his voice and Sir Charles gave him his full attention, suddenly fearing he had gone too far . . . perhaps it would have been better to allow the viscount to think he could have the chit—". . . has nought to do with me. You may dispute your differences over the . . . er . . . smuggler at some other time . . . that is, if you are still planning to play at cards with me, sir."

"Of course, of course, my lord. But I would but make one alteration," suggested Sir Charles slyly.

"Really?" said the viscount, already aware of what Sir Charles had in mind. Completely prepared for this event, he smiled to himself.

"Indeed . . . let us change the game from picquet . . . to faro!" Sir Charles attempted a friendly grin.

"Excellent notion . . . but shan't we need a dealing box?" asked the viscount innocently.

"I have it in the library. Come, I'll have Harris bring our libations to us there," said Charles, nearly rubbing his hands together with anticipation.

All this while, Cassie who had moved to stand with her face to the fire and her back to the gentlemen, had been quietly seething. To be so affronted in the presence of the viscount was the outside of enough! She knew not how to behave and dearly wanted to smash something, preferably over her guardian's odious head! The viscount called to her now and his tone was strangely gentle. "Miss Farrington . . . do come, or have *I* too incurred your displeasure."

She attempted a faint smile. "You? Of course not. Yes, I should like to come . . . *and hope I may give you luck*," she said, suddenly casting a defiant look at her guardian. She took the viscount's arm and allowed him to lead her across the hall to the library and see her seated there beside him at the card table.

Harris brought forth an elaborate contraption ornamented with a tiger. It was known in faro as the dealing box and was designed to eliminate cheating. This was presented to the viscount for his inspection and after a quick but thorough investigation, he was satisfied that all was in order. Cassie watched with interest for she had never before seen faro played.

This time Sir Charles did rub his hands together, and he wore a wide beam across his thin face. "Eh now . . . what are the stakes to be?"

"Shall we make the tokens represent ten-pound notes?" answered his lordship blandly. "Or is that too steep for *bucking the tiger*?"

Sir Charles frowned slightly, for truth was he was down on his cash. He had not received nearly half of what he had expected from his . . . business connection, but faro was a game he considered peculiarly his own. "Done! Ten pounds per token then." He directed Harris to bring forth a sealed deck of cards and proceeded to place these before the viscount for his scrutiny. This done, they cut for the deal, and Sir Charles could have hooted when it went to him. 'Twas fair knowledge that the dealer had a ten percent advantage. His ward might be seated in the viscount's lap for all he cared, thought he viciously, 'twould do Kirkby Welford little good, for luck was with himself, and there he meant to keep it.

Sir Charles shuffled the deck of fifty-two cards and placed them neatly in the dealer's box. He brought forth the first card and placed it to his right. It was the black jack of spades, and he held his breath.

Cassie whispered, "What do you do now?"

His lordship smiled, for her childlike manners were winsome in the extreme, and he found it difficult keeping up a barrier between himself and the girl. " 'Tis the soda . . . or so it is called; no place bets are taken yet."

Another card was dealt and put to the left. The viscount picked up five tokens and placed his bet to lose. To his mind it was a small bet, but when the next card came up a heart, Sir Charles blanched considerably. Several turns went by in this fashion with the viscount ahead at the end of one hour by some four hundred pounds.

Sir Charles brought out his handkerchief and wiped his brow before his unsteady hand went to his glass of brandy. He noted wryly that the viscount had barely touched his own glass.

The following turn brought them to the last three cards in the box, and the viscount smiled knowingly to himself. He knew his game well, he had been watching the cards, remembering what card was in which pile. Luck was with him now, for if he could bet on the right order of these last three, he could triple his bet. He coppered the equivalent of his total winnings of the evening (four hundred pounds) on the first of the three cards. It turned up correctly, as did the next. When the third came up to prove him a winner, Cassie exclaimed with some excitement.

"You did it! Why that was prodigiously clever of you, my lord!"

"Damnation, girl! How can you be so unnatural. Don't you understand . . . he has won twelve hundred pounds from me?" ejaculated her guardian.

"So he has," said Cassie. She hated Charles and was incensed over his jibes linking her with Jack before the viscount.

"You'll take care to remember who feeds you, chit!" thundered her guardian, much infuriated. " 'Tis time you retired . . . take yourself off!" for he was beginning to wonder if she worked as a jinx against him.

The viscount watched this exchange with some puzzlement. They had a strange relationship, these two! But, it was becoming somewhat clearer. It was apparent the girl was under the thumb of this scoundrel and there was evidently little feeling other than hatred between them. That much was obvious. It was just possible that her actions . . . what she had done . . . had been to protect herself. That explained it but did not excuse it. And then he remembered the reference to the smuggler and her relationship to the man.

Cassie's color heightened, but she did get to her feet; however, Kirkby Welford's hand reached out and caught hers, detaining her. He placed a warm kiss upon its smooth whiteness, and his voice was low, "Good-night, Miss Farrington, and believe me indebted to you for the charm of good luck you held over my cards. May your ray continue with your departure."

To spite her guardian she said sweetly, "Indeed it will, my lord. 'Tis a secret I have well guarded. In truth, I am a witch, and have cast my sorcery over the cards . . . you cannot lose!" with which she giggled, cast a haughty look towards Sir Charles, and took her leave.

Sir Charles made a low sound in his throat, "Drat the jade! Let's get on with it." He believed now, especially with Cassie gone, the viscount's winning streak would end. It would have to give out, he told himself. He attempted to recoup his losses.

"Shall we raise the bidding, my lord?"

"Certainly, whatever you choose. Though you have been given fair warning by your ward. I cannot lose, Sir Charles!" said the viscount. His tone, if nothing else, should have forewarned his opponent. But, Sir Charles was not given to wisdom.

"May the fiends seize the chit and carry her off! We'll make each token worth one hundred pounds and set a minimum . . . this time no maximum," returned Sir Charles.

"If that is your wish," agreed the viscount, silently thinking the man a fool and wondering where he had ever acquired the fancy that he had a skill with the cards. For while he knew Sir Charles was a gambler, he also found him a bungler.

The deck was reshuffled, but the deal this time went to the viscount. The soda was put aside as the win pile, and

48

the first card overturned was the two of diamonds. Rashly, Sir Charles, looking for a coup, bet five hundred pounds on a win . . . and a black came up next. He cursed aloud. Again he bet another five hundred, switching this time and placing it to lose.

It took no more than fifteen minutes to put him back an additional ten thousand pounds. He sat back in his chair, his handkerchief discarded, his brow wet, and his mind a jumble. He hadn't got it. All he could think was that he hadn't that sort of money . . . anywhere! He had to win it back. There was nothing for it. He would have to chance the entire thing.

Cassie was in no mood to hide herself away in her room. She meandered over the house, landing finally in the parlor. She picked up a book she had started earlier and turned over its pages for some time before setting it down and starting for the stairs. A chill brought her hands round herself, and she recalled leaving her shawl behind in the library.

Sir Charles sat forward again, it was the last three cards of the deck. He had tried to remember . . . if only he hadn't taken so much drink . . . but he had hoped to encourage the viscount to do the same. He placed his bet, ten thousand pounds. The viscount raised a brow but accepted.

The first card came up correctly and Sir Charles nearly exploded with excitement. "Hurry up, man . . . the next . . . the next . . ." he cried almost triumphantly.

"I am afraid you will find you miscalculated." said the viscount as he turned the card over. He had not seen it, but he too had been watching the cards, and he had *not* been drinking.

He put it down on the table to give evidence of Sir Charles's loss and the squire pushed away from the table, giving the viscount his back. "My God, my God . . . Esperida . . . oh, God, things haven't been right . . ." He turned on the viscount. "You knew . . . you knew I would lose, yet you accepted that bet! You are a fiend!"

"May I remind you that gambling debts are debts of honor, sir," said the viscount, suddenly harsh.

"Indeed, remind me. What good shall it do? I haven't any honor left to me . . . and I haven't the cash! All I have left to me is Farrington Grange!"

"Very well, then, I accept the mortgage of Farrington in lieu of the thirty thousand-pound debt," said the viscount slowly.

"Good God! It is worth three times that much!" ejaculated Sir Charles.

"Ah, is it? But I understand it has a heavy mortgage on it. Therefore, my thirty thousand pounds more than makes up the difference. Get the papers, Charles. . . *now!*"

Sir Charles cursed him, but he moved to a cabinet and brought forth the documents. As he put quill to paper, Cassie arrived on the scene. She had heard only the last of their discourse and knew that somehow the Grange was being offered to the viscount.

"What are you doing, Charles?" she demanded.

He laughed. "Ah, 'tis the one good thing . . . I have the last laugh over you, chit!" His eyes were full with fever, for he was near to madness. There was a nauseous sensation within, and his head ached. He signed over the mortgage and threw it at the viscount. "There . . . it goes to the viscount. I have lost this fiendish place at last!"

"You cannot mean it? You never bet the Grange? How . . . how could you have done such a thing?"

"Shut up, chit. It was mine to lose!" He thought a moment, before a low wicked smile coursed his face. "But it may yet be won back. Leave us and go upstairs."

She hesitated and he glared at her, but there was a meaning in his glance. Perhaps he could win it back, she thought, perhaps there was a way. She looked at the viscount and found his eyes wavering over her. Indeed, she thought, Kirkby Welford was not so evil . . .

"Very well, Charles . . . I will go back upstairs, if you

promise to do whatever is necessary to get back the Grange!" she said quietly.

"Aye, chit . . . now get whatever you came for and begone!" he sneered.

She scooped up her shawl and went to the door, but just before she departed she turned and found the viscount's eyes scouring her back. What was he thinking? she wondered. Why did he look so oddly at her? She had no way of knowing then that the viscount fully understood Sir Charles's meaning a moment ago and believed she too had understood. She left them.

Sir Charles turned and faced the viscount squarely, "Well, my lord . . . the Grange is at stake . . . and you know I have nought but one thing left to me."

"Indeed?" sneered the viscount, for he found this end of the gaming repulsive.

"You have shown yourself . . . interested in my ward. She is a lively piece, that I will grant you . . . and she needs just such a man as yourself to tame her shrewish tongue . . ."

"You are suggesting that you would wager your ward against the estate?" supplied the viscount curtly.

Sir Charles flinched but a fleeting moment, "Yes, the girl for the estate."

"You place a high worth on her head!" sneered the viscount. "I have yet to find a woman worth such. What makes you think I would take such a gamble?"

"Because women are relative things with regards to worth! I'd not pay a sou for any I've seen since . . . but had it been Esperida . . . I would have staked that and more. I've seen the way you look at Cassandra. You're itching to get into her bed. Here is your chance," offered Sir Charles daringly.

"You do not take your guardianship very seriously, do you?" said the viscount contemptuously. "I have no desire to take an unwilling wench, and you have already said the girl has a lover . . . some smuggler."

"What does that signify? If I lose, you will have the

51

estate and full control of her until she is one and twenty . . . should you want her that long . . ."

"But as I have said, I have an aversion to rape," retorted the viscount backing Sir Charles into a corner. He wanted to know if Cassie was in on this. Had she understood when she left the room? Was that what she meant when she said, "Do what is necessary to get back the Grange."

"Rape? Did you not hear her when she left? She knows I wager her . . . she will give you no fight. All that matters to her is the Grange. If the Grange goes with you . . . so will she."

It was true, he had witnessed the exchange of the significant looks between guardian and ward. Perhaps they had a further plan. Perhaps they meant for him to lose . . . to go upstairs and claim his prize . . . perhaps they meant some villainy between them? Very well, he would play their game.

" 'Tis done then!" said Kirkby Welford.

A few moments later it was over, but before the viscount made his way upstairs, he turned on the squire. "Now, Charles, tell me. This Eaton you spoke of . . . did he court Miss Farrington?"

Charles brought himself up from his stupor. "What? Eaton . . . stupid puppy . . . he fumbled after her, but she paid him little heed. I told you, her heart is with that smuggler . . . go on, go upstairs, and leave me be!"

"No, Charles, not quite yet! You are now a guest in *my home.* Be certain I have no qualms and would turn you out in an instant should the fancy strike me. So you will answer my questions. When in London you spoke of a gentleman . . . someone you do a great deal of business with . . . profitable business. Can you put me in the way of him . . . for a fee, of course."

"Damn you . . . get out . . . I . . . can't think now . . ." said Charles, sure he was about to give over the insides of his belly.

"His name . . . I would first have his name!" snapped the viscount.

"Would you? Then, by God, you will have it tomorrow! Now leave me be . . ."

The viscount glanced over him curiously. He could see the man was unwell; all right then, he thought. He had waited this long. There was nothing Sir Charles could now do. The squire would have to cooperate with him. He would wait until morning . . . but for now, he would go upstairs and see what his prize had in store for him. He would ferret these two out if it was the last thing he did.

The viscount made his way to Cassie's room with grim determination. He would have to be careful. He fully expected Sir Charles or one of his servants to come charging in on them with pistol ready . . . calling rape. Thought he, the girl herself might have the implement concealed . . . ready to use. He had to know.

He found her room unlocked and it furthered the sneer in his heart. He opened the door quietly, closing and bolting it at his back; he cast his eyes about the dimly lit room. She sat curled up before the fire, cascading billows of flame-colored hair falling down her back. The fingers of the fire lit up her face, and there were tears streaming down its pale softness. She wore a flimsy white nightdress, and the light from the flames caught at its transparency allowing him an excellent view of her voluptuous charms.

She watched him and her mouth opened to speak, but then he was flinging off his coat, unbuttoning and casting aside his silk waistcoat. "What . . . ?" she started, but he was already above her and she could see the hard line of his jaw. Then suddenly he was raising her off the floor, and his voice was breathing in her ear, low and tinted with anger. "Tell me, beauty, in what manner may I expect to be betrayed?"

"Betrayed? Have you lost your mind? Get out of my room!" shouted the maiden, her body trembling at his touch.

"The door is locked against intruders, and I can well see . . . you hide nothing on your person . . ." said he, his eyes raking her. "So how then . . . ?"

"Let me go! Get out of the room. Do you hear me? How dare you?"

" 'Tis no longer your room, my love. 'Tis mine, as is everything in the Grange . . . including yourself. Your guardian has signed over your care to me."

"My faith!" breathed Cassie, she could not believe this to be true, not even of Charles. He would not give over his ward like a common harlot . . . not even he . . .

"Indeed, you play your part well. You don't mean to try and bamboozle me, do you. It won't fadge, m'girl. You knew just what Sir Charles had in mind when he sent you out of the room. You were his trump card! Ah—but then, perhaps you did not expect *him* to lose." Suddenly his arms were pressing her soft pliable body against his chest. His lips descended almost violently upon hers, parting them, exploring their sweetness with a heated fervor. She felt her breasts against the hardness of his chest, and it flashed through her that he was as firm as Circe's wand and far more powerful than Zeus's thunderbolt!

Oh, God! Even now, she wanted him. Was he man . . . or sorcerer? Confound him! He was a devil! What did he mean by this sophistry? What in faith's name did he want from her? She struggled within his embrace, attempting her freedom, but his laugh came low and harsh, and his words lashed at her senses.

"Is it me you fight . . . or the fact that you have lost? Come now, love, the scene has been played out, you need not pursue the role longer," he said raising his hand to the neckline of her insubstantial nightdress. With the single movement of his hand it came away with a tearing sound, falling to her hips. She gasped with the shock and put up her arms at an attempt to conceal her nakedness. His eyes ravished her and he sucked in his breath at the sight of her perfect white round breasts with their rosy nipples. Her waist was small and curved voluptuously towards hips that were round and wondrously sensual. He groaned as with one hand he took both of hers behind her back. His free hand went swiftly, skillfully to fondle one breast. He lowered his mouth to the rose-colored peak, and his tongue etched a circle enticingly, exciting it to firmness. But she struggled too ferociously to keep up such seductive methods. She kicked at him with her feet and tossed her shoulders in a desperate effort, yet every fiber of her yearned to relent to his touch. He lifted his head and saw in her green eyes a light of fear, and he frowned. It was no act. The girl was frightened. Could it be that she loved this smuggler of hers . . . that she had never been taken by another? The thought pinched at him and he held her a moment at arms length. "Tell me truly, Cassandra . . . are you indeed sighing for your smuggler? Has no other possessed you?"

She wanted to slash out at him. She wanted to rail at him. How dare he suggest that any man had taken her to his bed. How dare he? How could he? Instead she spat, "There has never been anyone else!"

He stiffened with the words. He had no intention of taking an unwilling wench, though she deserved rape for her deeds. But that was not his way. He would see her punished . . . but not that way. As he began to step back, the furrow on his brow, the sneer in his eyes as well as his lips, a blast from a pistol pierced the air and brought his head round with a start. The viscount stopped and pulled himself away, suddenly realizing what the sound of the report portended. He cursed as he moved forward, rushing to the door. "Damnation!" she heard him shout, "Damn his soul to perdition for escaping me!" and he was gone from the room.

She felt bewildered. Her head seemed a thing apart from her body with no will to function. What was happening? Then slowly, things began to take shape and substance. It had been the explosion of a gun that had sent the viscount from her! A gun? But . . .? She ran to her door and, holding her torn nightgown about herself, peeped out of the crevice and saw Meg rushing toward the stairs. She called her maid's name, and the woman turned to her at once. "Meg, what is it? What has happened?"

" 'Tis the squire . . . Lord preserve us . . . he has shot himself . . . he is *dead*, miss!"

Cassie closed the door and put a hand to her head. Sir Charles dead? The Grange . . . now in the hands of the viscount . . . and . . . oh, faith, *she was in the hands of the viscount*! Making an abrupt decision, she ran to her wardrobe and yanked out a simple blue muslin. She wriggled into the dress, caught up her brown cloak and tied it round her shoulders. Stockings were slipped on and then covered with her riding boots. She had to hurry . . . for there was no saying when he would return . . . what he would do.

She went to her window and flung open the lattice, climbed onto the sill and took possession of the strong vines that clung to the building's stone surface. She had no fear, she and her brother had often managed it easily.

A few moments later she was in the stables and stroking the white star on her horse's forehead. She cooed to him as she slipped on his saddle and tightened the girth for her weight. With expert nimbleness she was on his back and meeting the cold night wind. In her haste she never noted the presence of another. She missed the small gruff man standing in the shadows. Chips, the viscount's man watched the mistress of Farrington Grange ride her horse to the drive and followed her a bit on foot and discovered that she veered south. He scratched his chin thoughtfully and wondered what was toward at the house, and what the viscount was about letting this one run off like that?

5

Cassie took the south pike for Christchurch, frenzy guiding her pace. The moon was high and bright in the dark but cloudless sky, and the path was one well known to both Starfire and his mistress. She made her way beneath the overhanging willows shadowing the road, took a fence flying, and put a field behind her, cutting her travels by some two miles. She could feel Starfire kick up clumps of earth and grass and knew her pace was far too dangerous for nightriding. She slowed him to an easy trot and he whinnied, for he had liked their speed and would have his head. She assuaged him with soft words of comfort and then lapsed into silence.

It was then, like the fall of an avalanche that her thoughts collected, expanded, eroded, and collapsed. The Grange . . . her Grange . . . it was lost to her forever. Sir Charles had in less than one evening taken a home, lands, tradition that dated back more than a hundred years, and lost it on the turn of a card. Fiend seize his soul! she thought bitterly. By God, how could he have done it? She had heard so many stories of men losing their fortunes, their ancestral homes to hazard, faro, picquet . . . but she never believed Farrington would go that way. Tears formed in her eyes for it struck hard knowing the last threads of her past had been torn asunder. And he . . . her cousin Charles . . . he was dead by his own hand—another blow to the proud name of Farrington.

A vision formed before her eyes. Its colors were shrouded in feathery wisps of mists, with only the black eyes sharply distinct, and the mouth . . . sneering its mockery. Kirkby Welford! God—had she been blind to what he really was! She, who had always prided herself on her intuitive powers, she had been taken in by a common adventurer . . . only out for himself.

How stupid she had been with her fancies, her girlish hopes. All these years Cassie had kept her dreams to herself. She never shared her innermost thoughts for fear that she would be ridiculed or that they would be shot down from her sky. Then he . . . he came, this Viscount Kirkby Welford. A man whose fire ignited her own, and for no reason at all, she found herself drawn, trusting, *wanting* to trust, because her heart told her it was right. Ah, the heart. It pumps, it works ceaselessly and in return requires but one pleasure . . . love. But it is oddly selective, using no known logic in its choice and ends sobbing for respite. Blind . . . I was blind! Cassie shouted in a storm of silence, reproaching her emotions, chastising her brain. She caught the pain in her throat, felt it grow mercilessly. She felt the torture of the degradation pass through her body and leave her weak. 'How—how confound him —how could he have brought a smile to my heart when he was no more than an immoral rake?'

She veered, taking a wooded path and heard an owl calling to its mate echoed in the forest. At any other time, the sound would have drawn a grin, but she heard nothing as she put distance behind her. She had to get to Jack . . . he was the last being left on whom she could rely.

The white stone walls of Jack's thatched cottage glowed

in the darkness, and Cassie saw it a veritable haven on the crest of the hillside. The breeze meandered through the budding branches and played a music that Cassie heard as soft and welcoming. She guided Starfire to the stable where she slid off his back, unsaddled him, quickly rubbed him over with a cloth, and saw him stalled for the night.

She tried not to think of the pass that brought her here, forcing herself to think only that *she was here* . . . and safe. She made her way to the cottage, stopping to peer through the small window. It was too dark to make anything out so she continued to the door and pulled at the latch. It opened easily enough and as she stepped inside she called quietly, "Jack . . . Jack?"

There was no response. She moved to the wobbly table next the stove and found there a tallow candle and matches. This lit, she gazed about the large one room cottage and found it empty. No doubt he was out sporting the night away with one of his pretty wenches. She smiled at the thought, for it was a part of Jack, his merry popularity with the women. He belonged, it seemed, to all, and yet to none . . .

The door opened at her back and she spun round with some fear but relaxed almost immediately. "Jack!" She ran into his lanky embrace, but for the first time in many years, this brought very little comfort.

"Blister it, girl!" snapped the hero of Cassie's youth in some exasperation. "What in thunder be ye doin' 'ere at this hour of the night?" He shrugged off his navy wool shortcoat and dropped it near the fire to dry out the damp.

"Oh, Jack . . . he . . . he lost the Grange at faro to the viscount . . . and . . me as well . . . like so much chattel . . . and then . . . he shot himself! He is dead, Jack . . . and the viscount . . . meant to have all his winnings . . ."

"Bless ye, girl!" interpolated Jack taking up her shoulders and holding her before him, "ye best slow down a bit and give it to ole Jack easy."

She began her explanations in detail, leaving out but one scene, the last between herself and the black-eyed viscount. It would not do to tell Jack her feelings during her near-rape. She did feel, however, that she had to impress upon him the fact that she could not return to the Grange and hence ended her story by saying with something of a blush, "You see . . . my cousin . . . chose to pledge me . . . as a wager . . . in an attempt to win back the Grange . . ."

"How much did he lose to the viscount?" interrupted Jack.

"Thirty thousand pounds," said Cassie lightly.

Jack whistled. "Lordy . . . this black-eyed devil of yers must want ye pretty bad. Took the Grange for the money . . . took ye on against the Grange . . . whew!"

"That is not the point!" snapped Cassie, thinking he was not seeing things as he should. "The point is that the viscount won both the Grange and me . . . and he is not a gentleman! He meant to collect his winnings . . . in full!"

"Aye," he said. He turned from her and thought on all she had told him before releasing another long low whistle. "The devil fly away with the squire's soul! For there never lived one less worthy of his name. To be going and betting his own blood . . . like ye was a prime mare . . ."

". . . and . . . and the viscount . . . to accept such a bet . . ." said Cassie, her eyes swelling with tears suddenly.

He looked at her sharply. "Aye . . . but that, m'girl, is only natural. Ye looking like ye do . . . and his being a man of honor—he had to give the squire a chance to win back his holdings."

She cut him off fiercely. "But Jack . . . I tell you he meant to have me!"

"Did he now? How then did ye get away?" asked Jack, taking a chair and straddling it, placing his chin upon the peak of its back and giving her an open stare.

She blushed. "He . . . he . . ."

"He came to yer room, I dessay . . ." offered Jack helpfully.

60

"Yes he did!" returned the maid heatedly. "And he . . . he . . . tried to . . ."

"He tried to lay wit ye . . . how far did he get, lass?" asked Jack, torn between amusement over her expression and a ready sympathy for what she had been through.

"He . . . he tore off my gown . . . and would have . . ."

"Lordy, girl, spit it out. I know what he would have done, what I want to know is *why he didn't?*"

"I don't know. He stopped suddenly . . . I was nearly crying . . . and he looked at me all at once . . . and asked about you . . ."

"About me? How the devil did he know about me. . . and why . . . ?"

"He had some notion that you were my lover," said Cassie grinning all at once. She too took up a seat and plopped down, watching his face.

He roared with mirth, and she waited for this to subside. "Charles . . . he told him that I had a smuggler in the village whom I paid visits to . . ."

"Aye . . . so he asked about me did he?" said Jack, his mirth spent, his tone thoughtful. "Wonder why it should bother him . . . especially at such a time?"

"Don't be odious! 'Twas dreadful," snapped the lady.

"Sure, m'darlin' . . . but then . . ."

"Oh, horrid man, you are hungry for the lusty details aren't you?" she grinned pulling a quick grimace at him. "That is all really. It stopped him."

"Why?" asked her tormentor unrelentingly.

"If you must know you big oaf, he misunderstood something I said . . . and thought me . . . thought that you and I . . ." she faltered.

"He already thought *that* . . . remember . . . you said Sir Charles told him you had a smuggler for a lover . . . so why the turnabout?"

"It seemed to make a difference, when he thought you my *only* love . . ." managed Cassandra, her cheeks burning, her eyes deeply engrossed with the dark flooring.

Again the full gusty laugh. When Jack next brought his

chin down upon his knuckles and gazed across at her she had put up her chin, and he said with a chuckle, "So the flash cove didn't want the taking of a girl whose heart was snabbled to another, eh? It makes a pretty tale, don't it . . ."

"And then Sir Charles shot himself . . . and here I am."

"And back ye go," said he amiably.

"But Jack . . . I cannot. The viscount is there . . ."

"And ye already said he won't take ye as yer 'eart belongs to me," grinned the man before her, and she was struck by the devilish glint in his eye.

"And there is no saying he won't think better of his scruples!" retorted Cassandra hotly.

Her savior looked her over and put up a brow that told he thought she might be right there. However, no further discussion of the matter continued at this point as the door of the small cottage burst open to admit a young man with a long mane of unruly dirty blond hair.

In some distress, the lad waved an official looking document in their faces, until he spied Miss Cassie, whereupon he stopped short and blinked back in some confusion, "Miss . . . Miss Cassie." At that point he remembered his manners, stepped to her chair, picked up her hand, and began shaking it with some vigor.

Jack sighed with resignation and said lazily, "Unless you mean to take the lass's arm off . . . leave go, Tim!"

The young lad blushed beet red to the roots of his hair, dropped her hand with some force, and began shuffling his feet in a most eye-catching manner. Open-mouthed, Cassie watched this for one amused moment before urging gently, "Tim . . . how pleased I am to see you again. But 'twas not me you came to see as you had no notion I would be here. Perhaps you would like some privacy with Jack?" she suggested.

"Oi don't needs privacy to say what it is Oi got to say," sniffed the lad.

"Then say it!" snapped Jack Rattenbury, his kind heart growing weathered with impatience.

"Oi come to say good-by. 'Tis to the fishes Oi go . . . Oi aim to throw m'self into the seas and let the little divils 'ave at me, Oi do!" announced Tim with some determination.

Jack thought this worthy of his mirth and released it with gusto. Tim looked on, monstrously shocked by his friend's callous attitude, and so it was left to Cassie to comment.

"Oh, Tim . . . would you reconsider? I am sure that if you think on it a bit, you will find that notion not at all comfortable. I daresay you have never felt fish nibbling at your flesh, but I do assure you, it's not at all what you would like!"

This struck Tim Sayers most profoundly, and he weighed it without wondering how it was that Miss Cassie knew what it would feel like to have the creatures of the deep bite at one's flesh. Her fancy seemed most plausible to him. He relented a mite. "Well . . . mayhap Oi would drown first . . . and then Oi wouldn't feel it . . ."

"Lordy, Tim! If ye don't want to be thrown out on yer pink ears, ye better make some sense," exploded Jack suddenly, his amusement at an end. His night's rest was being badly cut up between these children, and he would settle their lives and get to sleep. "Ye can't drown coz ye been able to swim since ye was no bigger than a tot! What are ye trying to bam me for?"

"Oi ain't bammin ye. Oi want to die. If Oi can't drown in the sea that Oi love . . . well then . . ."

"Oh, lordy, lad . . . we'll be 'aving ye think up plans fer yer dropping off all night. Wot's got into yer head?"

" 'Tis Molly . . . she dun run off, Jack . . ." he cried plaintively, adding after a moment's pause in a tone that told how much worse he thought it because of her choice, ". . . with a . . . *military man!*"

"Oh, that *is* dreadful, Tim. Was she someone you . . ."

"We were to be married. Lordy, she sent me after the license, she did . . ." he began, putting his hands through his hair.

Jack swished the air with his hand, indicating his opinion of the tragedy. "Molly were ever a tart, Tim, and ye be well rid of her!"

"Oi don't likes ye calling her that, Jack. No . . . Oi don't."

"Like it or no, she was and is a strumpet!" returned Jack, giving it to the boy starkly. "I didn't say nuthin' before coz I seen 'ow ye was dangling after her. But lordy, son, there ain't a man that sails our *Sweet Mary* that ain't had a samplin' of 'er . . ."

The boy in his misery and sudden anger lurched out with an unsteady swing, missed Jack by some measure, and got himself caught up backwards in the big man's hold. "Steady, lad! Did ye ever know me to lie to ye? What purpose would I 'ave fer giving ye a tarradiddle now? Fiend seize ye, stop yer wigglin', and I'll let ye go."

Tim called upon some inner strength and ceased his struggles. He was set aside and regarded from Jack's bright eyes. "There now, Tim . . . what say ye?"

The boy shuffled about, not meeting the older man's eye. He knew what Molly was . . . knew it the first time he had taken her in his virgin arms and allowed her to teach him all she knew, which turned out to be considerable. He managed a sheepish smile. "She did not . . . not with 'em all. Blister it, Jack! Dan O'Shanter's too dang old and ugly!" At which both men began to chuckle.

Cassie had been listening to all this with wide-eyed curiosity, for they seemed to have forgotten her presence. Marveling, she watched them chuckle over the boy's near escape and wondered how he could be transported from wishing death to himself to such laughter. Did not men's feelings go as deep as the soul? Were such heart-rendings merely for women, poets and artists?

"Fiend seize the girl! You know, Jack, Oi been all over these parts trying to get this blasted license . . . and it put me down ten pounds, it did!" complained Tim suddenly. Then again, recalling for whom he was jilted, he shook his head and said with disgust, "For a *military man!*"

"Here, lad!" said Jack taking out a ten-pound note and placing it roughly into the boy's hand. "Take this and let us hear no more of fish and drowning . . . and give that license over here . . ."

Cassie had removed herself to Jack's cot and put her head down upon his pillow . . . just for a while, she told herself. She could hear their voices trailing off and tried to raise her head and open her eyes to see what they were about, but she could not. The events of the day had come to rule, and Cassie drifted off into a troubled sleep. It was filled with shadows, dark and ominous. They seemed to surround her and when she called for help, a man's face appeared. Black eyes glinted at her through a hazy mist and a mocking smile tortured her. She awoke with a scream to find Jack above her. He re-covered her with the blanket and put a hand up to smooth her hair, "Hush, lass . . . go back to sleep." She felt him kiss her cheek, felt him hesitate and move his lips to hers. Felt the soft, tender pressure and knew no response. She heard, felt, knew his sigh of disappointment, and kept her eyes tightly closed.

The sound of busy clatter permeated the fog loitering about Cassie's head. She stirred on the cot, groaned quietly as she rolled over, but managed in spite of all this to maintain the tranquility of unconsciousness. A pewter plate fell to the wood flooring with a reverberating thud and the unmistakable tone of a youth's oath took to the air.

Cassie blinked and her green eyes saw a dull gray wall, stark and unfamiliar before her. The aroma of coffee and bacon wafted her way in seductive waves and she sniffed. Where . . . ? was the first question that came to her mind, but as soon as the query was fixed in her thoughts, so was the answer. Oh—of course!

Cassandra Farrington turned over and propped herself up on one elbow, allowing the horsehair blanket shrouding her shoulders to fall negligently to her waist. Her hair fell in flaming torrents about her shoulders, and she brushed some wayward locks away from her neck with a casual movement. Her green eyes scanned the corners of the room and found Tim, pan in hand, staring in open admiration. She bestowed a sweet smile and a sleepy good-morning on him, and he stammered in some confusion, "Oi . . . Oi . . . didn't mean to wake ye, Miss Cassie . . . bless me, Oi didn't . . ."

His eyes took in the vision before him traveling over the lovely face, down the length of white neck to the full swells beneath the open lacings of Cassie's blue muslin. He gulped, and Cassie followed the route of his inquiry with a blush. She noted that someone had undone her lacings during the night, allowing her bosom the comfort of freedom. Quickly, she hastened to set herself to rights, attempting light conversation all the while as Tim seemed not at all disposed to turn away.

"Hmmm . . . is that coffee that I smell, Tim?" she asked, smiling at him.

"Aye . . . aye . . . Jack said Oi was to . . . to . . . wake ye and have ye eat yer breakfast . . . but Oi didn't mean to wake ye so soon . . . the eggs . . . they be . . . oh, lordy . . . !" he ejaculated, suddenly realizing that his eggs were near to burning and running headlong to the stove.

Cassie giggled and her eyes found Jack as he entered the large one-room cottage carrying a linen-wrapped loaf of bread. He waved it at her. "Shake yer shambles, child . . . up with ye. Yer wash water be set on the bureau . . . the coffee is piping . . ." He sniffed. "The eggs are done . . . damn, are they done! And I got ye fresh bread!" he added with some pride.

"Where d'ya get that, Jack?" bantered Tim knowingly, "from pretty little widow Hawkins?"

"Shut yer mummer, Tim. I'll have none of those sly looks from ye, and, yes, the widow was nice enough to bake me an extra loaf."

Cassie sent Jack a wide grin, and he looked away, unable to conceal the twinkle in his eyes. He threw over his shoulder nevertheless, "Up with ye, slug–a–bed!"

She jumped up and proceeded to the bureau, screeching

gleefully that Jack was the best of goodfellows for he had thought to provide her with toothbrush, hairbrush and comb. These she used to some advantage before returning to the cot, her stockings in hand. By this time the food had been served, and Jack and Tim had taken up positions at the center table facing Cassie. Both were in the process of lifting a forkful of food to their mouths when this action was halted in midair.

As it was necessary to lift her skirt in order to don her stockings, Cassie had not deviated from the habitual custom, thus affording her audience with an excellent view of calves both slim and alluring. Cassie noted their interested stupefaction and put up one austere brow, cowering them. The gentlemen shamefacedly regarded their plates until she was finished.

"Faith, I do wish I had a change of dress though," she said looking over her wrinkled gown. "I really shouldn't have slept in this last night."

"Bless ye, woman . . . how much do ye think flesh and blood can stand? It weren't in me to let ye sleep naked! Why, the thought of it sets me to burning. And poor Tim here . . . jest look at him!" teased Jack for indeed Tim's hue was the color of fire. "But ye come and eat now, coz after ye'll be changing all right . . . but not into a gown. Lordy, no . . . we'll be packing . . . and ye'll be leaving dressed as a lad . . . though truth has it no one that takes a good look at ye will take ye for anything but a woman!"

"Change . . . pack . . . leave . . . ?" cried Cassie coming to the table.

"Aye . . . ye got that, 'ave ye. Good . . . always liked a bright lass," said Jack.

She took up a piece of the fresh bread and dunked it in her black coffee. "Hmmm, your widow's bread is fine, Jack," she said mischievously.

"It is that," agreed Jack.

"That ain't all the widow does right fine, is it, Jack?" beamed Tim unwisely and received a rap across the head.

67

Cassie giggled but turned sober after a moment. "But Jack . . . really, where do we go . . . and why?"

"Can't stay here. Stands to reason, lass. This viscount of yours . . . ye mentioned his knowing of me. Well then, if he wants ye . . . he'll be after ye . . . willy-nilly."

"He is not *my* Viscount, and I don't think you are right there. He wouldn't dare come for me here. And besides, he doesn't know that I've flown to you . . . or where you are."

"Might though. Can't chance it. Don't fret it. As it happens . . . Christchurch wearies me . . ."

"But what of your widow?" interrupted Cassie naughtily.

"Ye can get a spankin', ye can . . . and there be widows in Dorset," said he amiably.

"Dorset? We go to Dorset? Why?" asked Cassie with some surprise.

"Coz, me lads are sailing the *Sweet Mary* there . . . docking her in Weymouth Harbor. As it happens I'll be getting a shipment in next week . . . thinking of dropping it off in one of them nice little coves thereabout. Besides, got a ken we can stay at north of Weymouth, near the Spithead. We'll pack up and leave soon as ye see fit to finish yer eggs. Eat lass, we'll not be stopping along the way but to water our horses!"

6

The coast of France lay in sight, for it was to Cherbourg the *Sweet Mary* and its free-trading crew were bound. It was just about a week since Cassie had gone to Jack, and it had taken nearly all that time to convince him to allow her this trip at his side. The moment she heard them making plans to sail for a shipment of brandy, she had begged, nagged, cried her way on board.

The *Sweet Mary*, her sail at a right angle, ran with the wind taking the white caps of the bay steadily as she cleaved her way to the Cherbourg harbor. Gulls squawked above their heads, and Cassie watched their frenzy as they dove and rose. The sun shone through a variegated sky of blue, gray, and white. The air was heavily laced with the month of May. Spring had infected the spirits of the *Sweet Mary*'s crew as well. The five-man set of the neat sloop had sailed under Captain Rattenbury for many years, and they were much a family. It was good to be at sea again after a cargo, for their last trip had been over a month past. They jested jovially with one another as they went

69

about their business. Cassie smiled at their antics, but her mind was elsewhere.

She wrapped the warm, blue wool coat about her person tightly and walked the deck moving into the bow of the boat. She discarded her dark floppy hat, allowing her long red hair to be swept into the seabreeze. She felt the salt zephyrs against her cheeks and gazed out to the French coastline ahead, but there was something about her that spoke of despondency. It was strange, she thought to herself. For so long, all she had ever wanted was to be free of her cousin, Charles. For so long, all she had wanted was to run away and sail aboard the *Sweet Mary* with Jack to protect her. Now, all at once, it seemed not enough.

" 'Tis perverted you are!" she told herself rancidly. "You are free . . . Jack is by your side . . . you are actually sailing to France . . . a dream come true . . . and all you can think of is . . . what . . . ? You don't even know!"

A near memory feathered her blood, tickled a response, and she visualized herself in the viscount's arms that first time. That first kiss, when she had so wanted more . . . she tried to force the memory away, but his black eyes haunted her. Then she thought of Farrington Grange. She thought how he had stolen it from her . . . how he had come to her room to take even more. She hated him! She *hated* him . . . and one day she would have her revenge . . . somehow.

An arm went about her shoulders, and she smiled up at Jack's cherubic countenance. He was a man well into his late thirties, yet he had the youthful face of a lad. His hat was well back on his dark head, and his bright eyes were shining with inquiry. "What be ailin' ye, lass? Ye look deep into the dismals, ye do."

"I . . . I don't know . . ." she said quietly.

"Ye ain't been the same since that viscount of yers come down on ye!" he said thoughtfully, his eyes scanning her face.

70

"What has he to do with anything?" she snapped. "Discounting the fact that he stole all that was ever my home!"

"Ho there, lovey, no sense getting hipped wit me," said her free trader, grinning at her broadly. "But still . . . it do seem ye be a might piqued lately," he added, allowing his voice to trail off purposely.

"I am just fine!" then turning the subject abruptly, "imagine, Jack . . . sailing right into a French harbor . . . in broad daylight!"

"Aye. Always queers me to do it . . . seeing as half me life we had to come in by moon, and then into *no* harbor."

"Where did you get your brandy then?" asked Cassie, idly curious.

"Lordy, girl . . . we'd have to wind our way, light the lantern, and wait for an answering call . . . then we'd row into a sandy cove, load up, and make the trip back in the same night. Whew! But it *was* a mite more fun," he declared.

"But now we can do a tour of the village . . . and eat French pastry . . . and look at French shops and . . ." she was saying with a degree of animation.

"Blister it, Cassie!" he cut in hastily. "We ain't here on a spree! We be going in on business!" he admonished.

"But, Jack . . ." she wheedled, putting her hand to his lean chest and looking full at him, her green eyes wide, "Can't we mix the two . . . your business *and* my pleasure?"

She sparked him off without being aware just how she had done it. His rough hands went around her small waist, pulling her to him. She felt the firmness of his lean muscles pulsate against her soft body, and his voice came low and far less jestingly than was his wont. "You light m'hunger, girl, with those sea-green eyes of yers. Pity me, darlin', if ye don't have it in mind to lie wit me, best then be watchful how ye use yer arts!"

It was meant to warn her off, to frighten her or at least make her aware that he was more than just a big brother.

71

However, it had not accomplished its purpose. His tone, his remark had more than half pleased her. She liked knowing that she was capable of stirring a man's heart, and as she was perfectly safe with Jack Rattenbury, she took a mischievous delight in his lusty flirtation.

She purred accordingly, "Now, Jack, m'fine big blade . . . all I ask of you is a bit of French flavor . . ."

He heard the lively banter beneath the music of her voice and fell in line, ever ready for her sport. His hand dropped from her trim waist to her rump, and he coddled it through the faded breeches with some appreciation before she managed to gasp and jump out of his reach. She took a swat at his arm as she went and rounded on him, hands on hips, eyes glaring amiably.

"You take a liberty, sir!"

"Do I? No, m'darlin', 'tis not one ounce what ye well deserve . . . sweetness that ye be," he returned. "But, lordy, love . . . don't be getting yer bristles up. If it's French sugar and spice ye be yearning for, 'tis that ye'll get." Then a pause as a wide grin spread over his smooth cheeks. "But I'll be expecting payment, ye know . . . 'tis only right."

"Oh?" she bargained, "what sort of payment, sir?"

"Aw, now, lass, trust me to take what's fair!"

"Fair? Well, m'fine buck, 'tis exactly what ye'll get. But it will be to *my* way of thinking, not *yours!*" she said dryly, pleased to be well out of his range.

He laughed and picked up her hat from atop the sand bucket and threw it to her. "Put this on, Cassie lass, I don't want every ugly cull on the dock falling into a faint from setting his poppers on ye! Make sure that flash hair of yers be up tight. And, lordy, girl, try and keep a straight line without swinging that pretty butt of yers. I'll be hanged if ye don't look more like a wench in breeches than ye do in a skirt," he grinned broadly.

She picked up her hat and began to tidy her hair. Suddenly Tim called out, "Cherbourg!" and she felt a tinge of excitement run through her. The docks loomed up as they drew closer, and she could already see the busy wharf with the dark-clad people moving about, each one bent on his own purpose.

They veered into an empty portal and began the necessary work of docking. She watched silently as Jack called out orders, and observed the swiftness of his skill as he moved to and fro. Within minutes they were ready to leave the boat. Jack spoke to an older crewman, Dan O'Shanter, and told him to stay behind on the *Sweet Mary*. The man grumbled about wanting to go have a round with a French wench or two which drew some ribald remarks from his younger mates.

"Don't we have to go to a customs house . . . or something?" asked Cassie.

"Lord love ye, child, think me green, do ye? Customs house!" he scoffed. "That's been settled long ago . . . me and them fellows *on this side of the channel* see eye to eye. M'gold takes care of that! They knows the *Sweet Mary* and what we come for . . . and they don't give us no trouble." This he said as they waved at the uniformed men in the customs building and sidled past unmolested.

Shades of browns and grays loomed before Cassie's wide scrutiny. The shabbiness of the wharfside was nothing to its booming activity. There were young maids in mobcaps and aprons, slinging their heavily weighted pails before them as they made the rounds. Sailors in bright blues and stripes were going to and fro, each with a set purpose. And the sounds . . . They were bustling with the loveliness of the French mystique. It poured its way through, the French language, clicking as Cassandra's tutored knowledge found its way past the accent to the meaning. She loved every sight, every scent, and her heart felt overcome with the wonder of the new world she had entered.

Her hand clutched at the sleeve of Jack's coat, and she hurried to keep up with him. She noticed Tim and Ollie looking like young pups with their handkerchiefs tied at their throats and their caps set rakishly. They sauntered up to a full-bodied woman and Cassie eyed them askance. They chortled with the woman in an easy familiarity just as though they were not meeting her for the first time. Cassie turned to Jack expectantly and noted with an uplift of her chin that he was laughing at her.

"Ye might say the wench makes her livin' by . . . er . . . entertainin' their like. A pleasant enuff female . . . but we ain't got time for it now." He put up his arm and hailed, "Tim . . . Ollie . . . lord love ye lads . . . *another time!*" It was merrily ordered, but the two boys knew well the firmness behind the command. They sighed with some reluctance as Cassie watched them fall into line with the other members of the crew.

"I . . . I suppose Tim has forgotten all about his Molly by now?" asked Cassie thoughtfully after walking in silence a moment.

"Bless ye, woman . . . what was there to forget? She were nothin' but 'is first toss in the hay! Took but for 'im to realize that," said Jack grinning.

"Oh," said Cassie frowning. She paused and then heaved a sigh, "Does that mean . . . that a man . . . can . . . and not care . . . at all?"

He stopped on the dirt road beneath his feet and put an arm about her shoulders, his gaze intent on her face. "Now there, missy . . . there be a question to trouble the sages. I be a simple man, no learning past the sea. But I'll tell ye this. All men be cut differently. When it comes to women . . . they don't need to love 'em to lie with 'em! Though there comes a time . . . when a man feels the call to settle down."

She sighed, "It's so different for a woman—at least for me."

"Aye," he tweaked her nose. "And that's 'ow it should be. Don't ye go letting a cove mount ye unless ye got his heart."

"But how will I know?"

"Easy enuff! Ye got me lass . . . heart, soul . . . whatever else goes with it . . ." Again his hand slipped round her waist, to the exquisite surprise of many a passer-by who took a secondary glance over the young lad in the sailor's arms.

"Oh, but Jack . . . I love you in such a different way," she said fretfully.

"Aye," he said with a sigh, "aye."

They had reached a long rambling stone building on the wharfside. Its gray walls overlooked the dark harbor. Encrustations clung to its damp surface, giving it the aroma of the sea and in spite of its shabby appearance, Cassie felt a thrill of delight as they entered through its undersized wooden door.

The tavern galley was nearly empty, discounting the few stragglers—fishermen—seated with their wine at various round tables. Jack motioned with his eyes to his crew of four. "There, lads . . . be at ease for a spell. The lass and I will go in and see the monsieur."

The four men made their way to the tables, hailing the barkeeper jovially. Cassie noted before they left the large galley, that two women whose dresses scarcely covered their voluptuous bodies had found Jack Rattenbury's crew very good company indeed.

He took her elbow and steered her to the back hall, where a well-polished door, much in contrast with its surrounding walls, brought up Jack's hand. He pounded on it and called out, his voice showing his spirits, "Get thee out here, ye old dog! 'Tis Jack . . . Jack Rattenbury!"

She heard the scurry of footsteps, then a chair scruff across the wooden floor behind the door, heard the latch and then was staring across at a small, well-dressed man with a balding head and small bright eyes. "Jacques . . . you wonderful devil!" cried the man embracing the captain of the *Sweet Mary*. Releasing him, he ushered them into the room, talking all the while, "I expected you last week . . . and when you did not arrive . . . *mon Dieu!* I said to myself . . . they have caught the poor Jacques! But no . . . you are here, and all is well, *non?*"

"Yes, all is well," said Jack, closing the door at his back.

The Frenchman noted Cassie's presence, and his eyes scanned her with interest, before he released a low, knowing chuckle. Cassie's disguise would fool no one upon a second glance. Her lines were all too feminine.

"Oh-ho . . . you have with you the little woman, eh?" said the Frenchman, intrigued.

"My lass," said Jack suddenly pulling Cassie next to him. "Aye, she is more sister to me than if she were born from m'mother's womb." There was a hint of hardness in his voice, spelling a warning the Frenchman was quick to understand.

"But of course, of course. It is with much pleasure that I greet you, mademoiselle," said the Frenchman, still beaming wide. "Please . . . be seated . . . join me in a glass of wine," he said, returning with the offered treat as his guests took chairs around the covered table.

He poured, but his speech never tired. "Ah, you will find this most excellent . . . just as you will find the shipment awaiting you."

"I need seventy tubs, Louis," said Jack quietly.

"No, you need seventy five . . . 'tis what I have . . . 'tis what you will take, yes?"

"Yes. At nineteen," said Jack.

"At twenty . . . prices go up."

Jack started to rise. The Frenchman put out his hand and detained him. "But . . . for such a good friend . . . nineteen. Though it leaves me very little profit."

"Ha!" said Jack.

" 'Tis a bargain, yes?"

"Done!" said Jack, downing his glass of wine and taking up Cassie's and gulping it down as well. "Now m'sister 'ere has a mind to see a bit of France before we take to the sea. I'll leave m'lads here and be back to get m'shipment in an hour," he said, rising and taking Cassie's hand.

The Frenchman nodded and hurried to open the door. "It has been a pleasure, *mon ami* . . ."

As they walked out into the salty air, Cassie breathed, "Gracious, Jack! It seems so odd that but four years ago we were at war with France."

"Aye, but their tiger is caged!" he said quietly.

"Does that sadden you?" she asked incredulously.

"Lordy, girl, I don't mix with politics. What good would it do me to bother? But that Napoleon . . . he was a devil of a man, someone the Frogs could look up to. Now they got themselves a fat king robbin' them of their cash and their pride. Why, it don't bear thinkin' on!"

"Hmm, the Bourbons do seem to be about to make the same errors over again, but . . . Oh, Jack, let's take this avenue!" she cried with some excitement.

They walked down more fashionable streets lined with stores sporting the new bowed windows, displaying silken gowns, plumed hats, and intricate jewelry. Cassie oohed, aahed, and sighed with appreciation and Jack grinned all the while. His heart was fairly chaffed with longing. He wanted her; if ever he *could* settle down and have him a son, he'd like to do it with Cassie Farrington. But he was one for facing truths, and truth was, she was not in love with him. And his was not a selfish love.

Cassie's countenance became riveted to a window displaying sweetcakes in alluring shapes and colors. Jack glanced at her, gave over a hearty laugh, and pulled her inside. A few moments later they were again strolling down the street, and Cassie was gobbling up her French pastry. A bit of cream dotted her nose and once again Jack laughed, swiped at it with his finger, and sucked it away. "Ye ain't nought but a babe!" he declared teasingly.

She smiled, not minding this chastisement at all. They toured the streets of Cherbourg until Jack consulted his timepiece and declared that they would miss the tide if they didn't start back. "Come on, lass, we had best shake our shambles!"

"Oh—so soon?"

He pinched her cheek and pulled her along without further comment, until they were once again standing before the little gray tavern. Inside, Jack stopped a moment to glare at the remainder of his crew. Barkes and Widdons grinned sheepishly.

"Where be Tim and Ollie?" demanded Jack, his brows drawn in a frown.

Barkes shrugged and pointed upwards with his thumbs. "They be . . . takin' a bit of . . . dessert."

Jack's eyes went to the stairs and he shook his head ruefully. "Damned fools! Hoary-looking those morts were!" He turned to Cassie, and his voice was stern, "Wait here, lass!" With which he took the stairs, two at a time. He came upon the first door, listened awhile, shook his head again, for he had discovered both lads to be within, and then proceeded to give the door a hearty banging. "Get up, ye good-for-nothing lubbers! Avast there, ye bobs, out wit ye. Ye've got five minutes to finish the business and into the cellar wit ye!"

This made him grin, for he could hear the shuffle within and, satisfied, he descended the stairs and took Cassie's arm. He saw her wide-eyed expression and the question on her face, and he gave a short laugh. "Lord, girl, but ye be learnin' a sight more than I intended. Come on, lass o' mine, this be no place for a lady!"

He led her down the hall they had traveled before, past the Frenchman's open portal to yet another door. Here Louis produced a large iron key and threw wide a heavy oak door. It opened onto steep, narrow steps which led to the cellars beneath. Two tallow candles were lighted, and Cassie wrinkled her nose over their scent for, unlike wax candles, they were made from animal fat and gave off a not altogether pleasant odor. At the bottom of the stone steps they found yet another door of metal and wood. This opened ino a tunnel and along its walls were stacked tubs of French brandy. Torches were lighted along the damp dark walls before Jack and Louis put their heads together and began counting out the payment for the kegs.

"*C'est bon!* I go up now and tell your men to come help with the load, yes?"

"Yes, and send a few of yours as well . . . they will be paid and it will make the thing go faster."

"Yes, I will do this!" said Louis, leaving them alone.

Cassie gazed around the dimly lit tunnel. The torches

made an amber glow, and the stale salt water clinging to the damp walls gave off a pungent odor. The rapping of water against stone beat a cadence, but she could not as yet see the canal.

She held tight to Jack's sleeve and he led her farther into the tunnel. "Jack, Jack! Where are we going . . . where does this lead?"

He pointed before them. "Right smack up to the harbor, lass. 'Tis a prime ken Louis 'as. 'E built 'is tavern wharfside, for easy reach to the sea. This 'ere leads right beneath the docks. We'll be puttin' these tubs of brandy right onto the *Sweet Mary* as soon as m'lads get their butts down here!" he said with some impatience.

Two Frenchmen speaking hastily to one another went past them before Ollie, grinning stupidly, and then Tim brought up the rear. Widdens and Barkes, two large quiet men, made up the last of Jack Rattenbury's crew. Tim attempted to set to work, avoiding his captain's cocked brow, but Jack thought it best not to leave go and continued to stare hard at the young boy, who had just attained his nineteenth year. Tim flushed and managed, "Oi . . . Oi . . . well . . . Hell, Jack!"

"Get thee to work, lad! Ye be nought but a young fool. Ain't I told ye to be careful who ye takes a toss with. Those morts were two sickly ones . . . twice yer age . . . and *you* . . . !" he pulled a face at the ginger-haired Ollie. "Ye be a sight older than the lad . . . thought ye would know better! I'll crack yer heads fer ye if ye come down with the hoary ague!"

They mumbled something about the wenches being clean enough, before Jack smiled and told them to keep their mummers shut and get to work. "Now, I'll be meetin' ye at the *Sweet Mary,* I'd best go pay me respects to the Customs House."

He took Cassie's hand and turned with her, going back up the double flight of stairs to find Louis awaiting him. "Well, *mon ami,*" said the Frenchman, beaming. "You go with the brandy . . . and you are pleased . . . yes?"

"Yes," said Jack laconically.

"Ah, you Englishmen . . . you are a strange lot . . . but I like you well. Go in peace, *mon ami* . . . and let me see you again. Perhaps next month I will have another shipment for you."

Jack nodded and pulled Cassie along. They reached the white stone building of the Customs House a few minutes later, and he left her sitting on its stoop. He yanked hard on her floppy hat, pulling it low over her eyes and admonished her severely. "You keep your pretty little arse down on these steps, mind now . . . don't ye look up, or round, till I get back."

"Aye," she said sticking out a dainty tongue, just in case he took her acquiescence for meekness.

He grinned broadly. "Keep that up, m'fine lady, and see if ye don't find yeself over me knee!" With which he disappeared into the Customs House.

Some forty minutes later Cassie sat astern beside Dan O'Shanter at the tiller and watched Cherbourg with its narrow dirty streets and its French fascination shrink into a shadow and a memory. It had been a splendid adventure, but it was good to be heading for English soil again. For no reason at all, a glinting pair of black eyes bedeviled the horizon, and a mocking smile poured heat into Cassie's veins. "Oh, faith!" she thought with some desperation, "will I never get his face out of my mind? Why does it plague me so?"

Sweet Mary, reaching with the wind now abeam, made her speedy path towards Weymouth. It was good having the wind thus, for it meant the sloop could make excellent time. Jack was busy shouting orders to his men, as well as bending, jumping, lifting—very much a working captain. The neat sloop was one of the finest smugglers' boats in Dorset. She was equipped to transform herself into a homely looking trawler, or a simple trader out for a cargo of culm. She was furnished with a change of different-colored sails, lest she need to disguise herself, and it was to that end that her captain was now engaged.

The seventy-five tubs had been stowed on board, but they were not visible. They had exchanged their dark tunnel for the bleak recesses in a double bottom and a false bow. Here they lay with their special tackle in waiting. To be sure, one could traverse the sloop and see no sign of them, but still, the crew of the *Sweet Mary* would not chance that to the careful inspection of an exciseman. They had additional precautions rehearsed, timed to a nicety and would, if necessary, implement them.

Cassie cast her green eyes over the old, dark man and attempted to draw him out of his silent vigil. "What are we about now, Dan?"

"Eh? What else, we got to make our time and get to those scurvy porters . . . damn their souls!"

She was shocked at this and stared wide-eyed at him, hoping for an explanation. He didn't offer any as he continued to work the tiller, but Jack dropped down beside Cassie with a broad smile. "Dan 'ere . . . as do most of us free traders, think the porters a bad lot. All they do is carry and slink, breakin' heads wherever they find trouble, and more often than not throwin' us poor devils to the revenuers to save their own 'ides!"

"Porters? What are they?" asked Cassie, intrigued.

"Lord love ye, girl, they be the land-carriers . . . land smugglers!" answered Jack, surprised by her lack of knowledge.

"Oh? And they are not a nice set, I take it?"

"Humph!" said Dan O'Shanter.

"You take it right, lass. There's been more than one or two of 'em that's cried 'rope' on a free trader to save himself, but we need 'em to take shipment inland. Nothin' for it but to work with 'em, you know."

Jack moved off again, leaving her to her thoughts, and she watched the crew work the tackle. Beneath the scudding clouds they began affixing a strange-looking necklace to the tubs. It was made of rope and rocks, linking each tub of brandy to the next. She addressed Dan again. "What is that the boys are at?"

" 'Tis the sinkin' rope," he said curtly. "Lordy, girl, but ye do 'ave a lot of questions. Stop plaguin' me. I'm an old man and don't have the mind to jabber wit ye!" he said roughly. He was of the opinion that women had no place on board a boat. They spelled trouble . . . and superstition had it they were bad luck!

She moved away from him, not at all affronted. She understood his nature and knew it was not herself, but his own code that caused his rather gruff manner. She went to Jack, who had taken a moment to scan the northwest light. "Jack, what is a sinking rope?"

" 'Tis what we do with the tubs if we sight a cutter!"

"You sink the tubs?" she asked incredulously.

"Aye . . . we wait till we catch sight of our bearings . . . and then over they go. Can't take us in if there be no contraband on board. Then later we come by with our grapnel and pick it from the brine!"

"But doesn't the brandy . . . become spoiled?"

"Not if it ain't down there too long. Lordy, if we leave it past its time, the thing turns into a *stinkibus!*"

"Hmmm. I imagine it would," she agreed. She sighed then. "Jack . . . don't you want to give it up though? Isn't it all too risky? And after all . . . it is against the law!"

"Laws, Hell!" said Jack with much feeling. "There ain't no life in pound dealing! Laws, ha! What 'ave they to do with the common folk?" Nuthin' and well ye know it, lass. They be made to better the quality and no others. 'Tis good honest work to fight against bad laws. And that's what me and mine be doin'!"

"Aye!" agreed Tim. "Who likes taxes? They be stranglin' our fine country with their damnable taxes . . . and their corn laws!"

"Lord, ye said a mouthful!" agreed Ollie, picking up the spirit. "Corn laws! Devil's laws they should be called. If ever a set of laws were meant to choke the life out of good honest workers . . . Why, m'sister, she be a weaver up north, but she barely gets enough—her and her family—to feed their mouths!"

"Aye," agreed Jack. "The thing is the taxes and the corn laws need change, but the gentry like things the way they be. Wot do they care if our babes go hungry as long as theirs don't?" He shook his head. "I'll not buckle to pound dealing till m'country thinks more of the people that work it!"

She saw the expression of the men and realized that they were more than a little violent in their emotions over this. She didn't know much about such things, but suddenly she had a deep desire to learn more.

However, for the time being, they had to make tracks to Lulworth Cove, and the men turned their attention to the sea. The cargo they carried would first have to be landed, and this would take some doing. Three hundred gallons of French brew sat waiting its fate as the *Sweet Mary* sped water. Visibility was becoming less and less with the oncoming dusk. The weather was churning up suddenly, misting over. The swells took on size as they lapped the sloop, sending their spray to tease the crew into submission. But they were sailors all—even Cassie, who had often sailed with her brother when they were young.

The moon rose, but it gave them little guidance as it lay hidden behind dark thick masses of clouds. It peeped capriciously at them now and then, fording their path.

Jack was at the wheel, and his face was set in hard lines, for he had seen an unmistakable outline. He said nothing to his crew, as he veered the sloop towards its bearings, but then again, his last hope was run through. There she was—a Revenue Cutter—and Cassie pointed with a hushed whisper as she saw it astern.

Jack cursed softly to himself, for she veered, and he was certain she had spotted them. "All right lads . . . we'll have to move quickly," he said with quiet urgency.

"Did she see us, Jack?" asked Tim softly.

"Aye, but we'll make it. Get the sinkin' rope ready, for we'll have to dump our load."

"Hell!" said Dan O'Shanter with some vehemence. "Damn their eyes, the scurvy lot of 'em!"

"Never mind, Dan," said Jack soothingly. "We'll get our tubs over in time. See if we don't!"

"Aye," said the old fellow, shaking his head at the thought of all the extra work they were being put to.

Cassie stepped out of their way and kept a watch for them at the stern as they dropped the necklace of tubs overboard. It was secured both astern and at the bow as the *Sweet Mary* put water behind her and made for the chalk cliffs ahead. Cassie watched the tubs in the sea. They bobbed between the swells as the sloop made for its shore bearings. The circular cove was just before them, promising their cargo sanctuary, and then there was the flash of a blue lantern.

"The porters . . . they be there on time. Damnation! And we not able to give 'em their due. Hell!" complained Dan O'Shanter.

Then suddenly Cassie gasped, "Jack, Jack! There she is . . . coming out of the mist!"

Jack turned to find the cutter coming at them fast, and he cursed hard. His voice when it came next was harsh, "Cut the lashings, lads!"

In a moment the lashings were cut, and the necklace took its course down to the bottom of the brine. The galley was looming up larger, and Dan O'Shanter went to the tiller again. A new and deadlier game had begun as the *Sweet Mary* veered round from shore and headed toward Weymouth.

"I . . . I don't think they saw us sink the cargo," said Cassie tremulously.

"No. Oi don't think they did, Miss Cassie, but we'll be headin' toward Weymouth to lead 'em away jest in case," offered Tim as he worked the tackle.

The sloop led the cutter but it was evident that they stood little chance. Cassie went up to Jack and he took up her hand, pressing it to his chest. "Do ye fear, child?"

"Aye, for you," she said quietly.

He laughed, "Don't then, for there ain't a cutter or a captain alive that can hold ole Jack Rattenbury. Got me reputation to live up to. Besides, we can't be taken in. The evidence be at the bottom of the sea!" Then he frowned to himself, and after a pause his hand went to his waist and untied a leather purse. He put this into Cassie's hand and said gently, "Hold this for me, girl . . . coz . . . see her coming on us. The captain is bound to board us, and he won't think to search a wee thing like yerself!"

"All right Jack," she said softly. She had a sick feeling in the pit of her stomach. Something awful was going to happen—she just knew it!

It was inevitable. They were overhauled by the *Duke of York*, and the captain of the revenue cutter with two of his armed sailors came on board the *Sweet Mary*. He walked up to Jack and glanced over him with a sardonic twist of his mouth. "You, I presume, are the captain of this . . . questionable vessel?"

"I am and would know what business you have boarding her?" said Jack daringly. He had pushed Cassie between his men and told her to keep her face averted. She was doing precisely that when the lantern held up by the captain's first mate was swung her way.

"What cargo are you carrying?" asked the captain of the *York*.

"None, sir!" said Jack.

"None?" he turned to his men, "Search the hull! And keep your eyes open for a false bottom . . . all these smugglers seem to have them!" He returned his attention to Jack. "What do you call yourself?"

"M'mother give me the name of Jack . . . m'father, Rattenbury. Lord knows that makes me Jack Rattenbury!" he said inclining his head.

The captain of the *Duke of York* looked impressed. "Upon my soul! They say you have escaped more revenuers than ever a smuggler before you has sighted. 'Tis said you are the devil himself. Well, well, I have caught me a grand fish. Jack Rattenbury, indeed!"

"Begging your pardon, Captain," suggested Jack. "But, seein' as ye ain't got evidence to hold me, ye be foresworn to let me and me crew pass!"

"That is true, Rattenbury. But I seem to recollect a colleague of mine wanting dearly to get his hands on you. It seems you evaded him . . . and there is this document he has allowing him to arrest you on sight!"

"Meanin' no disrespect, Captain, but it queers me how he is to manage it when he ain't here to do the job, nor is the papers ye speak of," said Rattenbury, keeping his cool demeanor.

But the man he spoke to cared little for rules and to be able to say that he had captured Jack Rattenbury was too good a thing for him to pass up. "As to that, Rattenbury, don't worry your head about it. We'll bring you all together . . . at Bodmin!"

"Bodmin?" ejaculated Jack, much surprised. "That's in Cornwall. You don't have the right to transport me there without papers."

"Don't I?" said the captain, his smile vicious. "We'll see." He turned to his first mate. "You and Mr. Leeds see that they maintain silence, while we tow them into Weymouth."

Cassie's green eyes narrowed with the flurry of thoughts that crowded her mind. Something would have to be done. She watched as the amber lights of the harbor loomed into view. Soon, they would be dockside. Suddenly, she was up and her head was over the side, giving every indication that she was violently retching.

Mr. Leeds came forward and meant to tap her shoulder with his musket, but Jack put his foot in the goodfellow's path, thus tripping him up. He rounded on Jack with a snarl, "Watch it there, cully!"

"Damn your soul, seaman!" returned Jack amiably. "Can't you see the poor bairn is sick. 'Tis his first trip on the sea."

Cassie had slipped out of her wool coat and, while she maintained an excellent account of herself for the sailor to hear, she allowed the coat to slip to the floor. Then suddenly she was gone. She had slipped over the side making a neat splash into the dark water below.

7

Think not that Viscount Welford who, as it were, started
Cassandra Farrington on her unlawful escapade, sat idly
back. He was a man of tenacious stamp and meant to
carry out his plans in the face of any obstacle. Now, since
it happened that Cassie played an important role in the
conclusion of his schemes, he had to find the wench. And
one could almost feel the fire of his determination to find
her and bring her under thumb.

Several things chanced to get in his way and slow him
down. There was, of course, the untimely and unexpected
demise of one Charles Farrington. The circumstances surrounding his death very naturally called down questions,
and a magistrate from Southampton appeared. However,
this worthy gentleman seemed to think all was in order
and soon took his leave. Then there was the question of
the viscount's newly acquired ward, Cassandra. It was put
about that the viscount had sent her to Bristol to stay with
some female relatives until the gossip regarding her cousin
had subsided. This was readily believed by all, excepting

Meg and Harris. These retainers regarded their new employer from beneath knit brows and knew better.

Thus it happened that nearly a week had gone by before the viscount was able to pursue the quest for his missing ward. It was just about the time that Cassandra walked the streets of Cherbourg with her smuggler that the viscount stood in the stables with his man Chips.

"Damnation, Chips! That was one unexpected piece of bad fortune!" grumbled the viscount to the older man.

"Ay, that is was," agreed the small stout fellow. He had been in his lordship's service some eleven years, and they enjoyed a closeness few in their situation ever attain. "More's the pity, but never ye mind it, sir. Truth will stand when a thing's failin'."

"The thing is . . . I never thought the blackguard had it in him to do away with his stench-filled life," growled the viscount. "Well, there is nothing for it but to proceed as best we can. First, we shall have to discover where the girl is hiding herself."

"Ay, the wee bonnie. She took off in the murk she did . . . lowping fer the laigh, I'd say," said the Highlander thoughtfully.

The viscount frowned at his man who had a habit of dropping into his brogue now and then. "She did what . . . where?"

"That night, m'lord . . . run off on her high prancer . . . for the lowland . . . toward the sea." He saw his employer eying him askance and added apologetically, "Seen 'er, I did . . . forgot aboot it till now."

"And the town south of here is?" asked the viscount, one brow still up.

"That would be Christchurch . . . aye . . . Christchurch," offered the groom.

The ebony eyes narrowed, for the name of the town had sparked off a memory. Cassandra's lovely countenance with her well-defined cheekbones and her sweet full lips zeroed into focus. This set off an irrational sensation that coursed through his blood, and he tried to ignore it . . . tried to ignore the bewitching quality of her voice as he recalled her words. That day, the second day of his stay at Farrington, she had been gone, and when she returned she mentioned Christchurch. He had assumed she had gone shopping, and she had blushed . . . actress that she was . . . and had admitted to visiting a friend. He wondered at her foolishness for but a fleeting moment before exploding.

"Of course! Hell and brimstone, Chips! The wench has gone to her free trader . . . Jack Rattenbury!" He mounted his horse, and his groom hurried to do the same, calling plaintively.

"Lordy, where may he be?"

"I think we may discover him easily enough, Chips." With that he was off, giving his groom job enough to follow.

The ride to Christchurch was not a long one, and the viscount trotted through its cobbled streets easily until he spied a tavern that looked to him as though it might be one friendly to a free trader.

He exchanged a glance with Chips, whose look told him that he was much of the same opinion, before he dismounted and sauntered into the unsavory-looking inn.

It did not take overlong for the viscount to discover the way of Jack Rattenbury's cottage. A diplomatic question, a friendly smile and a proffered coin produced the required instructions. And once again they were to horse.

Welford and Chips approached the hill cautiously, for he had no idea what sort of fellow the smuggler might be, but even at a distance, he knew that they would find the house empty. It had just such a look about it . . . and he sensed that it would not hold that which he sought.

Nevertheless, they stabled their horses and made for the small cottage. A knock upon its weathered door seemed to echo back at them, and with a sigh the viscount took hold of the latch, bent his head, and entered the one-room dwelling. Once inside a quick scanning confirmed his suspicions. Jack Rattenbury was no fool. He had taken his prize and made off. But had Cassandra been here? He searched the room for a sign and found one at last. In her haste Cassie had not bothered to remove the hairs from a brush left behind on the bureau. Its cinnamon gold dazzled in the light. Welford looked at it strangely for a moment and once again reminded himself what it represented to him. He would have his vengeance, whatever the cost.

Chips shrugged his shoulders and said cautiously, for he could see his lordship was in a vile mood, "Methinks our birds 'ave floon their nest, m'lord."

As the viscount turned, a shadow cast itself into the room catching the viscount's eye. He looked across to the doorway and there found a tall, well-rounded girl of no more than eighteen. She wore her long brown hair loosely about her shoulders, and a half-apron was tied to her waist, over a plain, drab servant's gown. Her face was fair, her lips full and moist, but the viscount found the look in her bright eyes not to his taste.

"Well, dear me," she said as though startled to find strangers there. But then she had a moment to survey the viscount, and a full smile swept her face, for she found him very much to her liking. "I didn't mean to . . . I . . . I was looking for . . . someone," she offered.

"Indeed," prompted the viscount, "then you don't live here I take it?"

"Gawks, no!" ejaculated Molly, much struck by this. " 'Tain't likely! Jack now, he can't abide the sight o' me, though one of his men . . . well now, that be a different tale . . . and 'twas after him I come," she said, winking at the viscount.

"Ah, I see," said that gentleman. Then releasing a sigh, he gave the place one last look. It would seem this was a closed port.

"Well, now," pursued the maid. "A flash cove like yerself . . . what would ye be doing here at Jack's cottage? Ye can't give me no round tale coz I jest wouldn't believe ye to be revenuers."

"No, we are not excisemen," smiled the viscount.

"Well, then, mayhap . . . *I'll* do in Jack's stead . . ." offered the wench, coming forward, swaying her hips invitingly.

"What is your name, and what are you doing here?" asked the viscount authoritatively.

"I'm called Molly, and I come to make it up with m'beau. No crime in that . . . is there?" she asked, twirling her long hair over her finger and moving close to the viscount.

"Your beau . . . he works for Jack Rattenbury?" asked the viscount, coming to the point.

"In a manner of speaking . . ." She sent her eyes over the cottage and exclaimed, "Goodness! What bobbery are they at now? This place 'as been clean swept, it 'as!"

"Exactly so," agreed the viscount.

"Bless me! I've only been gone a few days . . . had a notion to marry a military fellow, but he . . . Never mind him. Thought I'd pick it up with Tim. But now where can Jack have spirited them all off . . . ?" she said putting her finger to her mouth in thoughtful perplexity.

"Happen the free trader 'as another ken!" put in Chips. "He's flit there . . . make no mistake!"

"Hmmm . . ." said Molly. A light shot into her eyes as she thought of the Spithead, but she said nothing. However, the viscount had seen the momentary gleam and quietly produced a gold coin, holding it up before her. She licked her lips and reached, but he pulled it away.

"First, Molly . . . where is his other ken?"

Molly touched her lips fingering them seductively, her eyes inviting his lordship to peruse the line of her neck.

"It queers me to know for certain. Jack now, he had a brace of prime kens scattered about, but I do seem to remember me Tim speak of one in particular." She smiled indulgently over her former beau's memory. "The twiddle-poop would get all goggle-eyed when he spoke of it. This ken had some secret room—the blue room he called it—laid out some hundred years ago . . ."

"And that would be?" inquired his lordship impatiently.

She held out her hand to him and pursed her lips, "As I said, I couldn't be certain . . ."

The viscount smiled and dropped the coin into her eager palm.

"And now . . . ?"

" 'Twould be the Spithead. It lies some two miles or so north of Weymouth Harbor. Lordy, I remember onct when Tim . . ."

"Thank you," said his lordship, cutting her off short. He nodded over his shoulder at Chips and was gone through the doorway.

Chips cast the girl a long look of appraisal, tipped his peaked cap, and gave the chit a wink before following. She smiled to herself, pleased with this attention. She sighed presently. Her military blade had taken her best and left her without a wedding ring on her finger. Sure now, he had been the better catch but Tim had been in her pocket, and now she had neither. 'Twas a sorry pass indeed. However, she thought of her many charms and a moment later was cheered. She'd have Tim round her finger again soon —and if not Tim—someone else.

In the stable the viscount cast a frown at his groom. "Weymouth . . . that would be at least half a day's ride from here?"

"Aye. Leastways, I think it be," agreed his groom.

"Then we'll return to the Grange, pack an overnight portmanteau, and then proceed."

This attended to, it was well into the afternoon before they set out for Weymouth. It was not an unpleasant ride, for the roads were good, the air fresh, salty, and invigorating. The flowers blooming in the landscape gave a pleasing touch of color among the vales. Their route took them along the coast, and now and then they were able to catch a sight from the high white cliffs of the sea-green channel below. The road wound through stretches of thickly plumed vales, and trees everywhere sported their new spring foliage. They passed orchards full with the hint of future crops, yet all that loveliness had no effect on the viscount.

Kirkby Welford, did not really enjoy the passing landscape. Nature had lost its power to lift his flagging spirits. He was a man lost to his obsession. He was in a fret. He knew only one purpose, to get his hands on that chit, Cassandra Farrington.

She was the only link left to him, the only chain that would lead him to Nathan . . . and he had to get to Nathan! The very thought that he might be near to coming upon her excited him. He told himself, 'twas because she was vital to his motives, vital to his plans . . . but, irrationally, the thought of her did something to his blood, and he was all too aware of this. Damn her! And damn her again! he thought viciously. How can anyone lie with her eyes all truth and innocence? How had she managed to perfect the art? Well, she knew who this Nathan was. He was certain of it. She knew the man's full name, and she knew his whereabouts . . . and soon, he would too!

The viscount made several stops to refresh the horses, and each time Chips noted with thoughtful interest the fidget his master was in to be off again. It was just about the time the viscount with his groom reached the Spithead, that Cassie was diving to freedom into the bay at Weymouth.

8

The *Duke of York*'s first mate as well as Mr. Leeds pushed the crew of the *Sweet Mary* out of their way in an effort to look overboard for the daring lad. But it was useless, Cassie was too good a swimmer to show herself. She kept under water, making in the general direction of the docks. She popped her head up, sucked in air, and was down again. The weight of her waterlogged boots slowed her down, but she made it to the battered wharfs and held onto the oak stanchions while she regained her breath.

Her escape had caused much commotion on board the *Sweet Mary* and the *Duke of York*. However, the cutter's captain, upon hearing it was no more than a green boy who had taken to the deep, was inclined to let it pass. He had both his cutter and the *Sweet Mary* docked without any further ado and went himself to secure post chaises and constables.

Cassie remained beneath the wharf for some time before she sensed it would be safe to make for the beach. She swam through the salty calm of the bay until the village lights were left behind her. She scrambled to her feet in the gentle breakers, exclaiming only once when an oversized crab decided she looked like a tender morsel and attempted a sample.

Sinking down on the pebbly beach she removed her sodden boots. Her hat was gone and her hair dripped the icy water onto her shoulders. She was suffering with the cold and the damp, but she could not take time out now for such concerns. She had to do something, or Jack would be taken to Bodmin Prison.

Carrying her boots in one hand, she raced up the beach to the road. It took but a moment to get her bearings, and she began crossing the field to the little cabin she had shared with Jack this past week.

An hour later she was in her blue muslin gown, her hair piled on top of her head. She had dried her boots by the fire, but when she put them on again she found them still terribly damp. No matter, there was nothing else for it. She went to a trifle box that Jack kept beneath his cot and produced the special license Tim had procured a week ago. She held it a moment and organized her thoughts, for she had a plan. A good plan, she told herself.

She found Jack's knife in its sheath and slipped it into the strap of her boot. Then she donned her hooded cloak and went to the makeshift stables for Starfire. He was ready for a run, for he had been cooped up in his stall since the previous afternoon. It was already late night— Cassie guessed it to be nearing ten or so—when she hit the main pike to Weymouth. However, the sound of coaches approaching sent her into the forest brush, and there with her hand over her horse's mouth, she waited.

Two post chaises had been procured for the journey to Bodmin. Each held a driver, a constable, and three prisoners. The windows of the coaches were locked tight and she imagined the crew were roped one to the other as was the custom for prisoners. They passed by her, and she saw Jack's face pressed against the window pane of the first coach.

It came to her suddenly that now it *was* late, really

quite late. Would they not have to stop for the night? She drew some inner calm and power from this hope. However, she received her first surprise when they arrived at a posting house along the road and instead of putting up for the night, appeared merely to be making a water stop. It was a drab little inn with but two ostlers available to tend the coach horses. The drive swung in a semicircle brushing the stone inn and wooden stables before joining the road again. It lay fully exposed to Cassie's view as she watched from Starfire directly across in the woods.

She maintained her vigil from the darkness of the woods and saw the two constables go off toward the shabby inn. They were arm in arm and much inclined to be jolly. They had, after all, the singular honor of delivering the most famous smuggler in England to Bodmin. In addition to that, they were being given traveling expenses, and they meant to use it wisely . . . on traveling. This meant sampling the libations of as many inns as they could along the way.

The drivers remained seated, each on the coach he guarded, each with a long pistol in his lap. The windows were tightly locked and Cassie could see no way of getting the knife to Jack. It was basic to her plan, delivering the knife into his keeping. She knew that the prisoners would be expecting something from her, for could they believe she would escape and not bring them aid? Then she heard a loud commotion coming from Jack's prison coach.

Jack and the companions of his coach who were Tim and Dan O'Shanter, began at his command a loud thumping with their feet and heads. It brought their driver down, and he unlocked the window. "Bless ye, lads, are ye going daft in there?" He was not a wicked fellow, this driver, having himself spent some time in various prison establishments during his less profitable ventures, and he was well disposed to sympathy.

"Aye!" said Jack desperately. "We be going addle-brained with the stench in here! Poor lad 'ere, he couldn't hold himself . . . nature dun called and got answered. Lord 'ave pity, gent, leave us the window open. We all be too big to crawl through!"

"Eh, that ye be! Well, Oi don't see no 'arm in it," said the driver hooking the window open. "There now, lads. Let's 'ear no more!"

Cassie had not heard all of this exchange. However, she did see the driver hitch open Jack's window and silently blessed her free trader for a thinking man.

A few moments later the two constables reappeared singing some lively song. They mounted their respective carriages and once again took to the road. Cassandra kept the sound within hearing, rather than the coaches in sight. 'Twas not a bright night, but she could not chance their catching sight of her on a turn in the road.

Resigned that there would be a long interim before they stopped again, she settled in her saddle and was much startled and puzzled some forty minutes later when the coaches turned off. A rambling posting house of yellow painted stone with a large well-lit tavern room loomed out before her. It was flanked by thick woods, and its stables were roadside. Cassie crossed hurriedly and did a tour of the rear of the building, approaching the stable from the back and in time to overhear the constables.

"Hell! This be Nell's place . . . and she do 'ave more than ale to give us. Come on . . . what's the difference if we stop for an hour or so? Lord love ye, they'll be all right trussed up in there!" argued one of the constables.

"I dunno . . . mayhap . . . we best not," said the other, unsure.

"That's coz you ain't seen m'Nellie. She be a woman with the biggest, prettiest set you ever dun laid your poppers on. And wot's more . . . she got a gal that works for her. Lordy . . . can she please!"

"I suppose it don't make a ha'porth o'difference if we rest up a bit, do it?" grinned his partner.

"There, thought ye'd see it m'way. Come on then."

Cassie watched the two men saunter into the inn. She heard the unmistakable sound of hearty greetings and as the laughter within swelled, she returned her attention to the matter at hand. Jack's open window lay barely ten feet away; there was nothing between her and it—discounting the driver who still remained seated on his perch. What to do . . . what to do? she thought desperately. This was almost immediately answered. Drivers are living things. They have flesh, blood, and bones . . . or so Jack's driver thought as he climbed down from his perch and grumbled into the stables, calling for a livery boy.

Cassie waited only long enough for the second driver to follow suit, before she sped the distance to the window and dropped in the knife. "Hurry, Jack . . ." she said and once again returned to the side of the stable. She listened and heard the driver order the one livery boy, who could not have been more than ten, to fetch two bumpers of ale. She waited for the lad to pass before going to the rear of the stables and remounting Starfire. She led him to the road and then spurred him into a canter, smashing at a spanking pace as she made for the stable doors.

Two pair of bloodshot eyes looked up at her with some astonishment as she came down upon them. They saw before them a fiery beauty with hair the color of flame. It seemed to light up the face it framed, and her eyes—the color of green stars, bright with unshed tears. "Oh, sirs, sirs," cried Cassie as she slid off her horse and came toward them.

"They tell me Jack . . . my Jack Rattenbury is in your charge. That he is to be taken to Bodmin to stand trial."

"Aye. But . . ."

"Oh, please, you must let me see him," she cried plaintively.

"Can't do that, miss. He ain't to have nothin' to say to nobody. That be our orders!" said the driver of Jack's coach gruffly. His companion agreed, though rather doubtfully, being a bighearted fellow himself and inclined to relent before a woman's tears.

"But, you don't understand," said Cassie, entrapping their attention as her hand swooped into the bodice of her gown and produced the special license. "We were to be married . . . in the morning."

The second driver pushed his wool cap back on his

head and proceeded to play with his straggly curls. "Lordy . . . poor chit!"

"It don't make no mind, Alfie!" said the first driver, "we got our orders, we do."

"Aye," said Alfie regretfully.

Cassie was prepared for this, prepared to go the limit. "I . . . I am so ashamed . . . but I have to tell you then. I must see Jack, we must get married . . . for, you see . . . I . . . I am . . . with child," she sobbed, going into Alfie's chest. She had chosen her mark well, for the poor man nearly burst into tears with her. He cast his partner a pleading look, and the first driver relented a might.

"Bless ye, ma'am . . . I feel for ye, I do . . . but there be nuthin' for it, ye know . . ."

"At least, at least . . . allow me to see him . . . speak to him . . . he must tell me what I am to do . . ."

"Christ!" ejaculated Alfie. "She be right there. Poor wee thing . . . let her speak to him."

The first driver frowned but by now was inclined to have this thing off his conscience. "All right then . . . come on," he said rather gruffly, going for his set of keys and making for the carriage. However, at this particular moment the young boy returned with two bumpers of ale. Cassie swiftly took charge, taking the ale and setting them down, placing a coin in the lad's hand without the drivers' noting it and whispering for him to keep mum. He vanished into a stall, his instinct for survival telling him to keep out of sight. The drivers had by now reached Jack's door and were fumbling with the key. At last, the door swung wide.

The two men never knew what hit them. It was as though a cannon had been fired and they were the target. They took the impact full and lay winded on their backs as they were mounted by two fierce-looking savages. Tim astride one driver, Dan O'Shanter over the other, kept them still and horrified as Jack worked at the ropes. They were gagged and tied without too much bustle or noise, and Cassie pursued the business at hand, very much as though she had been born to it. She scooped up the set of keys and rushed at the other coach. Ollie, Widdens, and Barkes were set free, whereupon they began to release the four coach horses.

With the drivers neatly ensconced in the coach, which was once again under lock and key, and the constables playing their games in the inn, the night saw five horses set off. A drizzle was falling, yet its mist had no sting and was met with the joyous sound of laughter, the laughter of free men.

Jack sat behind Cassie on Starfire. Tim had doubled with Dan O'Shanter on a coach horse, and they all took to a side road on their way back to Weymouth. They paused a moment in the dark of the woods, and the crew of the *Sweet Mary* awaited word from Jack. "Well, m'hearties. Ye know now what needs to be done. We got our shipment waitin'. We'll have to round up our porters and 'ave them ready. We'll have to get hold of a galley, for 'tis sure the revenuers will cut our poor *Sweet Mary* into threes. But never mind. 'Tis a new day comin', and we need shelter and food if we are to get through it. I say the Spithead . . . what say you?"

This was wholeheartedly thought to be the only safe haven at that time, and it was toward the Spithead that they rode. However, Jack clasped Cassandra's hand as his boys went forward in the lead. His wiry arm tightened round her waist, and his voice sounded husky. "Aye, lass, ye be all a man could be wantin', and the Lord knows I want ye! 'Tis how to spark yer blood . . . for tis hot-blooded ye be. I feel it now holdin' yer body close, ye be wantin' a man to take strong rein, ye be wantin' a man to lie with . . . ah, Cassie . . . I wish ye would burn for me." His mouth descended upon hers with his hoarse plea, sucking away her breath with the violence of his kiss. She felt his need surge through her, engendering a spark within her own vitals. He was right. She was hot-blooded. She was past the age and much in need of a man's arms to

100

warm her. And Jack—she cared for him, had long thought of him as a hero—but not her hero. Not in *that* way! He was a leader in his own right, and he was masterful . . . scampishly heart-winning, and she cared for him . . . *but not that way!*

She took his kiss wishing she could feel more, but nothing happened, no explosion, no melting away, no seering need. She heard his words and wanted to please him. She did not want to hurt him but had to draw away. His kisses covered her face before returning to her lips, and she sought desperately for a way to stop him without causing him pain. But it was unnecessary. He did it for her. Jack Rattenbury was no fool, no boy scarcely breeched. The moment his lips had touched hers he knew. His was a heart that loved without expecting anything in return. He opened his embrace with a rueful sigh. "Ah, lass . . . ye burn . . . but 'tis not for me!"

9

The viscount's brow went up as the Spithead loomed before his visage. Its frame though large wanted a fresh coat of paint. Its wooden casement windows seemed to be set in stone that was near to crumbling. A dirt drive led to several constructions at the rear, the largest of these being the stables and carriage house. However, upon inspection (no hostlers came out to take charge of their horses), the viscount found that the stables housed but one vehicle and that a supply wagon.

This may have been considered at variance with the harbor town below the Spithead's, for Weymouth was still the idyllic vacation spot the king had made it some fifty years ago. True, all the fashionables flocked to Brighton now with the Prince Regent, but many Tories and those wanting a quieter vacation still came to Weymouth. During the season, which had already begun, the small harbor town boasted full occupancy, and its hotels did a thriving business. But the Spithead was not designed for that sort of business. Nor would any of the fashionable have deigned to cast a glance at the dingy inn.

It was well situated for easy access to several roads. This was important to its clientele who were made up for the most part of seamen. Tom Crewes, owner of the Spithead, was a particular friend of Jack Rattenbury, because many years ago Jack had saved him from a press gang. They had sailed alone on a small galley, met up with some others, and concluded a few deals involving smuggled brandy which enabled the man to become the present owner of the Spithead.

The viscount encountered the beetle-faced, broken-nosed Tom as he entered through the back door. This portal led directly into a pantry room off the kitchen, and the large heavy-set man stood before the viscount suspiciously.

"Ye be wantin' somethin'?" he asked harshly. It was blacker in the pantry than it was outside, and he had not yet seen the cut of the man he addressed.

"Lord, yes, but not in your pantry, my good man. I simply took the closest door from your stables."

Tom Crewes heard the quality in the big man's speech and relented. "Aye . . . well ye be welcome to pass through the kitchen if ye 'ave a mind to," he said, leading the way.

Once in the kitchen region which, unlike the remainder of the Spithead, was well-lighted with tallow candles on the walls and in a hanging brass fixture, the beetle-faced fellow turned to look at the viscount. "Gawks! Ye be a flash cove if ever I clapped eyes on one. Ye got yerself lost? Weymouth be but another couple of miles south of 'ere!"

"I am not lost," said the viscount authoritatively. "What I want is your best ale—and one for my groom out in the stables. You do have someone to take it to him, I gather?" He eyed Tom's broken nose.

"Aye . . . but . . ."

"Also, I'll have a plate of that delicious-smelling stew

you have cooking there—and one for my man as well. You may bring it to me in the tavern, and ask my groom to join me there. There, that's a fine fellow!" said the viscount, dropping a coin in his hand.

"Aye . . . but . . . I think ye would find . . ."

"Now," said the viscount, in a tone indicating that he would brook no argument.

Evidently the tavern owner was trying to steer him away from something. What, he knew not, unless the fellow had something to hide, which was likely. He would not stand a chance putting his questions about, but he might be able to pick up something if he kept his mind and ears alert. He made his way past yet another pantry with several cabinets before he found the dark hall leading to a flight of stairs on one side and an open galley on the other. The room was dimly lit, its counter made of dark rough oak, its ceilings beamed with the same. Fishnets and such ornamented its walls and, as he made his way to a round table in the center, the buzz of animated conversation seemed to abate.

The occupants were garbed in wool caps and short coats. Some had removed their outer garments to display threadbare shirts of rough cotton and belcher scarfs with faded polka dots. Their over-all appearance was unsavory, and their suspicion of the newcomer was plain on their sullenly silent visages. The viscount found it disconcerting to be so conspicuous among them and wished he had at least changed into his buckskin rather than wear his blue superfine. He shed his riding cloak and put down his top hat on the table, deciding it would best serve to ignore the hush. Chips came in and, seeing all eyes on his lordship, said gruffly to the company at large, "Och! Shut yer mummers, ye filthy pack of rats . . . what ye be gapping at?"

This set a few of them off, and before long the buzzing began again, with only a scattered few casting their eyes dubiously over the viscount. However, the viscount's presence was soon forgotten altogether when a scrawny barefoot urchin, clothed in rags, came running into the tavern shouting as though his heart would burst.

"Tom . . . Tom Crewes!"

"What be the trouble, lad?" asked a nearby sailor. "What ails ye?"

" 'Tis Jack . . . 'tis Jack!" managed the boy, quite visibly out of breath.

"Jack?" asked the tavern owner coming forward and taking up the boy's shoulders in his fat hands. "What about him?"

"Coo, gov'ner, let me . . . catch . . . me breath . . ." he paused with a hand to his chest. "There now . . . they got him, they do . . . the redbreasts got him and his crew off the *Sweet Mary*!"

"Coo!" responded a one-eyed man from the recesses of the room. "Never say they got ole Jack Rattenbury . . . not with a shipment, they didn't!"

"No, 'tis said he sunk his tubs . . . coz the *Duke of York* picked her up without nuthin' bein' found," responded the boy excitedly.

"Then they can't give him over to the redbreasts! No evidence!" said the tavern owner.

"But they did . . . they mean to take him to Bodmin . . . where he be wanted to stand trial for somethin' else."

"They can't do that!" said the tavern owner again.

"Well, they did . . . but one of his men got away!" reported the boy with fervor. "A young lad, they say . . . spunky *I* say! Dove overboard before they harbored . . . swum clear out of their sight! And him . . . his first time on board the *Sweet Mary*!"

"Aye, that may be . . . but what of Jack?" asked another man, shaking his head. "It don't seem right."

"Hell! Go on! There ain't a redbreast alive that can take in the devil . . . and we all know Jack be the devil himself! Ain't never been held more than a day. Always escapes—see if he don't again!" predicted the tavern owner with feeling.

The viscount exchanged a glance with his groom. This was all very interesting. Jack Rattenbury had been captured, and some young lad had escaped after being on the *Sweet Mary* for the first time. The viscount had often been called omniscient by his friends. The thought occurred to him that this escapee might just be Cassandra. But no, to dive overboard . . . a young slip of a girl, to brave the waters fully clothed, and manage the thing? Why, most girls did not even have the knack of swimming. Yet the thought continued to nag at him sharply.

A tray of food was brought out by a serving girl, and the viscount pulled at his lips thoughtfully as he watched Chips take to his meal.

"Eat hearty m'lord," advised Chips quietly. " 'Twouldn't do not to in this set!"

"Aye," his lordship agreed.

Tom Crewes noticed the viscount again and sidled over. "I suppose ye'll be wanting a room. They say the Windermere be a prime ken. That would be . . ."

"We'll take rooms here," decided the Viscount, casting him an amused glance.

"I can house yer man above the stables. Ye can have the first room at the top of the stairs," said the tavern owner resignedly.

The viscount and his groom enjoyed a few more ales after their dinner and continued their vigilance in the hope of picking up more information, but none was forthcoming. Finally, Welford got to his feet, shrugged, and pushed his wooden chair backward. He placed a hand on his groom's bent shoulder and bade him get some sleep.

Cautiously, and with an eye over his shoulder for any would-be assailant with a mind to have his purse, the viscount made his way up the stairs to his room. There he found his overnight portmanteau on the neat bed. He was surprised to find a pitcher of fresh water for washing and poured it into the basin to commence his nightly toilet.

Sometime later, he lay naked beneath the sheets, his

hands cupping the back of his head as he stared into the darkness.

"Cassandra Farrington . . . with cinnamon-gold hair . . ." It was like a line he had memorized from a page! But his heart hardened again just before he dropped off to sleep.

Then quite suddenly, he was awake, staring into the darkness. There—the sound of horses snorting! He jumped up and rushed to the window where he crouched and, ever so slowly, moved aside the flimsy hangings. The window overlooked the rear court, and there in the moonlight were five horses bearing seven riders. One horse led them and, though the night held clouds to dim the faces of the riders, it could not conceal the markings of this particular horse. It was blood chestnut with unmistakable lines—and a white star on its forehead. Starfire!

In an instant his breeches were on and, without boots, without a shirt, without sense—for he had no plan—he rushed out of his room. Hell and brimstone! Thoughts tumbled into his brain as he took the stairs much like a great cat—stalking. Cassandra . . . with her smuggler! Here for the taking—but just how that taking was to be accomplished he knew not—yet. He sped through the dark hall at the bottom of the stairs and dove into the pantry room before the kitchen. Suddenly a booming noise started up at the back door. The viscount glanced around for a place to conceal himself, found a closet, and jumped right in to keep the brooms company. He closed the door, yet was able to peer through the cracks and see Tom Crewes, candleholder in hand, nightcap askew, coming forward.

"Who in hell be bangin' on me door like that? I'll have yer neck, I will," yelled the man as he opened the door. There was a moment of silence and then a loud gleeful exclamation. "The divil himself! Bless ye, Jack . . . ye got away! Lord preserve us . . . 'tis that glad I be, ye confounded blade! Ye gave me quite a turn!"

Jack ushered his men into the kitchen and sank down

upon a chair, grabbed Cassie's arm, and pulled her down onto his lap. "We're that hungry, my man . . . what can ye do for us before puttin' us to bed?"

"I'll fetch me Sally. She be a good wench as ye well know, Jack!" winked Tom. "She'll heat up the stew."

"No Jack, not I. All I want is a bed to sleep in," said Cassie wearily.

"Aye, darlin', and well ye deserve it!" said Jack turning to Tom.

"See that the lass here gets a room with a bolt across the door. I don't want none fumblin' into her room . . . catch m'meaning Tom?"

"Aye, when ye put it so plain, Jack. 'Tis no way I couldn't," grinned the tavern owner. "Come then, Miss," said he, leading the way.

Cassie passed by the door where the viscount was hiding, and he saw her lovely face. He was near enough to reach out and touch her. He saw her give Tom Crewes a wide, soft smile, saw the old brute melt beneath her charm, and he smiled ruefully to himself.

He heard her free trader, Jack, call out to the yellow-haired wench, Sally, and felt a sudden curiosity to see the smuggler. He opened his door a trifle and saw only the back of Jack's head. Sally put on the stew before Jack caught her hand and put it to his lips, "Sally . . . ye ain't welcomed me yet!" he admonished.

"Aw, go on, lovey. I was jest settin' about to feed ye."

"Then feed me. These lads of mine can serve themselves . . . and then 'tis the blue room for them. But, darlin', 'tis yer room for me . . . what say ye?"

For answer the girl wrapped her arms round the man's neck and brought her lips up to his. This very naturally caused much revelry among his men. He paid no mind as he picked up the wench and carried her to a door off the side of the kitchen. There he opened the door, put the girl down, and then turned to grin widely for the entertainment of his men.

They laughed and joked among themselves until Dan

O'Shanter grumbled, went to the fire, took up the pot of stew, and pressed a blue stone near the fireplace. There, what appeared to be a solid brick wall, suddenly seemed to rend itself in two. Tim and Ollie, still chuckling, went and grabbed hold, opening it wide enough for the men to squeeze through. The crew of the *Sweet Mary* eased themselves through the narrow crevice into the blue den on the other side. Hoots of laughter rang out when the bricks nearly took off Dan O'Shanter's arm as he tried to squeeze through with the big round pot of stew.

Quietly, the viscount retraced his steps to his room and leaned against his closed door. Cassie was in the only other room abovestairs, right beside his own. But damn, he thought, he couldn't just break down her door and ride off with her. Not in this house, with six worthies below to bar his path. So, he would need a plan to do the thing neatly.

She was here with Jack Rattenbury, and evidently she had been the one who escaped from the boat and therefore must have had a hand in Jack's own later escape. Interesting. He would have to learn more of this at another time. Then he thought of Jack Rattenbury. Not a very faithful lover to Cassie—taking another wench right beneath her nose. Why didn't they occupy the same room, Cassie and her free trader? Puzzling indeed!

He had not been able to see much of the smuggler, but what he had seen told him that Jack Rattenbury, though slender and fully ten years older than himself, was certainly a bruiser of a fellow who would know how to handle himself in any given situation. He would have to move wisely. In truth he could not see what Cassie might find so devastating in the man, but there was no accounting for a woman's tastes . . . or passions.

He needed a plan. And then he thought of Cassie in the next room, lying beneath the covers . . . probably naked. His blood warmed and he began to ache for her. Damnation! Why in hell did he want her so? She was but a woman, much the same as any other—and he had satisfied his appetite with many beautiful women. Blister her! he thought viciously. Wanting her went against every fiber, every principle.

Then a plan came to him. He went over it again and again until he knew it would work. Only then, did he drop his breeches and climb into bed, seeking rest. But his dreams were filled with the honey of her voice, the sway of her hips, the bewitching green of her eyes.

10

A ray of sunshine filtered through the hangings of the viscount's room and came to rest on his face, absurdly youthful in repose. He blinked, rubbed his eyes, reached over to the nightstand for his timepiece. "Six?" He groaned quietly and hastily set out his shaving supplies.

Some twenty minutes later, garbed in an open-necked white linen shirt, buff breeches and hessians, he crossed to the stables, sped up the outside steps to the room above, and demanded admittance. Chips came about sleepily and found his lordship in earnest spirits.

Ten minutes passed before the viscount emerged and went back to the inn through the rear portal. He heard a sound and had scarcely enough time to get out of the doorway and lean into the side wall when five men came shuffling out. He saw them make their way toward the stables and breathed a sigh of relief. This was working out even better than he had hoped. Now for Jack Rattenbury.

He sauntered through the pantry into the kitchen, his black hair billowing about his handsome face, coming up short as he found the free trader leaning into his wooden chair, a cup of coffee poised in his hand, and leveling an inquiring eye his way. There they stood, each measuring the other and finding a worthy adversary.

"Well now . . . mayhap, lad, ye be wishful of a fresh cup of coffee?" asked the free trader casually. "If ye like, I can call Sally to fetch ye a cup."

"No need for that, sir. I can pour it myself," said the viscount with a smile.

The free trader watched his movements, a frown forming between his eyes. Then the viscount turned, and his black eyes seemed to penetrate the free trader's mind. All at once Jack recognized him. Never before had he seen eyes so dark, and Cassie had described the blade well. He let out a low whistle.

"Well, now . . . I been wonderin' jest when we'd meet . . . coz . . . I had a feeling . . . deep in the pit of me that ye wouldn't give up so easily."

"Indeed?" said the viscount, somewhat taken aback.

"Aye. Stands to reason, don't it? I mean jest coz the lass bolted, don't mean ye'd be the type to give over—not from all she told me," responded Jack amiably.

"Then I need not introduce myself?" tested the viscount.

"No, m'lord,"

"How very astute of you. Perhaps then you may be able to tell me where Cassie is?" he asked, beginning to put his plan into operation.

"Saints! Ye don't mean to bamboozle me do ye . . . coz it won't fadge, lad. I weren't breeched yesterday. Might say I got a goodly year or so on ye," chuckled Jack.

The viscount looked him over and even in the bright morning light, Jack's features took on the aspect of a younger man. Also, Kirkby Welford found himself liking the lanky free trader.

"Then Miss Farrington is here?" said the viscount as though he had not the slightest indication to that effect.

"Ye already know that, jest as ye know who I am.

Never thought to ask. Knew me right off . . . before I closed on who ye were!" said Jack laying it out flat.

"Very well, Rattenbury. Then you must realize, I mean to leave with her," said the viscount easily, not at all perturbed.

Jack shook his head and the frown showed even in his bright eyes. "Certes be! I jest don't gleam your ken, big 'un. Ye be a flash cove—I'd say used to having yer own way—though, I wouldn't a put ye as an ogler. Yet here ye be with the lass in yer eye and meanin' to have her. It don't figure . . . it jest don't. But there it is."

"You have misread your man. It doesn't figure, because it isn't so! I am not here because I want to bed Miss Farrington!"

"No? Why then?"

"I'm here for information, and one of you—it matters not which—is going to give it to me," said the viscount, straddling a chair and lifting hard coals of darkness to the free trader's face.

"Lord love ye, lad. What kind of information is it ye think we have?" asked Jack, somewhat startled.

"Not here—someone may come in," the viscount responded in a low whisper.

"Where then? Though truth has it I don't know what devil is eatin' at ye."

The viscount cast about for an appropriate corner before saying lightly, "Out back . . . behind the stables."

"Aye, if ye have a mind to it." As he rose alongside the viscount, the free trader paused. "But ye did say ye mean to take her back with ye?"

"And so I shall, but not for the purpose you imagine. There has been a great deal of speculation regarding her cousin's mode of expiration. If her family name is not to meet total ruin, I must get her back to the Grange—under proper chaperonage to still the wagging tongues."

"Aye, that sounds as pretty as any ye might give me. But I'm not buyin'," said Jack, smiling all the while.

They strolled into the rear courtyard where Jack stepped among a pack of cackling hens and one bantam

113

rooster. The hens set up a series of outraged squawks which won him a dangerous glance from the irate rooster. Free trader and rooster eyed one another warily before Jack was allowed to proceed. All this met the amused observation of the viscount, who found himself more than half won over by Jack already. He sighed over it, thinking it a shame that he was going to have to double-deal the fellow.

They sidled round the stables when an expanse of glen led off into thickly plumed woods, and Jack stared ahead of him a moment before turning to meet the eyes of Kirkby Welford.

"Ye know, lad, I hope ye ain't got anything in mind. 'Tis the milkiest of men that I be—until roused. Ye don't mean to rouse me now, do ye?"

"I merely want some information," replied the viscount quietly.

"Such as?" answered Jack, truly puzzled.

"Such as . . . who is it that finances your enterprises?" put the other bluntly.

"There ain't nobody that sports the blunt for Jack Rattenbury. I ain't owned. My sloop is me own, and I don't answer to no one!" he stated with some pride.

"I don't have the time or patience to argue. All right, your boat is your own. But someone puts up the blunt for your shipments. I want to know with whom you deal."

"Ye be either dimwitted or blind. Ye got the wrong free trader," said Jack, moving warily.

"Well then, I am not dimwitted, and I am not blind—and I am inclined to believe you. That leaves Miss Farrington—for she *will* know of whom I speak." He started to move off but was arrested by Jack's hand.

"Where be ye going?"

"Where do you think?" The Viscount was ready for this,—it was exactly as he had planned.

"I mean ye to leave the lass be," said Jack firmly.

"And I mean to take her in tow and return to the Grange," retorted the viscount purposefully.

"Over me dead body," said Jack grinning broadly, putting up his fist. "Come on then, lad. Up with yer dabblers, for 'tis clear ye be sportin' fer this!"

"By all means," said the viscount, bringing up his fives in a swift hard movement that sent the free trader flying backward. Jack bounced right back, smiling once again as he brought through his right past the viscount's guard and landed the younger man a facer. The viscount recovered immediately and laid his opponent a blow to the body before taking yet another flush hit across his bone box. Readjusting his jaw, his lordship grinned ruefully and then bustled his man, sending Jack sprawling backwards, when suddenly out of nowhere, Chips appeared and brought down an empty bottle over the free trader's head.

Jack was out. The viscount's visage took on the hue of fury as he rounded on his groom. "Damnation, Chips! What in hell did you do that for?"

"Nuthin for it, m'lord. A number of redbreasts—soldiers—be riding down the main pike . . . saw 'em from me window."

This spurred the viscount into immediate action. "Very well, let's get this old sea dog out of sight. We don't want him taken."

Jack was dragged to a nearby shed, where he was tied and gagged. "Keep a look out that no one comes near him . . . I'll be back later," instructed the viscount, rushing to the inn.

Unaware of these proceedings, Cassie Farrington had ordered a hot bath, and now sat in the wooden tub in her room, luxuriating in its warmth. She had much to think on, but her mind drifted away from the present and discovered a host of memories. Black hair gleaming with blue lights, a handsome visage, and black eyes that devoured her hungrily. She saw the viscount as clearly as though he were there with her, and for a moment she wondered what he would do if he could see her now . . . naked in her bath. It was a titillating fancy, and her blood warmed from its provocative conclusions. Then, all at once Kirkby Welford was there in the flesh, with his sardonic smile.

"How . . . how . . . ?" she stammered as she

crossed her hands over her breasts in a vain effort to hide her nakedness. She sank deeper into the tub but the wretch of a man came forward in his ungentlemanly fashion.

Cassandra brought up her wet head almost defiantly and her large green eyes opened wide with disbelief at his arrogance. Her flaming tresses clung damply about her glistening body and the viscount did not fail to take in the sight. His eyes found the lovely pink points ornamenting her full ripe breasts and, in spite of himself, he felt his blood surge. Damn! That's not why I'm here, he told himself furiously. Yet, he felt his own intake of breath, just as she was gasping with indignation before his perusal.

"Your maid neglected to relock your door. Ah, Cassandra, how good it is to be reunited with my dearest ward," he said, folding his arms and standing above her, his smile mocking her all the while.

His coolness in the face of her nudity brought her to rage, which in turn eclipsed all thought of fear. She could not speak, nor could she scream, so acute was her wrath. All she could manage was a tiny squeal. She felt her cheeks scorch, her mind lost in a turbulence. She leveled a full-scale attack upon him with her hot green eyes and he, he was benumbed above their blazing beauty.

"How dare you!" she hissed at last. The lady's glance found a towel lying uselessly some distance away, and she gave her back to the viscount, not waiting for an answer to her reprimand. She pressed against the tub, attempting to reach the cloth. This position afforded him an excellent view of the graceful lines of her back, small waistline, and well-rounded derriere. With an inner anguish, borne of the need to control that which rose within him, he groaned, stepped round the tub, picked up the towel, and knew if he were not to go mad with desire, he must give it to her—quickly.

She accepted the prize with eager hands, holding it loosely before her and stepping into its folds, but not before his lordship had discovered the sensual limits of desire. His assistance with the towel both disconcerted and surprised her, and somewhere in the haunts of her subconscious, somewhat piqued her as well. Now, rather more modestly attired, the lady's thoughts began to take shape, and her eyes flew to the door. He had already bolted it and stood between her and it. She could never rush it, unlock it, and get out. She could scream. But where was Jack? How had he gotten past Jack? Of course, Jack had no inkling what the viscount looked like—discounting her description. Still . . . what if the viscount had done away with Jack . . . oh, God!

"Jack—what have you done with my Jack?" stamped the little lady, her damp hair curling round her shoulders as her head moved.

"I found it expedient to my purpose to have him . . . held . . . for my pleasure," returned the viscount wickedly.

"I . . . *I hate you!*" she spat at him in a surge of impotence. "You are an evil man!"

"Nevertheless, you will cooperate with me. There is a small band of soldiers on their way here. Undoubtedly, they are in hot pursuit of Rattenbury, after his daring escape last evening. And his fate remains in your hands," said the viscount, intimidatingly.

She looked him over with loathing. How could she have ever thought him wondrous? How could she have ever thought him handsome? He looked satanic. So, he meant to have her. 'Twas a toss with her in bed . . . or Jack's life. Yet, even so, she could not believe that it was desire that had brought him here. There must be more to it than that. She stalled for time. "What . . . what do you mean to do?"

He took a step toward her, his hand reached out and took a ringlet of hair in a twirling motion, "What think you I mean to do?" he asked, his voice low, hushed. His desire was proving more and more nerve-racking.

"You . . . you could not be so cruel as to give him over . . . you have no fight with Jack. He has done nothing to you," she pleaded.

"Your opinion of me is remarkable," he said quietly. "But it doesn't signify, for it serves my purpose well. You are afraid I will turn him over. Perhaps I will, if you don't cooperate with me!"

She turned her face from him, giving him the line of her lovely profile. She was torn by conflicting needs. The need to preserve the last of her dreams—to keep her physical ardor for the man she loved—and to save Jack. If he had put such a proposition to her, when there was but herself on the scaffold, she would have gladly died rather than give over her pride. But there was Jack. And what was pride next to her own Jack? Oh, Jack, she thought sadly, how you would fret to know what is toward. She knew only that her Jack held all the best of her good emotions and that he had to go on being free. He had to go on living the life he cherished, being the legend of his time.

Then suddenly they heard a banging belowstairs, heard the soldiers at the front doors, and the viscount raised his black brow in question at her. He moved as though to go to the door, and she found herself flinging herself into his arms.

"My lord, I beg of you, do not . . ." she sobbed. "I . . . will do anything you wish."

She had misread the situation entirely. How could she have done otherwise? She knew nothing of the torment driving the viscount. She knew nought of his purposes, his long-range purposes! She knew only that he had attempted to make love to her and that she had at first wanted him to. She knew only that he had won her in a game of chance and had meant to collect. By some fiendish way he had discovered her direction and had put Jack beneath his thumb. Well, then, if that was what would save Jack Rattenbury, so be it! "Please my lord," she pleaded more, not aware of his surprised expression. "I will gladly submit to your bed—if you will but spare Jack."

He held her away from him, her shoulders feeling the strength of his grasp. His dark brows were heavy, his black eyes intense. She had hit him with an unexpected attack. He had not come with such intentions. It had never crossed his mind to ask for such a boon. Once he had found that Jack and Cassie were lovers, he had not the spirit to intrude upon their relationship—not by force. He asked her somewhat dubiously, "You offer me a toss with you for your smuggler's freedom? Ah, but, sweetness, that is not what I had intended. First, I want your promise that you will return with me to the Grange—and Cassie . . . before those soldiers find their way here . . . I want some answers!"

She frowned, totally dumbfounded by his rejection and again, somewhere in the recesses of her mind, she felt piqued. "Answers?"

"Yes, woman, answers—and a promise."

"Very well, then. I promise. Now . . . what answers would you have?"

"Who is Nathan, and where may I find the elusive devil?"

"Nathan?" she said the name quietly, tilting her head in some quandary, though the name was not unfamiliar.

He grew angry abruptly and shook her. "Don't think you can go on sporting your games with me. Nathan—'tis but part of a name, and I would have the whole—now!"

Suddenly she heard an imperative command and knew the soldiers to be in the inn, knew they would soon be taking the stairs. Nathan, Nathan . . . of course, she remembered. She knew not why the name held out so much importance, but if 'twas what he wanted . . .

"Assure me that you will not give him over," she pleaded still.

"Blister it, sweetness, you needn't be melting in fear. You have given me your word . . . you have mine!" he said, softening somewhat for her anxiety was real.

A knock sounded on their door, and she felt her knees buckle beneath her. Suddenly she was uplifted in his arms, felt the power of his hands, and then he was sliding her into the bed, covering her to her neck with the blanket, and putting a finger to his mouth for her silence. She watched him go to the door.

"Who is it?" he asked, sounding very irritated at the interruption.

"Lieutenant John Pike of the Fifth regiment. Open this door at once!"

"May you be damned first!" returned the viscount.

"Sir . . . I am here on His Majesty's business," said the young officer.

"Not in *my bedroom*, you are not!" retorted the viscount.

"I was told a young woman occupied this room," attempted the lieutenant tentatively. "I should like to confirm that information."

"You have it confirmed," said the viscount, a twinkle lighting his eyes.

"If you do not open the door, I regret to advise you that I shall have to break it down!" said the officer, getting up his courage.

The viscount opened it a crack, purposely allowing the young soldier a quick glance at the occupied bed. "You young scamp! I could have your head for this!" whispered the viscount amicably.

"So sorry, sir. The innkeeper told us a viscount was staying here. I take it you are he? You see I had to make certain of it, as we are searching out an escaped smuggler."

"You won't find him in this inn, I assure you. I have been here since yesterday, and he has not come this way. I have heard talk though . . . below . . . and I gather from all reports that he has flown north where it is thought he will lie low for some time."

"I see," said the lieutenant thoughtfully. "My lord, what, may I ask, are you . . . a man of your consequence . . . doing in such an . . . out of the way . . ."

"You have no right to an answer, but as I have nothing left to hide . . . you have *seen* the reason for my . . . out-of-the-way jaunt!"

The lieutenant smiled at last. "I see. Well . . . again, please accept my apologies."

"Lieutenant Pike, stay a moment longer," said the viscount after a second's thought. "If I should get information to the contrary regarding the smuggler, where may I get in touch with you?"

"Oh, we have temporary quarters in Weymouth at 94 Bristol—horse guards, you know—but we shall be leaving tomorrow morn."

"Thank you," said the viscount, closing the door and gazing across at Cassie who remained wide-eyed.

"Now, sweetness, his full name," demanded the viscount, moving to sit beside her on the bed. "And please to remember that I have the soldier's direction and am quite capable of recalling them should you prove uncooperative."

She looked at him with some surprise, wondering if he had read her mind, for it *had* occurred to her that she was a bit safer now with the soldiers gone. "Look, I know his name only because a letter arrived at the Grange from him. It was meant for my cousin, but poor old Harris delivered it to me in error. 'Tis his eyes. They grow old and he refuses to buy spectacles. I didn't open the letter but gave it straightaway to my cousin."

"His name, if you please," repeated the viscount patiently.

" 'Tis Nathan . . . Nathan Asbatol," she said, frowning over it.

"Does he sponsor your smuggler's activities?"

"Of course not! Jack answers to no man but himself!" returned the lady proudly. "He has never even heard of Nathan Asbatol."

"Good," said the viscount, unaccountably pleased. "But never mind . . . tell me, where may I find this Asbatol?"

"How should I know that?" She was stalling for time, hoping Jack would miraculously come to her aid.

"Because his return address was on the envelope, and you must have noticed it when you noticed his name," he replied blandly, aware of her purpose.

" 'Twas in Bristol . . . though I don't know his exact direction," said she, frowning.

Again they were interrupted by a heavy banging upon

121

the wooden door, and a sturdy man's voice rang out. "Miss Cassie . . . miss. . . ?"

It was Tom Crewes, and the viscount eyed her warningly before allowing her to answer. "Careful now," he whispered.

It flashed through her mind that she could shout out to Tom that she needed help . . . or that Jack needed help . . . but it might mean Jack's ruination for there was no telling whether or not Tom could do aught. She sighed, "Yes, Tom?"

"Be anything amiss, lass?" asked the man.

"No, Tom." she said quietly.

"Aye, then I'll leave ye be. But ye holler if ye be needin' me for Jack and the lads be off somewheres." He sidled away in some puzzlement. He had heard the lewd chatter of the soldiers and knew that the viscount was closeted with Miss Cassie. It wasn't like the good girl she was to be entertaining a strange man in her room, but, gawks! Ye never could tell what vagaries a woman would take to.

So, she thought, he had trussed up the crew of the *Sweet Mary* as well. What sort of man was this Kirkby Welford, that he could bring seven men under his thumb? She gazed at him quietly, expectantly, and he moved closer to her. One large strong hand reached out towards her hair, and she stiffened. He ignored this response, as he picked up one bright tress and played with it, "You have done well, Cassandra." His eyes were like glittering black onyx as he appraised her. He hadn't meant to take her up on her offer, but, God! he ached for her. Suddenly, he found himself bending over her, thinking if he took her, if he possessed her, perhaps he would be free of his fever for her.

She pulled away, pressing herself up against the oak backboard of the bed, one hand clutching the towel to herself. One delicate brow arched over eyes gathering a storm. "So, it was a lie! I should have known better, but I truly believed you when you said a toss with me was not what you were here for!"

"I find that a toss with you is precisely what I am here

for," said the viscount, his voice low, seductive, and she felt herself stirred in spite of her anger.

"You are no better than Shakespeare's Angelo!" railed the lady, "but then, I should be thankful at least that you have sent the soldiers away as you promised."

"Did you think, like Angelo I would promise you the free trader's liberty and deliver them his head? No, Cassandra—and this is no stage we walk upon. I am not one of Shakespeare's characters, and you are not Isabella to trick me with another wench in the dark! You offered your body in bargain, and I have decided 'twas a fair price . . . though I did not mean to accept it. But damnation, woman! *I want you!*"

His arms brought her halfway up to meet his burning lips and they took her own with a wild, exultant fever. She felt the power of his touch, felt the embers within her raked into flame, and knew a moment of madness when all was forgotten but his mouth on hers. He was startled by the heat of her response, but not more so than she was herself.

All this time, from the moment she had looked up to find that he had invaded her room, she had been watching him, thinking him almost a god . . . or a demon. She told herself she was giving her virginity in exchange for Jack's freedom. But it gnawed at her spirit—lies always had. She knew well why she would give herself to this Kirkby Welford. For lust! He made her body burn, apart from her mind and heart. Her body yearned for his touch. There was something in her blood that responded to his desire. When his lips met hers, she had put her arms round his neck, drawing him down upon her.

His whisper in her ear was enchantment, igniting her long-checked passion. "Cassandra, sweet beauty . . ." there was urgency in his voice that incited her to wantonness. He felt her quiver beneath him and kicked off his boots. With another movement his shirt was flung to the floor and there was a flash before her eyes of the taut powerful lines of his shoulders, chest, and arms. Then suddenly both towel and blanket were gone. She felt his eyes burning her body with their perusal. "Damn! You beauty, you," he breathed hoarsely. His hands went to her hair, stroking it away before they found the way to her full round breasts. His hands fondled those treasures, gloried in them, his lips teased their coral peaks, his tongue tutored her into anticipation. He went on, his frenzy curbed by skill, and he found the curves of her calves, and he allowed his fingers to work them, discovering her pleasure points and massaging them with sensual, perfectly timed seduction. There was a rhythm in his every movement, and then his hands spread wide her thighs.

Cassie tried to hold back, her mind racked by past lectures. She heard some of his blandishments and attempted to stiffen before his onslaught. She *would* not enjoy this! She *could* not enjoy this, she told herself. But his voice came low and vibrantly seductive. "Oh sweetings, don't fear, relax, my lovely . . . here . . . and here . . ." He allowed his fingers to move up between her thighs . . . and Cassie knew she was lost.

His mouth once again found hers, his tongue making her understand what he meant to do, and she felt the wonder of his scepter between the softness of her thighs. Hard, large, and pulsating, it took over the exploration, but had not yet quite entered her . . . and it was sweet torture. She wanted him to take her. She wanted, needed him to fulfill their desires. She felt him take position closer and closer to love's portal, and then his hands grasped her swelling breasts almost violently. She awaited the moment, barely breathing.

He managed his passion skillfully with an eagerness he could no longer contain. He whispered her name, his admiration of her body. "Ah, Cassie . . . you ripe young beauty! I love your small waist and your big white fruits . . . and God, Cassie . . . your little honeybox was made for me . . ." He entered tenderly at first, but his passion sent him plunging, excavating his way into her depths.

She clung to him, partly from her own hunger, partly in fear, and yet, a portion of her mind and body held back.

124

He had awakened all her normal desires, but she told herself there was still her soul—she could still keep her soul from him, she would give only her body, but oh! oh! She met his fierce penetration with a hitherto unknown heat and then suddenly, with a cry of exquisite pain, she opened frightened eyes to his face.

Just as suddenly it came to him that she was an innocent . . . never before taken. He nearly stopped in midmovement, astonished by his newfound knowledge. He looked at her face. "Devil a bit! Cassie! *You are a virgin!*" he accused, much upset.

She nodded, and one tear ran down her cheek. He wanted to withdraw from her but even as the thought came to him, he could feel the tightness of her, and he groaned. His kiss was warm, gentle, and tender before he whispered, "It's too late, little beauty . . . but have no fear . . . the worst is over . . ." Again he was moving within her sweetness, hungrily taking her all. Again, the pleasure of his movements returned to her, and soon the tempest left her panting. She felt her body tighten in ecstasy and then quite suddenly grew weak in his embrace as she descended from the heights. He smiled, well pleased to have satisfied her, and his voice was wondrous to her ears. "Ah, sweetness . . . you are perfectly formed for this . . . so snugly do you hold me in your depths . . ." The cadence of his movements picked up speed, and she saw passion flit across his handsome face. He brought his mouth deliciously over hers, she heard him groan and knew another kind of satisfaction as he found his release.

He brought his head down to the swells of her breast and buried his face between them before easing himself out of her. Then he dropped a kiss upon her mouth, her neck, and her ears before sliding off her warm body onto his back beside her. He lay quietly, frowning a moment, and then propped himself up on his elbow and surveyed her luscious form. She blushed and raised the blanket to her chin and he gave over a short laugh.

"Will you never cease to surprise me, chit? Modesty?

At this point 'tis a bit late, don't you think?" he teased. "But now, ma'am . . . will you tell me how you happened to be a virgin?"

"What made you think otherwise?" she asked, blushing all the more.

He touched her hot cheek gently. "How could I think you were? You said yourself that Jack Rattenbury was your lover."

"It doesn't matter," she said quietly.

"Oh, but I am afraid it does. I am not in the habit of ravishing virgins," he said with a frown.

"If you are ravishing a woman, you are violating her. What matter whether 'tis her first man or no? A violation is but what it is," she finished pugnaciously.

"And did I *violate* you, Cassie love . . . or did you welcome it?" he asked softly, kissing her earlobe.

"I am flesh and blood . . . and I am twenty. Think I was not ready?" she defended. "If it was not you . . . 'twould have been someone else—soon."

That he did not like. For some illogical reason this rankled, and he pulled her to him roughly. "But it *was* me —and there will be no other so long as you are with me, Cassie!" he said hoarsely.

She cowered at the fierceness of his tone, but she stared with some temerity at his wild black eyes and saw them grow warm once again, just as his lips lowered to take hers. She pulled away, and he chuckled suddenly. "Is it too soon for another bout? Very well, we'll talk. I'm curious . . . what is Rattenbury to you?"

"Jack and I are closer than brother and sister. He likes to tease me about marriage . . . says how much he wants it with me, but he doesn't, you know. He would hate it, being tied to one woman—especially a jealous woman!"

"Are you a jealous woman?" asked the viscount with a twinkle.

"I . . . I don't know really . . ." she answered, trying not to meet his intent gaze. His finger traced an invisible line down her arm, journeyed past and found the beauty of one taut nipple. He fingered it predatorily before taking the entire breast in his hand. His smile was full with his designs, but she wondered still what he was about. "Cassie, love, you will be sore enough tomorrow, so we might as well play today," he said, remounting her.

"But . . . but my lord . . ." she objected.

"Hush, my beauty . . . you are far too tempting and even in your innocence far too good a toss to leave go after only one sampling," he said, quieting her with his mouth. His kiss touched her heart, and his hand took hold of hers, guiding it down to the hard extremity of his needs. She drew back in some confusion, but his gentle urging forced her fingers round the throbbing muscle as he guided it between her well-shaped thighs. A keenness permeated her inner being, and she felt an almost violent emotion thrust her toward him, making her bite at his lips.

He whispered huskily, "Now, Cassie . . . feel it enter now . . ." Caught up in a white heat, she had no thought, no battle of mind and heart. There was only sensation, wild, passionate, seering sensation blending into united needs and fulfilling satisfaction. His hand went under her hips, manipulating her movements so that she rotated beneath him. He raised her legs to his back, stopping only when she cried out in pain. He soothed her and said it would not always be thus . . . 'twas but her virginal soreness that interfered.

It seemed to give him an intangible joy to refer to her virginity, and he did it a few times during their play. Then all words ceased as they melted into one sensual beat that left them laboring for breath in each other's arms.

Cassie hid her face in his chest and wondered at the pass that had brought her to this. She wondered at her lust and at her future and shed a tear for the destruction of her dream.

11

Jack groaned in a senseless, groggy darkness before the oblivion dissolved into acute discomfort. He blinked, shook his head, and groaned again, noting with only partial awareness that the sound of his grunt was strangely muffled. It was at about this moment that he realized he had a length of dirty cloth pressed between his teeth, and then he remembered. He closed his eyes and, as the throbbing in his head attained ferocity, he attempted to comfort himself by putting his hand over what he was sure was a bump as large as an apple. Another realization thrust itself forward as he discovered both hands were tied at the wrist. He peered through the darkness, found his ankles similarly bound, and sighed.

Well, ole bucko, that's what ye get for trustin' a flash cove! Now where be ye? He looked round and, by the light that filtered through several empty knot holes in the wood, discerned that he was being held in the tool shed. He began the painful procedure of pushing himself on his back toward a wall. This done he brought up his feet and began thumping against the wood with all the strength left to him.

Chips, sitting leisurely on a bench outside the shed, jumped to his feet and came to the door. "Lord love ye, free trader! There ain't no call to take on so! Ain't goin' to keep ye there much longer."

He was met with further, far more violent thumping and he grunted, before replying, "Lookee 'ere, there weren't nuthin' personal aboot this . . . but I jest got to keep ye delved awhile longer. 'Tis fer yer own good."

Jack was not in accord with this thinking and exhibited his opinion most fervently on the thin worn walls. Chips responded by flinging open the door, cursing all the while. The light from the bright sun swept over the smuggler's face, and Jack blinked from the blinding effect. Chips surveyed him with some sympathy and grumbled, "May me fathers forgive me! You do look a peesweep, and I can see that be a nasty bump I give ye—but 'twere nought fer it." He paused a moment, rubbing his stubbled chin. "If ye 'ave a mind to give me yer word not to holler and put up a fuss, I'll give ye free to drink a bumper with me. What say ye, free trader?"

Jack considered this and decided he would not have to shout in order to save himself from the small stout man. He nodded. Much relieved, Chips removed the gag and aided the smuggler to a sitting position. He then went outside again, produced his bumper of ale, and brought it to Jack's mouth, "There . . . that's the dandy."

Jack rested a bit after the warm soothing brew cleared his parched throat. "Be ye the viscount's man, then?" asked he at length.

"Aye. Close on to eleven years now," said the groom.

"Ye served me a blackguard's trick. Was it at *his* calling?" asked Jack, curious about this point, for he had not put his lordship down as such a one and had been much surprised by it.

"No. I laid ye low on me own . . . and I ain that it weren't to me likin' . . . but nuthin' fer it, free trader. Them redbreasts were coming doon on ye, and there were no time to settle the matter without a fuss. Thought I'd put a quick end to it."

Jack snorted. "I can think of a sight better ways of having done the thing, and I give ye fair warning, sport, I'll serve ye the same when I get a chance at it."

"Aye, ye might be free to try—when we get done 'ere," said Chips, eying him thoughtfully.

"What be yer name, highlander?" asked Jack smiling suddenly. "Ye are a Scot, ain't ye?"

"Aye . . . from Pitrochley. John Chiprony. But been known as Chips more than half me life! I come south with the Highlanders' Brigade to fight Boney! Met up with his lordship then . . . over in Spain."

"His lordship served in Spain?" asked Jack with some surprise.

"Aye. No ordinary colonel he weren't either . . . fierce —and smart too—won his title ten times over. I was proud to serve under him. We sold out in '14 but then when Boney escaped and marched in '15, we went at him, we did. What a bloody thing was Waterloo! Took all the heart out of war, it did," said the groom sadly.

"Never knew there were a heart in war—but then, never fought one . . . being a peaceable sort," grinned Jack.

The elderly groom smiled. "Ye don't seem the sort to hitch up wit a jade of a wench . . . how come ye to it?"

"Jade? Who might ye be speaking of?" asked Jack frowning, truly at a loss.

"Why, the Farrington wench. Who else?"

"Belay that, sport," said the free trader, his tone menacing. "Ye best not speak of the lass in sech a fashion. She be better than ye can ever know. But I *am* curious . . . why would ye and yer lordship be thinkin' her a jade?"

"We got our reasons . . ." said the groom warily.

"Do ye now? What would they be, fer its plain as pikestaff the lass never gave ye cause to it!" said the smuggler.

"Not directly . . . but in a manner of speaking the

harvest of what she done . . . ah, now . . . I dun spake more than I should and think I best leave it go."

It was just about this time that Tim, Ollie, and Barkes jumped off their mounts and gave them over to the young ostler at the stable door.

"Where be Jack, young 'un?" asked Tim, brushing the dust off from his breeches.

"I dunno," said the boy, "ain't seen him."

Tim turned to the shaggy, ginger-haired Ollie. "I don't like this . . . those soldiers in town were here and said there were no sign of him. But still, Ollie . . . I got me this ill feeling . . ."

"Don't be a noddy. He be in the blue room sure as me mother birthed me," said the lanky youth in response.

Barkes, a good deal older, narrowed his eyes and scanned his surroundings. "Stay here, lads. I'll be after inquiring on Jack." He sidled off and when he returned some minutes later, his grayish features looked grim. "Aye, lads, it don't look good. Tom says he ain't seen Jack all morning. And what's more perplexin' is that Cass be up there with some lord. . ."

"What?" shrieked Tim, his eyes popping. "What then . . . the viscount she be running from? We got to save her, Barkes . . . I tell you . . . we . . ."

"Hold there, noddy! She been up there the better part of two hours! I'd say she were past saving. And what's worse is . . . what then of Jack?"

Fortunately for them, regrettably for Chips, he chose this particular moment to amble out of the tool shed and make for the tavern to refill his tankard of ale. The three bothered men turned at the sound of his steps and stared. It was Tim who found his voice and squeaked, "Who be ye?"

Chips put up a gray-black brow and though some inches shorter than Tim, looked down upon him with his glance. "Humph," was all the answer the lad received.

Barkes took over at this juncture and having years to match Chips and some girth and height over him, it behooved Chips to take notice. "The question was put to ye, covey . . . we be waiting on an answer!"

"Eh? Don't know 'tis any of yer affair, but I be groom to the Viscount Welford!" snapped Chips, attempting to proceed on his way. Instantly he was surrounded.

Barkes took up his neat blue collar and hissed, "Then ye'll be telling us where our captain might be."

"Captain? I don't know where he be . . . no . . . why should I?" bluffed the groom.

"Best gather him up and bring on back of the stable, Barkes," suggested Ollie.

"Aye," agreed his mate.

They linked arms with the grumbling groom whose wrath became resonant in its violence. Jack, sitting back in his dark cell, heard some of what the groom bellowed and shrewdly deduced it time to make his move. The groom had regagged him, so there was nothing for it but to begin thumping at the wooden door which he did with some force.

Tim pulled up short and commanded his mates to silence. His austerity had no effect whatsoever on the groom however, who continued his blandishments. "Hush up, ye old gager! Damnation, but what in hell is that? It sounds like it be coming from . . ." Then his face lit with realization and he stared hard at the groom. "Ye swine!" with which he ran to the shed and flung open the door. "Jack!"

Some moments later the captain of the *Sweet Mary* walked into the sunshine, groaned, and held his head, he turned to Barkes and with a soft smile and asked lightly —for it had never occurred to him that Cassie might not be free, "Where be my lass?"

Tim blushed as Jack met his eye, and the youth turned away. Jack's glance took on gravity as he asked Barkes again, "Where be the lass . . . or is it ye be dumb?"

Chips began squawking, and Jack turned his attention on him again. "Was I forgetting ye, Highlander?" with which he stepped forward and landed the fellow a facer that sent him sprawling backward. "Take care of him, boys," he snapped at Tim and Ollie before turning on Barkes. "Now . . ."

"Ye ain't gonna like it none, Jack, but she be upstairs . . . with that lordship she been worriting herself about," said Barkes, avoiding Jack's eye.

The free trader felt an intake of breath as his emotions betrayed him. His Cassie—beneath the hands of another —it stung somewhat . . . He then thought of the viscount and remembered the flash cove's words. Hadn't he said he hadn't come for her? What a fool to have believed the man! Well, he would pay for ravishing his poor innocent—but how? He started forward, but Barkes detained him. "Jack, 'tis been on two hours now . . . 'tis too late . . ."

"Too late, is it?" growled the free trader. Then suddenly his eyes went bright, and he dived into his boot. "Devil fly away with me for not thinking on it sooner!"

Ollie and Tim having trussed up the groom in the shed, appeared beneath the smuggler's eye in time to receive his order. He waved the special license Cassie had used so cunningly the night before. "There now, Tim, ye'll be fetching our friend, Vicar John, and bringing him here within the half hour. Run now!"

Tim asked no questions though his mind was busy over this latest fetch of Jack Rattenbury's. Barkes gazed on his captain's face and grinned as Jack said, "Let's wash up a bit. And have Tom send up some food to his lordship to keep him awhile—for 'tis a wedding we'll be having!"

Cassie had for the time forgotten herself in a new and wild dimension of warring emotions. Her heart became a battleground, and her conscience leveled its attack. She peeped over at the viscount's features for he lay upon his back, lost to his own deep musing, his gaze fixed on nothing in particular. Faith, she thought taking in breath, the very sight of him set her inner being pulsating. She dare not let her body touch his. She lay there in her confusion

—in her shame—for she could not deny the passion that had passed from his body to hers.

Kirkby Welford turned his head round suddenly to gaze upon her, and his frown dispelled before the sight. She was such a soft, childlike woman . . . with her green eyes forever probing. He propped himself up on his elbow, feeling absurdly youthful and irrationally happy.

"Tell me, sweetings, was it you who jumped overboard yestereve?"

She moved and stared up at him with some surprise. "How . . . how did you know about that?"

"Then it was, by God! Damn, but you are a wonder of a woman! Swam for the beach, did you? But how did you manage the rest of it, for I was given to understand that Rattenbury and his crew were on their way to Bodmin with an armed guard?"

"And so they were, but there were *only two guards*," grinned Cassie.

His eyes lit with amusement as he flicked her nose. "And of course *two* armed guards were no match for Cassandra Farrington!"

"Bah! They were fools busy with their wine and their women. They left their prisoners to the drivers. 'Twas done in a brace of snaps!" she said rather proudly.

He laughed aloud. "Tell me, little minx . . . just how did you manage it?"

She smiled, pleased with his attitude, feeling suddenly very close to the handsome buck beside her.

"You see, I had this . . ." A knock sounded at the door, and the viscount brought up his head from the contemplation of her sparkling eyes. "Damn your soul!" he shouted merrily. "Who is it?"

" 'Tis only Tom . . . with your lunch, your lordship," said the man gruffly on the other side.

"Lunch, is it?" grinned the viscount, feeling jovial. He cast a look on the soft creature beside him. "Aye, lunch . . . I've worked you, sweetings . . . I suppose I must feed you!"

Though he chuckled amiably, his statement had brought

134

the color to Cassie's cheeks, and the fire once again to her spirit. "How dare he?" she thought wrathfully. "How dare he tease me as though I were a common trollop!" She glared at him which sent him off into a peal of laughter. He attempted to pinch her chin affectionately, but she pulled away, and he continued to chuckle as he rose and donned his breeches. "Very well, Tom, we'll take that lunch. Just leave it outside the door!"

She watched him from beneath her dark curling lashes and noted the height and breadth of him with reluctant admiration. He was certainly a fine figure of a man. No doubt he had had his pick of women.

Kirkby shot her another rakish grin as he undid the latch and swung wide the door. He stepped into the hallway, picked up the tray of food, and with his hands full turned round to find Jack Rattenbury standing before him.

A fist was planted across his jaw, but the viscount was a worthy match for the smuggler, and the attack left Jack with a tray of hot food in his face. However, Barkes and Ollie had by now brought up the rear and, between them, the viscount was shoved into the bedroom and the door bolted behind them.

Cassie pulled the covers tightly up to her neck and ejaculated in some embarrassment, "Jack!" but found she could utter little else.

The viscount shook off his attackers and whirled round to face Jack's pistol. His brow went up. "Well, free trader, do your best then, for I take full blame . . . I forced her to it!"

Cassie suddenly thought Jack was going to kill him. He had never before killed a man, and she couldn't let him do it now. She nearly jumped out of bed in her frenzy to stop him and pleaded desperately, "No, Jack . . . 'twas not his fault. Why, he even sent the soldiers off. You mustn't shoot him!"

Jack stopped suddenly and eyed her a long moment before saying quietly, "So—'tis like that, is it, lass? Well now!"

"Please, Jack . . . you will hang for murder. You mustn't . . ." cried the girl fervently.

"I don't aim to shoot the viscount unless he forces me to it." He turned on him. "Though ye dismal me greatly, lad . . . thought ye would have it that ye meant to leave the lass be."

For no good reason the viscount felt a twinge of conscience. He had allowed the smuggler to think his interest in Cassie was not sexual, and, at the time it hadn't been. However, he made no excuse for himself. "What are your intentions, Rattenbury?"

"First, you will oblige me by getting back into bed," said Jack glibly. "You were there before we interrupted ye . . . so find yerself a nice comfortable spot and take it up, lad!"

"I have no intention of humiliating the lady before your men and am certainly surprised that *you* should find it necessary to do so!" snapped the viscount angrily.

"Don't be sportin' yer precious proprieties," retorted Jack, suddenly incensed. "Wasn't it ye who ravaged the lass?" He walked up to her and touched her nose lightly. "I'm that sorry, Cass, but I'll make it up to ye." Once again he faced the viscount. "In wit ye now . . . I'm in no fit mood to argue!"

"You might as well shoot then," started the viscount, but Jack signaled Barkes standing behind Kirkby and Welford was laid low with the butt of a horse pistol.

Again Cassie shrieked. "Jack, what have you done?" and knew not why she was so disturbed. She certainly should have been pleased to see her violator laid unconscious before her. Jack remarked upon this odd circumstance with something akin to a grin before advising her to rest easy.

"Now . . . put him in bed . . . and ye keep still, lass. There now . . . if that ain't John coming up now . . ." he said going to the door and making for the stairs. A moment later he reappeared with Tim and a dark-clad elderly man of undersized proportions with a clump of neatly trimmed white hair.

"This be Vicar John!" beamed Jack.

Cassie sank lower into her sheets, blushing crimson and cursing Jack beneath her breath. Whatever was he about, displaying her shame to the world, introducing her to a vicar as though she were dressed for the theater? She ignored the introduction and the vicar commented with some concern, "Oh, dear!"

" 'Tis good to see you, old friend," said Jack. "And on such a happy occasion. Ye might say that the lass there . . ." he motioned toward Cassie "is something akin to me sister, and the man beside her . . . he be the groom!"

"Jack!" said Cassie nearly frothing. "Jack! Stop! Have you gone daft?"

The vicar doffed his low-crowned top hat and attempted a smile at Cassie before returning to Jack. "But . . . oh, dear! Tim led me to believe that I was wanted to perform a wedding. And really, Jack, whatever are we interrupting this young couple for. My, the poor groom does look a bit worn out."

Jack gave a shout of mirth before tapping the good vicar on the back. "Lord love ye, and he probably is, but they ain't married yet . . ."

"Oh, dear!" breathed Vicar John. "Then—regrettably —I am too late, it seems."

"Aye, but we can make it up. All ye got to do is marry 'em!"

"But Jack—even for you—though under the circumstances I really believe they should be married . . . but . . . well . . . these are delicate matters and quite frankly, I cannot do it without the necessary papers!" said the vicar, more than a little flustered.

"Lookee here, John. We been friends longer than I got memory seeing as ye baptized me . . . befriended me . . . and I'm tellin' ye me poor child was ravished by that blade. He be out of it now, coz I had him knocked over the head. When he wakes, I want him married. That is to say, I want him to wake up to find himself gifted with Cassie as wife!"

"No, not for all the friendship in the world. Not without papers—and not while he is unconscious! Hell and the devil, man! I wouldn't do that to Beelzebub himself!" announced the good vicar.

"Here be the license," said Jack, slapping the document into the vicar's hand, "and by midnight tonight ye'll have a keg of the best in yer cellar. What say ye now?"

"Wake him then, for I won't do it otherwise," compromised the vicar.

Cassie sat open-mouthed throughout this exchange and finally managed, "Jack . . . you idiot . . . you can't mean to carry this through?"

He didn't answer her, instead he turned to Tim. "Fetch that pitcher of water and see to his lordship."

"Aye," said Tim, avoiding Cassie's eyes. He threw the contents of the pitcher into the viscount's face and stood back as that hard-used blade spluttered into wakefulness.

"Damnation!" muttered Kirkby Welford as he blinked into semiconsciousness. "Are you trying to drown me?"

"No, marry ye . . . to the lass here," said Jack, slapping his face and getting his hand smacked away.

"The devil you say!" started Kirkby, putting a hand to his head and groaning in spite of his determination not to.

"Ye abused the child—'tis only fitting," remarked Jack blandly.

"Do I take it that the young man is against the marriage?" inquired the vicar.

"Aye, evil sort," remarked Jack confidingly, "and she quality."

"Quality?" asked the vicar, opening his faded blue eyes.

"Aye. She be Cassandra Farrington, and that be the Viscount Welford—her guardian!" said Jack laying his half-truth in a manner bound to win the vicar to his side.

"Oh, dear! This is dreadful!" the vicar exclaimed before turning his gaze upon the viscount's wrathful countenance. "Young man . . . my lord . . . you really have no choice in the matter."

"Like hell I don't!" started the viscount, making an attempt to rise.

Jack laid a hand on his shoulder, detaining him. "Now, now, my lord, there ain't no use in gettin' miffed! Ye ravished the lass—or do ye mean to tell me she weren't no virgin?"

Cassie gasped and turned her head away, feeling this was just too much, and his lordship was not immune to her plight.

"I don't deny it," he said quietly, his eyes troubled as they scanned her.

"Well then, lad . . . 'tis time to pay yer comeuppance!"

"A wedding cannot be performed without a special license," said the viscount hopefully.

"Ah! Ye were out when I give it over to the vicar," said Jack, reaching for it and placing it in the viscount's hands.

Kirkby Welford perused the document silently before looking up. "The date indicates that this was procured the very day Cassandra left the Grange." He frowned darkly as he turned on her, suddenly believing he understood. He had been tricked. Molly had been no accident. She had been awaiting his arrival to send him hither. Cassie giving herself to him to save Jack had been but the bait in the trap. She knew full well the crew would return and, had he been less besotted, he would have realized it as well. "By God!" he hissed at her. "You have duped me well, *jade!*"

"Here now! That ain't no way to be speakin' to your future bride!" put in Jack defensively.

"No, and she is not to be my bride!" returned the viscount. "You aim your gun. Very well then, free trader, use it!" said he, getting up to his full height and making for the door.

Jack sighed and with some reluctance motioned to Barkes. His first mate came up behind the viscount who whirled suddenly and landed the large man a blow to the body. Welford was immediately set upon by both Ollie and Tim and, though they put up an excellent struggle, it was Jack who finally managed to put in his hand and bring down the butt of his horse pistol on the gallant's head.

He sighed again and turned to the vicar who shook his

head sadly over the incident. "Well, John, as ye can see, the viscount would rather sleep through the ceremony."

"This is not what I like," said the vicar. "He should be awake during his own wedding . . ."

12

Some ten minutes later Jack stood at the door ready to follow his men. He turned and gazed thoughtfully at Cassie, giving her a wry smile for he could see she was furious with him. She sat still, the covers held to her neck, her unconscious husband at her side.

"Tis for the best, lass. I'm off now for Wilkes be waitin' on us with the porters, and there be plans to be made for those tubs. But if ye need me, ye but have to get word to me and I'll be there," he offered apologetically.

"Oh, Jack! You don't know what you've done," she said morosely. "I . . . I am now the wife of a man who likes me not . . . oh, Jack! Can't I come with you?"

"No, lass. He be a man of a different stamp. I don't need him breathin' down me neck. If ye be thinkin' he'll do ye harm, ye be out there, for I ain't seen no bruises on ye."

She blushed. "No, he uses far subtler ways. Oh, Jack!"

"Hush there, lass. Give him time to get used to the idea . . . he'll come round—onct he gets to know ye.

Lord, girl, ye be woman enough for any man. Jest make him know it!" He chuckled and waved his farewell. She sat staring after him a long while before she released a long heavy sigh.

Well, she supposed her first duty as wife would be to bring her husband round. She slipped out of her bed and picked up an overturned chair. As she rose she caught the reflection of her naked figure in the looking glass. Somehow, she felt she looked different. Then she caught the sight of the unconscious Kirkby behind her and hastily sought her clothes. Once more dressed in her blue muslin, she found a piece of cloth and dipped it in what was left of the wash water. This she applied gently to the viscount's bruised head, calling his name softly and hoping for a response.

His lids fluttered, and she winced at the pain in his black eyes. He groaned and she refreshed the cloth, touching it again to his forehead and allowing its coolness to do its work. A moment later he blinked as Cassie's lovely features hazed before his eyes. He tried to rise, but dizziness overcame him. She pushed gently and he relaxed a moment against the pillow, trying to recall who and where he was. Then with another groan, he recalled everything. As she applied her ministrations, one long gleaming red tress brushed his cheek, and he opened his eyes again. He stared at her long and hard and as her hand came near with the wet cloth he took hold of her wrist and held it to him roughly. "Tell me, jade," he seethed, ". . . did they dare it while I was out?"

"I am sorry, my lord. Yes, they did," she said quietly, feeling every bit as victimized as he.

He threw her wrist from him and looked away, but his voice came low and harsh. "Blister their souls! May they rot unknelled!"

She attempted to ignore the hurt his bitterness etched in her heart and once again brought the cloth to his forehead. He pushed her hand away angrily. "Enough! Damnation! Are you already playing the wife? 'Tis a travesty! Enough of your tricks!"

She pulled away, her face long in sadness. " 'Twas not of my doing . . . I played you no trick."

"What then of the ready license?" he spat at her.

" 'Twas Tim's . . . he had meant to marry . . . but . . ."

"Keep your lies to yourself. Sooth your conscience if you can with them, but give them not to me! You are a shrew—nought else! Why can you not admit to it once and for all and have done?"

She gave up. "Confound you, then! Believe what you like, but know this. I am Viscountess Welford," she rose and stalked to the bureau, returning with a set of documents signed by Vicar John and the men of the *Sweet Mary* as witnesses. "These papers prove it . . . and think not Vicar John has no copy, for he made a duplicate himself and means to record it all in the register!"

"You unscrupulous hussy!" he spat.

"Very well, then, hussy I'll be. But I'll have Farrington Grange, and I will be known as your lady!" she returned in fury.

He threw the papers away from and grabbed her arm, pulling her down beside him. His face was close above hers but his lips hissed the words. "Fiend seize your vile soul, you brazen bitch! My God! To think I would end with such as *you* for wife. May Heaven preserve me yet and make you barren that I may be spared the curse of an heir in your likeness!"

Odd what force of violence words can take. Words without substance, intangible—yet they have the power to kill the heart and mangle the soul. Cassie was still an innocent. She had been thrust from a world of happiness at an early age into an emotional desert, but she had maintained her heart. She clung to her dreams and her hopes and thought, maybe, just maybe, something good would still come of her union with Kirkby Welford. Had she not lain with him? Had his kisses not stirred her blood, had she not known passion in his embrace? Could he feel nought for her after all that?

His words cut through her tender heart like a knife. She

bled, not so that it could be detected—no red droplets marked the wound, yet she bled. Her green eyes swam with rushing tears and her body trembled beneath the blow. Even as a wounded animal turns helplessly round to meet its end, yet fights to the last, she turned to her foe. "Very prettily said, my lord. I can find nought to match it. You think yourself tricked and saddled with a wife you would have none of. 'Tis done, but I vow that should you be willing, I would not stand in your way . . . it may still be undone. You could divorce me—charge me with what you like—and end it."

He leaned away from her as she stood up from the bed, averting her face. He sneered his disbelief. "I do not know what game you play, chit, but I do not trust you."

"What game is there in it? Pray, how can such an offer be yet another trick?" she asked impatiently.

"Divorce is not readily available to us. I have my family name to think of . . . and there are other reasons that make it difficult."

"Yet I offer it freely. And know this, you represent the end of all I ever wanted from life. *Your wife?* 'Tis a mockery of all I ever cherished. I hate you, with every beat of my heart I hate you . . . and warn you, my lord—never—ever will you bed me again!" She crossed to the door, but his voice halted her.

"Where do you think you are going?" he thundered at her.

"To Farrington Grange, my lord," she answered quietly.

He said nothing, but allowed her to depart, thoughtfully staring after her, wondering what next to do. This set a wedge in his neat plans, and he would have to deal with it. "Hell and brimstone!" he ejaculated in the silence after her departure.

Cassie's hurt slowly fashioned itself into a barricade, and she found herself filled with sudden indignation. In her rush to be gone, she noticed neither the tavern keeper nor Chips as she passed them in the courtyard. Tom had just released the grumbling groom as instructed by Jack Rattenbury, and the viscount's man stood a moment watching as Cassie stomped into the stable. He waited long enough to catch a sight of her astride Starfire, her cloak billowing in the breeze as she cut across the pike. He then went in search of his master. He had not far to go, for Kirkby Welford was already coming outdoors.

"Chips! So there you are, you rascal! Well, fine mess we've made of it between us, but never mind. Get my portmanteau, and make haste. I'm for the Grange."

"My lord, the girl . . . she did not take the coast pike but cut through the fields," offered the older man in some consternation.

"Indeed?" rejoined the viscount. He then turned on his heel and made for the tavern once again where he accosted the innkeeper and persuaded the fellow to put him in possession of the shortcut to the Grange. Some moments later he was in hot pursuit.

Unlike herself, Cassie took no time to sooth or pet her stallion. She rode him hard, not letting up on her spanking speed for some twenty minutes. She took the field gate flying, and her hood dropped away from her head allowing her long red tresses to fly in the breeze. She headed eastward until she reached a small road which would save some time on the way home. She knew the way well for she had often romped about the country with her brother —oh, God! she thought desperately, it seemed a veritable century ago! Was there ever any other life but the one she now led? Had her childhood been but a dream?

Starfire enjoyed the heady gallop, but after a time, Cassie slowed him into a canter and then down to a slow trot. It was cool this spring day, and the breeze brought her the scent of wildflowers swaying in the tall grass beside the road. It was a quiet ride, with but nature to keep her thoughts company, and Cassie needed this quiet.

However, her eyes discovered a man ahead of her. His dress denoted a gypsy—a person not uncommon on the backroads though they usually traveled with their wagons. As she approached, she noted a swarthy face beneath a dark wide-brimmed hat. He was bending over his horse's fetlock, picking at the shoe in an effort to dislodge an oversized stone. He looked up and smiled a greeting, and Cassie could see that he was not unattractive. His face was oval, his eyes dark, his lips full, yet she felt a sudden wariness.

"Ah! Good-day to you, lovely child," said the man with the accent of his people, intriguing her for she had never before spoken with a gypsy.

"Good-day, sir," she replied with reserve, attempting to pass by quietly, for though intrigued, she felt instinctively she should not linger.

"You ride the Frome Road?" he pursued, standing in her way.

"Yes, but only for a short span. I shall be cutting through the fields after a pace."

"I will accompany you, yes?" he smiled disarmingly. "Such a lovely day . . . a lovely woman . . . one must not let such treasures pass by . . ."

"There is no need, really," said she, quickly hoping to dissuade him without being rude.

"Ah, but there is much need. You should not be riding out alone," he said, taking to his saddle and urging the horse forward. "Come, we will ride leisurely. You go to . . . ?"

"To Farrington Grange, sir," she said curtly.

"Ah, but such a distance . . . I have heard of this place when we passed through some years ago. It is near Christchurch, is it not?

"It is. A few miles north of it," she said, telling herself she was being silly for distrusting him. After all, he meant her no harm.

"My caravan is at Wimborne. I go to meet it, but will be pleased to see you home," he said after a moment.

"Oh, no, sir. I am some ten miles past and could not let you . . . I wouldn't dream of such a thing," she said.

He snapped his fingers in the air. "So much for the distance. It is nothing when spent with beauty."

She blushed and felt uncomfortable again, but he soon set her at ease by speaking of his people, enticing her with tales of his adventures, making her laugh with a casual anecdote. Soon her initial instinct had been swept aside.

Not very far behind Cassie rode the viscount, his pace somewhat slower for he tracked her own. He left nothing any longer to trust and therefore, though he had received this alternate direction to Farrington, he stopped his horse now and then to investigate the tracks and assure himself of her direction.

Fool! You behaved like a boy getting his first toss in the hay, he told himself bitterly. *How could you have allowed yourself to linger with the chit . . . chit . . . now your wife! Damn! Did you not see? Where had your mind gone a-begging? You should have realized his crew would return. How could you have thought they wouldn't come back until nightfall? Fool!*

These chastisements occupied much of the first twenty minutes before giving way to other thoughts which took on a far different line. *Married! Sweet fever, married! And to whom? Cassandra Farrington, that's who now bears your name. The very girl who sent your brother to his grave!* Peter Eaton, whom she had spoken of so casually, was now dead—and all because of her betrayal. A stepbrother, but closer to Kirkby Welford than blood could have made him. The words were etched deep in his memory—his brother's words—and two sentences struck at Kirkby's heart: "Ah, Kirk," the boy had written, "she has hair the color of cinnamon gold, eyes as sweet and refreshing as a fresh water lake. Cassandra Farrington is her name." And then there was his last letter . . . but he couldn't think of that now. All he could think was that he had made such a jade his wife! Hell and fire, how *could* he have lusted for her?

Then he thought of the innocence he could not doubt, for he had taken her virginity—there was no lie in that! And there was that childlike wonder of her eyes . . . and the hurt there too. Her eyes . . . how could they lie? What an art she had perfected! Still there was more to her than he had thus far fathomed, he was sure of it. The

147

thought suddenly struck him that the road she would soon take was not safe for a girl alone, and he spurred his horse into a faster gait. He could still hear those last words of hers, still see the pain in her eyes. She had said their union was the end of all her dreams. Why then did she allow the marriage? Damnation! She planned it! Or did she? Could it have been the work of the smuggler? Confound it! There was the license—she knew about that license. How could she not?

Cassie and the gypsy had been conversing easily for some time before he inquired casually as to her name. She blushed and said that she was Lady Welford. His eyes automatically flew to her gloveless hand and found there no ring to support her statement. However, he allowed this to pass unchallenged. Instead, he appraised her horse with frank admiration. "A fine stallion is he . . . Spanish, I would say."

She smiled warmly. "Yes, he is Spanish. However did you guess?"

"We gypsies know something of horseflesh. But . . . if you do not mind my saying so, I think he is thirsty."

She frowned, for they still had another hour's ride to Farrington, and she did not wish to stop alone at any posting houses. "Yes, I suppose he is but . . ."

"If you will permit, there is a stream . . . through these woods. We could stop, take a rest and allow our horses the same pleasure."

"Oh, I don't like to leave the road," she said hesitatingly.

"It is no great distance from the road. See? There," he pointed toward the dark of the woods.

She frowned again, but a look over Starfire's coat confirmed that he needed a rest and a long drink of fresh water. "Very well, then," she said, though inwardly she felt troubled over her decision.

He smiled blandly as he jumped off his horse and came around to catch her as she alighted. There was no need for his hands to go to her waist for she was already touching

148

ground, and there was no need for his hands to slide to her shoulders as though to steady her, but she overlooked this, pulling gently but firmly away. He took the reins of both their steeds as he led them to the narrow freshwater stream some ten yards into the thicket.

She watched Starfire quench his thirst and bent to cup a handful of the clear water. She sipped it and came up smiling to find that the gypsy had removed his hat and vest. Her eyes flew to his saddle where the articles of clothing hung limply, and her brows went up. He chuckled softly as one hand reached for her arm, "Come, young beauty, this is a place made for love."

She wrenched out of his grasp and he laughed all the louder, "You resist? But why? Do you think I don't know how to please? Come, let me show you?"

"No! How dare you!" she said, attempting to reach her horse. He stood in her path and his eyes took on a hard look, his mouth sterner yet. "How dare I? Because you are alone—and even if you wish to tell afterwards, I will be long gone." Both his arms went round her, and she kicked at him. As she struggled her cloak fell away, giving her the opportunity to slip out of his embrace. She ran, but he was upon her, grabbing at her hips and bringing her down to the ground. She landed heavily, and it winded her. His mouth came down mercilessly on hers, but she bit his full lips. Furious, he slapped her face, leaving a red mark on the white cheek. She squirmed and managed to use her knees as a lever to push at his body until he fell backward, whereupon she kicked at him and got to her feet. As she ran, he grabbed for her and, though he missed, she screamed. It was useless, she knew . . . the road was only a back one, almost untraveled. Yet when he reached her and got hold of her bare arm, she screamed again, with all the terror and revulsion she felt.

His hold bruised her arm and as she fell again, the thorns of a thistle bush scratched her. She felt his hand reach into the bodice of her gown and heard the material tear. "Please let me go, please! " she begged.

Suddenly the gypsy was lifted from her as though he were a rag doll. She looked up and saw the viscount, his powerful body like a luminous bolt of lightning as he stood between her and the animal who had attacked her. Kirkby Welford threw off his cloak and hat and waited for his prey to lift himself from the ground.

The gypsy got to his feet, his face red with fury. "Who are you to interfere with a man and his woman? This girl is mine."

He was given no further chance to speak as Kirkby's fist gave him first a body blow that doubled him over. Next that same fist followed up to the man's jaw, laying him on the ground. Cassie watched in awe as the viscount stood waiting to deal out more of the same. But the gypsy had had enough. He rose quickly, ran off, and took to horse. The viscount stayed in position for a moment before turning to find Cassie trying to get to her feet.

Odd, she thought as she tried to rise, odd that her knees trembled so, making the task almost impossible. He came to her abruptly, staying her a moment as he surveyed her for damages!

The burning imprint of the gypsy's vicious hand was evident on her pale cheek. The bruise on one arm was growing darker as it swelled and on the other forearm blood was running down from the long thin scratches she had sustained. Kirkby Welford's expression, though grave, gave no hint of the concern in his heart. He had a sudden urge to stroke her tangled hair and reassure her trembling body with his embrace, but instead he helped her to her feet and said, "In the future, madame . . . *you will not ride out alone!* I will not have *my wife,* and thus *my name,* so hardly used!" He saw the tears in her eyes, and his tone softened as his arm went supportively round her small shoulders. "Now, come . . . let's get you set to rights."

She turned her profile to him trying to hide the tears staining her cheeks. To be in a position where she would have to be grateful to *him* . . . of all people! It was more than heart and soul could bear! But . . . fiend seize him!

she thought, she *was grateful,* for never before had she known such terror.

When she had offered herself to the viscount that very morning, *she* thought all was lost. Afterward when she lay in his arms, she knew the first chapter of her dreams for a future had been spoiled . . . but that was nothing compared to what might have just happened. She could think of no more horrible fate than to be violated by an animal and the gypsy had been an animal . . . nothing more! His touch sickened her, his lips revolted her, and his body on hers had disgusted her beyond thought. Then the viscount appeared like an avenging god, and she had wanted to throw herself into his arms, cry out her pain and humiliation, and feel whole again. But she had her pride to think of . . . her pride to save her from such a paltry thing. How could she give over so easily—certainly not before a man who only wanted to be rid of her. She kept herself coldly remote as he led her to the stream.

He bade her sit beside Starfire as he dipped his handkerchief into the cool stream. Quietly, gently he pressed it to her arms where the lacerations were already swelling beneath the oozing blood. He cleaned the wounds and then once again dipped the linen into the stream, rinsing it out before bringing it to her forehead and slowly, tenderly, washing her face. He avoided her eyes for only one glance their way had made him absurdly weak. He gave the wet cloth to her and began with long strokes of his hand to untangle her hair. He smoothed the thick red strands, sighed, and stepped back to view his handiwork.

It was then that his eyes fell upon the torn bodice of her gown, and he felt a sudden surge of murderous anger well up in his chest. He leaned over and flipped the material at her, his voice gruff. "Can't you do anything about this? I don't want you riding the roads half naked!"

She blushed and glanced down at the ruined bodice, noting self-consciously that her breasts were almost completely exposed, and she tucked the material in at the sides. She glanced round for her cloak, but her husband had already retrieved it and was placing it round her shoulders. He tied its ribbons in silence, put the hood over her head, and bade her keep it on. She didn't allow herself to feel his touch—it was all too thrilling, far too comforting, and totally confusing. She could only think, "Thank God—oh, merciful Heaven, he came and saved me from that animal." The experience with the gypsy had forced new perspectives upon her. She had always been comfortable with Jack, and when Jack had kissed her, she felt only sadness that she could not respond with the fire he wanted from her. Then, she had given herself to the viscount, telling herself it was for Jack's sake, but she had responded to his lovemaking with a wantonness she had not thought herself capable of. And now she had learned of repulsion. The gypsy's hand on her had made her ill. The thought that he might take her had brought her to nausea, and she knew in that moment that she would allow no man to take what she had given to the viscount! After all, though he did not want her now, she was his wife . . . and until he got rid of her she would be faithful. But she would hold herself aloof from him still, for his words were deeply branded in her heart.

And he, Kirkby Welford, his thoughts formed a pattern. He had heard her scream as he took the Frome Road. In that instant he recognized Cassie's voice and knew her trouble was not of any minor issue. When he reached the pair in the woods and saw Cassie brutally flung to the ground and attacked, he felt an instinct to kill. He had rushed upon the gypsy with a ferocious lunge, sending the man flying some five feet before he landed. It had not been enough, he had wanted to kill him. His hands had itched to do the deed. He had felt almost a madman, so acute was his distress. He told himself it was because until a few hours ago Cassandra had been a virgin. He told himself it was because no wench . . . not even she, should be taken against her will. It was after all, what any gentleman of honor would do. Thus, he answered the why to his wild emotions, thus he answered the why to his mad outrage and his sudden tenderness towards the chit. But damnation! He would pull himself out of such gentle thoughts! He would remember she was the instrument that had brought his brother low. He could think of her in no other way—*he would think of her in no other way!*

13

The fields of sprouting crops passed by unnoticed as Cassandra and her husband rode on. Their pace was easy, and the viscount's horse was just a head in the lead. Cassie gazed at him thoughtfully. He was her husband, had been for a short space this morning a lover—and yet a stranger. He had come from London, swooping down as a hawk when it sights prey, taking what is necessary, and then rising to the air again. So had he, this Kirkby Welford. The Grange had become his, and it was by no mere chance but the result of a determined pursuit that it had become his. Somehow she felt—she knew this. For some hidden reason he had made the Grange his object—her uncle his victim. Why?

He had not meant to be trapped, and she knew she would suffer by this last of Jack's. Though the free trader had her welfare at heart, he surely had made an error. Her eyes went to her husband's profile. Lud, but he was handsome! Absurd—that his looks should so affect her. His top hat was set at an angle over his gleaming black hair.

His brows, stern now in thought, hovered above those dark curling lashes, and she knew well how those black eyes could flash, and his shoulders . . . *but stop! stop, you stupid girl! He is a rogue, and you have vowed to keep him at bay!*

The viscount's lips curved in a sneer as he thought of his ambition, his project. It lay there, waiting just outside his grasp, and he was set on attaining his end. He had given his word as a man of honor, he had made his vow as a brother aggrieved, and he meant to achieve his purpose. He thought of Leander for no reason at all. Hadn't that worthy taken on the Hellespont, crossing its depths, passing its terrors? And for what, the heart of a woman! Bah! Not so with him, nor would it be! True, every man had his Hellespont to cross—his goal as it were. For some it would always be money or power, for others it might be love, but not for Kirkby Welford. His Hellespont led to revenge.

Nevertheless, he had been detoured and it irked sorely. He cast a sidelong glance at Cassie and noted in spite of himself that the chit was in some measure quite remarkable. She had eaten nothing all day, he knew that, and yet she begged no favor, no respite. He had himself grabbed a loaf of bread at the Spithead and eaten it as he rode; and still he felt hunger pangs, but he was a man! Poor chit, he thought for a fleeting moment, watching her ride, head erect and uncomplaining. He knew of no similar female of his acquaintance. Not one would have endured such a pass in silence. And there—she had been subjected to a rather rough experience as well, an attack on her person—and then a sudden idea entered his mind. Over his shoulder he said, his stern voice cracking the silence of their mood, "What the deuce were you about going into the woods with that gypsy?"

His question bolted like a shock through her, and she put up her chin, wondering why he must always think the very worst of her.

"Lud! Need you ask, my lord? Is it not obvious? I went with the gypsy into the woods for one sole purpose—*to be ravished!*"

He shot her an angry look but gave no ground. "Then, you are saying *you accompanied him willingly?* Why?"

Her answer came like rushing lava, thought having no part in it. "I have no more answers for you!"

"Indeed?" he said on a hiss. He stopped his horse on the word and reached out for her reins. Starfire did not like this and pulled up his head, but knew instinctively it was useless to fight. The viscount knew well the taming of flesh and blood. "When I ask you a reasonable question, woman, you will have the goodness and civility to answer, or trust not the consequences!" His voice was low, harsh, and yet strangely contained.

She felt a quiver of fear, but defied him still. "The consequences? What then. . . ? Will you raise your hand, my lord, as most of your kind are wont to do when crossed? Will you tie me to the rack until I yield?" Her voice raked him with derisiveness.

"Nay, madam, yet I will be answered!" he said, and there was a threat both in eyes and tone that frightened her. This was no man to fight and, though she knew she needn't be afraid of a beating at his hands, there was something in his mien that spelled danger. His eyes seemed almost to pull an answer from her and she gave over irritably. "Oh, faith! If you must know, the fellow said he would escort me to my destination. You see, he thought it unsafe for a gently bred female to journey alone . . ." she paused as she remembered, and her tone was sardonic in its lilt, ". . . then the dear brute suggested Starfire needed respite. He came along to water his own horse by a stream he said was nearby . . . and . . . shall I continue, my lord?" she said sweetly, her cheeks flushing in spite of her sangfroid.

He ignored this and spat out at her, "Why in all that is sane would you go into the woods alone with him to water your horse when a posting house would have served the same purpose and far more safely?"

"Lud! Am I on trial?" she spluttered.

"*Why*, Cassie?" His voice had taken on a suddenly softer tone.

She heard the change, but her blood was still on fire, her pride still hurt. "But have I not already told you? I thought it would be interesting to be ravished by the brute!"

"Why, Cassie?" he pursued, his voice gentler still.

She found his eyes, almost mesmerizing in their intensity. What was he about now? Why suddenly so gentle, so concerned? She did not trust him, but she relented a fraction. "What would you have me answer—that I was stupid? That I trusted . . . that I never expected? Shall it be your choice? Take any . . . all . . . for, yes, I *was* a fool for trusting and not expecting a stranger to attack me! But how could I think in such terms . . . I have never before come across such as he and *you are both quite new experiences for me!*" She ended almost on a sob and turned her head away.

He said nothing to this, but released her reins and proceeded quietly. Cassie's statement had struck a blow to his gut. He took a moment attempting to fathom this new sensation. He had until now regarded her as a witch to be tamed, a jade to be punished! He had never taken the time to wonder what she might think of him! It had never entered his head that she might think him a scoundrel, and it was obvious now that she did. She had just placed him on the same level with the gypsy. It stunned him into silence. True, he knew she disliked him . . . but still . . . Well, no matter, what did he care for her opinion? he thought angrily.

Their thoughts seemed almost to answer each other, for he would scowl and she would frown, and thus they reached the Grange an hour later, having said nothing further to each other.

Harris opened the front door wide, and his pleasure at finding his mistress standing there overrode his misgiving at his master's countenance. "Your lordship . . . Miss Farrington . . . it is so good to have you home again!"

"Is it?" responded his lordship instantly. "Ah yes, I take

it you are relieved to find your mistress safe. Did you think I had done her mischief?"

Harris had not been butler to the family all his adult life without having learned the way of the quality. He was perfectly composed in his response. "My lord, had I thought so, I would not have remained here. It would have been my duty and my way to set an inquiry about." It was a warning as well, and the viscount realizing it, beamed wide, liking the man for it.

"Indeed, Harris. I see I have taken you far too lightly. But never mind. And, by the way, your mistress is now . . . the Viscountess Welford."

The butler, startled, stood open-mouthed a brief moment before he managed the polite, "My felicitations . . . my lady . . . my lord . . ."

Cassie, on whom the exchange had passed over, had stood in mute mortification. This was but the final blow. She choked, hid her face from view, and took to the stairs, leaving the two males to stare after her, each with very different thoughts.

The viscount frowned, for he did not like a scene before servants, and his voice exhibited his displeasure. "Her ladyship is tired after a long day's ride. Kindly have a tray brought up to her. 'Tis past tea, I know, but make it a pot, good and strong—and send her a dish of cheeses, biscuits, and jams as she has not eaten well today. I would like a tray also . . . in the library."

"Very good, my lord," said the butler, inclining his head.

"And . . . Harris, as soon as my groom arrives, have him come to me in the library."

"As you wish, my lord," said the butler going off to follow his instructions.

Cassie bolted the door behind her and threw herself on her bed. She lay across it, burying her head in the protecting circle of her arms. She was home—humiliated, it was true—but home . . . that was something. The day had been cool and by now the wind had picked up. Cassie

158

listened for a moment, then raised her head and sighed. She went to the fireplace and lighted the kindling, dropped on the hearthrug, and sat staring into the growing flames. This was her room and she loved it—even its fading wallpaper with the pattern of trellises and green ivy. The green brocade drapes were drawn open, and she could see the rear lawns from her window.

A knock was sounded, and she quickly wrapped her cloak about her. "Yes . . . who is it?"

" 'Tis Meg, darlin' . . . open the door . . ."

Cassie rushed to open the door for her maid who was carrying the tea tray. She planted a kiss on the older woman's round cheek in undisguised pleasure. Meg . . . oh, Meg . . ." was all she could trust herself to say.

"Let me put this down and 'ave a look at yer bonnie face, child," said the other, placing the tray on the round table near the fire. "There now . . ." She gave Cassie a long look and ended by sustaining a bear hug. "There, there . . . what's this about your being Lady Welford . . . be it true?"

"Yes," said Cassie dully.

"Be ye happy, child?"

Cassie started to open her mouth, then thought better of it, "Of course, Meg. I am only tired."

"Aye, I see that. 'Tis that weary ye look about the eyes. But . . . there now . . . have your tea . . ."

"This is very sweet of you," said Cassie, eying the tray. "Thank you, darling Meg. I am somewhat hungry."

" 'Tis not me ye should be thanking, but that fine strapping husband of yers. He told Harris to send ye up tea and more besides . . . Harris was that surprised, didn't put his lordship down as thoughtful—in that way. But there . . . there's never no telling," mused the woman. "Go on now, I'll leave ye to it . . . and, child, take off yer cloak, do. Ye be home now!"

Cassie ushered her out of the room and leaned back against her door with a sigh of relief. Another moment and Meg would have seen her torn gown . . . and then there would have to be lengthy explanations . . . Oh, she just wasn't up to it!

She poured some tea, and its fragrant warmth began to soothe her tangled nerves. Carrying it with the plate of cheese and biscuits to the rug, she sat by the fire, legs tucked in beneath her. Suddenly she was very hungry. Her life had turned upside down and inside out and in such a peculiarly uncomfortable way it was impossible to think of food. Yet now that she was home she heard the plea of her stomach and duly answered it.

She nibbled on shortcake biscuits, relishing the buttery flavor, and sipped the bolstering brew—wondered at the man who could be so coldly unfeeling one moment and then so considerate the next. What was he about? Did he seek to lull her wariness? If so . . . why? Well, at least she would not be taken in by his tricks . . . not she.

The viscount dropped a substantial portion of brandy into his dark tea. He sipped it hot and felt the fiery libation soothe his inner being before he sat down. His black hair fell over his forehead as he scanned the mail and found a letter from London. He popped a slice of cheese into his mouth as he broke open the wax seal and pored over its contents. The frown over his eyes darkened, and he pushed away the food and stared into the fire. The news was not good. The flames lapped at the air above them, and he watched and thought suddenly of Cassie. He cursed beneath his breath, but his attention was brought round by the presence of Chips in the open doorway. The groom cleared his throat and stood shamefacedly, for he had still not managed to wipe himself of blame. He felt responsible for his master's mishap with the smuggler and that it was his fault the viscount was now tied to a woman he would rather see in hell—and he was uncertain how to face him.

"Chips! Blister it, man, don't stand there looking like a lamb! Get in here. We must talk!"

"Aye, yer lordship, but I ain I'm that hipped over wot happened at the Spithead and don't know how I can face ye," said the groom, sticking his stubbled chin into his neck.

"Nonsense! It was no fault of yours, my man. I have no one but myself to blame for it. Now come on in here. Have you eaten?"

"No, your lordship." said the man, eyes still down.

"Well then, come here and share my fare. I will ring for another cup," said the Viscount going to the bellrope.

"I canna do that. . ."

"You are trying my patience. Don't preach proprieties to me, Chips. It was more than a dozen times we drank from the same bottle, knee high in mud and wet through . . . and I don't have time to send you off for a proper meal in the kitchen. You'll have to grab dinner later on when you stop for the night."

"Where might I be goin', my lord?" asked Chips, once more at ease.

"To London, my man, to London!" grinned the viscount.

Some forty minutes later Cassie sat gazing out of her dressing room window, waiting for her bath to cool. She started up and pulled the damask hanging round her and watched, for she could see the stables from this window, and master and groom were making their way in that direction.

She remained fixed until some few minutes later she saw the men part at the end of the drive, and she watched the viscount until he was out of sight. She moved from the window and dropped her wrapper beside her marble tub. She caught a glance of herself in the long glass and stood a moment before her reflection. Did she look a woman now that she had become one? Did it show—her loss of innocence? She blushed as she remembered and quickly slid into the tub.

14

The tavern in Christchurch was dimly lighted but this in no way inhibited its occupants, many of whom were quality and cits bent on enjoying a night's freedom. The viscount sat among them, refreshing himself with a bumper of ale and a plate of mutton stew. He had finished his business in the town some thirty minutes past and had decided not to dine at home. It would do his young bride good to wonder about him, he thought with a smile. For no particular reason he rather enjoyed the fancy that she was up waiting and wondering about him.

A yellow-haired serving wench sauntered over to him and brushed her full breasts against his arm as she bent to inquire what further would please him. He smiled at her and replied that he was quite contented. "Aw . . . go on now, m'lord . . . sure now, I could content ye a might more."

"I'm sure you could, but I think I'll pass tonight," he said, pinching her chin. "You see, tonight is my wedding night."

"Gawks! Never say so! What? Did ye have a spat with yer lady?" she responded, much startled.

"Something like that," he answered, his eyes twinkling.

"Well then, ye jest forget it. Ain't nuthin' worth givin' up yer night for. Lord love yer handsome face . . . I'll bet yer lady be weepin' her eyes over ye this very minute and willin' to make it up. Go on now—give her a chance . . ."

"You know, woman . . . I think you are right," said the viscount, getting to his feet.

He stood some height over her, and she gazed up with a sigh, "Bless ye, but if she don't give over, come back to me. I'll be that pleased to take her place."

He laughed, pinched her chin again, donned his hat, and once again was on the road to Farrington Grange.

Her bath over hours ago, dinner consumed, a selection of books tossed aside, Cassie paced in a state of absurd agitation. It was a most provoking thing to be thwarted when she thought she had the ideal notion. Cassie had formulated a plan and meant to institute it, but how could she when the victim was not present? Where was he? Why did he go out? Wasn't he tired? Of course not, demons never tire! Where was he—and who was with him?

Her white nightdress floated transparently away from her body as she walked back and forth before her fire. Her green eyes were alive with her thoughts, and her long red tresses flowed free around her lithe figure. She had her own revenge to inflict and earlier she had steeled herself to carry out her plan. He would come to claim his marriage rights, but she would give him none. He said he wanted no heir in her likeness. Well . . . he would get no more of her. She was safely locked in her room, and he cared too much for what the servants might spread about to force his way. However, it was close onto ten and he was not back yet. Then all at once she heard the clip-clop of a horse on the drive-way and she rushed to her dressing room window. But the night was too black and the stables too far to distinguish anyone. She waited at the window, but she could see nothing.

She returned to her bedroom, opened the door, and listened. She was rewarded by the sound of his voice as he sent Harris off to his own quarters. She waited until she heard him come up the stairs, until his footsteps were almost outside her door, then closed it loudly and snapped the bolt into place. Smiling, she leaned back against it and folded her arms.

Kirkby heard her ploy and stopped, a wide grin on his lips. That move was contrived to irritate him, he had no doubt. Now, to make his decision. He could walk off and allow her her moment, but that might cause complications. She could take it into her head that she had won the first round and give him more trouble than he wanted. He could demand admittance—or break the door down. Hmmm . . . or do something altogether different. His smile broadened, and he came close to her door and said, in a bland voice, "Darling, as I shan't be *needing* you tonight, try and get some sleep. That's a good girl," with which he hurried off to his own room. She turned on the heel of her flat slipper and stared at the closed door. How dare he? Blister his soul! What did he mean *he didn't need her*? *He couldn't have her*! She unbolted and unlatched the door to fling it open and so have him understand, but he was already gone, the hall empty and dark.

"Of all the gall! The arrogant!" she sputtered as she refastened the door. She snuffed out the single candle at her bedside and slid between the covers where she closed her eyes, but opened them again in indignation, then determinedly closed them again.

The viscount's grin still spread over his face as he placed the candleholder on his nightstand and dropped his clothes onto a nearby chair. He went to the washstand which held a fresh supply of water and cleansed himself before going to the large four-poster bed. He sank down into the coolness of the sheets and glanced at his low fire and again he smiled. But suddenly he felt an urgency in his loins as he thought of the beauty of Cassie's form.

164

Against his will, he half-rose, than sank back and determinedly closed his eyes.

His lordship and her ladyship discovered that tightly shut eyes do not a sleeper make. Both had painstaking difficulty in attempting to find the rest they so badly needed. Cassie told herself delightful fairy tales, in which she was the heroine to be rescued, but this made her more interested than sleepy. She then paced the room and told herself she loathed her husband. But this made her cry. Finally, exhaustion took over and, without realizing it, she dozed off somewhere near four in the morning.

The viscount, though less dramatic in his attempts at rest, was just as determined. He moved about his wide bed furiously, pounding his pillow violently. He attempted fantasy, but the devil would have that the only female he could conjur up was Cassie! He rose, lighted a candle and went to the hearth. He tossed on a log and stood staring at it as the flames warmed his naked body. He was much in need of a woman, but damn! He was not going to take that witch! He snuffed out his candle, returned to bed, and all at once he too drifted off, somewhere near that magic hour of four.

Morning found them both groggy and only the viscount willing to leave his unsatisfactory respite. He rose, stretched, rang the bellrope and advised Harris that he would have his breakfast in his room, after a hot bath. Cassie stretched and noticed by the table clock that it was past eight. She groaned and turned over but a steady knock at her door brought her to attention. "Who is it?" she called drowsily.

" 'Tis Meg, m'lady . . . with yer coffee pipin' hot! Come now, yer door be bolted tight, and I 'ave me hands full, I do."

Cassie jumped out of bed and opened the door wide. "So sorry, Meg," she offered, rubbing her eyes.

"Lord love ye, child . . . I don't mean to pry. But ye never bolted yer door afore, and . . . well . . . Harris says . . . his lordship be in the master suite . . . and . . ."

"Never mind," said Cassie firmly, one brow up. "You may put the tray by my window." Her eyes dismissed her maid for she was in no mood to answer such questions.

"Now don't be puttin' on airs with me, child. Ye'll remember that I swatted yer butt now and then when ye was a wee thing," retorted Meg somewhat gruffly, evidently hurt.

Cassie went to her at once and put an arm about her. "Oh, Meg . . . it's just that I am tired and out of sorts. Don't worry . . ."

Meg grunted and patted her hand before taking her leave. Cassie plumped herself down on her chair and sipped the hot dark brew with pleasure. Before her lay the lawns, dismal beneath a gray mist. Gray-white fingers of fog picked at the lawn and twirled round the trees, and Cassie felt a sudden chill. She reached for her wrapper and glanced round to find that her fire was completely out. She moved to the hearth and spent a few moments kindling it, for it would be a cold day, and she had no plans to go downstairs—not with *him* in the house. Then she heard the sound of heavy boots in the hall. Her heart seemed to stop, and her breath caught in her throat as his steps stopped outside her door.

She heard him begin to whistle a lively tune, and then the door opened wide to admit him. She glared. "Don't you believe in knocking, my lord?"

"Charming, aren't you, first thing in the morning. Damn, but I think I've married a shrew," he said, closing the door at his back and taking long wide strides across the room. He reached her, and his black eyes sparkled with amusement. "Sleep well, Cassie?" he asked, his voice suddenly soft.

"Yes, quite well," she said, nose in air.

His finger went to her chin and turned her face to himself. "Bold liar!" he whispered. "But never mind, no doubt you will sleep better tonight," he said, his mouth light and sensuously charming.

"Oh? Are you leaving the Grange, my lord?" she asked sweetly.

"*Touché!*" he laughed, "No, love. Well, that is . . . not tonight, though I shall presently. I have come to bid thee good-morning before going off. Have a good day, sweet vixen," he said and turned on his heel.

Her tone halted him and drew his smile over his shoulder. "But, my lord . . . I mean . . . where do you go?"

"To the same place I went last evening," he responded mysteriously.

Good, she thought, we come to last night. "And just where is this place? After all, you are master of the Grange—and what if you were needed?"

"I doubt that I could be found. Good-day, my bride," he said lightly and left the room.

She jumped to her feet and ran to the door, thinking to demand his intended destination. Then she thought better of it and settled instead for stamping her foot. He was the most provoking man—a veritable devil! Then she sighted her countenance in the looking glass and went closer to scan her face. She was, in fact, exquisite, and had she known with what will power the viscount had held himself aloof, she would have been far more at ease. As it was, she wondered why he no longer found her desirable. She would change that. Before long, she would have him begging for her favors!

First, she would go through her mother's things up in the attic. Her mother had remained a beauty to the very end, and her figure had been much the same as her daughter's. Cassie was bound to find something that would not be too outdated. With a little help from Meg, she would make herself ravishing to him! Indeed she would make him gasp for breath . . . and grovel at her feet . . . then she would look at him as though he were no more than a . . . a . . . common rogue.

The viscount's plans had been slightly delayed by Sir Charles's suicide, but no matter, he now had the full name —Nathan Asbatol. He would go to Bristol and set up housekeeping in style. His wife would need clothes to suit her station. This had been taken care of yestereve at Mrs.

Bootles'. He had some other things to finish up there to-day—the ordering of shoes, hats, some jewels, and other necessities. It was important to his ends.

And what about Cassie? He was married to her for the time being. Perhaps if he had attended to the matter immediately, he could have wangled an annulment. There was still time. But no, he had to go to Bristol and ferret out Asbatol. By the time that was over, an annulment would be out of the question. That left only divorce. The word stuck in his gut. There had never been a divorce in his family. It was unthinkable . . . it would ruin his ambitions forever.

Damn! And damn again! He would just have to make the best of it. At least he would use Cassie in Bristol. As his wife she would be his hostess, and sooner or later she would raise her covers and let him in . . . though it didn't matter. He cared not a fig for her, not he. Thinking of Cassandra was dangerous and confusing, and he wouldn't . . . not now! He had an errand to discharge, his appointment with Mrs. Bootles. Then soon they would be off for Bristol . . . and Nathan Asbatol. There too, he also had a fancy to pick up word of Jack Rattenbury.

15

The attic was a large, dark room, cluttered with priceless though somewhat damaged relics of years gone by. However, at the moment, Meg and Cassandra were interested only in the trunks full of gowns. For what was now several hours, they had been sorting the contents into several piles. One consisted of gowns that would not do, another of those that would, and a third of those that had possibilities.

Cassie shook out an attractive gown of rich, dark brown velvet and held it up to herself. "What say you, Meg? This looks as though it might be made to fit to wear for tomorrow . . . don't you think?"

Meg, her mobcap askew, tilted her head for a moment before giving her considered opinion that it would do quite well. Cassie laughed almost happily and draped the gown over her arm. "Well then, shall we bring those others down with us? You may fit me in my room for, faith, Meg, 'tis stuffy up here. I wonder that you have borne with it and me . . . just because of my nonsensical notions," said Cassie on a grateful note.

"Nonsense?" returned the woman with some surprise. "I don't see any nonsense in a bride wantin' to be dressed proper for her husband, no, I don't. Wonder is that ye ain't smoothed things over with him," mused the maid, for she was being eaten by curiosity. She marveled over her mistress's recent marriage to a man the girl hardly knew . . . though, looking at the viscount 'twas no surprise the lass would take to him. But, the fact that they had spent their wedding night in separate rooms simply confounded her. After all, it was not usual—even for quality—to spend the *first* night apart.

Cassie had some very excellent reasons for wanting to look her best, but it would not do to tell Meg her plans. The woman was a romantic and there was no sense in distressing her. Oh, Cassie meant to win his lordship's heart —and feed it to the nearest beast.

They reached her room and some time was spent pinning the gowns that needed alterations. By the time Meg had left with the dresses and Cassie was once again wearing her old schooldress of pale green printed muslin, it was well into the late afternoon. As she smoothed her hair at her back and tied it with a green ribbon, she wondered where his lordship was, but quickly dismissed this from her mind. He could be lying in a ditch somewhere expiring and she would not care, but this was no balm to her nerves. After a moment's hesitation and a troubled glance at the sky, Cassie picked up her green spencer and straw bonnet and made her way outdoors.

Her half boots were beyond repair—the salt water had seen to that. She had no others, and she found that they were no longer capable of keeping out the damp. The sodden grass very soon made itself felt through the kid, and she hurried onto the narrow dirt path that led through the Grange woods. However, though the packed dirt made it somewhat easier going, in spite of the fact that she had to jump puddles, the droplets from the trees began to make her feel she would soon be soaked through. She sighed and left the walking path for the main pike. Here at least she had packed earth underfoot and no trees overhead to shower her. She wanted to walk and walk! She had gone a good mile when a light drizzle warned her homeward again. It was on her way back to the Grange that she finally heard the birds singing overhead and smiled at the sound. She looked about her as though seeing for the first time the beauty of spring fresh with diamond dew glistening in the gray light of growing dusk. Then all at once she thought of Jack, and her smile grew. *What are ye doing now, me swarthy buck?* she wondered idly. Surely he was safe. He must be . . . he was the last of her past she could cling to when her future looked troubled.

Then all at once the sky seemed to rumble with displeasure and two dark clouds stood at bay ready to come to blows. She glanced their way and hurried her steps, nearly shrieking as the lightning flashed across the sky. Then all at once the downpour commenced and her thin clothing was soaked through and clinging to her running legs. The wind seized her straw bonnet and she whirled after it, but it was lost to a tree branch out of reach and she gave up. Drenched to the bone and out of breath, weighed down by her clothing, she ran toward her front drive.

The viscount looked up as he felt the drizzle tap his face, and he cursed softly as he scanned the sky. Nothing for it but to make a dash as he set his roan into a steady canter. He was well protected by the tiered riding cloak, but was nevertheless relieved to see the drive to the Grange as he rounded the curve in the road. The force of the rain had already begun to soak through his hat when he looked up and found before his blurry vision a woman who appeared for all practical purposes to be totally nude —and exquisitely so!

Narrowing his black eyes into focus, he discovered that the owner of these magnificent proportions was Cassie. Again he cursed low in his throat and urged his horse her way. He halted before her, and she looked up to find his wet black locks clinging about his handsome face and his mouth set in an angry line. He had to shout over the force of the downpour, "Give me your hand!"

"I can walk back very well, my lord," answered she with as much pride as she could muster under the circumstances.

"Little idiot!" he exclaimed depressingly as he bent over and caught her round the waist. He brought her up onto the saddle, cradled her in his arm, and to protect her further, unbuttoned his cloak and forced her against his body as he wrapped her in its heavy folds. She said nothing to this for he had already sent his horse into a trot, and she was forced to hold onto him to keep her seat. In such a position she found it difficult to deny his masculinity, and she released a weary sigh, wishing she could for a moment let her guard down.

He felt her pressed against his body, felt her tremble and wanted to say it served her right for going out in such weather. But he refrained from this, for he was beginning to know her and fully expected she might do something foolish—perhaps refuse the protection of his cloak. He wanted no struggle now for it was hard enough seeing his way in the rain. They arrived home, and he slid off his horse, reached up and again took her in his arms, carrying her like a babe up the steps. Harris appeared and opened the door wide.

"Have a lackey take my horse to the stables and see to it properly. Then advise cook that her ladyship and I will be taking our dinner early. And Harris, we will be having it in her ladyship's chamber."

With that he was taking the stairs, Cassie clinging to him lest she fall. She had looked up into his face at the orders to the butler, thinking what the deuce did he mean *they* would be taking dinner in *her* chamber? But she refrained from an argument before the servants. He carried her to her bedroom, pushed open the door and set her on her feet. Closing the door with a backward movement of his foot, he threw off his hat and coat, glancing up at her as she stood undecided before him.

He grinned, "Hadn't you better get out of those wet clothes, madam?"

She ignored the question. "You don't really think you are going to have dinner with me *here*, do you?" she asked.

He made no answer, discounting the lift to his brow, as he proceeded to remove the blue superfine and blue silk waistcoat.

"Well . . . do you?" she pursued.

"Don't you think I should?" he teased, his black eyes suddenly alight. "No, I can see that you don't think so but, nevertheless, we shall take dinner together here . . . for we have much to discuss before we retire—and I would prefer privacy. Now come here, let me help you with your buttons."

"Go to the devil!" she responded at once.

For answer his lordship strode across the room, reached out, and brought her to him. Her wet body was nearly touching his, and her breasts were full and tantalizing as her nipples peaked hard and alluring before his eyes. "Madam, if you don't mean to be raped here and now, allow me to help you with your buttons so that you may change into something decent!"

She glanced down at herself and blushed for she hadn't realized how she looked and without another word she gave him her back, holding her long wet hair out of his way. He laughed suddenly, marveling at her quick turnabout, and his voice softened as he undid the last button, allowing his finger to trace the center line down her back to her small waist. "There now, sweet vixen, you may retire to your dressing room and return suitably attired, so that we may enjoy a bracing meal and—talk."

She said nothing but stalked out of the room, chin well into the air. As this only made him hoot with mirth, she blushed furiously and slammed her dressing room door.

He went to the grating, put on a log, and kindled a flame. In that flame he saw her face, her green catlike eyes, and he had to steel himself.

She threw off her wet muslin spencer and gown and

dried her body vigorously. She stood before the long mirror staring at her lush naked form, wondering what she should wear. Ah, Cassie girl, has your mind gone a-begging? Didn't you vow to bring him low? To win his heart and slice it with your own hand? With a sly smile she slipped on her nightdress, making sure her body glowed beneath before donning the matching wrapper and closing it loosely at the waist. She stepped into her slippers and sat at the vanity brushing her wet hair, catching it at the top of her head with a ribbon and allowing the red tresses to curl to her neck where she pinned them in place. She curled short strands round her face before standing up for a final inspection before the long mirror.

The viscount looked up at her approach and gasped involuntarily. She *was* luscious! As she swayed toward him he poured some madeira. She took the proffered glass, sipping it, and bringing her green eyes up to his black ones for a long adventurous moment.

He let his eyes roam over her body, resting a moment on her breasts, her slender waist, and the curve of her hips. He remembered her in his arms. . . But he must concentrate on the business at hand. She came closer still to put her glass on the table. Oh, hell! . . . His hand moved with a will of its own and drew her to him. She felt herself go weak at his touch as a wild thrill rushed through her and she knew an urgency to yield to whatever he demanded. They clung at each other, and his mouth descended upon hers, hungry, demanding.

She felt his hand move from her waist, his body burning against her own. Suddenly he was fondling her breast, breathing her name, his desire. She had to break this spell. Was she some trollop, to yield to a man she loathed . . . simply because her body ached—lusted? No, she would be no animal. She would remember how he had used her. She shouted, "Stop it! Stop it!"

He released her at once. He was on fire still, but he would take no unwilling wench. That was not his aim. He wanted her to want him . . . to come to him. He had thought when she returned to the room dressed seductively, her eyes warm . . . but he should have known. It was just another of her tricks—a tease, and he would not be teased.

"As you wish, madam," he said coolly.

She was still having a hard time composing herself, and she glanced at him sharply, marveling at his composure and piqued by it as well. "You . . . you said you wanted to talk?" she managed.

There was a knock, and the viscount postponed his answer as he crossed the room and opened the door wide to admit a lackey, followed by Harris, both laden with trays. Harris commanded the boy to lay his things near the fire, while he himself began to set the satinwood table for dining.

The viscount waited until the dishes and silver had been put in place before dismissing the elderly man. "Thank you, Harris, you may light the candles and go, for I have a fancy to serve my bride tonight."

The butler raised not a brow, but accepted this and motioned for the boy to follow. Cassie, who had gathered her wrapper round her during their presence, released it once again. The viscount observed this with a twinkle in his eye. "Come," he offered gently, his head slightly inclined, "take a chair, madam, and allow me . . ."

She sat down but maintained an aloof silence in spite of his gallantry. He overflowed with charm as he brought a plate of hot soup to her, speaking easily, lightly. Just before putting a spoonful of soup to his own lips he said glibly, "Ah, you will be interested to learn that I have had word of your free trader." Having thus forced her to raise her lovely eyes, he proceeded to take his soup, one spoonful following another.

She waited as patiently and as long as she thought reasonable before exploding, "Well?"

"Well what, my dear?" he teased.

"You are horrid!" she snapped, out of humor. This was no way for a man to act before a beautiful woman. Was she not beautiful? Jack had thought so, others had thought so. Why did he not think so?

"If I were truly horrible, I would never give you news of him," he responded, his black eyes alive.

"Please! It is inhuman to keep me on tenterhooks," she pleaded.

He laughed. "Sweet vixen, you should use such wiles more often, they work far better than stamping feet and flashing eyes . . . though, do not mistake . . . they too have their charms."

"Then you will tell me what has happened to Jack?" she asked eagerly.

"I had intended to from the start, impatient puss. I collect that your free trader has furthered his legend. He made off with the *Sweet Mary* right under the noses of the guards and has sailed, the locals think, for Devon and Beers!"

"Oh, wonderful! Oh, is he not grand? But how did he do it?"

"A clever fellow, your Jack. I should like to have him on my side in a tight situation. He created a diversion. Apparently, he had a female of doubtful reputation entertain the guards with her antics and promises when all at once she began screaming at the top of her lungs that her little babe had run off. She got both guards to run off down the road after the little tot, during which time in sails a sloop that is nothing to the *Sweet Mary*—but in it comes—while out goes the *Sweet Mary,* right under their very noses. The tot is found and the guards return to duty none the wiser, until this morning when they were relieved by the day guards!"

"Then he got his tubs from the brine?" she asked, her face wreathed in happiness.

"If he got the *Sweet Mary*, madam, one must assume that he got the tubs," grinned the viscount. His jealousy of the free trader had vanished the moment he had taken Cassie and found her untouched.

"Oh, that is good," she sighed.

"Now, to *our* business," he said, pushing aside his soup. She looked up a moment from hers, but returned to it immediately, saying quietly, "Go on."

"Tomorrow morning you will receive a visit from a Mrs. Bootles of Christchurch. She is . . ."

"Mrs. Bootles? But I haven't ordered any gowns. She is the dressmaker on Aberlmane Street, is she not?" said Cassie, interrupting him.

He sighed, "If I may be allowed to proceed?"

She blushed and inclined her head. He smiled mischievously, almost forgetting that she was to be held at a distance, for he found her irresistible.

"She is coming here at my instructions. I have ordered a quantity of gowns and female trappings for you and, as I was only able to judge by eye, she will need to have fittings."

"You have done what?" she shrieked. "How dare you! I . . . I won't accept them." As she said it, she knew she was being absurd. He was her husband. But it was a fact so hard to dwell on and yet impossible to forget. Caught in her confusion, she lowered her eyes.

"Exactly," he said quietly. "I see that you have already perceived the foolishness of your words. Now, if I may, I shall explain. Don't imagine I do this from pity. I am, of course, aware that your cousin did not see fit to clothe you as your position entitled. *Neither would I,* if I did not find it necessary to my aims. Think not that you have latched onto a wealthy lord, for that is not the case! My name is an old one, but I was unfortunate enough to run through the family fortune rather quickly, you see, and must now depend on my wits to continue the manner of living that pleases me. Do you understand thus far?"

"I understand that you are a rogue libertine!"

"Good. Then you will not be surprised to learn that when my groom returns . . . you may not have noticed, but he is not at the Grange. When he returns, we will then be off as soon as possible and in much style for Bristol. I mean to set up house there and entertain the rich *ton*—all of whom still believe me to be affluent. I mean to keep up appearances until such time as circumstances make this true. Do you still follow?"

She frowned. "You are an adventurer? But why Bristol?"

"Because Nathan Asbatol is there, and together I think he and I will do well—don't you?"

"I don't know him—and I think you are wicked!" Her voice was quiet.

"Nevertheless, you will accompany me as my wife and play the hostess to the many parties and routs I plan to give," he said blandly, but there was a hint in his voice that told her of his determination.

"No," she said firmly. "I won't be a party to any of your schemes. I will remain at the Grange."

"You would have remained at the Grange had you not seen fit to link our futures. Now, you will go wherever I fancy to take you. Mark me, woman, I won't be balked in this."

"Do you mean to drag me willy-nilly across the downs to Bristol?" she flung at him incredulosly.

"Tush, hot vixen, calm yourself. My ways are not so crude." He paused a moment and gazed from her to his plate before pushing it aside. "Let me see now, what was it I wanted to ask of you earlier? Ah, yes, I recall. Meg and Harris—two trusted servants, are they not?"

"Yes," she answered, feeling inexplicably afraid.

"And I imagine you would like them to remain on here, secure in their positions at the Grange?"

"Of course, but what has that to do with . . ."

He cut her short by raising his hand for silence. "I, however, am used to servants with far more cultivation. You see. I might find it expedient to remove your faithful lot and replace them with servants more to *my* liking . . ."

"Oh, faith," exclaimed Cassie, suddenly breathless, leaning forward on her elbow, her green eyes imploring. "You, you would not turn them off . . . surely . . . even you would not . . . ?"

"But why not?" he asked, his face a mask.

"Please, my lord, no matter what *our* differences, do

178

not heap your spite on them. They have done you no harm." She was begging now.

"I might find myself able to give you this boon, providing you find it possible to repay me what I ask in exchange," said he, suddenly intent.

She saw at last. Her mouth dropped and she gazed at him long. "Ah, it is that way. What a fool I was not to have seen from the start that you played a game. I would have capitulated without pleading my case. Very well my lord, it seems you have discovered my price . . . again." Her voice was low, her eyes limpid pools of seawater, and he felt his heart contract. He frowned over the sensation, for he did not like his method. But there was nothing for it —it had been a bluff, and it had worked. Yet he saw the contempt in her eyes and it gnawed at his spirit.

He bolstered himself. What did he care for *her* good opinion? Remember what she was to him. Remember how she had betrayed his young brother . . . what had been her price then? He hardened at once. "I see your soup is not to your taste, madam. Let me remove it and bring you the main course. It has a most enticing aroma."

Her heart felt that it was breaking, and her mouth was too dry to open, but there he stood coolly serving their meal. She would not crack before him. She would be every bit as hard as he. She raised her chin. "I do hope she has made potatoes with that chicken . . . ah, I see that she has . . . yes, I will take more, thank you." Something in her mien made him glance twice at her face.

They finished the meal in silence for the most part, only the touch of silverware against the plate breaking the quiet. At the end, he got to his feet, took up the decanter of port, and bowed low to his wife. "I bid thee good-night, my vixen bride."

She watched him go, bottle in hand, and stared after the closed door a long while before dropping her head into her elbow and giving vent to her overwrought emotions.

16

Nathan Asbatol stood with his hands grasping the finely ornamented back of an Oriental chair. He had the appearance that is usually defined as average-looking—neither tall nor short, fat nor thin. However, his childhood had rendered his features far less than average. He had come through small pox and the disease had left its marks on his dark brownish skin. Age and dissipation had done the rest, and because of that, he commanded a strange presence in a room. He stood now in quiet contemplation, for he had that morning received a disturbing letter from a friendly cohort in London.

What to do? Well, he would wait for his mate. Leila was a cunning woman, and he relied much on her advice. He was fortunate in that he had already attained much of his wealth some five years ago just before he met her. Leila was ever greedy and their union had nothing to do with love—at least not on her part.

The door to their richly furnished salon opened, and a lackey held it wide for Leila to enter. Her ivory satin rustled softly as it moved close to her tall slim body. He surveyed her and found that even at eight and thirty she still had the power to tease his lust. He liked her new hairdo which she had clipped close to her head in tight yellow curls. She smiled a welcome before dropping into a chair. "Nathan . . . it is not good," she announced. "I have already ordered my maid to pack our things and make ready to depart. We will leave with our coach, but I don't think we should close the house down. No . . . that might not look good and . . ." Her face and voice were serious.

"My dear," he said coming to sit beside her, "I have been waiting to discuss this matter with you, but it seems you have already made up your mind." There was the hint of the Middle East in his accent, but many years in England had rendered it nearly undetectable.

"Well, Nathan, really! We have no choice," she exclaimed impatiently.

"But Bristol works well for us. We have Nancina's house . . . and a ready clientele forever on the lists . . . we have our very lucrative shipping arrangements with the States . . ."

"For pity's sake, Nathan! All that can be handled from Liverpool—and we must leave." She raised her light brown eyes. "Dearest, it is far more serious than you think. That Linton boy—Frank did not obey orders. Instead of hiring a post chaise to return him as you wished, he tried to save himself some blunt and took the common stage. It is all in the *Herald*. Some old geezer remembered seeing a boy on the stage—he thought the lad was sleeping —until he heard of the Linton case . . ."

"Damn Frank for a fool! He was only supposed to use laudanum on this one. We expressly told him no opium— not this time. It was too chancy because of Eaton."

"But the point is, he used the opium, and the child did die . . . and someone saw them both. A description has been given of Frank, and it is just a matter of time before they catch up to him."

"Blast the fellow! May he rot!" cried Nathan, incensed.

"He will, darling. I don't mean for him to be caught, for

181

he would give our names within the first five seconds of his capture. But never mind. By tomorrow night Frank will be disposed of. I have arranged everything."

"How?" asked Nathan his eyes lighting up.

"An accident has been contracted."

"Good. Good. You are a treasure," he said, putting his arms around her. "But, Leila . . . all this . . . 'tis a bad omen. First Eaton—by gad, that was close. Then Charles, doing away with himself in that strange manner. Most odd that fellow winning all of Charles's holdings. And now, that dratted boy dying on us."

"Just be thankful that we have been able to get word on all these doings!" said Leila. "Never mind now, darling, we will soon be well out of it. And Lord, we can take a little jaunt up to the Lake district and visit Coleridge. He should be wanting a few taels by now!"

"Eh? The old fool . . . thinks he keeps his addiction to opium a secret!" chuckled Nathan.

"What does it matter just so he pays us higher than most."

"Thing is . . . don't like Liverpool. Damnable place —overrun with Irish!" said Nathan thoughtfully.

"Precisely why I have choosen it," said Leila, her eyes taking on a catlike glint. "Just think what we could do with those starving creatures, what lengths they would be ready to go?"

"Very well then, darling. We will leave for Liverpool as soon as may be!" he answered, pushing his hand into the bodice of her gown and fondling one small breast. She submitted to his caress for she had long ago learned to steel herself against his touch—and her mind wandered to another time . . .

At Farrington Grange, Mrs. Bootles fitted and pinned Cassie into the numerous gowns the viscount had ordered. Cassandra stood on a stool at the mercy of the woman's jolly ministrations. She had to admit that the viscount's taste in women's clothing was impeccable, for he had chosen the ready-made gowns with an eye to fashion. In addition to this the gowns were perfectly suited to Cassie's high coloring. "Tch, tch, such a small waist ye have, m'lady . . . all right this one can come off," said the woman, lifting the gown over Cassie who leaned forward to aid her.

Mrs. Bootles disappeared into the dressing room for some things she needed, leaving Cassie, naked to the waist, standing on the stool. Thus she stood when the viscount chose to enter her chamber. He stopped, transfixed a moment as he gazed up at her. Her red hair was pinned loosely at the top of her head and fell in lazy ringlets about her lovely face. His gaze went lower to the full ripe fruits so casually exposed to him above her petticoat before she had time to think and cross her arms to shield herself from his sight.

A slow smile spread over his countenance. Sweet life, he thought, she was too beautiful for him to continue his monk's existence. He ambled forward playfully. "You know, I have always thought such fittings were dull work. I see now how wrong I have been. Fiend seize my eyes if I lie . . . you are the loveliest creature I have ever beheld. Give over, Cassie, do . . ." he said reaching up boldly to cup one of her breasts in spite of her efforts to stop him. She blushed furiously, but his other hand had already caught her hip and his mouth had found her flesh just above her waist. She felt her blood race, and though she wanted to—or told herself that she must want to—shake him off, she could not. She stood still allowing his mouth to trace its own path over her flesh. She felt a groan well up within her but suddenly she was set free.

Mrs. Bootles' voice barely preceded her body as she trudged in on them, not in the least embarrassed by their play. "Tch, tch, young groom ye may be . . . and her a lovely piece, 'tis true . . . but out wit ye . . . I can't work with a man underfoot. Out, *out* . . ." she ordered.

The viscount grinned widely and put up his hands in surrender. As he reached the door he stopped and turned toward Cassie. "I came to ask you whether you had any desire for Starfire to accompany us on our trip?"

She cast wide green eyes at him and there was a hope in them. "Oh . . . I had . . . oh, yes my lord," she said breathlessly.

He frowned but his voice was soft. "Did it worry you, sweetings? You could have asked me . . ?"

"No, I couldn't," she answered.

He looked at her long, the frown deepening over his brow before he left her to Mrs. Bootles. He took the stairs to the library. He had passed another restless night—his thoughts were all of Cassie. He had not liked the ploy he had used to convince her to come to Bristol. In addition to that, he was a red-blooded young man with a longing for a woman. Not just any woman, but for *one* woman. She was his wife, not many doors away, and yet he was not able to go to her room and take her. His will power, though much abused, much cursed and flogged, came out the victor. She would have to show herself willing to lie with him. She would have to come to him—a little more than half way. It was important that he win this first battle. But he was fully cognizant of the fact that he would have to exert some effort to bring this about. He could not rely on his masculinity alone for the girl already had an aversion for him—she thought him an adventurer. So be it, he needed her to think so, but this would not aid his cause. Evidently she looked for some white knight to rescue her from herself. Well, he would charm her into thinking he was just such a knight.

That was only a small part of his ultimate goal. But first he would have to get to Bristol . . . and it lay there . . . so close now. He expected Chips back on the morrow. The gowns should be done by then, he mused silently. If all went as planned, they would be off, and he would find Nathan Asbatol.

Cassie had passed a night of contradictions, first wanting Kirkby Welford, then hating him, and finally crying from anger and frustration. She had risen early and breakfasted alone in her bedroom, until suddenly Mrs. Bootles descended upon her. The viscount's entrance and his subse-

184

quent fondling left her in badly troubled straits. She wanted to be honest with herself, but every time she tried to face the truth she blanked it out. She would not, *could* not, lust after such a fiend.

The viscount rode off on his roan unaware that a pair of hungry green eyes followed him from an upstairs window. The sun had dispelled the rain and there was something he had forgotten the day before. He was deep in thought and had no idea how well he looked astride his horse. Cassie was far too aware of it.

Finally, she bade Mrs. Bootles good-day and donned the brown velvet she had found in the attic the previous morning. Its neckline was scooped low over her bosom and was trimmed in ivory lace which formed a rose above her cleavage. The short puffed sleeves carried the same lace, the bodice was high waisted, and the skirt fell straight lines to her ankles showing off her graceful form. It was definitely a gown of the high Regency days, and Cassie fancied she could almost remember her mother wearing it . . . but she must not think of that. It seemed so long ago.

Bristol. She wondered what it would be like. Then again she was thinking of him and wondering what *he* was about. She went down to the library when it occurred to her that she should send word to Jack that she would soon be leaving the Grange. Quickly she scribbled a note to him, found an envelope, and sealed it with wax. This done, she went in search of Harris whom she found puttering in the garden.

She stood in quiet conversation with him as he tended his primroses. He loved gardening, and the beautiful flower arrangements they enjoyed in the Grange were due to his fine hand. After some time she produced the envelope. "Harris, I want this delivered by hand. Do you think you can spare someone? It is quite a journey to the Spithead, but 'tis the only place I know where it may be safe."

"Aye, it will be taken care of, m'lady," said the elderly retainer. She reached in her pocket for a coin, for she still

185

had some left to her from a pocketful Jack had supplied her.

"Give him this for his trouble," she said, placing both the envelope and the money in the butler's hand.

"Do I intrude?" asked a male voice.

She spun round, feeling strangely guilty, and it showed in the color of her cheeks. She wondered if he would stop the letter from reaching its destination, for she was sure he had seen her passing the envelope into Harris's hand.

"Oh! No, of course not. Harris was just explaining the fine arts of caring for roses," she said attempting to sound light and taking a step toward the house.

Kirkby detained her. "Come, Cassie, it is a fine day. Walk with me . . . do," he pleaded, smiling at her.

She was so relieved that she accepted quickly, far too quickly, and he felt an irritation. He had indeed seen her pass the letter, and though he did not overhear its destination, he had a fairly good idea to whom it was addressed. He had a very odd longing to hear her confess it of her own accord. She attempted to engage him in light conversation. "Did . . . did you ride into town, my lord?"

He grimaced. "You know . . . I am your husband . . . and it will not do to continually call me 'my lord.' I have a given name, and it is Kirkby. Do you not think you could try to use it?"

She smiled. "I will try. But did you?"

"Yes, I did. It occurred to me that we were rather thoughtless at our wedding . . . did the entire thing without benefit of a ring to seal the business," he said blandly.

She blushed. "A ring? What is a ring to a ceremony conducted for a mute bride and an unconscious groom?"

He laughed at this openly. "You are, madam, a constant source of amazement."

"I believe you have told me that before. It pleases me that in our *long* acquaintance that has not changed!" she returned.

He reached into his inner chest pocket, produced a small velvet sack, and placed it in her hand. When she looked up at him and frowned, he smiled reassuringly.

"Don't fret, sweetings. 'Tis but a simple thing. I did not want to put a strain on my funds. 'Tis but a band of gold . . . to keep you honest!"

She put up a brow. "If I were intent on dishonesty, a gold band would not stand in my way!" She avoided his eye as she slipped the plain gold band on her finger.

"I am sure it would not," he said drily.

"You purposely misunderstand. I mean by that, it is not the object on my finger that would keep me faithful, but my own principles."

"Principles?" he said dubiously. "Have you a set?"

Her anger gathered fire. "You may learn in time . . . or being thickheaded, you may just go on thinking what you like."

He was taken aback. "Indeed! But tell me, Cassie, do your principles extend to honesty between man and wife?"

"Do yours?" she countered.

"They did," he said softly.

"But not in our case? Eh, my lord, not in our case . . . due to the circumstances! 'Tis understandable, but then you must not expect what you cannot give."

He eyed her a moment and then came to the point. "To whom did you write that letter you gave into Harris's keeping?"

So, he had seen. Well, he might intercept this note, but sooner or later, she would get one through. Her cheeks were flushed with anger. "That is none of your affair!"

"To whom, Cassie?" he said quietly unrelentingly.

"My lord," she mocked, "are you not all-knowing? Do you mean you cannot guess? How strange! I thought you knew everything there was to know."

"I could put Harris in the awkward position of answering me and thus making him feel a traitor to you," he said, still softly.

"You needn't resort to threats! Did you think I was afraid to tell you? Don't be absurd. The letter goes to Jack at the Spithead. If you don't believe it, do approach Harris and take the letter from him. Satisfy your curiosity. That is all it is," she returned bitterly.

He had known all along, but he had wanted her to answer him freely. Her reluctance piqued him. "It isn't wise to keep up correspondence with a smuggler. Shouldn't you cut the connection now that you are a married woman?"

"I would rather brave the fate of Milo than give up Jack as my friend," she answered furiously. "You cannot make me."

He put up a brow and though he smiled, there was no mirth in it. He felt irritated by her loyalty to the free trader.

"My dear love, I have not the least intention of doing so. I have no objection in the world to your friendship with Jack. But . . . would you continue to write to him if I did object?"

"Of course, my lord. He is—has always been—my *friend!* Why, if Father were alive and took it into his head to stop either my brother or myself from communicating with Jack, we would each take a flogging—though Father would never do that—but that is neither here nor there. I am my own woman and will make and keep whatever friends I choose."

He smiled and his finger went to her chin. "You are most certainly your own woman. And may I take this moment to tell you that you look enchanting in your gown. It is not one of the gowns I selected, is it?"

"No, my lord. It was my mother's. Meg and I found it yesterday morning in the attic," she answered simply.

A brisk breeze made her tremble, and she held her bare arms against its coolness. He noticed and frowned. "You are cold, Cassie. Why did you not tell me?" His strong arm went round her, and she blushed, all confusion again. "Oh, no, my lord . . . not until just now . . ."

"Come, sweet gosling. Let us go into the library. You may choose a book and read by the fire while I go through your cousin's papers. What a domestic scene we shall present, to be sure!"

17

As it happened the day grew dreary and a low mist clung to the lawns, giving the library with its cheerful fire an atmosphere of even more coziness. To all outward appearances, the viscount sitting at the desk before a stack of papers and his lady curled up like a kitten next to the fire seemed the domestic ideal. But 'twas not so. Cassie, though comfy and staring at the pages of *Don Juan,* had not been able to get her senses clear of the viscount's presence. She cast a quick glance his way and sighed to herself. He was so devilishly handsome . . . if only he had not that trick of smiling with his eyes . . . if only those sensuous lips would not mock . . . if only . . .

Kirkby Welford went through Charles Farrington's papers, looking for Asbatol's correspondence, hoping for something, but evidently he had burned anything that had come from that quarter. But then his hands lit upon a sliver of ivory paper, and on it was an address in Bristol. No name accompanied this, but the viscount pocketed it, smiled to himself, and cast his eyes over Cassie. Egad! she was a lovely thing! And her hair . . . superb! He rose and walked softly to the fireplace, dropping on the floor next to her and gently stroking her long flowing tresses. " 'And there sat *Hero . . . Hero the fair* whom Apollo courted for her hair . . . ' " he mused near her ear.

She turned her green eyes on him, and he felt a sure warming of his blood. "Hero? I don't think I have ever read that. What is the story?"

"Ah, you have never read of poor Leander and Hero? Well, Marlowe tells a pretty version of it. Hero is a beauty, a virgin priestess who dwelt on Sestos. She shunned all lovers including poor Apollo, and remained chaste and faithful to Venus. Ah, but then she had not met Leander, you see. Tch, tch . . . he was *her* price as it turns out." He paused, chuckled at her blush, and continued, "Leander lived on Abydos and the two fair creatures —for he was as handsome as she was lovely—were divided by the Hellespont, a cruel wide sea. However, he overcame it, swimming to her every night to lie in her arms."

"Oh! That is lovely! What happened to them?"

" 'Tis sad. Leander caught the eye of Neptune, but did not want the god for lover. As I recall, there are reprisals . . . and it ends badly."

"Oh, no! But what then?" she cried.

He laughed and flicked her nose. "As the legend has it, the poor lad drowned on one of his journeys," he lowered his voice, and his eyes twinkled. "Personally, I have always suspected Neptune of foul play."

"Oh, how dreadful! And she—Hero—what did she do?"

"Upon hearing of his death, she threw herself into the sea. Quite proper, don't you think?" he teased.

"Indeed, yes, what else could she do? He was dead, was he not?" she said seriously.

He laughed and cupped her chin playfully. "Ah, I have a romantic for a wife!"

"And you, what do you think?" she asked shyly.

"She should have grieved, of course, but then gone on as all great heroines must."

"But what for? She will never find a love like his again —why drag out a loveless life? No, you are quite wrong," she said, sounding a veritable innocent. He had a sudden longing to kiss her and did in fact place a gentle kiss upon her lips. "And you are very naive, but sweetly so," he said, his black eyes full with something she did not understand.

"I am not so naive, my lord. I once told you that love was the only ideal I still clung to. And in spite of what has happened, in spite of what you think, it is the last truth, the last beauty a human being can hope to attain in the world. I prize it as sacred."

"I believe you, Cassie. Tell me more of what you think. I like hearing you speak," he encouraged hoping to delve into her mind.

"No, you wheedle things from me, my lord, but I know nothing of you. I want to know why we go to Bristol. I want to know why meeting Nathan Asbatol is so important to you?" she asked seriously.

He stiffened. "Because he is involved in a field I find fascinating. You need know nothing more on the subject." He looked away and Cassie sighed. Then suddenly he was all smiles again and going to find a deck of cards. She marveled at his quick change of mood but welcomed it too much to put him out with further prying.

"Let us play a rubber of piquet, my lady," he said, dropping to his knees and shuffling the deck in his hand.

The time ebbed away lazily. They took their dinner on the floor, finding they just didn't want to leave the coziness they had managed between them. It was with reluctance that the viscount pointed out the hour. Cassie gasped. "Midnight! Faith, we have been at it for hours." She rose and brushed out the smoothness of her velvet gown and gave him her hand. He surprised her by kissing it lightly and then sliding it through his arm.

"Come, gosling, think I am not gentleman enough to see my wife to her room?"

191

"It is not necessary," she said shyly.

"It is most necessary," he said, picking up the candelabra and leading her out.

They reached her door and he put the branch of candles down on a wall table. She turned to feel his hands on her shoulders. She gazed long into his eyes and felt a sudden thrill as she realized he was about to kiss her, and she wanted him to do so. As his mouth descended upon hers, her arms went round him. She felt the silkiness of his black hair in her fingers as his tongue delighted her senses. His granite-like muscles pressed against her, and she heard his groan as his mouth shifted to her ear lobes. His whisper was hoarse with anxious desire. "Do you invite me in then, Cassie? Do you? Answer me, sweetings, for I am on fire."

Suddenly her senses returned. The vows she had made to herself wedged their way into her heart. She wanted to entice him, but here she was chasing him! He evidently thought . . . well, she would show him. Invite him into her room . . . into her bed? Oh, no, *not she*! "My lord . . . you mistake me! I had it in mind to thank you for the lovely gowns—and the pleasant evening—nothing more!" she said sweetly, pulling out of his hungry embrace.

Her words sprinkled cold water over him, but it sizzled on his burning flesh, and frustration lit his eyes for a moment. He made a slight bow. "You are most welcome, madam. But damn you for a bitch! May your rest be blighted and a fiend seize your charms! You have sent my rest to the devil!" With that he turned on his hessian heel and marched to his room.

She stayed a moment in the dimly lit hall looking after him, heard the slam of his door, and picked up the branch of candles. As she entered her own room a slow smile worked its way across her lips. Lady Welford was well pleased with the results of their exchange.

Two more days passed before the viscount and his lady set out for Bristol. Chips had arrived with a driver atop a well-sprung black coach of splendid lines headed by a pair of perfectly matched bays. Trunks were piled high, farewells made to Meg and Harris who were left behind to tend the house, and Cassie was seated in the comfortably upholstered interior. She sat in abject silence, clothed in her new finery, a traveling gown of blue muslin with a matching spencer, and a chip bonnet of yellow straw whose blue ribbon tied beneath her ear. Long ringlets of flame showed here and there and she looked quite adorable. However, her companion frowned and paid her little heed for they had not been on speaking terms these two days.

He had taken affront, it would seem, and Cassie was unsure as to how to solve this problem. She sighed and attempted charm, he growled. She cooed and begged a game of piquet, he declined. Feeling that he was behaving quite the spoiled child she pouted, "Faith! my lord! 'Tis unfair, I say! Fie on you! Did you not win all the blunt I had in the world two nights ago? Am I not entitled to a chance to win it back?"

He smiled suddenly for her good humor was hard to deny. "A sovereign? Madam, really! But if you must win it back, you must have a cache to play with!" he bantered.

"Well, I have that, sir!" she smiled mischievously.

"Eh? But you just said I won all the ready you had to your name? What trick is this, Cassie?" he grinned amicably, wondering what she was up to.

"True," she sighed, "I have no cash at present. But I have a husband . . . and he has some, you see. Would you not lend me a sovereign or two, my lord?" She smiled sweetly, and he reached over and flicked her nose.

"Vixen! Sly little puss! Aye, I'll lend you a coin or two, but if you lose, how shall you pay me?"

"In labor, my lord. I have nought else," she returned softly.

"Done! And I give you fair warning, madam, I don't mean for you to win," he added, a twinkle lighting his eye.

At the end of an hour, she had already lost several coins and threw down her cards in some irritation. "I declare, you are unbeatable!"

"I have been told that on several occasions, but I *did* warn you," he said, taking her chin and leaning toward her. "Come then, Cassie . . . pay up," he said gently, pressing a kiss to her lips.

She did not resist but took his kiss willingly until his hands pulled her out of her seat and laid her in his lap.

"My lord . . ." she objected.

"My lady? Labor did you say . . . define labor," he challenged, his hand beneath the folds of her gown, already finding the satiny smoothness of her thigh. He was there suddenly, taking strong hold of the tufted little mound he craved, and she arched into his touch, before attempting to stop him.

"Stop it! Stop it!" she cried frantically.

"Why? Do you not want it? Do you not feel, sweetings? How pliant is the opening, how ready to receive me . . ." his voice was husky against her ear, and his mouth took hers in wild, tumultuous passion.

She pushed at him desperately and begged for release. He cursed but let her go, and she moved away, sitting next to the window, avoiding his eyes as she set herself to rights. He eyed her moodily a moment before speaking, and then he was once more in control of himself. "Very well then, the lady will not define a toss with her husband as labor. 'Tis just, for 'tis no labor. But what then, will you scrub my back like a dutiful wife?"

"Aye, my lord," she said, throwing him a saucy smile, determined to win his arrogant heart, "if you won't blush for your modesty."

"I have no modesty—none whatsoever. So be it then! After that we shall see what next I can find for you to do."

"But I object, my lord. Is there no limit? There must be a limit," she cried half in earnest.

"You have lost a goodly sum, madam—ten pounds to be exact. You must work it off, and the scrubbing of my back is a thing I have got more than once without paying. But . . . do put a price on it . . . a half crown, shall we say?"

"A crown!" she countered, flushing, slightly irritated at

the thought of another woman having tended his back. "And what of the kiss you stole a moment ago? 'Tis worth a price," she bantered lightly.

"Aye, wench, that little encounter was priceless . . . but 'twas left unfinished. Well, then, it can't be listed for 'twas no more than a tease. There ain't satisfaction for a man in that! Maybe for a suckling lad—but not for a man!"

She blushed and offered no further comment as they were just then pulling up to a mellow-looking posting house for a late lunch.

"That's a good lad . . ." said the Viscount placing a coin in the lackey's palm and ushering him out of the chamber. A hot bath had been prepared, and the viscount turned to greet his wife with a broad grin. "I have been looking forward to this. Damn, but I have," he said, dropping his buckskin riding jacket onto the bed, his eyes twinkling at Cassie.

She had changed while he was belowstairs and stood before him in a pale green nightdress of sheer silk. Her matching satin wrapper was tied at the neckline and opened in soft ripples to the floor. Her deep green eyes watched him as he dropped off his clothes with unconscious glee, and she felt herself go hot and cold and then hot again as he stood before her in all his powerful, naked glory. He dipped his foot into the water, winced, but bore it like a Spartan. Then he was sliding in and groaning with satisfaction. "Well, madam?" he called. "Commence scrubbing!"

"I come, master," sallied Cassie, mincing forward and getting to her knees. She took up the sponge and began lathering his back. She felt the wide sinews covering his long back and she worked them well, eliciting sounds of approval from him.

"Very good, madam. If one did not know better, one would think thee born to it. There now—don't stop! If that isn't just like a lazy servant! Compliment them, and they take it into their head to wheedle out of their labors.

Ah . . . there . . . now come round, and do my chest," he ordered glibly.

She stopped in midmotion. "The bargain was for your back," she said raising a brow.

He turned his head round to look at her and smiled. "A crown for my back, another for my front. Come, Cassie . . . 'tis the least a lass can do for her husband's weary bones."

She walked round on her knees and dipped the sponge into his bath water, without dropping her eyes. She soaped the dark curling hair on his chest and worked at his shoulders and then suddenly found his eyes compellingly on her face. She stopped and returned his look and felt a wave surge through her being and leave her without air in her lungs.

She got to her feet and gave him her back, but he was satisfied to gaze there and his black eyes lingered on the round well-shaped buttocks as they swayed away from him.

"I . . . I am tired my lord . . . and I am troubled, for there is but one bed—and that a not very large one . . ."

"There was no other room available. We shall have to contrive," he said, his voice low, his eyes devouring her, moving to her breasts swelling full and high, bewitching his thoughts, inciting his passion. He wanted her—damn! but he wanted to take her now, now—now.

Suddenly he was out of his bath and striding toward her, his manhood prominent, his body glisteningly wet. "My lord! Let go, you are soaking me through," she objected, but it was only half-hearted, for her blood was pounding in her brain and her knees were mere jelly.

"Sweet vixen, do you say me nay?" he asked, his eyes intent upon her own, mesmerizing her with their lights.

"Yes, I do . . . say you nay!" she lied, and it showed. "Let me . . ." His mouth silenced her. Tenderly he took the nectar as does the bee gently, lovingly. His ardor engendered her own and she responded warmly to his touch, and his body burned against hers. His mouth moved across her cheek searing a path to her ear, and his whisper had the sound of passion. "Sweet liar . . . you want me, Cassie. Admit it . . . admit that you want me. Come, Cassie, deny me no more . . ."

"No!" she made one final, useless attempt to free herself. His iron grip held her and her arms would not take orders from her brain. Her mind said push away, but her body clung wantonly. She broke under the strain of her ambivalence, holding him for support. He heard her denial, but her words were quite contrary to her movements. Her arms held him still, her thighs pressed against his own, and his prodding staff could feel the tender lodging he longed to take. His mouth caressed her flesh on its hungry journey to her breast. His tongue danced round the pink tip before his lips did their magic. His knee came up and wedged itself between her thighs and pressured her ever so gently, ever so suggestively.

"Do you still say me nay?" he asked, his voice hoarse with desire.

She could not answer. She wanted to deny him, but her body was on fire. And he pursued, "Cassie, want me . . . want me, sweet gosling. I want *you,* please, please say you want me . . . do, Cassie . . . do . . ." he pleaded.

He sounded so much the young boy begging a boon and something within her burst. "Oh, yes, Kirkby . . . I want you . . . yes, yes . . ."

It was all he needed, for he was already a kindled torch. He lifted her triumphantly and took her to the bed. Her nightdress was discarded, and she gasped under his passionate gaze. She was beauteous as the candlelight flickered over her. He knew at that moment that there was only Cassie. His mouth took hers again, wanting her, all of her.

His hands played with her breasts and then moved to her legs parting them, stroking her thighs, building up her fire into wild abandon. She felt his hand move to the soft tuft of hair between her thighs and groaned as he grasped that sweetness in his hand. She arched in response to his strong hold and could not believe her own voice that begged, "Take me Kirkby . . . please . . . now now . . . *I do want you!*"

Her words echoed in his brain like the beating of exotic drums and the crescendo rose all around him until he felt he would burst. He had waited for this moment, to hear her sweet voice speak of wanting. It shot through him, lodging itself in his heart and exploding, but it gave blood and life. He uttered a wild exultant sound as he made his entrance, pushing his hard muscle between the tender lips. He tantalized them both with his deft lovemaking, maneuvering between the lips of her honeycomb, bringing her to such passion that she made wihmpers of delight.

"Kirkby . . . Kirkby . . . now . . . please . . ."

He penetrated deep within her, feeling the snugness of her perfect sugarbox and experiencing a joy he had never before known. "Oh, Cassie, my own wild vixen . . . how you please . . ." he breathed as he covered her face with hot kisses.

She moved beneath him, arching her back to match his turbulent motion. His hands went under her hips and raised her up as he thrust wildly, giving them both ecstasy. Never before had he experienced such high gratification.

He whispered his pleasure as he wrapped himself around her, begetting her responsive ardor. Then suddenly, maintaining himself within her, he changed positions, rolling over and bringing himself onto his back, so that she sat upright on him. She looked somewhat startled, but he grinned and reached up, fondling and reassuring her. "Ah, sweetings, gently now, I'll bring us to it soon . . . but not just yet, you're far too good, and I want to stay put awhile longer." He reached up and brought her long flowing hair onto his chest as he drew her down to him. Now she was the rider, and before long she had learned just how to move in this new position.

Then suddenly neither was able to speak as they moved

in unison in sweet intoxication, and Cassie knew her release just a moment before Kirkby breathed his satisfaction in her ear. He remained holding her to him, almost afraid to let her go and content in the afterglow of her desire. Then after a time she moved into the crook of his arm, happily receiving his kisses on her nose and forehead, and then staring up into his jet black eyes.

With wonder in his heart, he knew himself bewitched. It had been good . . . too good for his peace of mind. Yet her face so near his own brought him a soft sensation he had never before known. She was just a good toss, he told himself harshly, nothing more . . . but damn, she *was* more to him than that! She was in his blood, she was his wife. Trickery or no, that was a fact. She was his—all his. No other had ever touched her. This brought him a sense of preposterous jubilation. He smiled tenderly and flicked her nose. She opened her eyes, and his mouth met hers caressingly, gently. But the touch of her awoke and incited his heat. His hand was once more roving over her, fondling, teasing.

"Cassie?"

"No!" she answered firmly. "I am so tired . . ."

He chuckled and slapped her rump. "Ah well, rest then for a bit," he said pulling her to him, kissing her forehead, stroking her hair. He watched her doze off, his emotions vacillating between absurd happiness and wretched puzzlement. True, she looked a kitten now with her defenses down, but he had seen her claws. She had been a virgin, but he had won that at a price. Damn, he thought feverishly, no other man would ever touch her—not while she was his, and he meant to keep her for a time. And then suddenly he had to have her again! He knew he would never be satiated while she was beside him. His hands worked at her thighs, urging, enticing, his lips seducing. She groaned pleasurably but her eyes flew open and she upbraided him as a whipster. "Leave me be, you tyrant . . . I need sleep . . ." she begged, but already her body was arching towards him, already her arms were winding themselves round his neck and her lips were tempting him.

" 'Tis just what you will get, sweetings . . . *after!*" as his hardness knocked upon her door and rushed in without waiting for an invitation.

18

Bristol spread itself all around them as the viscount's coach tooled through the busy streets. Cassie was struck by the old timbered buildings, the taverns and shops with their tiled roofs, and she bubbled with excitement at her open window.

"My lord, oh, 'tis wonderful! Why, it is all I remember!"

"Remember? Then you have been here before?" he asked, frowning suddenly.

She giggled. "Indeed, yes, I did have a life of sorts before . . . before Charles came to the Grange. My parents brought me here for a shopping spree when I had attained my thirteenth year and was off for school . . ." Her voice drifted away, but she shook off the momentary sadness and exclaimed excitedly, "Papa took us to Cabot Tower, you know!"

He flicked her nose, his eyes twinkling with amusement. "No doubt a most exciting monument," he teased.

"Well, I thought so. John Cabot sailed for the New

World, you know. They erected the tower to his memory. It stands on Brandon Hill and is most lovely. Shall I show it to you?" she asked enthusiastically.

"If we have time, puss. If history intrigues you, I should be pleased to take you to Llandoger Trow," he said, his own enthusiasm kindled. "You would like that, I think."

"Would I? Whatever is it?"

"A pirate's den!" he dropped blandly.

She turned on him, her green eyes wide. "A pirate's den! Oh, that is beyond everything great! Do let us go immediately. Oh, I should love that before anything!"

He chuckled and put his hand on her cheek tenderly. "Perhaps later, gosling. At any rate, 'tis nothing more than a quayside tavern. Pirates went out with the seventeenth century."

"But . . . just think . . . it still exists! We could walk its floors and imagine some horrid pirate strutting about, his cutlass at our throats. Why 'twould be grand!"

"It would be no such thing, vixen!" he retorted with spirit, but his eyes laughed all the same.

She sighed and sat back. "Oh, but I can't wait. Do you know, my lord, I am most pleased I decided to accompany you to Bristol."

She sounded so childlike, so innocently sincere that she managed to capture his gaze for a long minute before he could reply. But he recouped his emotions and said only, "Indeed, I too am glad you made that decision."

There was ever a mock in his voice, and she cast her eyes reprovingly over his face but said nothing. He capitulated at once. "No, sweetings, do not look so. Truly I am."

She smiled and had an urge to snuggle up to him but was as yet still too shy to give way to her feelings. She held back and instead gave him her shoulder as she returned to the window. He sighed, thinking her miffed with him, but refrained from further cajolery. After all, it was not his aim to please her.

As per the viscount's instructions, his coach pulled up before a respectable brick building whose blue and white canopy extended to the curbing. Cassie eyed it for a long thoughtful moment, before putting a gloved finger to her lips and musing softly, "The Beacon . . . hmmm . . . no, I don't think it was here that we stayed, though 'twas something like it. But, faith! my lord, it does look expensive!"

"Very expensive," he answered grinning, for he found her naïveté both adorable and bewitching.

"Oh, dear! But you said you are not a wealthy man. Surely you did not win enough from Charles to sponsor an extended stay *here*?"

"No, but appearances matter in my business, and I have a sufficient bank—made from other less skilled card players to furnish us enough for our stay," he responded drily.

"Oh," she said, a troubled light coming into her eyes. She must not allow last night to cloud her thinking. He was an adventurer . . .

Then all at once the hotel lackey came forward and held the door open. The viscount descended the lowered steps first before turning to give his hand to his lady. As she alighted, her head tilted in order to spare her bright chip bonnet, her tresses of flame cascading down one shoulder of blue silk, she looked a dazzling beauty, and more than one gentleman cast his eye her way. Her ladyship was not at all aware of this; however, her husband was and though he hurried her into the richly appointed lobby, he felt a strange sort of pride well up within his breast.

He shrugged it off almost as soon as it entered his mind and made his imperious path towards the hotel desk, seating his wife nearby on a gold striped silk lady's chair. She watched him handle the clerk with adroitness, heard him quietly demand the best suite in the house, and smiled to herself over his arrogance. However, he seemed to be getting all he wanted and she cast her eyes about the richly decorated room. Ivory plaster cherubs pranced around the gold moldings near the high ceiling. Gold brocade hung at the windows and dark Oriental carpets covered much of the wood flooring. However, her attention was suddenly wrenched from her surroundings and centered on a tall, thin, fashionable and exquisite dark beauty calling her husband's name. "Kirkby . . . you devil!" exclaimed the woman in a voice as soft as rainwater.

The viscount turned, saw the woman with an uplift to his straight black brow. As she approached, gloved hands extended, he doffed his hat and tucked it in the crook of his arm, leaving his hands free to clasp the woman's. "Constance," he said, smiling and pressing her hands together he put them to his lips, "how delightful!"

"Kirkby! I declare . . . don't come on sweet with me after the trick you served me," she said, her dark eyes teasing and flirting with him.

Cassie watched this exchange with mute curiosity and no little jealousy. Who was this woman? An old flame? How dare he go on for such a length of time and leave her to watch? He was a . . . a . . . cad . . . he probably didn't want to tell the woman he was married. Horrid rake!

"Trick? What trick, Connie . . . for I swear I know of none," he said, his eyes taking in every detail of her appearance.

"You were promised to me . . . remember, we were to go to the Jerseys' ball together . . . and you suddenly vanished, without a word. I was obliged to go with Simon!"

He laughed. "I am sorry, but, you know, Simon *is* your husband, 'tis his place to escort you, not mine!"

"There you are, being a dreadful bore now," she pouted.

He laughed again. "What brings you to Bristol, Connie . . . at a time when Brighton must be wild and full to capacity?"

"Simon brings me to Bristol. Some dratted fellow dropped dead and left Simon, who was his only relation, a fortune. Simon insisted on my accompanying him . . . said it would be something of a second honeymoon. I can think of no other notion so nonsensical . . . he is a lunatic!" she said with some feeling.

The viscount had glanced at his wife and suddenly remembered his manners. He also noted the line of Cassie's mouth and was taken with sudden amusement; the chit actually looked jealous. He found this fancy utterly delightful, and it was with much inward mirth that he brought the two women together. "Connie, my manners have gone begging. Do come and meet my bride!"

The woman nearly fainted. She did close her eyes and open her mouth before she was able to compose herself. "Your . . . your bride?"

"Indeed . . . I have the pleasure of introducing my wife, Cassandra, to you. Cassie, love, this is a very dear friend of mine, Mrs. Constance Berkley."

They managed the usual polite exchange before the older, more sophisticated woman began to show her claws. "But how very interesting, my dear. You must tell me all about it, for until this very moment I was not aware Kirkby had a romantic inclination in this part of the world. Though, with all his women, I should have realized . . . but however did you manage the feat of getting his name?"

Cassie blushed, for she was no match for this woman's questions, and she stumbled for an answer. Her husband came surprisingly to the rescue. "Connie, you have but to look at my wife to discover how she accomplished the 'feat' as you put it."

Constance Berkley disliked his answer and snubbed him as she pursued her course. "And it must have been a whirlwind courtship. Why, 'twas no more than two weeks ago that Kirkby was in London . . . and I assure you he gave no sign of having been engaged."

Cassie answered before her husband could stop her, "That is because we were not engaged two weeks ago, ma'am."

Connie's eyes narrowed perceptibly. "Really?"

"No, she had not yet accepted me two weeks ago. And a recent death in the family prohibited a large wedding party or an announcement in the *Gazette*," returned his lordship deftly.

"Well, you must tell me all about it tonight over dinner.

205

Indeed, we will take dinner together and then the theater. Do not say 'no' . . . Simon would so like to meet your bride."

"Oh, I think not tonight, Constance," said his lordship. "I believe my wife will be tired after the long day's ride."

Cassie would not be put to blame and she interjected, "Not at all, my lord. If it is your wish, I should be pleased to make up a set tonight."

He frowned, but Constance had already exclaimed, "Good. It's settled. Shall we say eight, then? We will meet here in the lobby. There is a perfectly delightful restaurant on the quay . . . we went there last evening. I really must go now, ta-ta, darlings!" with which she floated out of their sight. Here was an intriguing tale if ever she had one. She could not wait to take up her pen and notify all London of the viscount's latest exploit. But drat the girl for being so lovely! There were bound to be those who might put her as a new *incomparable*, and she rather fancied keeping that title herself.

A few moments later, Cassie found herself in an elegant boudoir of blue and silver. The furnishings were done in the French country style of the seventeenth century. The huge bed was hung with blue silk and crowned over the center. She exclaimed over all this magnificence, Constance Berkley momentarily forgotten.

The viscount laughed over her ingenuousness and pinched her cheek. "It seems I shall find it very easy to please you, love. I have ordered you a bath. But though I should like to remain here and scrub *your* back, I am afraid I must go out."

She blushed, but her disappointment showed. "Oh! But where do you go?"

He frowned and said lightly, " 'Tis business," then turned on his heel and left her to herself.

Simon Berkley put his quizzing glass to his faded blue eye to better observe Lady Welford's entrance into the lobby of the Hotel Beacon. She was wearing an evening gown of white froth. It was sleeveless, with crystals trimming the thin white straps and ornamenting the low heart-shaped neckline. A fashionable white egret was fastened over one ear with matching crystals and her long cinnamon-gold tresses were done Grecian style. Long white gloves covered her arms to the elbows, and she carried a cloak of white silk. His eye took in the vision, noting the full, swelling breasts and the small waist, and his imagination decided on the rest.

"Upon my Soul! exclaimed the portly Mr. Berkley to his wife, "she is a rare beauty!"

"Do you think so, my dear?" she said blandly. She had dressed up her own dark beauty in red silk, and her gown was daringly slit nearly to the waist, displaying her small but firm breasts. Constance Berkley was some ten years younger than her middle-aged husband.

The viscount led his lady forth, quite aware of Cassandra's exquisite loveliness. Why, he had always considered Constance Berkley a rare diamond, but she was nought beside his gorgeous wife. Simon Berkley gushed over Cassie's gloved hand and before the viscount realized what the older man was about, he had the displeasure of seeing the man drape Cassie's cloak over her shoulders. Simon grinned amicably, plopped his top hat onto his graying locks, linked Cassie's arm through his own, and announced that they were off.

The viscount frowned over this, recovered, did the honors for Constance and followed Simon and Cassie out to the Berkley coach. Here once again, the viscount had cause to frown, for Simon seated Cassie and Constance and then rushed in to take up a seat beside her ladyship, leaving his wife to the viscount.

Simon Berkley felt much a schoolboy, infatuated with the new girl in town, and acted the part well. This rather embarrassed Cassie who blushed often and turned her eyes away. The viscount watched her and felt a sudden softness envelop his heart, for it was obvious that she wanted none of Simon's flirting. However, his own attention was soon taken up by the elegant woman at his side.

Dinner turned out to be somewhat of an ordeal for Cassie. She had constantly to give her attention to Simon and watch Constance flirt outrageously with Kirkby. Cassie felt wretched; she wanted to pull the woman's dark hair out by its roots, to slap Kirkby's face for so enjoying the flirtation. He would smile . . . and he would kiss the lady's hand . . . and . . . oh-h-h!

"We are taking you to a showing of Sheridan's *The School for Scandal*. I have heard that it is famous good fun," said Constance pulling on her gloves and coming to her feet.

Cassie gritted her teeth as she watched the woman lean into the viscount's chest to receive her cloak, and she turned a charming smile upon her own gallant which she instantly regretted for it sent him off again. They stepped outdoors to find their coach had not yet arrived. Simon had lingered with Cassie in the doorway, holding her back. Kirkby had stepped away from Constance to have a look into the street, and at that moment a shadow emerged. It was an undersized grotesque form, holding out a much battered pewter cup. His hair was a dark, dirty mass, his slim, bony arms covered in grime. His clothes were but rags, and he wore no shoes. He could not be more than twelve years old. He had stood in the darkness waiting for someone to emerge from the elegant inn . . . someone likely to be sympathetic and throw a coin his way. He had learned to be cautious in this regard for too many of the quality were apt to give him a kick rather than pity. But then he had seen Constance Berkley standing in the candlelight!

Her beauty awed him. Surely no human being so lovely could turn him down. He was hungry . . . so very, very hungry. He came forward, the hunch of his back causing him extra effort when he glanced up to her face.

"Please, mum . . . a penny?" he begged desperately.

Constance Berkley shrieked, and the hunchbacked child jumped a step away, terrified at what would now befall him. Kirkby had come round at once and stood taking in the scene with a frown. However, Simon Berkley grew red in the face and came forward raising his walking stick at the same time. It happened so quickly that the viscount hardly realized what was about, but Cassie had seen it all and instinctively, without thought for herself, jumped between the crippled boy and the stick. She took the blow and, though Simon had recoiled midway, it was enough to wring a cry of pain from her.

Cassandra held her shoulder where the stick had left its mark and saw through a flash the viscount wrench the stick from Simon and break it over his bent leg. Kirkby Welford's voice was a growl as he flung the broken wood at Berkley. "You stupid fool!"

He then turned to Cassie, turning her face to his, but she paid him no heed for the crippled child was trying to make good his escape. She reached out and took hold of his filthy arm. There was a repelling stench about the child, but she held fast, and her voice soothed.

"No, lad, no one will hurt you. Stay . . ."

The viscount did nothing to deter her, but stood frowning over the scene, for they were beginning to attract an audience. Simon Berkley was blubbering, "Not my fault. Meant it for that creature. How dare it approach my wife! Her ladyship had no business . . ."

Suddenly, the viscount turned on him and spat, "You and your lady get out of here! Immediately. I don't want to see your faces!"

"Well!" said Constance indignantly.

"Come, dear," said her husband, drawing her to their coach as it stopped before them.

The viscount returned to his wife and heard her gentle voice. "No, don't be frightened, child. I only want to ask you a few questions."

The boy looked frightened, but something in the woman's tone allayed his fears. He stared hopefully up at her. She had taken a blow meant for him . . . surely, she could be trusted.

"You are so young. Have you no parents?" Cassie asked, her delicate brows drawn, her mind in agitation. She had never before seen a child in such degradation.

Beggars she had seen . . . hard-used children she had seen—but never like this. None to equal this misery. Her heart nearly cracked, and there were tears in her eyes.

"Naw . . . I got nobbut meself mum," he said proudly, as though it were a feat.

"I see. And . . . you have no work?" she pursued.

"Naw . . . who would 'ire me? They says I be useless, they do," he said putting down his chin once again. "And they be in the right of it. I be twisted . . . they call me kin to the divil!" There was no bitterness in his tone, merely acceptance.

The tears in Cassie's eyes overflowed, and she had to catch her breath. "Well, they are wrong! You are a child of God—more so because of your affliction. And . . . *I* think you worth the hire. Come, tell me . . . do you like horses?"

"Dunno . . . guess so. They be animals same as me."

"Well then, you shall have the opportunity to discover they are not the same." She turned to the viscount who had been watching her in quiet consternation. What was this new facet of Cassandra's character. Why had he not realized this side of her existed? This was no act. Her taking the blow meant for the wretched child had been no act. Her tears now were no act. Then how could she have betrayed his brother?

"My lord," she cried, "I should like to hire this young man. I feel Starfire will need looking after if I am not to exercise him daily . . . and I am certain your man Chips could use an assistant. Please, my lord . . ."

"There is no need to beg, Cassie. 'Tis done. But come, we must get off the street." He raised his hand and summoned a passing hack.

The boy was helped up to a seat on the luggage rack before Cassie would allow herself to be seated within. The viscount climbed in beside her and released a sigh. He cast his eyes over her to find her on the verge of a battle with her emotions. "Hush, Cassie, it will be all right."

"But, my lord, how can people like the Berkleys exist? He would have struck the poor child . . . and he thinks himself in the right of it! Oh, God! Here we sit, our bellies filled, our bodies clothed—and children go about in such a state! It makes me wretched." Her heart could take no more, and she burst into sobs on his shoulder. He allowed her to cry herself out, patting her hand and finally bringing her lips up to his and kissing them softly, gently. But there was nothing he could say. Such things did exist—and staggered the mind.

At length he sighed again, wondering how to handle the problem he now had. Obviously, he would not be able to put up the boy in the same lodgings with Chips, without first bathing him. Well, he would see his wife to her room and then take the urchin to Chips and leave him in that worthy's care.

Thus resolved, he paid off the hack and turned to his wife.

"Cassie, I will take you up now and then return for the boy. I think we will give him over to Chips who will feed and bathe him and bring him round to you tomorrow."

"Yes, but he will need proper clothing," said Cassie, falling in with this plan.

"Trust Chips to see to everything," said his lordship. However, when he turned to the waiting boy, the child moved out of the viscount's path to hide behind Cassie's cloak. "Please, mum . . . don't leave me with 'im. Jest please give me a penny . . . a ha'penny will do . . . and I'll be off . . ."

"Nonsense. What is your name, child?" said Cassie firmly.

"Never 'ad one. They laughs at me and calls me Beau, they do. Don't like it, but 'tis what they call me."

"Very well then. From now on your name will be Thomas. Does that suit you?" returned she.

"Aye, that it do," smiled the urchin worshipfully.

"Very well, Thomas. You will wait here for the viscount. He will see that you are fed and taken care of—and tomorrow you will present yourself to me. Promise now —you will wait?"

"If it be yer will, m'lady," said the lad.

211

Cassandra gave the lad a reassuring smile, and he gazed after her, watching every move she made, already besotted. She was a fairy tale princess come to life. She was the embodiment of childhood longings, hopes, and dreams . . . and for a moment, a sudden whimsical moment, he thoughts perhaps, just perhaps a miracle had come to pass! Was he at long last turning from a frog . . . into a man?

19

The viscount had seen Thomas off, giving him into Chips's reluctant hands. He had watched the gruff old groom take the squealing boy in hand, and a smile had crossed both heart and face. What was this woman he was wed to? God save him if she had a mind to rescue every misbegotten creature they came across!

His mind flitted over the night's events and the picture was livid with her flying in front of Simon's walking stick. He remembered how she had cried out from the sudden pain of the blow, and how her sound had ripped through his soul. But never once did she utter complaint afterward. Her concern had been all for the boy. He frowned over this and resolved to examine her shoulder before the night was out. He hurried his steps as he turned the corner from the stable lodgings and made the hotel entrance. He found his heart beating at a ridiculous pace, for he wanted to get to Cassie, to be with her, to touch her . . . to wipe the horror from her eyes.

Cassie had changed into a nightdress of sheer silk. Its pale green hues floated softly about her exquisite body. Her waist-length hair trailed in thick golden-red waves, and her eyes were troubled. It had been an awful evening, with that odious Simon Berkley gushing at her and his wife gushing at Kirkby. The sight of the woman touching and clinging to Kirkby had driven her nearly mad.

Then that poor child, unkempt, starved, deformed, with no one to look after him. How many more were about the city? How many children begged and were kicked for their trouble? The thought brought tears still to her eyes. She couldn't bear the thought. She must not think about it. She had done what she could, but there must be more . . . more she could do for the others. Somehow, someday, she would find a way. And Kirkby? What sort of man was he turning out to be? She had thought him heartless. Verily, she had been drawn by passion to him. She could not deny her attraction to him, but he had been winning her affection, insidiously winding his fingers round her gentle heart. He had come to her rescue when that woman Constance Berkley had made sly insinuations regarding their marriage. He had shown himself capable of goodness and compassion with regard to the beggar child. No common adventurer . . . no common rake this!

She stretched out before the burning fire and waited for him, longing for his speedy return, for suddenly she wanted him. With every fiber of her body she wanted him to return and touch her, kiss her . . . love her.

He entered their boudoir to find her lying on her belly and he sucked in some air. She was a provocative sight. Her round, well-shaped derriere tempted him as she rolled over and lay on her back. Her full cherry lips parted in a warm greeting and her green eyes invited. By God, she was inviting his caress!

He felt a hard need rush through him and discarded cloak and hat in one sweep. His blue superfine too was flung aside, and he unbuttoned his silk waistcoat as he dropped down beside her. He gazed long into her glorious eyes, and they burned with passion. He took her waist in one strong hand as his mouth met hers furiously, searing them both. His tongue plunged with wild hunger, and his hand moved wildly over her body, tearing the material that stood in his path and fondling her breasts with a fierce need.

"Cassie," he groaned, "my sweet wife . . . how you make me want you!" His lips covered her ears, her cheeks, her neck and stopped suddenly at her shoulder, where his black eyes saw the bruise already turning blue.

"My God! I could kill him for that!" he breathed, his anger flaring.

"Never mind, Kirkby . . ." she whispered, reaching for his face and bringing it back down to hers, kissing his lips, pressing her body into his. She wanted him! Not revenge! She only wanted him, his heart, his soul . . . all that made him Kirkby Welford!

She gave herself full force, startling him into new awakenings. His spirits soared. Nearly mad with joy, he discarded the remainder of his clothing. The urgency of the need for consummation was uppermost as he spread her beauteous thighs and thrust himself wildly, deeply, sensuously into her very womb. His deft hands were all over her body, giving and taking pleasure. She cried out with delight and clung to him in her mad desire to give all —and more!

They burned as one, their rapture gaining force, their sweet reckless turbulence driven by their desire to please each other. She wanted to tell him then, at that moment of what she felt. She wanted to sing of her love, to tell him of its glory, to share . . . but something held her back. She heard him groan out his pleasure, "Sweet, oh, sweet! How you please me!" And still she held back.

How could she own her love of him? He spoke of lust, not of love, and it prevented her. Her passion began to ebb suddenly. He felt the change, frowned, and redoubled his efforts until he had rekindled her passion. His thrusts took on a violent force, and she arched into him, giving him her dancing body until his skill brought them to ecstasy.

Soon afterward he breathed easily and stroked her glistening hair. He spoke of satisfaction, of her beauty, and he frowned when he looked into her eyes. He lifted her and brought her to bed. She permitted his handling, she let his whisperings go unanswered and, as he climbed into bed and pulled the covers around them both, she allowed him to kiss her tenderly, but her sadness had made her suddenly cold.

She loved! The knowledge brought her pain, deep cutting pain. Jack had said that men can lie with a woman and feel nought in their hearts. So it was with Kirkby Welford. He made love to her—but he loved her not. Oh, the thought was bitter! She wanted him to love her . . . she must make him love her . . . but how?

He continued to hold her. Odd, he had never wanted to hold his women afterward . . . not in this way. He was not the affectionate sort . . . or at least had never been before. It was different with Cassie. Perhaps because she seemed such a child . . . perhaps because she had so tried to please him . . . or perhaps he was so fully satisfied. Never mind. What did it matter? There could never be anything real between them. He must always remember his brother's life lay at her door. This thought brought on a feeling of disgust of himself and suddenly he could hold her no more. He withdrew his arms and turned from her to face the opposite wall. She felt him depart, knew that his mind had somehow recoiled and it was as though a bolt of lightning had struck her. She caught a sob before it could make itself heard, beating it down with her pride. She would not let him know . . .

20

The viscount sat back in his comfortable coach, his fingers pulling lightly at his bottom lip as the carriage rumbled over cobbled streets. Street peddlers shouted their wares, merchants hurried about their business, sailors struggled to their ships after the night's festivities, and children played in the gutters. But all the noise and havoc of the morning blurred before his vision, they were as nothing, for Kirkby Welford was lost to another time. His mind was on his young stepbrother, Peter Eaton. He could hear him, see him as though he were before him still . . as though he had never looked upon his silent form and dead eyes. And the memory brought back all the pain, *all the guilt*.

"Kirk . . . what a dog you are . . . keeping all the fun to yourself! Indeed, I declare it a paltry show!" challenged Peter, his eyes gently mocking, an admonishing grin lighting up his pleasant coutenance. He had a way of smiling that always moved his brother's heart. Kirkby looked up from the papers covering his desk to find his sandy-haired stepbrother wagging a finger, and he grinned in response, "Now what, puppy?"

"Don't pretend to me that you don't know!" exclaimed Peter. "You've been on the Select Committee nigh onto two years. All that while I've been telling you, 'tis just what I want. I can't think of anything I'd liefer do than to serve with you, Kirk," he said pleadingly.

Peter adored his older brother, his mentor. There was but four years between them, yet the viscount often acted the father. He had come under Kirkby's roof when they had both been very young. However, it had never been Kirkby's father who had taken him under wing. As long as he could remember, it had always been Kirk. And his older stepbrother knew this, felt the boy's hero worship and rather enjoyed it as well.

"Now, Peter," he started somewhat patronizingly, "you've scarcely left Cambridge . . ."

"Nay!" interrupted Peter at once. "Don't be 'now Petering' me! If you won't give over and recommend me . . . then I'd as lief turn loose-screw and start flitting me life away! Now what do you say to that, you old devil?"

This sort of badgering had gone on and on, not ending until a week later when Kirkby Welford had relented and given Peter some minor obligations to carry out for the Committee. This had served to silence him for a time for the lad, though feeling he was being put off, thought reasonably that he must start somewhere. So, it was that within six months of being given these nominal duties Peter rebelled. Again the viscount looked up from his work to find his youthful brother wagging his finger at him. He sighed and awaited the lad's abuse.

"Demme, Kirk! I've taken enough! Why don't you stick a wooden plaque on my chest and label me 'Dunce'?" exclaimed the outraged young man.

"What now?" returned the viscount, one mobile brow going up quizzically, his lips parting in amusement, and his admiration for his brother's plucky ambitions gleaming in his black eyes.

218

"You can ask? What, Kirkby . . . am I nought but a . . . a . . . clerk? Any noddy could do what you've set me to! Lord, Kirkby . . . think you less of me than you do of John Drummond?"

"Of course not. What does that signify?" retorted the viscount breaking in on the harangue amicably.

"Signify . . . I'll give you signify . . . did not John Drummond receive the flash-house assignment? And I . . . what am I given, but shabby paper work!"

"Peter, John has led a life which enables him to disguise himself and rummage with whores, beggars, and thieves without the chance of being detected. He goes on in St. Giles and, if you were to see him face to face, speak to him as close as you are to me, you would not know him! I am afraid that would never do for you. For one thing your accent is too refined— and you have no knowledge of flash-house cant."

"Never mind the flash-houses. 'Tis not that I am after! I want a chance at the Linton Case!"

"Impossible! It is not just any case . . . it is, we believe, linked to all the other abductions that have occurred. I believe I am going to handle it myself in the end," returned the viscount gravely.

"Kirkby, we could do it together for that matter. I have a plan, for I discovered something . . ."

"What?" queried his brother, snapping this up.

"First . . . do I get to work on it?"

Again, he had finally relented and not without his having to sustain his stepmother's rebukes. He was fond of the dowager. A wise, lovely lady, she had been his confidante during his youth—she was so now—and had at last agreed that he could do nought else but let Peter have his head. He was after all, a man grown.

The decision proved, he thought at first, to be a good one, for Peter was unknown and far too youthful in appearance to be taken for an agent. He was bright and before long he had established a framework within which he worked. It was Peter who had brought an arrow right on target, for it was he who discovered Sir Charles Farrington. Coincidentally, it appeared, Sir Charles had had a tremendous amount of socializing with the families of the abducted victims shortly before their disappearance. Peter became suspicious and began cultivating the fellow, speaking to him of financial woes, crying about his ambitions to set himself up well, mentioning that he would be willing to do anything to attain his ends . . . and mentioning too . . . his social connections, leaving out but one person—the viscount!

Then arm in arm the two had gone off to Farrington Grange! That had been less than six weeks ago, during which time the viscount had received but two letters, parts of which he now knew by heart. An excerpt from the first read:

"Lord Kirk . . . Sir Charles is an *opium eater*! I always felt it was something more than drink, but never mind. The fact is that his estates are mortgaged to the hilt. He is most definitely the *connection*, but NOT THE MAN! He rambles when he has been drinking, but I have nothing more concrete. I have but one other thing before my scrap of paper is used up, and that is about Cassandra Farrington, cousin and ward to Sir Charles. She has eyes the color of a beckoning lake arrayed with water lilies and hair the shade of cinnamon-gold. *I think I am in love!*"

Kirkby had laughed at this last sentence, for his brother was always falling in and out of love. 'Twas nothing new and nothing to fear. However, his second letter coming a week later and from Bristol did set up his doubts. Its last lines ended thus:

"*The man behind* all these horrible workings—and Kirk, there are more than just the abductions—is named Nathan. I have not yet his last name or his exact address, though I have met him briefly and will again tomorrow. I have learned no more of the poor Linton child and fear greatly he will go the way of his predecessors . . . but perhaps I will be in time!

"There is one other thing troubling me, Kirk, for I have discovered that *I am in love*, but I fear my angel is no angel at all, but a very hard-hearted lady who has taken to

220

her bosom unspeakable deeds— simply for gold! Her hair of cinnamon-gold and her face have me fairly addled, for how can anyone so lovely be so evil? If only she will not betray me—for I fear she has suspicions!"

But she had betrayed him, for a few days after the receipt of this letter, Peter Eaton's body had been found in the quayside with a knife in his back. She must have betrayed him . . . how else? He had ever a gentle heart for a female . . . he was ever the young gallant. The viscount felt his eyes grow wet with the pain, and gruffly he pushed it all away. He *would* see his brother avenged.

Then quite suddenly, something intruded upon his mind, and he knew at once what had been bothering him since yesterday afternoon. Cassie . . . she had been as excited as child; her eyes glued to the window, taking in all the sights . . . and saying that she had been here but once . . . and that with her parents! But . . . if he were to believe his brother's letter, she had been here with Peter and Sir Charles . . . less than six weeks ago.

This was totally confusing. She could not have been acting. Why would she? He and Peter had agreed not to mention their connection, so she would have no way of knowing his purpose. Could his brother have been wrong in his assessment of Cassie? But why would she lie about Bristol? Was she as innocent as she appeared? Where was the lie?

The coach had stopped, and the driver atop sat idly wondering when his lordship meant to descend. Finally, the viscount became aware of his surroundings and opened the door to step down into the street. "I shall want you again inside fifteen minutes," he said quietly to his driver and walked up the stone steps of an impressive brick building. Chips had ascertained early yesterday afternoon that the address the viscount had found among Sir Charles's papers was Nathan Asbatol's. The viscount felt confident that, within a short span of time, all his questions would come round full force to give him the answers. He steeled himself, for he had a part to play—and play it he would!

However, though the butler, perceiving that 'twas no ordinary individual standing austerely before him, moved aside to allow the viscount admittance to Asbatol's marble hall, he quietly advised the visitor that master and mistress were away from home.

"Away?" repeated the viscount, frowning darkly, his irritation ill-concealed. "Damnation! For how long?"

Somewhat frightened by the viscount's vehemence, the butler hesitated. "As to that, sir . . ." he started, taking the card the viscount held out to him. "Oh . . . rather . . . my lord, as to that I really could not say." He paused, and then added as an afterthought. "However, they did take a great deal of luggage with them, so I feel safe in presuming they will be gone a considerable length of time." He eyed the viscount speculatively, wondering if there was a profit to be made here.

The viscount was quick to understand the look in the butler's eyes, and he held up a coin, playing with it, attracting the butler's full attention. "Very well, then. You will answer me as best you can. Where have they gone?"

"I don't think I ought to give that over. The master expressly forbade it. Said I wasn't to give it to no one but his particular clientele . . ."

"You may consider me . . . one of them," offered the viscount, producing yet another coin.

"I may, 'tis true, and as I have misplaced the list he gave me to review—you being a gentleman—well, I would be taking yer word for it . . . now wouldn't I?" he said reaching for the two coins.

The viscount held him at bay. "The address, if you please!"

"You'll find them putting up at the Grand Hotel, just a mile or so from Liverpool Center."

"Liverpool?" ejaculated the viscount, then thinking aloud, "Now, why on earth would they go up there?"

The butler, his face eager with the hope that there might be yet more to be earned replied, "Well . . . as to why . . . I couldn't say, but they did take off sudden like, right after the master got that letter . . ."

222

"A letter?" asked the viscount sharply, his mind flying to the letter Cassie had written before their departure for Bristol. She said it was for Jack Rattenbury—and he had believed her.

"Yes, your lordship, thought it had something to do with their haste . . ."

"Who was it from?" interjected the viscount, feeling as though he were on fire.

"Can't say as I remember . . ."

Again, the viscount held out a coin allowing the butler to grab and take hold, but catching his wrist in an iron grip. The butler's eyes flew to the viscount's angry eyes. "Not so fast, my greedy friend. The information, if you please?"

"Don't have a name I can remember . . . but 'twas a lady's hand . . . I'm sure of it."

The viscount felt a welter of irritation. "You are sure of that?"

"Aye . . ." said the butler.

The viscount released the coin, turned his back, and went out into the refreshing air. Once again in his coach, he became thoughtful.

The macabre thing about it all—the thing that stuck in his gut, was the fact that he was finding it impossible to think of Cassie as anything but an innocent. His brother had said his angel was a hard-hearted lady. Peter had been able to see through her in a relatively short time, and Peter had never seen through any female before. She must certainly have been blatant about it for such a fancy to take hold of his gallant brother. Yet he—Kirkby Welford, rake of all rakes, man about town, cynic—could not see through Cassie's guise.

Heaven allow it! let Cassie be innocent of his brother's suspicions and he might still come about. But now there was this new twist to things. The letter! He had believed Cassie when he came upon her sneaking off a letter and she said it was to Jack Rattenbury. He had allowed it to go. Damnation! Had she written to Nathan Asbatol, warning him of their coming?

There could be another explanation. What if the letter had come from a cohort in London. What if they had been warned about the Committee's finding a witness to identify their henchmen? By God! They would certainly rid themselves of anyone who could link them up to abduction and murder.

He sent his coach to the stable and rushed into the hotel lobby to purchase a copy of the morning paper, for he had been struck by a singular notion. He scanned the contents carefully, slowly, and finally came upon what he had known would be there.

It was a small insertion, but it amply described the body of a man found in a slum alley two nights past. It begged for someone to come forth and identify the body, and that was all.

The viscount stared at the insertion without seeing. The description exactly tied in with that given by the witness who had come forward to the Select Committee. Lord Sidmouth would have to be advised at once, and right there in the lobby he took up quill and paper.

The Asbatols covered their tracks well. They had done away with their one connection to the Linton boy—and perhaps those other hapless children. This would mean that his alternate plan would have to be instituted, and he would need his lordship's assistance.

21

Cassie had awakened to an empty room; she knew it even before she stirred. She lay in bed awhile, her forearm over her eyes and her thoughts all for the viscount. What manner of man was he? How could he hold her in his arms and then turn his back on her? How could he loathe her when his eyes would twinkle at her? But loathe me he must, she thought bitterly. Why else would he turn away? She had no answers.

She rose from her bed and groped about in the darkened room until she had found the drapery cord. The rays of a doubtful sun tiptoed into the room, and she gazed out on a gray-blue sky with large puffs of white. She sighed and wondered where he was, this great wild man she had found herself linked with. It was all so strange.

A knock sounded at her door, and she called out hopefully, but only a chambermaid appeared. The girl was carrying a tray and stood a moment until Cassie directed her to the terrace. It was a cool, comfortable summer's day, and July could almost be felt in the air. July? Almost, thought Cassie sighing, once again alone. She stirred her coffee. Confound it, girl! You need something to distract you.

Another knock sounded and with it Chips called out, " 'Tis me, yer ladyship. I brought Thomas fer ye to 'ave a look at."

Cassie jumped excitedly to her feet and rushed to the door. Chips pushed the diminutive lad through the doorway gently, encouragingly, as Cassie watched, her voice lost in surprised pleasure.

"Go on, lad . . . I ain ye be nought but a mowdie, but a sight better than ye was, and she'll be pleased enough . . . go on . . ."

Thomas was red-faced. He hid his dark eyes from Cassie but she had already taken up his freshly scrubbed hands with glee.

"Thomas . . . Thomas . . . how handsome you look. Oh, Chips, you have done well! Do you like your clothes, Thomas, for I declare you look grand!"

"Fine as fivepence, I keep tellin' him, but he . . . he says he ain't fit to come to ye," offered Chips after the lad's silence.

"What nonsense is this?" cried Cassie. "Thomas . . . I am *proud* of you! You have nought to be ashamed of, for from now on you will beg no more. You will do an honest day's work and receive an honest man's pay!"

Thomas smiled then, raising his eyes almost to Cassie's face, but found this too much for his shyness. He shuffled his new boots instead and pulled at the wide collar of his coarse blue shirt. Cassie smiled gently and then turned to Chips.

"I think, sir, that your charge will be more comfortable after he has done a bit of work. Why don't you take him and introduce him to Starfire? I am persuaded that my Star will be more than pleased to greet anyone ready to treat him with an apple."

Chips nodded. In spite of himself he was drawn to his new mistress. He knew that somehow she was connected with the matter which had brought his master hither. He

226

knew that his lordship had taken her at the Spithead and that the smuggler had forced marriage upon the viscount. Yet there was that in the lady's mien that touched his heart.

"Yes, m'lady," said Chips gruffly. "Come on then, laddie . . . ye got learning to do if yer to be any sort of horseman!"

Cassie watched them go before turning to her toilet. When she had completed this, she stood before the long looking glass and inspected. She had piled her hair on top of her head and twisted the tresses into long curls, pinning them all around. She wore a black velvet ribbon about her neck with her mother's locket. Her wide open neckline exposed the full swells of her breasts and her puff-sleeved, tight-fitting, green muslin gown set off her form attractively.

She considered her reflection. She was lovely . . . but probably nothing to what he was used to in London. Still, he had chosen her gowns well.

When would he return? Would he keep his promise? Would he take her to the pirates' den? Would they do a bit of sightseeing? Would he give her a chance to win his hard heart?

The morning drew on, and the answer loomed sadly before her. But still she was shocked when a chambermaid appeared and began packing the trunks she had unpacked the night before.

"What are you doing, girl?" asked Cassie.

"His lordship sent me up to see to yer trunks, m'lady. Said I was to pack 'em, for he was sendin' for yer coach."

"Pack?" repeated Cassie, dismay on her countenance to be swiftly replaced by consternation. She puzzled over it a moment before her anger suddenly took to flame. Confound him! How much did he think she could stand? This would not go unanswered. Swiftly she made her way into the hall, down the wide circular staircase, and into the hotel lobby. Several sporting gentlemen had gathered below, for they had assembled in Bristol for the express purpose of watching a pugilism match and were now in the midst of laying odds against the favorite. However, upon Cassie's entrance, a sudden hush swept them, broken only by a scarcely breathed, "By Jove!" from the youngest of the set and a "Quite!" by a gentleman at his side.

Cassie was fully aware that they were admiring her but no decent woman would acknowledge such boldness, and she would not have, had not the viscount chanced to look up and frown. This so infuriated her that she turned a dazzling smile upon her admirers. This was a mistake, for it encouraged their forwardness.

The youngest among them had already reached her and was offering his arm. "Flame of my heart! My only true love . . . command me, I am yours!" cried the gallant.

This so amused Cassie that she could only giggle. The youth attempted to gain ground. However, he was being boxed in by his peers and had first to dispense with them. He turned on his companions and frowned darkly. "Away, dogs!" Then to the beauty, "Come away with *me!* Such as you should not be subjected to such as *they!*"

He was totally surprised (though pleased) to find his group disperse, and he charged on, unaware how this had come about until he felt a heavy hand upon his shoulder. He looked up into the rugged face of a gentleman who was no doubt a *blood*, a corinthian . . . whose shoulders were enviable indeed.

"Sir," said the viscount, a twinkle in his eye, "I believe you mistake. My lady and I are not acquainted with you."

The boy gulped. "*Your* . . . lady . . . no . . . my . . . my error . . ." said the lad, hastening to back away and join his friends.

The viscount watched his speedy departure with amusement, but his eyes no longer twinkled when he turned them on Cassie. "Fool! Have you no sense? Had he been a bit older, you would have already received the most indecent of proposals for that little bit of idiocy!"

Cassie felt reduced to the status of a child. The color rushed hotly to her cheeks, but she smiled sweetly at him, maintaining her composure. "My lord, go to the devil . . . do!" she said, attempting to move past him.

"Where do you think you are going?" he demanded on a hiss, ignoring her latest remark.

" 'Tis none of your affair!" she snapped.

He took her by the arm and marched her right back up the stairs. With heart and soul she wanted to flout him, to pull out of his iron grasp and turn on her heel and run from him. This was impossible for she was not willing to create a scene, and she doubted if that would have served to free her. She glared at him, feeling the bite of his fingers on her delicate skin, and then suddenly she was flung into the room and the door was slammed at his back. He stood, his feet apart, his arms folded, looking a veritable forge of wrath. His raven locks skimmed across his forehead, his black eyes shone with wildfire, and his sensuous lips were drawn into a sneer. "Little slut! Are you trying to provoke me? For if you are, you have attained your goal! Where did you think you were going?"

"If you hate me so, why don't you leave me . . . go away and not look upon me?" she shouted at him.

His voice was a snarl as he strode across the room and took her shoulders. "It is because of that I keep you with me! A torture to you, is it not?"

His words ripped into her soul, and her green eyes went to the attack as a small sparrow attempting to fend off a storm.

"Torture?" she spat back at him, her voice trembling. "Aye, my lord . . . *'tis agony!*"

He flung her away. "Get your shawl! The coach will be here in a few moments and, madam—mark me—if you are not ready, if you do not come down of your own free will, I shall come up and get you—and it will not be pleasant!"

He stalked out of the room, and she turned and found a pillow. She picked up the hapless object and pounded it with both fists before bending over it and giving vent to her anguish.

The viscount returned to the lobby, his face drawn in

fury. He was in the bind of turbid emotions. He felt the battle rage, for *Cassandra was driving him mad!*

He made his way to the stables, curtly ordered his driver to hurry up, snapped at Chips, and told him to saddle his roan.

"Ye be ridin' then . . . what of her ladyship?" asked the groom curiously. "Should I be 'aving Thomas 'ere saddle Starfire?"

"Nay! Her ladyship will be in the coach," said the viscount roughly.

"Would ye be wantin' me to ride wit ye, my lord?" asked the groom trying to ferret him out.

"Nay! I ride alone. Tether your horse and ride at the back of the coach with my lady's tiger!" he said glancing at the hunch-backed child. His mood softened as the boy shuffled out of the viscount's path, and he cast the child a smile, but Thomas knew better than to trust the caprices of quality. He kept his frightened eyes averted.

The viscount paced impatiently as Chips readied his horse. Finally, mounted, top hat firmly angled on his head, dark riding cape tied at the neckline, the viscount regarded his groom thoughtfully. "Chips . . . my lady is sometimes given over to impulse. You will see to it that this does not occur by stopping at but one watering house!"

"I understand, m'lord," said Chips grinning widely, "Do ye go on ahead then?"

"Yes, though in truth I shall not maintain any great distance between us. If there is any trouble, you have but to send ahead for my return. Now, go on with the coach. I will tarry only long enough to make sure she gets . . . that all is in order."

"Aye, m'lord," said Chips, the grin never leaving his mouth.

The viscount scowled at him fiercely, but Chips merely took to whistling and soon afterwards Kirkby Welford saw his lady seated in the coach. Thus satisfied, he rode on ahead.

230

Cassie should have been pleased to find that he had chosen not to keep her company in their coach. After all, she had declared his lordship's company was agony—a thing he was recalling as he rode on ahead. But there is no saying how a woman will react when mind and heart do not find common ground. She watched the passing scenes as they made their way into the Cotswolds. Manor farms of weathered amber stones caught her eye with their starkness. A pond full of ducks fluffing their feathers in the warmth of the afternoon sun enchanted her. She smiled to see the tiny ducklings take to the water after their mother. The ruins of a fourteenth-century abbey loomed before her, intriguing both eye and imagination, but still her anger raged within her!

It was already late afternoon when they made their first stop at a posting inn skirting Gloucester. Cassie alighted, feeling the need for exercise. Chips called after her, and she stopped and waited, wondering why he was looking agitated.

"M'lady . . . meaning no disrespect . . . but his lordship . . . he said ye wasn't . . . well . . . he said we weren't to make any overlong stops. Means us to keep to his timing," he faltered noting that this only served to put up her back.

Cassie raised her chin. "I am certain his lordship had his reasons for his orders to you, just as I have mine for not . . . obeying!" She gave him her back, throwing over her shoulder, "Come, Thomas . . . you may attend me, child."

The boy glowed as he ambled after her. It was all he could ask of the forces of heaven, to follow in his mistress's footsteps. She was in a state of near convulsion, so acute was her irritation. She had meant only to stretch her legs with a short jaunt around an interesting looking square, but Chips's words had set her on fire. Now, now she would tour the city on foot. However, she was not lost to the proprieties that she would wander off alone. Thomas, however helpless in the way of protection, would at least afford her respectability. After a time she came upon a glorious cathedral dating back to the year 1100. She studied its cloisters, allowing Thomas to climb and jump about to his heart's content before laughing and bidding him follow.

Her bubble of anger had drifted off, and she was at length able to return to her waiting coach, where with much dignity she climbed inside. They returned to the main road, and she watched as they passed the docks of Gloucester, leaving the River Severn at their backs. She sat back and ignored the landscape as her mind's eye brought her husband's visage before her. Where was she bound? She didn't even know! She hadn't taken the chance of his carrying out his threat. She hadn't wanted to be carried out willy-nilly from the hotel, so when a servant was sent to advise her that her coach awaited, she had followed without further demur, thinking she would rant to her heart's content once inside the coach with her husband. However, once inside she found him absent. Neither was he anywhere in sight. A most depressing thing for a woman with a lecture to spout and no audience. He was arrogant, despicable . . . wicked! She hated him!

What she needed was a ride. Of course! She stuck her head out her window and called the driver to a stop. This accomplished, she alighted nimbly and turned toward Chips's disgruntled countenance. "Chips, where did his lordship instruct you to stop for the night?"

"Red Hart at Shrewsbury," he said slowly, wondering what she was about.

"Very well. Kindly saddle my horse. Thomas, you saddle Chips's blood, I am certain he will have no objection. You can ride, lad?"

"Aye . . . some . . ." said the boy doubtfully, for he had not done so often.

She frowned over it, but Chips's objections brought her head round. "Nay, m'lady, ye canna mean to do it?" he said dropping into a heavy Highland accent, so distinctly did he feel his master would not like this change in plans.

"Of course, I mean to, though . . . perhaps you

232

should accompany me until Thomas learns the knack with the reins."

"Aye, that I will!" returned the groom sharply.

"No, m'lady . . . Please . . . I can do it. Hang me if I let ye down! Please, m'lady, take me . . . take me . . ." cried Thomas.

"Oh, Thomas . . . I certainly shall take you, as soon as you learn how to handle yourself on a horse. But I don't want you hurt. You ride along with the carriage."

He wanted more than life itself to remain within her sight. She was his goddess, she restored hope to his small shattered soul, but she had given the command, and he had pledged never to buck her will. He dropped his head.

She felt her heart tug, but no, he couldn't . . . not just yet. She patted his shoulder and bade him saddle Chips's horse. Starfire was pawing at the ground, champing at his bit, for he wanted this run with his mistress. It had been days since she had taken him. No sooner was she mounted, but she was off in a heady canter, leaving Chips to struggle at her back.

Tuck her up in a closed coach, would he? Confound him for a bully! She would attend him indeed . . . in her own style!

The viscount had taken to the road at a leisurely pace. He had given Chips the command to bring the coach to Shrewsbury where they would put up for the night, and he had nought to make him race. He stopped in Gloucester a while ahead of his coach and lingered over his ale, brooding over his wife, before taking to horse again. By the time he reached the Red Hart in Shrewsbury, it was well into six and, though the days were already growing longer, the afternoon had lost its sun behind long masses of clouds. The viscount obtained a room for the night and then casually wandered into the tavern room. It was empty but for an elderly man snoring at a table and a set of two playing chess in the window seat. It was a small town, and its menfolk would not start coming in until later in the evening.

233

Taking up a bumper of ale, he meandered to a corner table and straddled a chair. His black eyes were bright as they gazed into his brew. He had to force his mind away from Cassie, but he was finding it near to impossible. Damnation! She was a witch to haunt him so.

When she had flaunted his will in the hotel he had wanted to spank her. His fury had been laced with near insanity for he had wanted to know where she was going. It mattered. He didn't know why at the moment, but it mattered enough to make him want to beat it out of her. He had never roughly handled any female before in all his life. Never before had he wanted to hit a woman, but he wanted to hit her. He had taken her by the shoulders, and the touch of her sent a warmth through his body, and all at once all he wanted to do was kiss her. God! He could feel that same desire still! He had heard her declare that his company was a source of agony, and he had flung her from him feeling all the while he was under attack by a thousand burning coals. It mattered not that he had told her he hated her. 'Twas but the words of passion. Hate . . . love . . . they entwined to make a man half mad. What did all of it mean? He only knew that when he had first taken her in his arms . . .

Hell and brimstone! He must be rid of her magic! How . . . how . . . how? Another woman? Damn if he wouldn't take another woman into his arms and forget the feel of Cassie's soft flesh! He glanced around and there! There was another woman to favor his wish.

Dolly sauntered out of the backroom, calling a greeting to the chess players and swinging her hips as she bent to pick up a wet rag from a wash basin. Her dirty blond hair was fluffy around her full pretty face. Her body was well endowed, and the hem of her skirt was tucked up into her waistband allowing the observant eye an excellent view of her long well-shaped legs. She came close to his lordship's table, winking at him as she bent over to wipe it down. Her white, low-cut peasant blouse fell away from her, giving the viscount a full view of her substantial charms. Her plump breasts swayed with her movements. He could just see her nipples, large and dark, intriguing . . . beckoning. He wondered how she would toss, and he felt his blood warm. Aye, she would do . . .

The woman gave him a smile for she was fully aware where his gaze strayed. "Can I be getting ye somethin', sir?" she asked coyly, tilting her head, and dimpling up at him as she straightened.

He ran his eye over her pretty face and then once again over her voluptuous charms. "Aye, love . . . if you are willing?"

"Willing?" chuckled one of the chess players diverted from his game. "Go on wit ye, covey . . . don't she *look* willing?" His friend snorted loudly over this, and Dolly shook her hand good-naturedly at them.

She then leaned over and planted a soft kiss upon the viscount's mouth. "Aw, darlin', wot mort wouldn't be willing with sech as ye in the offerin' . . . though I do charge a bit of a price . . ."

Her kiss did nothing for him, and there was the scent of stale gin about her. He remembered another scent—Cassie's—it was that of wild roses. He put up his hand and took her wrist, drawing her into his lap, "What's your price, woman?" he asked, more curious than tempted.

"A gold guinea."

He smiled and went to the first button of her blouse, undoing it. The second undone, he reached in and brought out the full soft melon and fondled. The chess players gaped and began making ribald remarks, but Dolly didn't mind . . . she reveled in it.

"Look at them fruits! Don't ye wish ye be young enough to suckle at 'em?" cried one of the men.

"Eh? I *am* young enuff . . . ye old dog!" retorted his friend. "Eh, Dolly girl . . . if that young buck don't please ye, jest come to old Willie. I'll show ye how it's done!"

She laughed loudly and flung her arms round his lordship. "Now, Willie, jest look at him. How's he *not* going to please me?"

However, she would have been much surprised to find

235

that the viscount had not yet been aroused enough to stir his manhood. It lay limp in his breeches, his desire unflamed. In fact, he felt as though he were immersed in slime.

She returned her lips to the viscount's ears and giggled. "Lord love ye, good-lookin' . . . but 'tis upstairs we should be goin'."

To stall for time, he took her face in one hand and brought his mouth down on hers. Hell and fire! Why wasn't this working? What was wrong with him? He kissed her furiously, his free hand going once again to her large breasts, fondling, teasing . . . hoping his blood would heat.

22

Cassie had reached the outskirts of Shrewsbury just about the time he had taken the tavern wench onto his knee. She reached the Red Hart but a few moments later and gave over her reins to Chips. Brushing the dust away from her dainty green muslin and adjusting her bonnet she strolled into the inn, her heart beating wildly as she cast her eyes about for the viscount.

Finding no one at the hall desk, she made her way toward the tavern room, and suddenly a gasp came to her throat and she pulled herself up short. The viscount heard her entrance and looked up, horror filling his eyes to find her surveying the cozy scene. He got to his feet without thinking, dropping the wench onto the floor. She screamed loudly over this, and he was obliged to aid her. During this time, Cassie had managed to steel herself—to disguise her pain with a sneer.

"Oh! How *clumsy* of me, my lord! It is obvious I am *de trop*! Please go on with . . . whatever you were doing. I shall bother you no more!" She turned and walked from the room.

"Cassie!" called the viscount. He only knew that suddenly his world was being blown to smithereens. He had seen the expression on her face, knew himself responsible for it, and wished himself dead.

He was detained by the plump wench at his side. She clung to his arm and screeched objections into his ears, and all he could think was to get to Cassie. By the time he had put the wench off he saw Cassie, key in hand, rushing up the narrow flight of stairs. He took the steps by twos and, just as she pushed the door open and attempted to shut it in his face, he blocked the move with his powerful arm and pressed his way inside. He closed the door at his back as he stood to face a wildcat hissing at him, and he thought he had never before seen her look so astoundingly beautiful. "Get out! You filth . . . you contemptible knave . . . you swine . . . get out . . . get out!"

"Cassie . . . wait! Let me explain . . ." he tried, not sure what he could say. He had been caught with the goods after all, and in such circumstances there is little a man can say. Still . . . he had the truth, he could always use the truth . . .

"Explain?" hissed the lady, evidently thinking this beyond his capacity, indeed beyond anyone's capacity. "What is there to explain? Surely I will lose my mind!" she said clasping and unclasping her hands. "He wants to explain . . . prithee, sir . . . what can you *possibly* say to me?" She did not wait for him to try, which perhaps was a good thing (for he had not yet thought of anything to say), but proceeded to give full vent to her feelings. "I . . . I thought once something could yet be made of this mockery of a marriage we share! I was wrong! You have shown me clearly just how stupid I have been."

He took a step forward. He only knew he wanted to comfort her, he wanted to soothe her pain, banish that look from her eyes. She seemed such a child . . .

She jumped before he could touch her, and her voice was wild with pain and rage. "Nay! Stay, you cur! No. . .

238

don't come near me! You boor! You womanizer! May your soul be eternally damned! Just go to your wenches and leave me in peace!"

"Cassie . . . listen to me . . ."

"God! I *did* listen to you, to your soft words as you held me at night . . . and I was a fool among many! I want no more. All I want is to be rid of you! Once you said you hoped I was barren that you may be spared a spawn in my likeness! By faith, I hope that wish of yours proves true so that I may yet be free to love! You have given your favors loosely. You have no heart to give, but *I* have. And I shall —when and to whom it pleases me. You have shown me how the game is played, and at last I have learned!"

Again he stepped near her. Her words whipped his face and breast. His temper took a wild bound forward. Unreasonably his anger surged. A moment ago he was all guilt and softness as he looked into her pained eyes. He had been ready to confess himself her slave. But now he was a man on fire! Give herself to another man? *He would see her dead first!*

He was almost on top of her and there was a threat that beat from his heart to his eyes. She dived out of his reach and placed her hand round a letter opener on the desk. The brass glinted in the candlelight as she pointed it toward her heart, and her green eyes were two pools of glazed ice as she spoke.

"Nay . . . come not near me, my lord. I swear the touch of you would drive this through me . . . *I swear it!*"

He stopped instantly, for though he doubted her ability to accomplish such a threat, he did not doubt a struggle might cause her some injury. He was wild, itching to lay hands on her, but he composed himself and his words came hard. "Cassie, love . . . make no mistake, *you are mine!* I'll not lie about what you saw. I'll say only that I have been wanting you out of my blood and thought *that* the way! Suffice it to say, it didn't work. Let that be my hell, and hell it is . . . wanting you! The wench didn't raise my blood . . . nor could any but yourself. I know

239

not how, but it seems you've worked your design upon me. Depend upon it, sweet vixen . . . whether I touch you or no, *no other man will!* No other, Cassie . . . do you hear me?"

"Hear you? Aye . . . that I do. But so you shall hear me—and understand me well. When and if I choose, I shall take a lover! And when I do, 'twill be with my heart, soul . . . and body! Kirkby Welford, you have told me to mark you, now mark me, all three items go as a whole . . . heart, soul, and body . . . and the man who receives such favors will be of my choice! Now get out of here, for *you* will get no more of me. You are an adventurer—corrupt and evil—I want you out of my room!"

He could have struck her at that moment. Her words taunted him. Yet he knew they were but words of anger. Frowning, he thought quickly. She was jealous. Jealousy was an odd sensation. It did many things—mad things—to the mind. She was speaking without thought. He knew women enough to know that. He calmed himself, brushed away her demented thunder. His voice tried to assuage her fever, he tried to submit.

"Cassie . . . what is it you want . . . what more can I say . . . or do?"

"Nought, nought . . . there is nothing you can do but leave me be. Can you transport me in time? Can you put me upon a smuggler's sloop . . . make me a girl again with nought to worry about but the excisemen? I sigh for that, and you cannot give it to me. Go away . . . go away . . . please . . ."

He stopped. This hurt more than her earlier threat. She missed her smuggler, Jack Rattenbury, and this was cause for Kirkby to feel the pangs of jealousy. There was nothing more he could do. He left her alone.

She watched him go, ran to the door, and bolted it. She hated him! There was but one thought, to get away. She must get away. She had to think . . . how . . . when . . . and where, where would she go? She could not return to Jack. Kirkby would go after her, find her . . . and perhaps cause

Jack trouble. She could not go back to the Grange. Kirkby would again find her and carry out his threats to dismiss the servants she held dear. She would have to find shelter . . . somewhere.

Cassie's thoughts took her along many roads and at last she found one that would have to suit. She packed a small portmanteau with but two gowns and a few other needs. She slipped her small pistol (it was only a one-shot gun, but it too would have to do) into her riding boot. She readied her brown velvet riding habit and though she wanted very much to cry, did not. Her world, her dreams, and hopes had come to an abrupt end. She hated him, this Kirby Welford, but what was worse, hating him hurt . . . hurt so intensely!

He did not make any attempt to come to her room. A tray was sent up to her with his compliments and though she wanted very much to send it back with hers, she did not. She had a long ride ahead of her. So, though the food had no taste, though it seemed to stick in her throat, she ate. Afterwards, she lay in her bed, alone, quiet, except for the times when her heart ruled and brought on a sob! Still she wondered what he was doing—and with whom!

Near midnight she dragged out the bed linens she had carefully knotted earlier and tied one end to the bed post. She was only two stories above the ground. It would be easy to descend. She dropped her portmanteau before her and winced when it landed with a heavy thud. However, soon afterward, dressed in her riding habit and hat, she scrambled out of the window. Holding tightly to the linens and bracing her feet against the building, she lowered herself by degrees to the soft ground below. That done, she picked up her portmanteau and circled the tavern to the stables. Here she found everything in darkness and stood a moment frowning, wondering how she was to find Tom, when he solved the problem for her. He stood above in the hayloft, straw sticking out of his hair in several places, a candle held tightly in his hand. "Gawks, mum! *You here?*"

"Shhh, Thomas . . . hurry. Collect your things and get down here to saddle up Chips's horse while I ready Starfire."

"Yes, m'lady . . . right away," he said hurrying to do her bidding. He had no idea what was afoot, but he would never question anything she chose to do.

Some few moments later just as Cassie was mounting her steed and Tom attempting to pull himself up on the horse she had chosen for him, a young, loose-limbed, and somewhat dirty fellow appeared. He was a stable ostler, and he frowned at them. He could see the woman was quality but what was she doing sneaking about at this hour? He scratched his head and attempted an inquiry.

"Eh . . . who be ye? Wot ye be up to?"

"Never mind! 'Tis none of your affair!" said Cassie severely. " 'Tis my groom, my horse, and my business!"

The young stableboy stepped out of her way. Clearly, he was in the wrong of it and had better stay well out of the way. Cassie and Tom walked their horses slowly out of the stables, leading them down the narrow dirt path onto the main road. They went at a slow pace for there was not enough light from the moon and stars to show the way, and the area was unfamiliar to Cassie. She wanted to head back toward the Grange. She had made up her mind to it, there was nowhere else she could go, and he would not follow . . . not yet, for he had his business to conduct in Liverpool. By the time he came after her, she would be gone. That was her plan.

They rode no more than two miles or so when the snort of a horse champing at its bit brought Cassandra up short. Her hand went back swiftly, stilling her small groom. "Hush, lad . . ." she whispered as he started to speak.

He watched astonished as she slipped off her horse and motioned for him to follow suit. She was out at a dangerous hour. The sound of horses came to her from not far off, and it could mean several things, but of one she was certain. It would not be safe to go on until she knew what was ahead. She led Tom and their horses into the brush, winding their way until she thought it safe to tether their animals. She turned to her groom. "Tom, keep them still . . . cover their mouths if you must, but keep them silent! I'm going to go on ahead and see if its safe to proceed in the open."

"But, m'lady. . ."

"Hush now, I'll be fine as long as you take care to do as I bid you," she said firmly already starting down a narrow path. Cassie's heart beat furiously. This was not to her liking. What if they heard her in the thicket? She could already hear the sound of muffled conversation and was certain it portended trouble. Her association with Jack Rattenbury had taught her much, and she suspected that the dark forms ahead huddled together at the edge of the road were highwaymen.

She got close enough to hear them speaking and crouched low, out of their range of vision. She could hear one man with a Yorkshire accent. He was somewhat out of breath, as though he had been running.

" 'Tis a well-turned out job, I tell ye . . . bound to have a fat purse on him. He were some miles south of the tavern. What's it to be, lads? We ain't got time if we're to get to the crossroads. . ."

That was all Cassie had to hear. They *were* highwaymen. What to do? She doubled back to Tommy, thinking all the while. It would seem that a coach was on its way and that this coach was the highwaymen's objective. They meant to attack at the crossroads ahead. She could hold back and wait for them to do the thing and leave the road safe for her. She had to go to the crossroads herself if she were to make her way back to the Grange. But how could she leave the coach an easy prey to these scoundrels?

By the time she had reached Thomas, she knew what she had to do. She went to his saddle and found there Chips's horse pistol. She looked it over and then, dipping into her boot, she took out her own small pistol and put it into her groom's hand.

"Do you know how to use this?"

"Better than I can ride, m'lady," grinned Thomas.

"Very well. We are going to the crossroads. There we will await the arrival of a coach and three high tobys. I will fire a shot from one side of the road. When you hear it, you will fire an answering shot. Aim to injure, not to kill. Now come along, we haven't much time if we are to reach the crossing beforehand!"

'Twas all she said, but he did not question it though his heart began to beat irregularly. Tobys . . . coaches . . . guns! Gawks! thought he, but he followed as she led him out of the thicket and urged his horse into a heady canter.

Lord Eric Widdons sat back in his handsome black coach. It was a late hour, and he had been traveling for some time. He was returning to Liverpool from London, having had three exhaustive meetings with Sidmouth. His top hat was on the cushions before him beside his raised feet. His hair, the color of marbled yellow and white, fell across his smooth forehead, and his pale blue eyes scanned the darkness out of his window. He sighed for he was worried. This thing Sidmouth proposed, this trap to which he had given his consent, involved his only son and, though he would be sending his boy to Scotland out of the way, it worried him. And then all at once he was shaken out of his thoughts by the sound of rushing thunder.

The coach was pulled up to a severe stop. There were shouts and the report of a gun. He threw open his door, thinking too late to reach for his own gun on the sidewall. And he found himself looking into the barrel of a horse pistol. The dark-clad man bearing down upon him was masked from the neck to the eyes as were his two accomplices.

"Your money or your life, gent?" said the gruff fellow amiably.

"It would appear I have little choice," said Lord Widdons, scanning the two men holding weapons over his driver and postilion.

And then again the air began to buzz, and all heads went round. The man holding the pistol to Lord Widdons found his hat shot off his head, and he spun round. "What in damnation?"

"Throw your guns down, lads!" said a rough, deep voice, "ye be surrounded!" Then thinking it time to use her second shot, since Tom had frozen and not used his gun yet, she fired again for emphasis, managing to hit one of the highwaymen in the arm. He yelped and looked in the direction of the sound, but Cassie was well hidden by the bushes. This time Tom did his bit by firing quickly and grazing yet another man just above the ear.

"Run for it lads!" shouted the leader. " 'Tis the runners, damn their eyes!" With which the three tobys tooled their horses into action, spurred on by Lord Widdons who had by this time thought to take up his gun and aim it at their heads, nearly nicking a man in the process.

Cassie let go a hoot of victory and urged her horse forward towards the coach. Her groom met her from across the way, and they both approached his lordship.

He looked up at Cassie in astonishment. "You are a woman!"

"So I have always believed. How do you do, sir? I take it you are unharmed?"

"But . . . by God!" he managed.

She looked at him. His face was attractive, his mouth open in a half-smile. His eyes she could not see, but his hair was uncovered and its thickness was such that added to his attraction. She smiled warmly, liking him without knowing why.

"You want to know how we came to be here so opportunely, and indeed I shall tell you. I am running away, you know. 'Tis a sorry thing but I have found that many truths are, never mind that. We heard those creatures up the road and hurried here ahead of them to take our places . . . and the rest you know," she said succinctly.

"Do, miss, I beg of you, dismount and allow me to thank you properly and learn further how all this came about," he pleaded on a chuckle.

"Very well," she said, slipping off her horse. She felt somehow festive, she could forget Kirkby now. Busy with her adventure, she could put away the hollow ache in her heart.

She smiled up at him as he fell in step beside her and they walked slowly. He said gently, "Now . . . you have said you are running away? Your parents?"

She cut him off with a bitter laugh. "Not, sir, from my parents! From my *husband*."

"I see," he said quietly. "I am sorry to hear it and, of course, 'tis none of my affair. But perhaps . . . if you talked about it . . . you might see your way more clearly . . . might change your mind."

"Never!" she snapped harshly. "Indeed I do not wish to speak of that. Suffice it to say that my taking such action put me on this road this night. I overheard those men planning to rob your coach at the crossroads. I have a gun . . . my groom has a gun . . . *voilà!*"

"Indeed, *voilà!*" he laughed. "But tell me . . . where do you go?"

She frowned. "You would not speak of it to anyone?"

"That would be a very shabby way of repaying you for such singular assistance," he said gravely. "I do not inquire because of idle curiosity but, believe me, in an effort to lend you whatever aid you allow."

She looked at him long. "The thing is . . . I wish to go somewhere *he* will not find me, and I fear that he may if I go home."

"Which is?"

"Farrington Grange. I am . . . or rather was . . . Cassandra Farrington and should like to be so again."

"I see. What you need is a place to think things out . . ." he mused to himself.

"Yes, yes, I do, for I must discover how I can rid myself of him and yet go on . . ." she answered.

"I was on my way to my estate in Liverpool . . . oh . . . do excuse me, in the excitement of the moment I neglected to introduce myself. I am Lord Eric Widdons at your service . . . Miss Farrington."

She acknowledged this with a smile but then frowned. "*He* is going to Liverpool."

"I was about to suggest the following. I have a widowed sister who lives some miles south of Liverpool. I was not going to stop there tonight for I had reasons for wanting to reach home by early morning. But *you* bring me to my senses. My driver must be dreadfully tired as he had but a nap this afternoon and, although I changed my horses at the last posting house, they too should be rested. Come, do allow me to take you there."

"Oh, no, I could not. I am very sure your sister will not want a strange woman foisted on her . . . and in the middle of the night!"

"You will find Isabelle a prodigiously good woman and most ready to welcome me and anyone I choose to bring to her home. I am her younger brother, you see, and quite a favorite." He was smiling reassuringly.

She hesitated, thinking it would be ideal. Kirkby would never find her there. Yet the thought gave her pain. However, she bolstered herself and made up her mind. "Very well, my lord . . . if you think it will serve."

"I do, Miss Farrington . . . now come, allow me to offer you the comfort of my coach," he said leading her back to the carriage.

"Thank you," she said, then turning to Tom, she had him tether the horses at the coach's back and climb to its top.

23

A new day came bringing with it sunshine and a sky to taunt the imagination. Its blue enveloped all and as the viscount stood looking out of his window, he thought of Cassie's Dorset with its rolling soft green hills and the scent of salt—and love.

"Fiend seize the fates!" he hissed softly. He had not had a good night. Much of it was spent in self-recrimination and rationalization, all of which left him out of temper with himself and with Cassandra. He told himself he should have stormed her door and forced her to give over — she was his wife. Now in allowing her to have her way he had in all probability created a monster. Well, he would not have it. So he told himself as he donned a brocade dressing gown over his nakedness. He would end this nonsense now. He strode on this note to his door, flung it open, and took the hall very much determined. There he found her door and knocked. There was no answer. He frowned, it was early morning still, less than twenty minutes to seven . . . could she be asleep? Irrationally, this irritated him. Sleep? How could she when he could not? He knocked harder still, adding his call, "Cassie!" It was firm but not yet harsh. Again, "Cassie!"

Still no response. She was acting the child, he told himself, pretending she was asleep. He had no patience for such antics. "Cassie, come, love . . ." Quiet came back at him.

"Cassie . . . you little fool!" he whispered in some exasperation. "Open this door!"

Really, thought he, 'twas enough to make a sane man mad. "Cassie, do you think I could not open this door? Cassie!" And there it was, the silent challenge. There was nothing for it but to step back and vent his fury upon the gateway before him. Giving himself room and leverage, he lunged forward with force enough to bring down the walls. The feeble door gave way and swayed pitifully on its hinges as he strode angrily into the empty room.

One glance told him a story. Not only was his wife gone but a look towards the open window and the knotted linens was enough to tell him the method of escape. He cursed softly as he made his way hastily back to his room. He would have to act quickly, for in all probability she had many hours on him. But where could she go? Liverpool? She had no one there. Bristol? No one there either. To the Grange? Perhaps . . . or perhaps to Jack! The thought made his mouth twitch, and he began dressing with unbelievable swiftness. He had a purpose, to find the wench he had wived and to bring her to heel. She was costing him. He had no time to waste on such things, for he had to get to Liverpool. Damn, but he was going to teach her.

Cassie had slept from pure enervation. They had arrived at Mrs. Isabelle Bamfield's home near the hour of four in the morning. That gracious lady moved about just as though they had not roused her from her sleep. Kindly she had ordered her brother to his usual room and taken Cassie to the guestroom, leaving her there with but a pat on the shoulder. She asked no questions, and happily seemed not at all put out by the intrusion. A gem, thought Cassie, as she passed out in her small clothes upon the soft bed. She awoke now with a start. It was but a few minutes past seven and she had slept only a couple of hours but still she felt refreshed. She glanced about her and was surprised to see her room was decorated in blue and pale yellow—last night everything had seemed brown. She went to the drapes where the sunlight peeped through between the center folds, and she drew them back by their cord. She looked out on the front lawns. They were not extensive, stretching out but a hundred feet to where a picket fence separated them from what appeared to be a narrow country road. She sighed and then, as her thoughts went to a black-eyed devil, she frowned. Oh, how she hated him!

She turned away from the window and went to her vanity stand. She poured some wash water into the basin. It was cold but refreshing, and she cleansed herself before getting dressed. She wanted to go out and have a look about before the household stirred, before Lord Widdons came down. She brushed her long bright red tresses and put them up with a brown velvet ribbon, so that their curly tips touched the ivory muslin at her shoulders. Picking up her spencer of matching ivory, she tiptoed out of the room and down the stairs but at the foot she was brought up short. There stood her new friend, and now she could see the color of his eyes. They were blue and twinkling—right at her!

The viscount knew well the needs of the hunt. He ordered Chips to follow him for that Highlander had a way with him. His groom could often ferret out information that he could not buy even with a gold coin. A further irritant stung him when he discovered that his lady took not only her own horse but Chips's as well. He quickly purchased from the tavern stables a fair nag and, though ordinarily he would have been amused by the expression that came over his groom's face, he merely ordered the man to hurry and get into his saddle. To his coach driver he gave a curt command to proceed to Liverpool where he would join them later that day.

"Chips, I want to know if you are aware of any . . . off-the-main-road inns?" said the viscount, mounting his roan.

His groom cocked his head sideways, and his eyes narrowed. "Aye, methinks there be a den of sorts . . . but not one meant for yer lady . . ."

"But it is south, on the way back to Dorset?" he interrupted.

"Aye, that it is . . . but . . ."

"Let's go!" said the viscount, roughly taking up his left lead and bounding forward.

His groom sighed. This wench his master had taken to wife . . . she was a handful, she was!

It was nearly an hour later when they veered off the main road. They had not far to go, though in truth the inn itself could easily have been missed, so far back from the country road it was and hidden by a grove of evergreens. As they drew near, it was obvious that the inn was *not* of the first stare. Its weathered walls were chipping and much in need of paint. Its roof needed repair and a shutter hung lopsided. The viscount turned a rueful smile upon his groom. "Off the main road, yes, but in business?"

"Tried to tell ye 'twas somethin' of a thieves' den. Ye won't be finding our lady 'ere."

"No, but if anything unusual has occurred on the highway, we may be able to find out. I'll go in the galley . . . you go have a word with the stableboys."

The viscount soon gave up making his discreet inquiries for the tavernkeeper was as closemouthed a fellow as ever he had come across. However, when he sighed and looked round, it was to find Chips standing in the doorway eying him meaningfully.

The viscount put down a coin for his drink and strode towards his groom. "What did you find out?"

"Let's ride, m'lord. I'll be telling ye when we are well away," said Chips, cautiously, glancing round.

Silently the viscount mounted, but they had not gone far when he rounded on his groom. "Now my man, if you will dispense with the secretive attitude you have adopted and tell me what it is you found out."

"That's the wheedle, m'lord. 'Taint sure it has ought to do with m'lady . . . but 'ere goes. This guid lad in thare, he be a talkative little cove, says 'ow these divils come raving into the place last night, all talk as 'ow they got nearly twigged! Seems they be these high tobys, meant to pluck a passing coach near the hour of twelve last night. Aye, had him cold, so the tale goes when up pops some other culls . . . come on shootin', these others did, so the tobys they piked off! Later, when they got to thinkin' . . . findin' out things for themselves, they come to think it *wasn't* the King's men that twigged their rig!'

"What the hell does that . . . ?"

"Beggin' yer pardon, m'lord, meanin' no disrespect . . . but one of the coves I been telling ye aboot, well he happen to 'ave looked back as they were loping off! Nearly fuffed his breath, it did, for he thought he saw the skirts of a woman swingin' a pistol their way! Didn't say nuthin' at the time thinkin' 'twas his old eyes that was queerin' him —that or the drink . . ." Chips stopped and eyed his lordship who had gone thoughtful.

Cassie . . . waving a gun at highwaymen? Yes, only Cassie. She had probably come upon them attempting to rob the gentleman in the coach. That was Cassie all over. He almost smiled to himself.

"Anything else, Chips?"

"Nought."

"This coach . . . which direction was it headed?"

"North toward Liverpool . . ."

Again, the viscount went thoughtful. He had a hunch that Cassie had not continued on her journey south. The gentleman in the coach would not have allowed her to do so. He would have insisted on helping her. And Cassie? Yes, she wouldn't want to go home if she could avoid it. She would want to stay somewhere out of his reach.

"Come, Chips. We'll take the road north and inquire

after her. She has two things on this journey of hers that should aid us. One, her young tiger—the poor lad is bound to draw eyes—and her horse!"

"And there's herself, m'lord. I mean, her ladyship do stand out in a crowd!" said Chips on a note of approval.

The viscount eyed him sharply for a moment but said nothing. Instead he spurred his horse forward, and again they were heading toward Liverpool.

"Why, my dear . . . I hadn't expected you up at such an early hour. But, come, this is marvelous, for I must leave and wasn't at all satisfied with the note I planned to write you," said Lord Widdons, smiling up as the titian-haired beauty descended the polished oak steps. "You see, I have business that takes me to Liverpool which is something more than half a day's journey, otherwise I would not have thought of leaving before you were awake."

Cassie smiled down at him and placed her hand in his outstretched one. Slowly, he raised her white fingers to his thin lips, and she reappraised him. His hair, unusual in its shades of yellow and white, was thick and long and fell down upon his forehead casually as it did about his ears. His sandy brows were thick and slightly winged. There were crow's-feet at the corners of his blue eyes and his sandy lashes made them seem somehow perpetually alight. She calculated that he was somewhere in his late thirties.

She was disappointed that he was leaving. They had fallen into an easy discourse on the four-hour trip to Whitchurch and she had come to regard him as a friend. A friend she badly needed now. "Oh! Then this is good-by, sir, for I shall not trespass on your sister's gracious hospitality longer."

"Nonsense! If you leave, Miss Farrington, my sister will find me sadly put out with her . . . a thing she would not like I warrant you. No, she has given me her word that when I return you will still be here."

He had already drawn her slender arm through his. He was patting her hand, and she looked up into his eyes.

253

"You are most kind, my lord, but it simply would not be right."

"What would not be right?" asked a firm authoritive voice at their backs.

They turned round to find a large woman of some forty-five years in a mauve silk wrapper and a lace nightcap over her light brown cropped curls. She was built along magnificent lines and had all the determination about the blue eyes of one used to handling the reins. She came forward smiling amiably at both Cassie and her brother.

"My dear, I understand from Eric that I am to have you as my houseguest. A treat indeed, for I never was fortunate enough to bear a daughter. I have been pining for a young female to brighten this dreary household of mine. Do you mean to tell me that you would rob me of such a thing?" It was a whimsical challenge, and it brought out a full smile from Cassandra.

"But, Mrs. Bamfield, you don't know anything about me," offered Cassie.

"I know that you came to my brother's aid last night. Unusual and most intriguing, and depend upon it, I shall drag the details from you presently. I know that you are lovely, well-mannered, and that you find yourself in some sort of trouble. Of that, 'tis your own and I wouldn't dream of dragging it from you. At least, I'd liefer you gave over of your own accord . . ." The woman's eyes were twinkling. "But *that* doesn't signify. You are my houseguest, and that is that!"

Cassie could not help herself. She found her arms go round the large, kind woman and she whispered, "Thank you."

Isabelle Bamfield frowned over the girl's head in some concern and met her brother's eyes. She stroked Cassie's red-gold tresses.

"There now. Take your leave of my brother, for I can see he is itching to be off."

"Not true!" countered his lordship, "I have not the least inclination to leave you, yet indeed I must, for there are obligations awaiting me in Liverpool."

Cassie turned to him and once again found her extended hand placed softly to his lips. His eyes met hers and he said, "I shall return as soon as may be. Try to rest, Miss Farrington. I am sure a turn with my indomitable sister will give you a new perspective on things."

There was nothing she could reply to this without being rude, for she doubted that anyone could change her mind with regard to her marriage. But she merely smiled, thanked him again, and watched him depart with something near to warmth.

"Now my dear. Breakfast . . . and then 'tis back to bed for you, for I'll swear you couldn't have gotten more than two hours' sleep, and I shan't have you losing that natural bloom in your cheeks under *my* care!"

Cassie laughed but followed her out of the hall to the small brightly furnished morning room. Everything was so different. She felt as though she were moving through the scenes of an unhappy dream for in spite of the shelter and the kindness of these people, her heart felt cold and tugged and pulled and ached.

24

The night fell heavily upon the viscount. A day's search had left him irritated, in the boughs, and ready for quarreling. The fact that he could not take out his temper on the one woman who deserved it further angered him. Where had she gone? How could his red-haired vixen, her young poorly formed servant, and her eye-catching steed have just disappeared?

He and Chips had stopped at every posting house and road tavern between Shrewsbury and Liverpool, making a long, full day's journey even longer, and yet they had not picked up a trace of her whereabouts. There was an answer, of course. Either she had not gone along with this mysterious coach, or they had taken a byroad to some country estate. A letter to an acquaintance in the vicinity of the Grange would, of course, tell him whether or not Cassie had returned home. But that would take time, and he wanted to get his hands on her now. His impatience nearly obscured clear thought. However, he had collected himself and by pure will power had drawn himself up and proceeded with his groom to Liverpool. He would have to give up the hunt tonight, for his original purpose had to take over in this instance. But he had not given up. He would find Cassandra if it was the last thing he did.

He arrived at the Grand Hotel, an elegant establishment in the more respectable section of town, to discover that his coach had already arrived. His room with his belongings had been prepared for his arrival, with an offer for a hot bath. However, he tarried at the front desk long enough to put in an inquiry after the Asbatols. This proved fruitful for they put him in the way of that elusive couple's direction. His body throbbed with livid anticipation as he sat down at the lobby desk and jotted off a hurried letter. It was brief and to the point, introducing himself and begging an interview for the following morning. Its tone was such that he felt the Asbatols would not dare refuse. This completed, he glanced at his watch. It wanted some minutes to ten. It was late, he could only hope the note would find them home. He summoned a link boy and, placing both a coin and the sealed letter in the lad's palm, he instructed him as to where to deliver it.

"And, lad . . . wait for their reply," he ended. This done, he thought once again of Cassie. Had it been her note that sent the Asbatols to Liverpool? Had it been a fit of jealousy that sent her flying from him yestereve—or fear of confronting the Asbatols? Hell and fire! He would make her answer.

Though pleasant, the day had been a long one for Cassie. She had spent nearly an hour after Lord Widdons' departure sipping tea with Mrs. Bamfield. They talked of many things though Cassie never allowed the conversation to become personal. The woman was naturally curious, but too polite to put any "tight" questions to Cassie, and she offered little other than her opinions on the mundane. She also declined Mrs. Bamfield's suggestion to retire to her room and catch up on her sleep.

"No, once I am fully awake 'tis nearly impossible for me to sleep again during the daytime. But, if you wouldn't mind, I think I should like to take a stroll about the gardens. I saw only the front courtyard from my room," she said, gazing out the small bowed window overlooking the side lawns of the house and the roses in bloom.

"Gracious me, my gardens are not very extensive. I am pleased that you wish to see them for I tend them myself," said Mrs. Bamfield proudly.

"Do you?" asked Cassie surprised. Somehow she could not picture the woman before her puttering about in the dirt.

"Indeed, yes. Oh, I have an excellent gardener . . . but I allow no one to play with my rose garden." She tilted her head. "You know, a walk among my roses may be just the sort of treat you need to pick up your spirits."

Soon afterward Cassie found her way outdoors through a rear exit and wandered about. The back lawns sloped some two hundred feet to the thicket, which seemed to go on for miles. There a narrow path started and, curious, Cassie made her way to it. It wound through the forest, and it was good, this walk. The scent of summer was in the air, and wild daffodils peeped up where the sun touched down through the trees. Great bushy ferns tickled her ankles—and she forced his black eyes out of her mind. She walked and walked but after a time gave up. 'Twas useless, the scent of him seemed everywhere as did the feel of his hands on her body. She hated him. And, she told herself, she would forget him—in time.

It was a bit later that she returned to the house, breathless and rosy cheeked from her exertion, and found there in Mrs. Bamfield's sitting room a young man.

He was in his early twenties. His height was no more than average, his uncovered Brutus curls were a golden shade of brown, and his eyes reminded Cassie of the woman who was her hostess, for they were just as alive and of the same bright blue.

"Oh, excuse me," murmured Cassie, stepping back, hoping she would be allowed to escape without further conversation.

He stared at her a full second, his eyes wide with surprise, and his words came out swiftly, bluntly, "But . . . who are you?"

Cassie blushed and felt the heat in her embarrassment, for she hated subterfuge, "I? I am Miss Farrington . . . Mrs. Bamfield's houseguest."

"Are you? But . . . devil a bit! When did you arrive? I was here until very late last evening, and I'll swear I didn't see you about," said the young man whose frankness had often been a source of controversy in his family.

"I arrived . . . after you left," she offered, stepping still further back toward the door.

"But m'mother never mentioned she was expecting anyone . . ." he said, frowning.

Cassie lost her sense of embarrassment simply because this was beginning to ruffle her quick temper. "Need she have?" returned Cassie on an austere note.

He looked at her then and remembered his manners. "Oh! So sorry! 'Tis my damnable inquisitive nature. I'm Guy Bamfield . . . your hostess's son," he said, coming forward, evidently about to take up her hand, "and most pleased to make your acquaintance." He ended by taking up her ungloved hand and giving it (much to her astonishment) a vigorous shake.

"It is also with pleasure . . ." started Cassie.

"You back, Guy?" came Mrs. Bamfield's voice from behind Cassie. "I thought surely I had packed you off to Liverpool." She was amused yet rather exasperated by the thought of Cassie watching her.

"And so I am, Mother, and so I am, but the devil is in it that after I left you last night I got word there was to be a *meet* this morning," he explained.

His mother's countenance took on a troubled expression. "Oh, no, Guy . . . you did not cancel your plans simply because . . ."

It was his turn to interrupt her. "No, no . . . been to it early this morning. Just thought I'd stop by and see if m'uncle sent you word when he would be back in Liverpool. Forgot to ask you last night."

"Oh. Well, as to your uncle, he stopped by last night . . . after you left . . ."

"Busy night!" interpolated her son, mischievously sending a look at Cassie who had taken up a seat in the background to watch their exchange.

"Hush now!" ordered his mama, "I was about to say that he left this morning for Liverpool and should be at Widdons' by afternoon tea. So do stop by and pay him a visit, he has been asking about you."

"Will do . . . after I have seen Mary Beth. I shall be putting up at the Grand, if you want me you have but to send word." He turned to Cassie, picking up his top hat from a nearby table and making her a slight bow. "Good-day to you, Miss Farrington. I hope you enjoy your stay with my illustrious mama. Don't let her bully you!" He ducked his mother's hand as he made his exit, leaving both women smiling at his back.

What he thought of Miss Farrington or her sudden appearance at his mother's house was left undisclosed. The truth was that Guy Bamfield thought very little about it indeed. He had other matters on his mind, and these kept his brows knit together on his journey into Liverpool.

Nathan Asbatol sat with his dove gray pantaloons crossed at the knees and looked at his guest with caution; what had this nobleman to do with him? He did not like it. When they had received the viscount's request for this interview, he had voiced his opinion to his wife, but she had felt it would not be wise to deny his lordship. She sat not far away from him now, playing with a short blond curl over her ear, her brown eyes watchful and intrigued by the man before them. The viscount was some ten years her junior but too attractive to leave go at that. She was well pleased with their decision to allow him admittance.

"Well, my lord, now that the genialities have been exchanged, perhaps we may get down to . . . if you will pardon my abruptness, the meat of the matter. Why are you here?"

260

"As my note indicated, Mr. Asbatol, you were recommended to me by the late Sir Charles Farrington," said the viscount, brushing at a white speck on the sleeve of his dark blue superfine.

"Er . . . yes, poor Charles . . . and just exactly how *did* he die?" put in Leila Asbatol, pushing herself forward on her chair.

The viscount smiled at her, caught the interest in her brown eyes, and thought here perhaps was an ally.

"It is a sad story, far too sad for such lovely ears. Frankly, had I known he was given over to such dejections, I would never have allowed him to bet the Grange or his ward."

"He lost the Grange and that cousin of his to you?" ejaculated Mr. Asbatol, somewhat surprised. "I had not heard that piece of news."

"Probably because of your . . . so hasty departure. However, 'twas the case . . . most pitiful indeed for the wretched man took his own life," said the viscount coolly.

"Never say you have taken Miss Farrington as your mistress?" interjected Leila. She thought it a very good jest indeed.

The viscount felt a sudden annoyance. For some unknown reason he did not wish Cassie discussed by these creatures. His voice was curt when it came. "No. I married Miss Farrington."

"Oh," said Leila thoughtfully. Too bad, but then a wife was no rival.

"But all this, though interesting, does not explain why you have chosen to come after me to Liverpool," said Asbatol, bringing things once again to the point.

"Sir Charles was aware of my . . . rather limited financial condition. We had discussed it quite thoroughly. You see, the family estates are all entailed. No mortgage can be had against them. At the same time I find myself without a sou—and have accumulated some rather heavy debts." He gazed at Nathan a long moment before continuing. "It may clarify things to advise you that I am something of a gamester. At any rate, my position in society allows me to travel freely among people who are amply endowed with funds . . . and . . . Are things becoming clearer?"

"No," said Asbatol, ever cautious.

"Very well," said the viscount, proceeding. "Some of these absurdly wealthy set have children whom they dote upon. Should anything occur to separate them from their spawn, they would do anything to be reunited. Are things unveiled to you yet?" asked the viscount in his blandest tones.

"But, my lord . . . what has all this to do with us?" returned Nathan, greed lighting in his eyes, yet wariness keeping him at bay.

"As I have mentioned, my family name is highly accepted amongst the *ton*—a far pinker set than Sir Charles knew. I am in a position to circulate, learn the daily routines, eccentricities of these people. For these efforts, I would expect a percentage of the rewards." It was suavely said.

"I think you mistake, my lord," said Asbatol.

"Come now, you are too cautious. Sir Charles told me all about the Linton boy. Very neat, indeed. As Charles is no longer available to carry on with his estimable work, it behooves you to align yourself with another partner. I am far more capable than the late Sir Charles, I do assure you."

Asbatol hesitated, but Leila moved in her chair. She sent a silencing glance toward her husband before rising and gliding closer to his lordship. Her ivory silk skirts rustled about her tall, thin frame until she came to a stop just inches away from his broad chest. Her brown lashes fluttered, and her voice was low, almost seductive. "How do you propose to start?"

Asbatol frowned but remained silent. The viscount smiled down at her, there was a hint in his black eyes that nearly stole her breath, and did in fact send a warm thrill through her veins.

"I intend to set up lodgings in Liverpool's finest quarter, and send out invitations to the *ton* for a rout. That should get things off, for as I have said, my name carries with it the usual intrigue. You have made the mistake of hitting only the quality. There are skirters . . . such as wealthy merchants, bankers . . . whose bourgeois inclinations make them even more frantic over their children. Well then, what do you say, Asbatol?"

Nathan pulled at his fat lower lip. "Hmmm, but . . . *if* one were to agree to such a thing . . . one would but pay . . . twenty-five percent of the income."

"Ha!" The viscount gave a snort. "You are not dealing with a stripling! You need me, my man. You need what I have to offer, and that is why you will pay me fifty percent."

"Outrageous!" returned Nathan, going red. "Sir Charles was getting but thirty percent . . ."

"Perhaps his lordship would settle for forty percent, Nathan. Let us not haggle," put in Leila, smiling sweetly at the viscount.

"Excuse me, madam, though I should like to do anything *you* ask, I am afraid I will not take less than fifty percent. You will both come to find that I will be most valuable to you—in many ways." Again that light in his eyes especially for her.

She sucked in air and the tingle of excitement he aroused in her swept away all better thought. A fancy to be held by him, lie beside him with his lips upon hers, suddenly flashed in her mind. She sparkled and turned to her husband.

"His lordship is a singular man, is he not, Nathan? We would do well to take him on."

"Very well, my dear. Your judgment in such matters is usually sound." He went to the viscount, hand outstretched and as Welford grasped it, he was shaken with revulsion. Though he smiled, he could not get the picture of Peter from his mind—Peter sentenced to death by this man! By God, he wanted revenge.

25

Lord Eric Widdons stood by his glass French doors. They overlooked a stretch of wide spacious lawns that veered off into some excellent riding trails. He had received an epistle nearly as soon as he had arrived at Widdons Hall and as the light grew dim outdoors he waited for the arrival of Viscount Welford. He sighed, thinking about the commitment he had made. It was a nasty business at best, but it had to be done and his sense of duty, a feeling that one must do more than pay lip service, had caused him to volunteer his services.

Oddly enough, he had put away these thoughts on his ride from his sister's home to Liverpool. He had no choice in the matter for all thoughts were shoved roughly aside to make room for the image of a spritely young woman with red-gold hair and flashing green eyes. Cassandra had won his interest with her unaffected ways and her fresh loveliness. She was the first to catch his real attention since the death of his wife some four years ago. But Cassie was a married woman and yet . . .

His fantasizing was rudely interrupted by his butler who entered the drawing room and announced in a dull monotone the advance of one Viscount Kirkby Welford. Lord Widdons turned round and smiled as he went forward, hand extended to welcome the tall, athletic young man. They were personally unknown to one another, though Widdons had often heard the viscount's name mentioned with some admiration in their common circles in London.

"How do you do, Welford . . . so good of you to make the trip out of town to Widdons Hall," said his lordship, giving the younger man a welcoming pat upon the shoulder. "I must confess I have only just arrived myself some hours ago and might have been tempted to postpone our meeting till the morrow had you wished me to come to you."

The viscount grinned. He had a knack of sizing up his fellow man quickly. The blue eyes before him were gentle, they hid little of the man's thoughts. There was a weakness to the chin—no out and outer here, but a good man nonetheless. Yes, he thought they would deal well together.

"I am spurred on by personal reasons, my lord," explained the viscount. He had gone from the Asbatol's to his hotel room where he had written his note to Widdons and had it taken over by a hotel servant. In the interim he had been vacillating between chagrin over his wife's disappearance and a consuming need for revenge against the Asbatols. He was in a strange temper, and it glinted in his black eyes.

Widdons noted a driving force about the man before him and was curious. He suggested graciously that as it was past tea time they indulge in a stronger refreshment.

"A glass of brandy might help," said the viscount, again grinning. There was a tact about this man that came through slowly. "No doubt Sidmouth has filled you in on all the details."

"Yes, but it would appear that things have changed since my meeting with Sidmouth in London. When we heard from you there you were in Bristol. In truth, I returned to Liverpool to tie up my affairs and make myself ready to join you in Bristol. I take it that is no longer the case."

"No. I had not realized from Sidmouth's missive that you were in London. He gave me your direction in Liverpool, and I simply assumed you were here. A lucky chance that you returned as the Asbatols have chosen to relocate in the vicinity," said the viscount dryly.

"But why, Welford? I mean, why would those dreadful creatures move their operation to Liverpool?"

"It seems they got word that things might not be comfortable for them in Bristol. All I know is that they received a letter, packed up, and have set themselves up in the heart of Liverpool. A most elegant establishment, I might add, which would tend to suggest that they have other sources of income besides the child hostages they have been trading!"

Widdons sighed, "I shall, of course, work closely with you, sir. My son remains with cousins in Scotland. Sidmouth assures me that he will in no way be in danger."

"Of course not!" returned the viscount at once. "His part is in name only." He put down his brandy glass. "My lord, I think now we had better discuss our future plans."

"Indeed, I suppose we must," sighed Lord Widdons.

For Cassie, that day, the next and still another were beginning to wear upon her vivacious spirit. Oh, at first she enjoyed the quiet repose, the time to dissolve her temper, but not for long was she suited to such ways. Mrs. Bamfield needed no aid in the running of her household, a modest establishment that took but a few hours of her time. The remainder of each day she received visitors, went walking or visiting herself. Cassie did not join her in these amusements, preferring to keep to herself. However, she was nearing the point of insufferable boredom and was therefore quite ready for Guy Bamfield's heady return.

It was on this third afternoon that the front doors of the Bamfield home were flung open to receive a dusty, bright-eyed young man. Cassie appeared from the library just in time to see him fling off his top hat landing it neatly on a chair and hear him ring out a peal.

"Mrs. Bamfield! I say . . . Mother . . . the prodigal son has returned!"

Cassie smiled as she went forward. "Mr. Bamfield, I am sorry, your mother is not at home. She is out visiting."

"Blast! Wanted to speak to her immediately," he sighed. "Oh well, I suppose you'll have to do."

She might have put up her chin had she not caught the smile in his eyes. "Well, sir, I must confess I have been pining to be of use to someone . . . so you are most welcome to my services." Her green eyes twinkled.

He caught his breath. "Egad, woman! If I were not in love already, I would have declared m'self smitten! And what an outrageous puss you are to be offering such things. . ."

She gasped. She had not meant anything saucy at all. He saw the blush come over her and laughed aloud. "Well, then . . . let us not be bantering about in the hall. Come, let's retire to the sitting room. . ." He turned to the butler who stood on in silent but paternal amusement. "Jones . . . have tea brought to us . . . and tell cook I'll take an extra helping of those special tarts she has such a way with. That's a good fellow." Again he turn to Cassie, taking her hand and pulling her along.

She liked him. He was a bright, merry boy, and he had come in time to cheer her day. They sat conversing on one topic after another until tea was brought in whereupon he fell to munching. But something was wrong. She sensed it in spite of his happy bravado. It was but an air he put forth to conceal his thoughts, she was sure of it!

"Mr. Bamfield . . . is there something wrong?"

"Yes. You should be calling me Guy! Everyone does, you know . . . and you are m'mother's guest . . ." He was smiling, but there was that in his eyes that arrested her attention.

"All right, Guy . . . but *something* is wrong . . ." she hesitated not wishing to intrude upon his privacy. "Some times it helps to talk about it."

He looked at her for a long moment, "Yes, there is a great deal wrong! I have come from Liverpool and have seen such poverty that cannot be described! And why? Because those in Parliament with the power to change such things will not listen!"

"What do you mean?" she returned, her brows drawing a frown.

"Where are you from, Cassandra?" he said, taking the liberty without getting her permission.

She smiled, he meant no insult, it was his nature to be forthright. "From Dorset, near the coast," she answered quietly.

"There you see, you are innocent to the troubles of the Yorkshire and Highland weavers!"

"But what has this to do with you? You are a landowner," she said, opening her eyes wide.

"Am I not a Christian? My brother's keeper? Must I stand by and do nought when I see children die in the streets for lack of clothing, shelter and food?"

She blushed. He sounded very much like a radical on a pedestal, but his words rang true to her own heart. However, she had always felt it was beyond her ability to do aught about such things. Here was this young man spurting fire . . . but what could he do? She posed just such a question to him. He answered by getting to his feet and shoving aside the tea table with some passion.

"Do? Why, everything within my power! Dorset, you say? Well, even in Dorset they must have heard of the Orator Hunt?" He did not wait for her answer but continued along the same vein. "He leads the less fortunate to rebel against their strife. We hold meetings, we draw up grievances, and we bring in numbers to our packs so that Parliament will stand up and take notice!"

"Has it answered?" she asked quietly, but concerned.

Suddenly the fire seemed to leave his eyes. He sank down upon the sofa beside her, and his hand rumpled his curls. "No . . . not yet! We aristocracy are so afraid of losing what we have that we would rather people starve to death than give them a meal. But it will change." He got up and walked away then, and she stared at his back. It was time to change the subject. His mother had spoken very little about the girl her son wanted for wife. Cassie was curious.

"Your mama tells me you are engaged to be married. I believe the lady's name is . . . Mary Beth?"

He turned around and smiled. "Aye, now . . . her name is Mary Beth." It was simply said, but it nearly reduced Cassie to giggles. There was a tease in her voice as she said, "And she is the sun, the moon, and the stars!"

"That she is," he said gravely, unaware of the laughing eyes.

"Then you have but to name the day."

He sat down beside her on the sofa, sighing heavily.

"If her family has anything to say to it, that day will never come!" He hung his head between his hands in the most dejected way.

My goodness, thought Cassie, he was certainly an up-and-down young man. "But I don't understand. Never say they object to *you?*"

"Aye, that they do! I'm a radical. They are staunch Tories!"

She looked at him a long moment. "And your Mary Beth—what of her political notions?"

"Bless her heart! She is for the people, the downtrodden, the lowly, the sickly . . ."

"Yes, yes," chuckled Cassie. "I can quite see she is a radical as well. But then there is no real obstacle in your path."

"No, you don't understand. If it was just that . . . but there is more," he cried tragically.

"Ah, a skeleton in the closet?" she was near to laughing, for he looked quite melodramatic.

He smiled ruefully. "Were it that and I titled and encumbered with wealthy lands . . . they wouldn't give a fig!"

"But I don't understand. Surely . . . you are not in straitened circumstances?"

"Do not let m'mother's cozy establishment fool you,

269

Miss Farrington. Though I am comfortably endowed with a living, I am but the son of a second son. Hardly in line to the title. My uncle you have seen and will admit—thankfully—he is a healthy sort, and at any rate my cousin stands between me and the title on that side. So you see?"

"Only too well! But is Mary Beth's family so high in the instep?"

"As to that, her father is a lord, but without a sou to his name. In addition, he has four girls to see married. Mary Beth is the eldest."

"Oh my!"

"Exactly so," he said dolefully.

"Upon my soul!" said a merry voice at their backs. "So this is what you've been up to? Hiding away the most beautiful girl in all of London!"

Cassie and Guy turned round to find a tall, angular young man of some twenty-eight years with a head full of ginger-rust for hair. His face was lean, his cheekbones well defined and sprinkled with distinctive freckles as was his straight aristocratic nose. His eyes were indistinctly gray and framed in that same unusual shade of ginger rust. On the whole, he looked puckish and somehow attractive as well.

"Egad! You devil! How did you get in here unannounced, Lyle!" demanded Guy, but Cassie could see they were friends.

"Don't blame me!" laughed Lyle coming further into the room. "Your butler wasn't on duty. Off somewhere on some errand, I gather. The door was answered by one of those sweet little housemaids of yours. Simply made the lass understand I knew the way . . ."

He had by this time brought himself up before Cassie, who sat looking up at him curiously. Before she knew what he was about he had taken her hand and was brushing his thin lips lightly against its delicate skin. His eyes twinkled naughtily, and she had the distinct sensation that here was a ladies' man.

"Your very obedient servant, ma'am," he was saying,

270

simultaneously swinging his booted toe into his friend's foot.

"What the . . ?" started Guy, then catching his older friend's glance. "Oh, quite . . . Miss Farrington . . . Mr. Lyle Stanton. Though we share lodgings . . . I hesitate to call him my friend . . . and what's more . . . don't you be making any mistake about him. He is a cad! 'Love 'em and leave 'em Stanton,' they call him in town!" chuckled Guy.

"You dog!" rounded Lyle. "Don't be believing the puppy, Miss Farrington!"

Cassie laughed, but something was bothering her. She didn't like this business of being introduced as *Miss* Farrington. She was after all a married woman, and it was very deceitful . . . which in turn was wicked of her! She determined at the first opportunity to tell the truth of it to Mrs. Bamfield and her son.

Guy interrupted, saving Cassie the need to reply to this sally. "But, Lyle, what brings you here?" Then aside to Cassie, "He and m'mother don't get along."

"Have a meet starting in an hour's time. I'm to be the Speaker of the day. When your man came by with your things, knew you were back and thought you would want to be there."

"By Jove, yes!" He turned to Cassie. "These meets of ours. We're preparing the poor souls for the orators' projected meet in August! Lyle, Sam Bamford, myself, and a few others have been touring the area giving speeches, organizing . . ." he stopped on an idea. "Egad, Cassie! Just had a thought! Would you be interested in attending the meet today? I'll grant you Lyle here ain't the best . . ." he was grinning at his friend, "but he is showy enough."

"Why, yes . . . yes, I think I should like that. Very much . . ." she got to her feet, allowing Mr. Stanton a view of her excellent proportions. "If you will but give me a few moments to change into my riding habit?"

"Of course, Miss Farrington. We'll have our horses brought round in the meantime," said Lyle.

"I'll have m'mother's mare saddled for you . . ." started Guy.

"Nonsense! I have my own stallion, and he has been wallowing about in your stables much in need of exercise!" returned Cassie as she moved out of the room. She had the satisfaction of seeing a look of some surprise cross over each man's face before they fell into excited conversation at her back.

These same days passed for the viscount, however, with little of quiet or boredom! His daylight hours were spent in tremendous exertion, some anger, and surges of bitterness. His nights, in a great deal of frustration. He had, though, in spite of these uncomfortable sensations, some success in his efforts regarding the Asbatols' affairs! Through diligence and devious means, he had discovered that Nathan and Leila Asbatol had some mysterious connection to a bordello known to the initiated as Nancina's. This, after following the seedy couple to the bordello's brightly painted doors. Mentally, he marked a decision to give the place a call, and see just what *their* visit there could mean. And there was still more. He had followed Nathan to the docks and was much taken aback to discover the man meeting a ship that had just arrived from Ireland. Just what it all portended he could not make out, but it did not sway his determination to discover their purpose.

Nonetheless, these minor successes did little to mollify his temper. His days were sickened by the nearness of the two people he hated above all others. They had sent his young brother to his death, and he wanted to lay hands upon them. Waiting it out was a burden he found difficult to live with. And Leila . . . he flirted outrageously with her, for she could be of use in her own ultimate end, but the sight and scent of her nearly drove his fingers to her neck.

And what of Cassie? Rarely did a moment pass that did not bring a vision of her to haunt him. He had been sending Chips into the countryside daily—each time in a different direction. Though the faithful Highlander inquired after a beauty with hair the shade of cinnamon-gold, looked into near-by stables for signs of a flame-tinted chestnut stallion and a deformed urchin, he came up empty-handed. It was driving the viscount into the boughs! And thus, what of Cassie? What part had she in Peter's end? He had *that* ever nagging at him. He had that to discover.

His letter to Dorset inquiring after her had been sent but it was far too soon to expect a reply. There was nought he could do but double his efforts by sending Chips farther south toward Shrewsbury, and himself comb first all the westerly towns and then the easterly.

Still, above all these things were the questions that plagued his mind. What was Cassie doing? With whom did she spend her days . . . her *nights?* And was she safe from harm? This last irked him far more than all the rest. Was she all right? It was almost maddening! To think, *he,* Viscount Welford, was bedeviled by a wench!

26

Cassie had accomplished two things on her ride to Bodwin's Field to hear Lyle Stanton's speech. The first she did by taking Guy aside and hurriedly explaining that she wished to be introduced (should the need arise) merely as Miss Cassandra. She further took him into her confidence and advised him that she was married. To this he professed much astonishment and demanded further explanation on the spot. However, she stalled him, saying only that she would tell him all in private. To this he agreed.

The second accomplishment was the retaining of much information regarding the cause for which they were fighting; and this in spite of the fact that disjointed sentences, with much fire and smoke, were flung at her awed head. Guy she found nearly ferocious, as is the raving of a youth with a cause. Lyle Stanton was far more tempered. It was Lyle's mention of the Corn Laws that really peaked her interest, for she had heard them mentioned when she was on board the *Sweet Mary* with Jack.

"Do you realize . . ." said Guy earnestly, "that the handloom weavers are near to working for nothing? Why . . . Good Lord, their wages have dropped from twenty-five shillings a week to *five* . . . 'tis inhuman!" he ended in disgust.

"I can't believe that to be true," said Cassie shocked.

"Believe it," said Lyle calmly. "The poor devils in Maybole get even less . . . they work for half-a-crown a week!"

"But that is quite impossible!" ejaculated Cassie, "Surely no one can live on that?"

"But they do not live!" returned Guy passionately. "They exist! And that just barely!"

"But, these meetings . . . what can they accomplish?" cried Cassie, distressed and as always wanting immediate action.

"To bring Parliament to their senses. They must be aware now that the people are tired of being trod upon. We meet and give word through these mass meetings that we will not stand for such shabby treatment any longer," answered Guy.

"But, Guy . . . you incite protest without the force to back it up. The government must retaliate with repression," frowned Cassie.

"They dare not! There is revolution in the air, girl. Oh . . . do excuse me, Cassie, but I get excited . . ." Her expression told him that once again he was shouting. "You see, they daren't take a forceful step for fear of ticking off a revolution."

"Nonsense!" said Lyle disgustedly. It was the first time Cassie saw him driven to heat. "They have nought to fear from us because too many like *you* rule these affairs!"

"What do you mean?" asked Cassie, for Guy had gone sullen.

"He means . . ." said Guy with some show of contempt, "that he would have the mobs *armed!*"

"And you do not agree?"

"How can I? How can any of us sanction such a thing?" asked Guy, somewhat shocked.

"I cannot answer that one for I have never been to a meeting. I will reserve my opinion until afterward."

"You will see that I am right. What we need is a movement that appeals to the men who make up the ruling body in Parliament. Arming the masses—which would be economically unfeasible—would only serve to alienate that group!" returned Guy.

"Perhaps . . . and perhaps a compromise would serve to shock them into caring!" offered Cassie quietly.

They had by that time reached an open field, somewhat enclosed by thickets on all but one side. In the center a raised platform had been hastily erected. There several people now stood, expounding their views to the gathering crowd.

Cassie slid off her horse and turned to find Lyle smiling down at her. "You should have allowed me to assist you to dismount . . . now at least allow me to see to the horses."

"Of course," she said feeling the blush steal to her cheeks. She watched him take the three horses off but then Guy was persistently tugging at her hand.

"I say Cassandra . . . about your being married . . .?"

"Shh . . . not now!" she warned.

Again he frowned, and more deeply still when Lyle returned from tethering the horses at the outskirts of the field and took up Cassie's arm.

"Come . . . I want you to have a place of honor beside me on the dais."

"Oh, I couldn't . . ."

"But you must," he chuckled. "Surely you don't mean to mingle with the mob?"

She laughed somewhat sardonically, "My dear sir! How in the name of everything you have been expounding to me can you still be so proud?"

"But Cassie . . . you miss the point," interpolated Guy. "We ain't saying *they* are our *equals!* Nonsensical thing to think! What we are saying is that they deserve a decent wage, a fair hire for their work. They are humans . . . not animals! But even so. . ."

"Not worthy our company?" She was annoyed by this, but there was no time for an answer. They had already stepped upon the platform where Guy found her a seat and Lyle took up the bullhorn.

Then suddenly the crowd of ill-dressed, hungry, noisy creatures went silent. Cassie looked down upon their faces and saw their eyes. The eyes . . . they stood out as one! Enlarged in bony bodies, all looking at the man before them with something of hope. It was what kept them going. And then Lyle's voice, mesmerizing them all. He started first with a harangue on government, calling on those in power to listen to the lament of the poor and, without realizing it, Cassie found herself caught up in his discourse. She gazed at Lyle's earnest profile and felt his greatness in that moment. However, she glanced at Guy and found him frowning. It bothered her but for the passing of a moment, for suddenly Lyle was a being of vibrant energy. He was shaking his fist, speaking impassioned words.

"We fought on the continent for twenty years! We fought the French . . . giving our sons, our brothers . . . our fathers . . . for what? Was it for Liberty . . . or against it? We have supported despotism under the guise of legitimacy! We have allowed the indolent aristocracy to take food from our mouths . . . subjecting the friends of freedom to spies, jails, and bastilles! And *they* . . . they would tell us, *hold fast by the laws*! But the Corn Laws are *unjust!* We call on the laws to end the squalor and hunger! We call on the laws to *represent the people* . . . and brothers and sisters, WE ARE THE PEOPLE!"

He was cheered heartily before he was allowed to resume, and then it was to call down rebukes upon men like Lord Sidmouth for not hearing their cries. " 'Tis noblemen such as Sidmouth who madden the spirits and the patience of the poor . . . and if ever a convulsion comes in this country, they will see their houses burnt over their high heads!"

He was cheered again and urged to go on, and then it was that Cassie saw him, really saw him. It was in that moment that she understood the look in Guy's eyes. Lyle Stanton was an opportunist! Something of a rogue, too!

His scampish air had drawn her interest but, unlike Jack Rattenbury, he had no principles. He was here because it served his purpose. He told these people what they wanted to hear, that the rich nobility were to blame for their troubles. It was partly true, but he put himself above them all —and for what, wondered Cassie . . . for what . . . power? She turned and met Guy's glance, and it was then they became fast friends, for an understanding passed between them as he whispered his acknowledgment.

"Yes, Cassie . . . that is Lyle's way. But never mind, it serves well enough."

"But, Guy, it will not answer in the end. Such speeches of unreasonable passion burn the spirits and rarely produce anything lasting!"

"He wants rebellion . . . less than but something of the French nature . . ."

"And look how they ended, the French! With a Bourbon on the throne!" she interrupted disgustedly.

"Aye. But it brings in the crowds . . . aligns them with the Orator Hunt, and as long as they turn to the Orator . . . all will be well," he answered on a sigh.

She said nothing to this but as she gazed about her she knew it was going to take more, much more. It was going to take organization. It was going to take *money*—and training, for if the crowds were to be more than just another savage mob, they needed to know how to behave *en masse*. And she had every intention of getting behind the movement.

Lord Widdons paced to and fro in his sister's sitting room. He had arrived only a few moments after Cassie's departure with Guy and Lyle. His sister watched him curiously but said nothing to his rather odd behavior. She hadn't seen her brother behave so . . . excitedly in many years.

"Just what sort of affair did Guy take her to?" he asked, his sandy brows drawing together.

"One of those dreadful political things of his," answered his sister lightly and on something of a chuckle. "Now calm yourself, Eric, the chit will be here soon. I suppose you fancy yourself in love with her?"

He turned sharply and had every intention of denying this but said instead, "You are an incurable romantic!"

"I? No! what fustian to be sure! *I*—a romantic? The only romantic in our family has always been you. 'Twas so with poor darling Delia. I thought you would die of a broken heart when you lost her. I know *I* never fretted so for my Henry!"

"Delia was . . . special. And the boy . . . he gave me reason enough to go on," said his lordship quietly.

"I know, dear . . . and only brought it up to show you how very vulnerable you are . . ."

He raised his brow. "I am a man quite capable of making my own decisions, Isabelle."

"So you are. Does that mean . . . you have made one?"

"I am also not a heady person. How can I have done so when I scarcely know the child?" Cassie was a married woman, yet he could think of nothing but making love to her. "But all these questions? Does it mean you have taken the girl in some dislike?" he asked frowning.

"Oh, gracious, no! She is a dear girl—something of a child in many ways—but more a woman in others! However, she is not a *miss* . . . is she?"

"Whatever do you mean?" he asked, surprised at her, wondering how she came to such a correct conclusion. Really, at times he thought Isabelle omniscient.

"I can't help feeling that the child is grieving over a broken love affair . . . and as I said, there is the blush of womanhood about her. She lacks a maidenly air."

"If you must know—though 'tis a confidence I'd rather have Cassandra tell you—yes, she is running away from her husband, a veritable brute . . ."

"She told you he is a brute?"

"Well . . . no . . . but why else?"

"A lover's quarrel perhaps?" suggested Isabelle.

He didn't like the notion. "That is impossible. A dutiful wife does not run away in the middle of the night. Besides, she told me that theirs was a marriage of convenience—not love!"

"Hallo, Uncle! You here?" said Guy opening the door and stepping in.

"You can see that he is, dear," said Mrs. Bamfield. "But where is Cassandra?"

"Went upstairs to freshen up before dinner, and don't mind telling you I am ravenous!" he said, giving his uncle's hand a hearty shake. And then much in his own blunt manner, "But whatever brings you here, uncle?"

"And since when does my only and very dear brother need an excuse to visit me?" laughed his mother coming to his lordship's rescue.

"Oh, as to that . . . well . . . he doesn't do it more than . . . well, what I mean is . . . he was just here!" floundered Guy.

"Lord Widdons!" exclaimed Cassie coming into the room. A bright smile curved her luscious lips for she was genuinely pleased to see his lordship. She had gone up only to wash and brush her hair, but as Widdons gazed upon her, he thought there was no lovelier woman in all England.

He went forward to take both her hands and put them to his lips, and it was then that Guy, watching him, understood. The younger man sent a quick look to his mother who acknowledged it but gave away nothing. Slowly, very slowly, and almost inaudibly, Guy released a sound of wonderment.

Viscount Welford was at that moment some miles east of Liverpool searching for word or sign of his wife. She was nowhere to be found and, when the viscount returned to his hotel in Liverpool two days later, Chips had similar information. There, too, no letter from Dorset had arrived. Perhaps he was being foolish, wasting his time searching the countryside. She had probably returned to the Grange. Where else would she go? Better to wait for the mail to arrive. He hadn't seen Widdons in three days, and it was time they talked. The viscount needed assistance. He had to find suitable lodgings and get a list of the *haut ton* that led society's fools in Liverpool. Widdons's secretary could help him with both. It was too late to start out that afternoon, but he made plans to do it the very next morning.

What a fine morning it turned out to be! Lord Widdons remarked upon it as he led Cassie along the wooded path. He knew he was faulting in his duty. He had sent a note around to the viscount before they had departed for his sister's home, advising Welford that he would be back at Widdons Hall this very morning. However, he had been unable to leave. He had taken one look at Cassie at the breakfast table and knew he just couldn't leave this day!

She was all fire and glory this morning, talking about her plans to set up a collection for the movement. She and Guy had decided to distribute the printed matter Mr. Stanton had managed to come by at the festivities that afternoon. And somehow he had said he would escort her. To this Guy readily agreed, for he had an errand elsewhere, but he would be sure to find them there.

Eric Widdons had decided to have Cassie—any way he could get her! He had been gaining ground these two past days, he was sure. Hadn't she admitted to Isabelle her married state . . . her desire for release? Didn't that mean something? He brushed away a branch, allowing her to pass through before following, but she waited for him to fall into step beside her. They went on, but as they reached the end of the walk he pulled back and she turned halfway to eye him.

"Cassandra," he said quietly, his voice low, "we have talked about many things, but there is one subject we *must* discuss. . ."

"Yes, I know," she sighed, " 'tis time I made plans to leave."

"That is not what I had in mind. Not exactly, for you know very well you can go on here indefinitely," he returned hastily. His ungloved hand held her elbow, and unconsciously he was drawing her closer.

She laughed. It was a bright sound though it held little mirth. "That is, though most kind, quite

281

impossible . . . and, I might add, somewhat absurd!"
Again the sigh. "No, my lord, just think how ridiculous
'twould be if houseguests were to go about the countryside
taking such unfair advantage of their hosts and hostesses!"

" 'Tis you, darling, that is being absurd! *You* are not
taking advantage . . . I am!"

The "darling" bothered her, but she brushed it aside. He
was a sophisticate. It meant nothing. So, she answered on
a gay note, "Now how am I to understand such logic?"

The nearness of her was driving him to *point non plus*!
He was losing control. Her lips invited as did the full
curves of her breasts swelling above the square neckline of
her summer gown. He could not answer her as his hands
went to her waist, and only her name escaped his lips as
he lowered his lips to hers.

She was not taken aback by it. She did not stop him. He
was an attractive man. Not in the wild, dashing manner of
the viscount, whose address drew the strongest of her emotions. No, this man whose kiss felt warm and yet passive
compelled her to respond to his gentleness, his kindness.
But that wasn't quite enough. She put up her hand between them. He stopped immediately.

"Forgive me, love," he begged at once lest he frighten
her.

Now what to do? He was her benefactor. He was a
good man, promising sincerity, security . . . yet it wouldn't
serve. She handled it by choosing to ignore it, which was,
of course, the wrong move. He took her want of chastisement to mean approval. What else could a lady in her
position do to exhibit her approbation without seeming
forward?

"My lord," she breathed, her eyes gratefully turning to
the woman coming toward them. "Here comes your sister.
Do let us drag her with us to that balloon ascension
today!" she said, hoping this would dispel any tension between them.

He was a patient man. Perhaps, he thought, it would
serve to make Cassie more at ease, and so they could become even closer. "Yes, indeed!" he agreed at once. "Isa-

belle, we have decided between us that we shan't take no for an answer!"

His sister, loaded with a basket of flowers, smiled benignly. She had seen them on the threshold of the garden. It would not do! Cassie was a married woman, and already the servants were talking.

"Won't you?" she quizzed. "I am so glad, as that makes us quite in accord with each other. I have no intention of giving you a negative answer, you see . . . but to what have I agreed?"

"Balloons in flight!" laughed Cassie.

"Oh, dear! Sounds dreadful! I warn you . . . the thing is bound to be an awful squeeze. But never mind, we shall make the best of it." He smiled and turned back to the house, ending their walk.

27

Just as Lord Widdons discovered the honey sweetness of Cassie's lips, Viscount Welford arrived at Widdons's doorstep.

He stood there, not yet entering the hall, because he had just been advised by the butler that his lordship was still away from home.

"Drat the man!" said the viscount softly to himself. Then noting the shocked expression upon the butler's drawn face, he relaxed, smiling ruefully. "Pray then, his man of business is no doubt at home. You may take me to him at once."

"Of course, my lord. If you will follow me."

In the stables, Chips proceeded to make himself at home. He smiled at the two young livery boys working in the stalls, and gave them a friendly greeting before he began inspection of the horses that stood at the other end of the carriage house. "Fine piece of flesh and blood his lordship has there!"

"What? Aye they be good nuff . . . but they be nought next to his high steppers!"

"High steppers is it?" laughed Chips, amused at the boy's puffing.

"Aye!" cut in the lanky fellow halting his work and eying Chips full, "better than the blood ye brought!"

Now the lad had gone too far! Chips was fully aware that the horse the viscount had bought for him after his lady absconded with his own was not up to par, but the viscount's steed was prime blood indeed, and so he would have this stripling know.

"Go on now! I'll have none of yer mucky pride! Wot ye know of the warld I could balance on me pinky! Mooncalf—to be talkin' to yer elders in sech a way!"

The boy shuffled his feet somewhat abashed but tried to regain his position. "M'maister's blood be a sight though . . . 'tis no bammin' ye I be."

"Aye. That's truth enough," said the other lad coming down from the lofts.

Chips eyed the fellow who was somewhat older and broader than the first fellow. "Well, I dinna heerd nobbut say different! I but had a fancy to know where they be?"

"Wi' tha maister is where," said the first youth, plumping down upon a pile of straw evidently ready to be friendly, for he proceeded to snigger in his cupped hand.

"Wot makes the lad laugh so?" inquired Chips.

"Nought, he be daft is all," said the other boy.

"Daft is it? 'Taint me be the one that 'as a tech of neeght in the 'ead."

"Who then?" asked Chips curiously, but only idly so.

The older boy put up his hand. "Don't pay the noddy no mind," upon which he glared at the younger boy. Chips waited, hoping for more, but the youth had indeed decided silence would be best.

"So then, his lordship be from home is it? The viscount, he won't like that. Had a note from his lordship assurin' him he'd be in by now . . ."

"Well, the maister, he canna be blamed . . ." offered

the youth in defense of his employer. "'Tis a woman's doin' . . ."

Chips raised a brow. "Do tell!"

"Ye be blabbin' out of turn!" snapped the elder. However, he too had taken up a sitting position in the straw.

"Aw, now, go on lads. Wot? Am I a woman to be goin' and openin' m'mummer to every passer-by? Ye have a tale to wile away the hour. Give over, do, and lets 'ave a time of it."

The older one considered this. "Well, it do be a tale . . . breathes like somethin' ye won't believe!"

"Well then?" remarked Chips.

Lord Widdons had not imagined things would turn out as they did. To the balloon ascension they went, he, Isabelle, and lovely Cassie. But the ride in his open phaeton was the only time he spent with her, and then separated by Isabelle, who somehow managed to get in between the pair. Once they arrived at the open grounds and viewed the brightly ornamented balloon, Cassie was lost to him.

For this piece of work, he had his nephew to thank, and he silently began to feel encumbered with relatives. Lyle Stanton and Guy hailed them as he tooled his rig into position. They were loaded down with single-sheet leaflets as they approached. Lyle shoved his stack into Guy's arms, reached up after giving a perfunctory greeting to Lord Widdons and Mrs. Bamfield, and caught Cassie by her trim waist, bringing her to earth.

"Good gracious! What a load you have!" exclaimed she as she fingered the pile in Guy's arms.

"Fiend seize you, Lyle! Take your portion back!" complained Guy.

Cassie laughed. "Here, give some to me . . ."

It was the last Lord Widdons heard or saw of Cassie for the next hour. She went off into the crowd, smiling and pleasantly handing out her sheets of political ravings to anyone who would accept them. Finally, the last of these distributed, she sighed and looked round. There, a merry pair of gray eyes lit upon her.

286

"All done, pretty girl?" said Lyle Stanton.

"All done. I see you are, too."

"Yes, so we are free to go and watch the ascension. I heard someone say the crazy fellow was about to cut the ropes!"

"Really? How exciting! But however will we get through these press of people?" she said frowning, for from her present location there was little chance they would see much until the balloon was well into the air.

He took her gloved hand. "Now aren't you glad you have me at your side?"

"I shall let you know about that," she returned.

He laughed aloud and Cassie could not help—in spite of what she believed he was—being attracted to the man. There was something very exciting about him, and she wondered if the attraction she felt could make her forget a pair of black eyes.

Both armed and eased by the information Widdons's man was able to supply him, the viscount requested a lackey to hail Chips. This done, he stepped outside, pulling on his riding gloves and settling his top hat rakishly upon his head. It was a warm day with a scent of spring flowers in the breeze. The languid, sensuous breeze brought thoughts of Cassie to him, and he frowned.

Chips, leading both steeds, appeared and something about his expression caught the viscount's interest.

"Eh? What is it, ole boy? You look as though you've just stumbled upon a horde of gold!"

"Mayhap I did . . . depending on how ye value her ladyship," said the groom softly. "But not 'ere, m'lord. There be ears about," he said, indicating the gardener working diligently among the flower beds not very far away.

The viscount glanced at him sharply but said nothing as he mounted. The two men left the Widdons house taking the drive at a brisk pace. However, it was not long before the viscount slowed his horse and allowed his groom to draw up beside him.

"Now, Chips, if you will, what the deuce are you talking about?"

"I could be wrong aboot this, m'lord, but it do sound much like yer lady . . . considering her nature . . ."

"Chips!" snapped the viscount.

"Aye, I be gettin' to the raight of it. The two lads in his lordships' stables . . . now they have this second hand, they do, as they weren't there that night . . ."

"Which night?"

"The night ye scared off m'lady . . ."

The viscount glared but decided to ignore this remark. "Proceed!"

"Well, it happens his lordship were on his way to Liverpool, from London, ye see, when jest before his coach reaches the Shrewsbury turnabout, out pops these toby coves, their barking irons lit by the moon. Well, the driver jest pulled up short, not knowin' what else he could do when faced with the very divil himself! Though it seems to me I'd of thought. . ."

"Chips!" admonished the viscount, "get to the point!"

"I be doin jest that! Now . . . where was I . . . aye, then all heads turned about for they was set upon by what they thought was the Kings men! But—beadles never do show up when they be needed. Dim-witted these coves must be . . ." he caught the look in the viscount's black eyes and cleared his throat before dropping this line of speech and picking up where he knew the viscount would wish, ". . . aye, but were no runners and . . . no light bobs! 'Twere a *woman* and a slip of a twisted lad! Though the bridle-culls didn't know that when they run off!"

"By God! She is capable of anything!" breathed the viscount. "What more have you, Chips?"

"Widdons . . . he took this woman . . . and her tiger to his sister's home in Whitchurch."

"He took her there? But . . . that is where he is now . . ."

"Aye," said Chips, avoiding his employer's eyes, but noting all the same the change of colors that flooded the viscount's cheeks.

In a matter of seconds, Kirkby suffered several emotions, all conflicting. Relief because he believed he had at last discovered her whereabouts; anger because she was under another man's protection; jealously for the same reason, and a burning desire to get to her at once!

"M'lord, I noticed a fingerpost on the way here. There be a road that connects with . . ."

"No, Chips. Not yet. I want to fetch the coach and retrieve my precious lady in style!" His torturous longing to lay hands on his wife was superseded only by good sense. Widdons could not know that she was married, and if he did, he did not know to whom. Of this, the viscount was certain. It would take tact and diplomacy to retrieve Cassie from the man without causing a scandal. To Widdons he would say . . . a lover's spat . . . a jealous wife . . . and it would be accepted. But Cassie . . . he would have to plan just how he would force her hand, for she would not come willingly with him. He would plan it all out on his way to Whitchurch. Bamfield . . . yes, that was the name Widdons's secretary had mentioned.

Lyle surprised Cassie by moving away from the center of the field where the great balloon was situated. He led Cassie toward the north woods, and she pulled his hand, holding him back. "Lyle Stanton! Just where do you think we are going?"

"Want a view of James Sadler's balloon, don't you, love?"

"Yes, but how do you suppose I shall get one from there?" she said, pointing.

"Wait and see. Don't you trust me, love?"

"No! And . . . you mustn't call me love." She hesitated. "I am a married woman," she said finally, incurably honest to the last.

He chuckled, "I know."

"You know?" she gasped, "Never say Guy . . .?"

He took her third finger beneath the white glove, touching the thin gold band that lay hidden. "You should have taken this off, love."

"Oh!" she said quietly. Somehow she had been unable to bring herself to it.

"Now don't be looking so down, sweetheart. It doesn't mean a thing to me. As a matter of fact . . ."

He never got to finish for there was a round of squealing and applause from the crowd at their backs, and Cassie spun round to see the deep-bellied galley of the balloon tilt sidewise as the ropes were set free.

"Hurry, Lyle," she breathed excitedly.

He brought her to his objective, a huge boulder. He jumped nimbly to the top and then reached down to aid her up. She set her foot in a groove of the huge rock and then found herself neatly protected by his arm. There was a moment in which she felt his eyes on her, the twinkle replaced by something darker though she pulled away and sat down. He excited her, this man . . . but he was wrong—it was wrong. He sat beside her and pointed out the sandbags attached to the balloon's boat-shaped basket,

"They will let them drop to gain altitude. Lord, listen to them scream!" he chuckled over the sound of jumping, waving, excited people.

"Oh, but it is thrilling, Lyle," she said breathlessly.

He looked at her lovely profile beside him. "That it is, sweetheart," he said, meaning something totally different. "Is this the first you've seen?"

"No, I saw another some nine years ago—with my parents and brother . . ." she said slowly. It was terrible to think of it now for they were gone. Never again would they share such excitement, and the thought made her realize how very alone in the world she was.

"Where are they . . . your family?" he asked curiously.

"Dead . . . and I don't want to speak of it," she said gravely.

"And your husband?" he pursued another road.

" 'Tis a stupid story," she answered curtly.

"Tell it to me anyway," he answered on a laugh.

"Oh, Lyle . . . I could say he was something of a fiend, and I ran away from him. But it isn't that altogether. You see, he didn't want to marry me. We were forced to it . . ."

"What made you run away from him?"

"I . . . I don't want to speak of it."

"Who is this shabby fellow?"

"He isn't shabby at all!" she snapped before she realized what she was about.

Lyle's thin rusty brow went up. "Oh?"

"What I mean is . . . he had his reasons for what he did . . . and I have mine!"

"What is your married name, Cassandra?"

"Why do you wish to know?"

"Because I have a strong hunch you bear a title and, if you do, it is important."

"Why?"

"Devil fly away with you, Lyle! Here is m'uncle madder than Ajax, looking for Cass this way and that!" shouted Guy at their feet. "Come down, I say . . . Lyle!"

"Hush, Guy, just look . . . it's lifting!" cried Cassie, pointing at the spread of yellow and blue cloth. It rose into the sky, and the sound of the crowd was almost deafening as it took flight. Cassie and the two men beside her seemed riveted with awe as they watched it grow smaller until at last it was lost from sight.

Guy remembered his errand and turned an admonishing finger upon them. "Now, Cass, come down, do, before m'uncle has m'head. He don't like Lyle. M'mother don't either, for that matter, and damn!—excuse me—I won't be blamed for this one!"

Cassie laughed and gave her hand to Guy as she jumped from her height. "There . . . no harm done," she said before turning to Lyle. "Will I see you later, sir?"

"You may count on it, love!" he returned before audaciously blowing her a kiss.

Guy frowned at him, took Cassie's arm, and hastily led her away. "Mustn't take him seriously, you know," he said gravely.

"Mustn't I?" she sallied.

"No, and don't be laughing at me, chit! I ain't blind," he snapped.

"Stripling!" she countered. "He is a charming scamp of a man! But no knight in shining . . . and well I know it for *I* am no fool, I do assure you!"

"Maybe not, but you are a woman, and there is never any saying what a woman might do! Forever falling in love with just the sort you shouldn't! And Cassie, mark me, Lyle Stanton is the wrong sort. Besides, hang it, girl . . . *you are married!*"

"How dreadful you are to remind me!" she retorted amiably, "but, sorry to say . . . yes, I am!" He looked so shocked that she was forced into a fit of wicked mirth, and it was thus that Lord Widdons received her into his waiting phaeton.

"My dear, whatever has this boy been saying to send you into such laughter?" he asked.

"I have offended his sense of the proprieties! But never mind," she waved it away as she greeted Mrs. Bamfield with a hug. "Hallo, have I kept you waiting? Was it not a marvelous ascension?"

"No, dear, you have not kept us waiting." She turned to Guy. "Do you join us for dinner, son?"

"No, I'm off immediately with Lyle for Liverpool," he answered.

"Liverpool?" asked Cassie surprised. "But why?"

"Sam Bamford is coming there in a few days to give a speech. He wants us there beforehand to see the thing organized."

"And you are no doubt overjoyed at the opportunity to see a certain young woman?" teased Lord Widdons, watching for Cassie's reaction to this. He was nearly certain the two were only friends but, anxious lover that he was, needed reassurance.

His observations pleased him. He leaned his shoulder gently against Cassandra whom he had managed to seat beside himself.

"I trust, my dear, you are not too wearied by your political endeavors?"

"Not in the least. But I am famished!" she responded merrily.

"Then 'tis to home!" he chuckled, whipping up the horses.

28

The viscount sat in his smart coach, his heels propped upon the leather seat before him. They had been traveling these four hours and more and were very near their destination. It was almost tea time, but he wanted no refreshment. Viscount Welford wanted but one thing! However, he allowed his driver and groom to satisfy their hunger when they stopped some time later to water the horses.

Observing his employer's impatience to be off, Chips gulped down his ale and mutton, adjuring the driver to do the same, and both grabbed a hunk of bread before returning to the waiting carriage. Thus amply fortified, they resumed the journey, leaving their lord to his thoughts within, and blessing the fact that there appeared to be little sign of rain. Summer was upon them, and it gave every promise of being a dry one. The viscount gazed out on the passing scenes, noting the sun was still high in the west, and he was struck with a sudden fancy to see Cassie's face lighted by its rays. What nonsense, he chastised himself immediately.

It was wanting some minutes to five when they reached Whitchurch and were given the direction to the Bamfield house. This was easily found and all at once, with a wildly palpitating heart, Viscount Welford approached the front door.

He gave over his card to an elderly butler who suggested he wait in the hall, while he gave notice to his lady. Welford acquiesced, making no demur and scanning the place for signs of Cassie. A moment later he was following the butler to a small and quaintly decorated sitting room. A woman of substantial size with a lace cap over light brown curls came forward, welcoming him with a smile.

"I'm Isabelle Bamfield. Now tell me . . . in what manner may I help you?"

He gave her a polite bow. "It is a pleasure to meet Lord Widdons's sister, madam."

"Oh, you know my brother?"

"Indeed . . . though we have only just met," he answered, his eyes surveying the room, going to the window which overlooked the garden.

"Then you have come to see him?"

"No. I have come to see my wife."

"Your . . . wife?" she asked cautiously. It was impossible, she thought. Cassie . . . a viscountess . . . running from such a man . . . such a marriage? The girl had never struck her as foolish. Yet, if it were true . . .

"Indeed. I believe you have been so obliging as to . . . entertain her during . . . my absence?"

"I would first know to whom you refer?" she answered.

"Is it possible that I am mistaken? Is not Cassie here?" he asked, somewhat surprised, though not doubting for a moment that Cassie was there.

"Your wife . . . Cassie? Upon my word!" was all Isabelle Bamfield could say to this.

Cassie was at that particular moment taking in the late afternoon air with Lord Widdons. They had wandered off together directly after tea and had discovered a path never before explored by either of them. They had talked of many things, and Cassie had been careful to keep the conversation away from herself. However, his lordship seemed otherwise determined.

"Cassie, here, sit down with me on this log for a spell," he offered, whipping out his handkerchief and laying it down against the bark.

"So gallant!" she laughed aloud, thinking he was from another age, but admiring the chivalry behind the action.

He took a seated position, turning himself on one knee to face her. "Cassie, we must talk about this marriage of yours."

"Ah! Must we?"

"I tried to broach the subject this morning."

"Very well. Do so, and then let us forget it."

"We cannot—until we have decided between us what you wish me to do?"

"Do? What can *you* do?"

"Cassie . . . that first night you said you wished to be legally separated from your husband. In order to do such a thing . . ."

She interrupted him. "I know, it takes money . . . which I don't have."

"It also takes power, Cassie. I have both," he said quietly.

"But . . . why should *you* bother?" she asked, frowning.

"Don't you see? I want you free . . . to be mine." His arms went round her, and he drew her near.

He was going to kiss her—she knew it—and as his lips locked with hers she felt she stood at an open portal. She had but to step through. There—a new world, perhaps a new life that could put away the silent heartache of these past days. Yet, it didn't mesmerize. She was not drawn by its beckoning. His kiss did not warm her blood. She pulled away. "No, please, my lord, do not . . ."

"Cassie . . . I want you . . . I believe I am in love with you."

"But I am a married woman!" she objected.

"I told you . . . I have the means to change that."

"No, no, you do not. I am married to a powerful man . . . . he has the means to stand in your way . . . to cause scandal."

"No, child, don't worry. I am not without influence."

"My lord . . . my husband . . . is Viscount Welford!" she cried.

He stopped then, for he had been ready once again to draw her near, more forcefully if need be, but her announcement stopped him cold. Not because of his awe to discover her married to an influential man, but because of a sudden sinking feeling that damped his fire.

"The viscount?" he whispered to himself more than to her. A fine strapping buck of a fellow with looks enough to win any maid's heart! With money and title to keep her. He had until this moment imagined her husband some monster . . . some brutish creature. However, he attempted to retrieve his position. Had she not run from him, this viscount? "Cassie, it doesn't matter," he said trying to embrace her.

"But it does! It does . . . oh, I feel so ashamed . . ." she said, jumping to her feet, racing away from him. He was unable to follow for he was too stunned by what he had learned.

She had closed the portal door. She had shut out the chance at a new life. Behind her was safety, security—but in her mind, ever taunting, stood a tall, black-haired, black-eyed devil of a man! And he, lord, how he beckoned, demanded—and with all her being she wanted her life to match his own! With every fiber of her throbbing young heart, she desired to own his, but even this caused her pain—quite thorough in its nature, devastating in its force—for she could never have this secret yearning of hers fulfilled. She ran, these thoughts driving the tears down her cheeks so that she didn't see that the path to the house was blocked. She ran head on, and into, the arms of her husband!

It was a sight worth seeing, enough to remember for a lifetime. The very air vibrated with their emotions. He held her at arm's length, staring down at her piquant, tear-stained face. She stood frozen in his huge hands, unable to move, unable to speak, yet nearly collapsing beneath the weight of her heart. He was here! He had found her! Part of her gave thanks to providence, another cursed the fates.

And then his arms crushed her to him, his free hand nearly tore at the bodice of her gown as he sought her breast, and his mouth gave her life. His kiss sent her to new regions. Paradise. She was sure that the earth had separated beneath her feet and that lightning seemed to crackle in the sky. She could do nought to stop him, was not quite sure that she wanted to, and then he was breathing her name.

"Cassie . . . you little fool . . ."

He had ever the power to bring her to her senses. It was as though fingers had been snapped before her eyes, bringing her out of her trance.

She hauled off and with all the force she could muster landed him a stinging slap across his cheek. He stared at her a moment as he tried to compose himself, gave up the effort as useless, and returned the blow. Her lightness of weight, rather than his force, sent her sprawling, but his quick hand caught her before she fell. Then almost viciously he took up the long titian hair trailing at her back and twisted it round his ungloved hand.

"Now . . . you will walk with me! Away from this path . . . away from *your Lord Widdons*, who I imagine should be following you down this path any moment. You and I, my wife, are going to have a tête-à-tête of our own! I trust you have no objection?"

Whether she did or not (and she did) made no difference, for he was already putting his hand over her mouth. Thus, half-dragging, half-pushing, he led her out of sight and deep into the denseness of the woods. When he felt safe enough, he dropped his hand from her mouth and let go her hair. Immediately she attempted to run. He thwarted this attempt by stepping in her path and shoving her roughly downward onto a pile of brown winter leaves and pine needles. To further insure her imprisonment, he went down first on his knees and took up her wrists. Then he sat down, leaning heavily upon her.

"Now my lady, I shall tell you what we are about to do."

"I won't!"

"Mind . . . I said I will *tell* you, *not ask* you! We are leaving together this afternoon and proceeding to Liverpool, as per our arrangement when we were at the Grange."

"I won't go with you!" she spat.

"No? Then know this. All prior agreements become null and void. If you don't uphold your end, you cannot expect me to honor mine. I have found a buyer for the Grange. The gentleman—an excellent businessman, though most certainly a cit—intends to convert the place into a boys' school . . ." he lied well.

"Oh . . . no! You couldn't!" she gasped.

Ignoring her, he continued, "Of course, your servants will have to go as he has little use for them in his scheme of things."

"Stop it! Stop it! You are a fiend! Why in heaven's name, why do you want me with you?"

"Because it . . . amuses me! Because you are my wife, and I will not have you under the protection of another man!"

"How I hate you!" she hissed.

He felt her body beneath his. He was on fire with hunger for her, her squirming only served to increase his appetite. Again his hand went into the bodice of her gown, only this time he brought out the full whiteness of her breast. She was so lovely. His head bent to place a kiss upon the rosy pertness, and his voice was husky, "I've missed you, vixen . . ."

"Devil take you! Let me go . . . would you force me? Have you sunk that low, knave?"

He brought his head up, and his black eyes devoured her face. "Would I be forcing you, Cassie? Would I?"

"Yes, I loathe you! Don't you understand?"

He got to his feet. "Indeed. So then you prefer to remain here. Very well." He was already walking away.

She propped herself up. "Kirkby?"

He turned. "Yes?"

"What are you going to do?"

"Do? Why . . . as I said, I am going to sell the Grange. Actually, 'tis better this way, I need the blunt!"

"No! Oh, Kirkby, you cannot . . ." she cried, running to him.

He caught her arms. "You will return with me to Liverpool?"

"On one condition," she answered, her eyes downward. She hated to be beaten.

"You are not in a position to dictate terms to me, Cassie." His low voice was tinged with harshness, but he tempered it. "However, I am curious . . . what is the condition?"

"That you sleep in a separate bed."

"Ah, marriage in name only?" his hold on her arms tightened. "Is that what you really want?" She nodded her head vigorously, and he released her with something of a sneer. "Very well, my lady! So be it. But you must remember not to take exception when I seek . . . recreation elsewhere."

For some inscrutable reason, it fevered her to think of him making love to another woman. She wouldn't stand for it . . . and she told herself it was a thing that would hurt her pride.

"No! If you humiliate me . . . I shall leave . . ."

"I would not do that. I have *my* name to protect. So then, my lady, we have made a pact," he said offering her his arm. "Come, we shall not be staying to dinner at Mrs. Bamfield's, and you will want to make your farewells."

She declined his offer, preferring to keep her hands to herself, but he stopped and took up her left hand in order to slip it through his arm. His fingers stopped, however, at the feel of a thin gold band, and he sent her a searching look. "Tell me, Cass . . . why were you running away from Widdons . . . why the tears on your cheeks?"

She wished he hadn't noticed the ring. She wanted him to think she had paraded herself as single. She put up her chin, " 'Tis none of your affair!"

"You are quite wrong. I could put the question to his lordship. You are, after all, my wife, and if he has been taking advantage . . ."

"Stop it! Must you spoil everything? Leave him alone. Lord Widdons is a dear, kind . . . lonely man! Leave it at that!"

"Very well. However, it may interest you to know that you haven't seen the last of his lordship," said her husband blandly.

"What?" she returned surprised.

"Indeed. In Liverpool you will be my hostess, or have you forgotten our original . . . compact?"

"But what would you want with Widdons?" she cried.

"A great deal!" he answered enigmatically.

29

The day waned as the Welford coach left Whitchurch. The road before them was ill kept, deeply rutted, and winding. It had gone from a bright sunny day into a dull, slowly graying evening that matched Cassie's mood. There was little in the passing scenery to catch her admiration as they had been detoured onto a road that took them through poverty-stricken villages.

Cassie sat at one end of the coach diagonally across from the viscount. Both were silent with their thoughts. Cassie thought of Thomas. He had looked almost pleased as she watched him tether Starfire at the back of the coach, but then the poor lad had come to depend on Chips and was no doubt happy to be reunited with the older groom. But Lord Widdons? He had taken it so horribly. He had said scarcely a word when he watched her take leave of Mrs. Bamfield, yet she could feel his eyes boring through her, and her heart broke for him. And Kirkby . . . Oh! he had behaved so . . . so smoothly! So unfeelingly! She had wanted to scream when he bowed to Widdons and said in that arrogant tone of his, "No doubt we shall have the pleasure of your company once we are established in Liverpool."

Lord Widdons had drawn in his breath. "Yes, of course. Things must proceed . . . as we planned."

"And Mrs. Bamfield, do please again accept my sincerest thanks for all you have done," offered the viscount.

"Having Cassie has been a pleasure, my lord, I do assure you," she replied, giving Cassie's shoulders a squeeze.

It had been almost too much to bear, and she could not stop the tears that overflowed. And then . . . oh, God! how she hated him! Look at him, sitting there, not caring! Oooh, but she would bring him down. Somehow she would make him pay for this.

The viscount stared out on the harshness of the passing landscape. It seemed to him that all softness had been left behind in Dorset. Drat the fates! This detour would cost them time . . . but there was nothing for it, they couldn't have gotten the coach round that fallen tree or the road workers repairing the damage it had done. Very well, he decided to himself, they would just stay the night at a posting house. It was in all probability the wisest thing to do under the circumstances as both his horses and his men were wearied from the long journey. He sighed and gazed at his wife. She was looking a beauty, all flushed and angry in her brown velvet habit. This cold politeness could not go on forever. He would have to bring her round. He made a brave attempt.

He pointed out the changing landscape, commenting on it articulately and at some length. He pointed out various notable buildings of ancient, historic, and architectural merit and commented on the unpredictability of the weather—several times.

His lady barely paid him heed. She did all she could to keep her heart set hard against him and was quite successful in her efforts. Every time his sparkling black eyes scored a win, she reminded herself how he had touched and kissed another female . . . and she hardened very well.

Thus, the evening turned into night, the moon hidden by the gathering clouds. The silence inside the coach became most depressing. The viscount sighed and lit the oil lanterns on the coach walls, leaning against her in the process. He grinned widely when a sudden lurching of the carriage sent him into her lap. She objected furiously and was surprised when he did not take advantage of the incident. He merely excused himself and moved away.

It was but a few moments afterward that Chips roared out the name of the town they were approaching: "Winsford!" and they felt the coach slow. The viscount tapped on the ceiling with his walking stick and called out that he wished to stay at the finest inn the town had to offer. His wife pressed herself to the window, for something had caught her eye.

Torches . . . many of them, it seemed—lighted up a dais of sorts constructed along the roadway. A hangman's edifice had its prize swinging for all to see, and Cassie shrieked as she realized that what she saw were two male bodies, their necks broken as they swayed from their ropes.

She jumped back almost instinctively and without thinking went into the ready arms of her husband. He held her a moment before he glanced out her window. His black eyes grew grim, for he could see that the bodies had been hanging there for a considerable length of time. Beside them was a sign attached to a high post. It read:

TWO MURDERERS: Here hang two murderers suspended between Heaven and Earth as they were fit for neither!

He read it aloud and Cassie gasped in horror. "But . . . but . . . that is inhuman! By what right does the law so subject their souls? That is for God to decide!"

"I don't think you believe their souls are contained in their earthly flesh. However, my concern is *not* for *their souls* but for the vulgarity of this crudeness! Before we leave in the morning, I shall make certain the bodies of those poor devils are buried."

304

She was heartily glad of it, but said nothing for she was in no mood to think him a good creature. She had to be wary of him, he was not to be trusted. This reminded her of a poem by Jonson:

> Trust him not, his words, though sweet,
> Seldome with his heart do meet,
> All his practise is deceit;
> Every gift it is a bait,
> Not a kisse but poyson beares;
> And most treason in his teares!

She allowed the words to sink in now, then again later when she bade him good-night at her door and closed it upon his hungry eyes.

Another day on the road brought them no closer together, in spite of the fact that they had been closeted in the coach while bleakness and drizzle outside made their confines all the more cozy. Cassie had managed to keep her head buried in, first, a novel by Jane Austen, and then for a change of pace she picked up *Don Juan*, which she had begun a day ago and Mrs. Bamfield had been kind enough to bestow upon her.

Observing this, his lordship tried once again to break through her veneer. "Do you enjoy Byron?"

"Yes," she answered, purposely laconic.

"*Don Juan*! That is superb. I look forward to receiving the next set of Cantos. We have a mutual friend, Byron and I—Douglas Kinnaird. He showed me a letter of Byron's he received about a month ago referring to those passages you now have there before you . . ."

As the viscount stopped there and seemed rather prone to silence, Cassie prompted, "Yes?"

"Oh . . . are you interested then? You seemed so preoccupied that I rather thought you were not listening," he said blandly, a twinkle in his merry eyes.

"I . . . I was listening. Byron has always interested me."

"Now then, what was I saying?" bantered the viscount.

"The letter to your friend . . . about *Don Juan*?" she prompted.

"Ah, yes. Byron seems a sport of a fellow. He refers to his *Don Juan*, saying . . ." He paused dramatically, and Cassie held her breath . . . " 'It may be bawdy, but is it not good English? It may be profligate, but is it not life, is it not *the thing*? Could any man have written it who has not lived in the world?—and *fooled* in a post chaise? In a hackney coach? In a gondola? Against a wall? In a court carriage? In a vis-à-vis? On a table and under it?' "

"I remembered that paragraph for it struck me as sublime. He goes on to tell Kinnaird that he means to finish his third Canto soon but is forced to modesty because of the outcry against it. I hope he may not be put off by the mob of hypocrites!"

"Oh, yes, for the satire is so strikingly a reflection of our times. It would be a shame to tone it down an ounce!" she agreed and then returned to it, once more shutting him out, and he sighed. There was nought else he could do but put up his legs on the seat opposite him near where she sat, tilt his hat over his eyes, and go to sleep.

They made slow going because the rains had created a great deal of flooding in some areas, and in others mud pools served to slow their progress still more. They made a brief stop for a late lunch and then were on their way once again, reaching the city of Liverpool after dark. It was a huge port, but Cassie could see little of it in the dark as it was still raining hard, further obscuring her vision. They passed through cobble-paved streets, and Cassie was spared the sight of gaunt children in wet rags racing home from the factories where they worked. As a great English port, Liverpool had thrived during the slave trade and continued to survive now as the industrial age was beginning. The canal connecting it with Manchester, further inland, allowed easy water transport of coal, tin, and cotton. Every day this brought Liverpool even more, for it brought the Irish, half-starved and proud, asking only for work—and not all found it!

Cassie saw none of this, for in the rain and the dark, nought but the amber lights of the fashionable Georgian and Regency streets stood out before her eyes. The Welford coach pulled up beside an elegant hotel much in the style of the Beacon in Bristol and, as Cassie was rushed through its wide portals, there was no suspicion of the dirt and poverty they had just rambled through some few moments ago. In the lobby was an array of Chinese pots filled with palms and crystal vases overflowing with summer flowers. Gold laced the furniture and the hangings. Link boys bustled, flunkeys bowed, lovely men and women strolled past, and the viscount and his lady were received with a flourish of quiet grace.

Cassie found herself some few moments later gazing about a bedchamber of pale green and gold. It was a spacious room richly furnished in French country style. Terraced windows stood open, and Cassie looked out on the stone balcony. The rain had subsided and garden torches allowed her a view of the hotel courtyard below. Designed for guests to take their constitutionals whenever the mood struck them, it was spaced with several squares of lawn framed with high evergreens and blooming rhododendrons. Its walks were composed in such a way as to allow several sets of individuals privacy at the same time. Stone benches were placed at intervals throughout.

A young couple caught Cassie's eye, though they were not within her hearing. There was something about the young man, something familiar that made her stare—and then he turned his face so that the light from the torch illuminated it.

"Guy!" she breathed to herself. That's right . . . he was coming to Liverpool . . . he said to the Grand Hotel! She hadn't noticed the name of the hotel when the viscount ushered her in. This was wonderful. And the woman . . . she must be Mary Beth. She determined to seek him out first thing in the morning. Thinking of Guy brought Lyle Stanton to mind. She wondered if he, too, were staying here, part of her hoping that he was.

The viscount had just seen out the last of the lackeys

and was closing the door to find his wife coming into the room, her face a mask of preoccupation. "Well?" he asked curiously. "Whatever has you looking so?"

She came about, remembering who and where she was. The frown descended upon her features, and he sighed with some show of exasperation. "Madam, draw your features like a cockatrice and you shall find wrinkles e'er you're thirty!"

"What are you still doing here?" she returned.

"This is my room . . . has been my room this past week!" he said curtly.

"I am afraid that is now impossible," she answered.

"You needn't be afraid . . . and I am pleased to advise you that you are mistaken! I have put up with your bad manners and your cold airs this day, *but no more!* Oh! Do not start, my vixen, I have no intention of laying a hand on you before you will it. However, there are reasons why I should like to keep up appearances. We are on our honeymoon . . . or so I shall put about. It is what I want society's fools to believe. Therefore, we shall share the same room—but not the same bed. My dressing room houses a daybed of sorts. I shall be unhappy but willing to use it—until circumstances alter . . ."

"They shan't!" she interrupted sharply.

"Very well, madam, I bid you good-night!"

She watched him for he did not make for his dressing room but for the hall door. She stepped forward before she realized what she was about, and her voice held a note she could not hide from herself. "But . . . my lord, where do you go?"

He smiled. He wanted to say, not to another woman, Cass. He wanted to say she was the only female he desired. But he could not. There was Peter between them. He said instead, "Why, love . . . worried? 'Tis your own fault. You have the magic to enchant my hours. You choose not to use it. I am no monk, love . . ." He had the satisfaction of seeing a hurt look creep into her eyes, and it drew a kinder note, "and still I go only to send a letter to . . . Mr. Asbatol."

308

His final words flooded her with a mixed sensation—pleasure that he sought no other woman; anger that she should feel pleasure at such nonsense; and irritation because he was still after such a dreadful man. She turned her back on him, reminding herself,

"trust him not . . . his words, though sweet,
seldome with his heart do meet . . ."

The viscount went purposely to the lobby below. He wished another meeting with Leila—alone. A hastily composed note was given to a link boy before he wandered into the hotel's refreshment galley where he orderd a brandy and sat back to drink it slowly, lost in thought.

Abovestairs Cassie found to her pleasure a team of serving girls had brought up buckets of steaming hot water for her hip bath. She dismissed them gratefully and eased herself into the soothing water, sighing as she felt the warmth assuage her aches. She had been through much these past two days, and her mood was querulous. He . . . now he was trying to turn her up sweet, trying to break down her defenses with his honeyed words. Well, she knew him for what he was . . . she had seen with her own eyes his betrayal . . . she felt her heart squeeze and wished . . . almost wished . . . she had not seen.

Her body went to sleep as it soaked and she closed her eyes, nearly dozing off. She was tired, tired of remembering, tired of feeling, of thinking, of wanting. She wished . . . but it was useless. Yet still she could see his large sparkling jet eyes twinkling at her. He was a devil, and though she loathed him, there was no denying she wanted him.

The viscount entered the bedchamber, dropped off his bucksin riding jacket, and slung off his neckcloth. A fire had been lighted, the terrace doors closed, and drawn against the damp night. Branches of candles added to the light of the fire, creating a soft compelling atmosphere in the pale green room. He heard Cassie move in her bath and smiled. He had ordered this bath for her as soon as they had arrived, knowing full well she would take to it with appreciation—knowing full well he would come in upon her. He was tingling at the prospect. His body was vibrating with need, and already his staff was hard and throbbing. Good Lord! She had the power to affect him so, and he had not even seen her yet. He moved slowly, coming quietly into the dimly lit dressing room. She had her back to him, but she was entirely visible due to the happy position of a long looking glass tilted conveniently in its satinwood frame before her. He gazed long, for her lovely lashes were lowered, shielding him from her vision, and she had not heard his return, so engrossed was she with her own thoughts. His gleaming eyes devoured her face and lips before dropping to the full high breasts floating tauntingly in the clear water. They were a rich handful, and his fingers itched to touch. He looked lower, deeper, and his blood fevered. He came up behind her and dropped to his knees. His hands flanked her neck, massaging with tantalizing firmness.

She stiffened at once, and her voice was hard, unforgiving. "Release me at once, Kirkby! Have the decency to allow me my privacy!"

"Nay, love, belay your anger. Let me ease your aches . . ." His voice was tender, coaxing. He had already brought himself round, his arms were gathering her wet tantalizing body to him, and his mouth told her hotly, wildly, of all the pent-up passion he had been controlling. His kiss excluded all other sensations. Cannons roared in her ears and music swelled in her bosom. Her body trembled with erotic pulsations, and her blood raced through her veins. Even so, she brought up her hand and surprised them both with the force of her slap.

His black glinting eyes reflected his anger . . . and something more—disappointment. Rage shook him as he got to his feet. Cassie watched him, unsure whether to gloat over her victory or cry out in dismay. But suddenly he was lifting her to her feet, and then up . . . up and over his strong shoulder, like so much baggage!

She was outraged. "Let me go! By God! You *are* a scoundrel! Let me go! Do you hear me, you villain . . . you knave . . . let me go or I shall scream!"

"And a pretty sight some fortunate gentleman would get if he were to attend your screeching!" sneered the viscount, not in the least disturbed by her threat.

It was difficult to carry on any reasonable discourse in her present position, so she continued to wriggle, kick, and fuss as much as she was able, until she found herself ruthlessly flung backward onto the bed. She had scarcely a moment in which to catch her breath before he was atop her, pinning her arms under her and grinning above her irate countenance. "A lesson, my vixen! Had I wanted to, now . . . at this very moment . . . with one single thrust, I could plunge myself into that little honeybox you withhold from me. I am your husband—by your own trickery—and it is my right! But I shan't. However, the time will come when you will ask . . . nay—*beg* for it!"

"Never! Cad . . . libertine!"

He grinned. "Shall I prove it then? Do you not believe me?"

"Nay, nay . . . I believe you," she said with some agitation. "You are stronger . . . any man can force a woman . . . is that what you want?"

"I have already said, sweetings, that it is not what *I* want. Though I think it *is* what *you* want. You would like me to force you, for your body hungers. I know it, Cassie. Your body betrays you, for I feel it tremble—and it is not from fear!"

She blushed, for it was true, but she fought the truth and him. "The devil fly away with you! I am a normal woman . . . but it is not for *you* that I . . . tremble!" she said, purposely baiting him.

He stiffened. "You are a liar . . . but I'll leave go, I want no unwilling toss, Cassie." He got to his feet and moved away from her, but his eyes still lingered on her luscious form, and his manhood fought at his breeches for release. His voice was almost a growl when it came again, "Get dressed, chit! Our dinner will be brought up presently and, though I have said I want no unwilling woman beneath me, there is only so much that flesh and blood can bear, and if I have to look at those rosebuds peeping at me over the table . . ."

She scrambled off the bed and found her nightdress and wrapper, hastily slipping them on beneath his watchful, hungry eyes. He had promised himself he would win her. Forgotten for the time was the fact that she had something to do with his brother's betrayal. He only knew a devastating need of her.

A knock sounded, and Cassie observed a coin and a letter exchange hands between her husband and a young link boy. Surprised, she watched as he opened the sealed, pink-tinted envelope. Pink, she thought wildly, a woman . . . it was from a woman! He had gone out before to send a message to a woman . . . and this was her reply. She was furious—nearly insane with jealousy as she watched his face, his eyes.

He put the note into the fire, watched it curl into wretched black ashes, and then left her standing. When next he reappeared, he was clothed in a silk brocade dressing gown of black and maroon design. His white open-necked shirt collar was spread wide over the robe's lapels. His black hair glistened over his forehead, his brows with their peculiar uplift at the corners added to the ruggedness of his handsome face—and Cassie was hard put not to yield to the demands of her own flesh.

Dinner was served almost immediately, and after a time they were once more quite alone. The viscount raised his fork to pick at his remaining prawns, but stopped and stared quizzically at her. The lights from the branch of candles between them lit up her beauteous face. Her red hair shone with all its golden glints, and her green eyes made him want to plunge right in. "Oh, Cass, there is so much about you that remains a puzzle."

"How so?" She had to remain on guard, she told herself.

"For example, where were you going that day in Bristol . . . in the Beacon. You sauntered down the hotel stairs as though you were about to go on some er-

312

rand or other. Just where did you think you were going?" Quietly he wondered again, had she made some appointment to meet with the Asbatols?

She opened her green eyes wide to his question. "Good gracious! Now you ask? It doesn't matter at any rate."

"But it does, and I would know," he coaxed gently.

She had to be wary of him, she told herself, what was he up to? Don't listen to the gentleness of his voice, but she answered all the same. "I was coming down after you. You had promised to take me to that . . . I've forgotten the name . . . the pirates' den. But then you spoke so rudely to me in front of that nice young man . . ."

He stared hard at her a moment. Was it possible? Could she be telling the truth? Was she such an innocent? God! Something inside him wanted to believe her. But Peter . . . Peter had described her—first as an angel, then . . . could Peter have been wrong? No, Peter was dead. However, his voice was tender when he spoke. "If that is true, Cass, I beg your pardon. I don't usually break my promises. It was imperative that I come to Liverpool. You see, as I told you yesterday . . . I need the cash . . . and if I am not to sell the Grange, I must strike up a deal with Asbatol!"

"Why? What can he do for you?" she asked, frowning.

"Never mind that . . . however, I shall endeavor not to break any more promises to you," he said sweetly, his eyes soft upon her.

She heard again Jonson's words taunting her, "All his practice is deceit; Every gift it is a bait . . ." and she answered lightly, "Of course, my lord, but now I want only to curl up with the remainder of *Don Juan* and then . . . to sleep."

He was being rejected, dismissed. It piqued him. He had been working hard to win her favor. He wanted her. He wanted to lay his hands on her breasts, to suckle her nipples, and taste her flesh. He wanted to feel those tantalizing hips, to place his staff between her thighs . . . and she . . . she wanted none of him.

"Granted, that poem is a lusty piece of work. But while

it may warm your blood to read about lovemaking, it will *not* satisfy your flesh—but, as you please!" He took up his glass of wine, bowed mockingly, and left her. She watched him go, saw that he left their communicating door more than half open. She hesitated. Should she close it? No, better not to try his patience.

30

Cassie rose, dressed in a blue riding habit, perched a blue top hat over her bright red hair, and sauntered down the staircase to the lobby. She was not staying indoors on such a fine day, simply because her husband had chosen to leave her without a word—or a penny for that matter. She had still some money left from the purse Jack had given her and which she had been wise enough to stow away. She had Starfire, she had Thomas—and, once she got hold of Guy, she would have one more friend in Liverpool.

At the lobby desk she inquired after Guy Bamfield and was told he was still in his room, whereupon she composed a quick note and had it taken to him. Before long she looked up to see Guy, neatly dressed in a tailored gray superfine, coming toward her, hands outstretched to take her own gloved ones. "Cass!" he said shaking her hands vigorously and, then lowering his voice, "What are you doing here, how did you get here?"

"My husband brought me," she answered, her eyes

twinkling at the expression of surprised stupor that came over him.

"Your husband?"

"Shh . . . come, let's take a turn outside. You can show me all the best places, and we can talk."

"Of course," he said ushering her along at a faster pace than she had in mind. Once outside he let go the questions once again. She waited until his fervor had subsided before replying.

"I am the Viscountess Welford and, no, don't look like that. 'Tis not what you think! He is not an ugly old brute but quite a handsome, young devil! We were not married for love . . . but for convenience as I explained to you the other day. I ran away because . . . he angered me. I have a wicked temper, you see. Now, however, for reasons I cannot explain to you, I have decided to join him . . ."

"How did he know where you were?"

"I . . . I don't know. I . . . somehow forgot to ask. It didn't seem to matter at the time . . ." she faltered.

"I see. Do you know, as it happens 'tis a good thing. I was going to return for you tomorrow—bring you and m'mother as your duenna. But as turns out . . . here you are . . . don't need m'mother now!"

"What do you mean you were coming for me?"

"For once Lyle has an excellent notion. Thinks you would be grand getting up subscribers to our cause. We need money to get the crowds to Manchester next month to hear the orator!"

"Then Lyle is staying at the Grand?"

"No, too plush for Lyle. He is not very plump in the pockets, you know. He is putting up with some friends. But he'll be pleased as punch you are here . . . and a Viscountess! Why, that makes everything all the easier!" he suddenly blushed hotly and stopped in his tracks, "Egad!"

"What? Guy, what is it?"

"Mary Beth . . . and her aunt . . . coming this way!"

"What is so terrible about that?"

"Her aunt don't know I'm here. Now she'll know . . . and make it harder for me to see Mary Beth!"

"Oh, dear!" sighed Cassie.

Mary Beth was a pretty girl, soft, round, and reserved. Blond curls peeped out beneath a straw bonnet, and her figure, full and youthful in her yellow gown gladdened her lover's eyes. Cassie saw at a glance that what they shared was very real and not a passing fancy. However, the aunt was a dragon indeed. Mrs. Osborne, a widow of many years, was determined to see her brother-in-law's child creditably installed. She would have scarcely given Guy Bamfield a nod, had he not hastened to introduce Casise to them.

Upon hearing the young lovely in blue was none other than Viscountess Welford, Mrs. Osborne's expression changed as though struck by a miracle. She fell into gushing, and Cassie saw for the first time that she could make use of her married name to another's advantage.

"I cannot tell you how pleased I am to make your acquaintance," said Cassie. "Mrs. Bamfield and Guy both mentioned your niece with such esteem that I feel I know her already." She smiled at Mary Beth's puzzled face. "It will be so pleasant to have someone near my own age to wile away the hours and keep me company. I would ask you to accompany Mr. Bamfield and myself for a stroll in the park—but I see you are on your way back to the hotel."

Mrs. Osborne was not about to lose the opportunity to push her niece into such exalted company. Why, this would mean invitations to balls . . . routs . . . all the right people. "Why, Mary Beth is not tired . . . are you, dear?"

"No, Aunt," she answered quietly, casting a hasty glance at Guy who dared to smile at her when her aunt was occupied with Cassie.

"Marvelous!" returned Cassie. "I shall take excellent care of her and return her to you shortly."

"Enjoy yourself, dear," said Mrs. Osborne, patting her niece's hand and waving herself off.

Three pair of eyes watched her retreating form before three young people turned to one another and let go a whoop of laughter. They were conspirators—and it was wonderful.

"Oh, Cass, that was the best piece of work ever I clapped eyes on. You played the viscountess—like a duchess!"

"But . . . I don't understand," put in Mary Beth. "Are you not a viscountess?"

"Of course she is, darling. Now come. Let us get out of sight!" he laughed, linking his arm through those of the ladies on either side of him and leading them to the park walks.

After much giggling and discovering that they all had much in common, Guy informed his love that Cassie was pledged to the cause.

"Why, that is beyond everything wonderful," exclaimed the blonde. "Then perhaps I may still be able to attend that meet with you at Lancaster Field," she said, looking at Guy. "That is, if I were to go with the viscountess . . ."

Guy's eyes lit up. "Of course. But, Cass, it would mean pulling the wool over the old . . . over Mrs. Osborne's eyes. Would you object to it?"

"No, I suppose we could manage the thing," she said hesitatingly.

"Oh, but what of your husband?" put in Mary Beth thoughtfully. "Will he not object?"

"*That* . . . doesn't really matter!" said Cassie, more confidently than she felt.

It was not until another hour passed that Guy returned the ladies to the hotel. He was promised to meet Lyle and, as Mrs. Osborne turned up in the hotel lobby, Mary Beth went to meet her, leaving Guy to make his farewell to Cassie.

"Well then, my lady," he bowed, the tease full in his voice. "Until later. I shall tell Lyle you are here. He will want to see you. Do you think it can be arranged?"

"I don't see why it could not be," she returned smiling, and then he was off. She sighed after him, turned, and started for the stairs, never noting that her husband had been standing not more than a few feet away, watching this, his blood curdling, and his black eyes glinting.

He lingered near the doorway as he watched Cassie take leave of her new friend, and then he followed her up the stairs to their room. It would appear, he thought, that his bride had had a busy morning during his absence.

Cassie entered her room, tossed off her hat, and picked up her brush. She neither heard nor noticed that her husband had slipped in behind her and was now leaning against the post of the bed watching her graceful movements.

"Good-morning . . . or rather good-day, my lady," said her husband. "Have you taken lunch yet?"

She swung round, her silken hair flowing with the suddenness of her movement. "Oh! You startled me. I never heard you at my back. No, I have had neither breakfast nor lunch, my lord."

He laughed. "You look a veritable imp with your hair all about and your eyes flashing at me. Angry still, sweetheart? Come . . . let us kiss and make up . . ." he said, going forward and taking her small waist in his large ungloved hands. He had dropped his cloak and hat onto the bed, and she could feel the hardness of his frame against her. She almost wanted to give in . . . but she remembered still how his lips had pressed another. She pushed him away. "Leave go, my lord."

He released her with a sigh. "Well, madam, what have you been about? Making friends?" his voice held a harsh note.

"Yes," she answered simply.

"Male or female?" he prompted, his eyes narrowing as he awaited the reply.

She hesitated. It wouldn't hurt to make him jealous . . . perhaps she had the means. "Both," she answered curtly.

"Indeed?" he said, his lip curling with an emotion he was not ready to understand. "Educate me, love . . ."

"Very well, if it amuses you," she said lightly, deliberately baiting him.

"It amuses me a great deal," he answered, now perfectly composed.

"I met a charming young woman, my own age. She was introduced to me by a friend . . ."

"A friend?" he interjected. "I wasn't aware you had friends in Liverpool."

"As a matter of fact, I didn't. Guy Bamfield . . . I met him in Whitchurch. He is Mrs. Bamfield's son . . . such a wonderful man . . . with such fire! One doesn't suspect it at first, but after a few moments with him, it is quite obvious. He is a radical, you see . . ."

"Is he?" asked the viscount, somewhat annoyed. "And you find radicals fascinating, no doubt?"

"Oh, indeed I do. They are all bubbling lava, and they have such high ideals. Reforms are needed, you know—and it is the radicals who will bring such reforms about."

"Ha! You know nothing about it. Radicals attempted a great deal two years back—in Nottingham—and it was put down as the Nottingham Riots! Nought came of it. Reformers are naive young fools who will make their innocence a weapon in the hands of their opponents. They know not how to handle their ideals."

"You do not approve of reformers?" she asked, curious.

"That, my dear, is a loaded question and requires a lengthy return. I certainly am not going to attempt to answer it on an empty belly. I'll just go rinse my hands . . . while you put up your hair, and perhaps we can settle the problems of our nation over lunch!"

She smiled in spite of herself. It was so difficult to hate him when he was bent on being charming. But she reminded herself what he was. An adventurer—using threats to keep her by his side.

Some forty minutes later Cassie was enjoying her quiche and salad in a local coffee house known as the Grotto, frequented by a horde of poets. It was a unique experience for her, and she sat wide-eyed as poet after poet of varying talents stood atop chairs and spouted their verses. They were urged on by their followers and fellow

320

scribblers as Cassie took in everything with undisguised awe.

The viscount picked at his food, for his attention was centered on his bride. Her eyes were alive with sparkling glints of pale green splendor. Her breasts heaved beneath the white soft material of her blouse. Her cheeks glowed, her full cherry lips invited without awareness, her expressions enchanted . . . and he acknowledged himself her liege.

The afternoon had been too beautiful to allow Cassie peace of mind. They had left the Grotto behind and wandered down avenues of fashionable shops. In the park they watched children at play and lovers communing behind the trees, and somehow Cassie had allowed her husband to take her gloved hand. It was only to lead her, she told herself . . . there was nothing in it.

They munched on fresh peanuts from a passing vendor and then found themselves at a puppet show laughing as if they were no older than the children around them. However, the afternoon ended. She had the memory of his unfaithfulness fresh in her mind, the bitterness of his threats ringing in her ears, the knowledge that he was an adventurer living off the misery of others. He had the memory of Peter's letter.

They reached their hotel room, and Cassie sighed as she cast aside her hat and spencer. She turned to find his black eyes pouring over her, and suddenly she was in his arms. He acted unwisely, giddy with his afternoon's success—after all, had she not allowed the illicit touching of hands . . . was that not a sign of her surrender? Taking this to mean that all was forgiven, he meant to end his monk's life. She felt his body burn against hers as he pressed her to him, and at that moment she nearly consented.

His lips took hers with a violence of feeling that left them both weak. And then, she recalled just how he had been handling that tavern wench! It was still all too clear in her mind. Cassie pushed at him with all her strength, and her voice came angrily, "No!"

He took her shoulders in his strong grasp, and his voice was husky, low, urging, "Come, vixen, you mean it not . . . come, Cass, quench my Priapean fire . . ."

His words roused her. The feel of his comet hard against her thigh excited her blood. But memories taunted her, and still she heard words, "Not a kisse but poyson beares . . ."

"No!" she said still, pulling out of his clutch, turning her well-shaped back to him.

He was beneath the spell of Priapus, and it was hard to let go his purpose. He came up behind her, his hands closing in on her small tight waist, his lips kissing the nape of her neck. "Do not say me nay, love . . . earth holds no other woman like to thee . . . I want only you, need only your . . ."

"Stop it!" Again she pulled out of his hold. "I will not listen to you. I know that you lie . . . have seen with my own eyes . . ."

His black eyes glinted strangely, but he controlled himself. It was too soon. He heard her refusal, but he had felt her in his arms and knew that her body was on fire. It was but a matter of time . . . and he had that. His voice came softly, tenderly. "You are wrong, sweetings. But I shall not press you." He turned from her, "I am going to the lobby to inquire after my mail. Why don't you relax? I'll order up our dinner."

She nodded for she didn't dare trust herself to speak. How could he suddenly be so casual? What was he made of, this wild, bold man? Why did her heart yearn so for him? Why could she not banish the feel of his hand on her? Oh, Cassie, her mind raged, you are a fool!

31

The night did not pass pleasantly for Cassie. Dinner had been quiet and strained for she had been all too aware of her husband's animal magnetism. He sat before her in his shirt sleeves, his long legs stretched out, his black hair glistening over his forehead, his dark haunting eyes compelling her to respond. She wanted him—and hated herself for her weakness.

She tossed fitfully and at one point threw off the covers and nearly went to him. Somehow she stopped herself, somehow her pride came to the rescue—and she cursed it!

The next morning saw her in a pale yellow sprig muslin whose shawl and matching bonnet made her appear a china doll. But the lord and master of her emotions was nowhere to be found. She was due to meet Guy and Mary Beth, so hastily she composed a note and, gloating over its contents, she proceeded to the lobby to find her friends. There she discovered Mary Beth looking pretty in a bright print muslin and a straw bonnet.

"Oh, thank goodness, you have come . . . before auntie

bowls down upon us. Guy is outside!" said Mary Beth, taking up Cassie's gloved hand, and leading her out of the hotel down the curbing to the corner where Guy and Lyle Stanton awaited them in a hired hack.

They were soon seated in the closed, cramped carriage. Guy called out the direction, and then took up a position beside his love. Lyle was smiling down at Cassie, the twinkle alive in his mischievous eyes. "Well, well, Lady Welford!"

"Don't be a cad!" she admonished severely, "I had my reasons."

"No doubt, no doubt," he answered, a mocking smile provoking a set-down from her again. However, Guy soon took over the conversation, and it was all about the projected meet and Sam Bamford.

"Sam writes that he expects something like forty thousand people to attend the Great Meet in Manchester!" said Guy enthusiastically.

"My word!" Cassie was impressed. And so it went on for the next fifteen minutes until they reached Lancaster Field. There, once again Cassie found she was placed on the platform, seated beside Mary Beth.

Sam Bamford was an imposing figure and well known to the hungry eyes before him. Cassie watched as the crowds gathered in numbers, she heard them chant the Orator Hunt's name, she looked down into their hope-filled eyes, and was moved by what she saw.

Sam Bamford's speech was unlike Lyle's. His called for peace . . . a peaceful movement. He stressed organization, drillings. They must learn how to march in order, they must do this, and they must do that, and finally they must march on Manchester on August 16, 1819. Later, other speakers took the platform, and Lyle worked his hand round Cassie's bare arm. "Come, love, we've heard enough."

"But . . . Guy and Mary Beth?"

"They will meet us at the carriage in a few minutes. After all, we ought to give the lovers some privacy . . . don't you think?"

324

"I suppose," she said doubtfully.

He led her away from the thick of the mob toward the clearing where the carriages and horses were waiting, then past these some distance to a wooded area, and linked her arm through his, patting her hand in a manner Cassie found somehow disturbing.

"Now there, m'lady . . . you are a boon to us, you know," he said.

"How do you mean?" She was puzzled by his tone.

"Well, as the Viscountess Welford, just think of all the subscribers you can get. You'll be entertaining . . . having ladies' tea parties . . . Venetian breakfasts . . . and you'll hit them all for donations. Lord! Are you ever a Godsend!"

"Oh, I see. But . . ."

"Don't be 'but-ing' me, love. We need the money for those poor wretches. Why, just think . . . just think how many of them will be needing a bit of something to eat during these drillings Sam is talking of! Marches . . . they can't march if they're starving! We could create a treasury . . . use the funds for such . . ."

"Yes, yes . . . that would be wonderful, Lyle!" she agreed excitedly, for this coincided with her own ideas.

His arm went round her shoulder, his other hand to her waist. It was thrilling having him touch her. She wanted him to, for she wished to rid herself of thoughts of Kirkby, so she lifted her face to his.

"Ah, love . . ." he whispered as his mouth closed on hers.

Armed with the list of suitable lodgings, the viscount had stepped forth early that morning. After a considerable tour and his morning spent, he settled on the best of these and instructed his man of business to prepare the necessary papers for signature. It was with some haste that he made for the hotel and Cassandra.

His previous night had been nearly sleepless. He had been frustrated for he had been able to hear Cassie's movements in the room next to his. The open door was a temptation he found difficult to resist and yet he held him-

325

self in check for fear he might lose what little ground he had gained that afternoon. But damn! he thought then, and again now, it would have to be soon. The notion of taking her into his arms, of even forcing her to it, excited him further, making sleep all the more difficult.

Some moments passed before the viscount's coach stopped before the hotel and he made his way to his chambers. However, upon reaching their rooms he found them neatly prepared and quite empty. His observant eye lit upon a note propped on the marble mantelshelf written in Cassie's hand:

> My lord:
> I am promised to Miss Osborne and Guy Bamfield
> for the morning. I trust you have no objections.
> > Cassie.

It was scarcely informative and just as polite. It was maddening! He picked up the hat and gloves he had just discarded and made his way to the lobby. He was unsure what he was about to do, but he could not stay in the room and do nothing.

Cassie had been quiet on the ride home—thoughtful beneath Lyle's gaze. She did not know what to think. He had kissed her . . . and it had been . . . exciting . . . and yet . . . It lacked something. Perhaps it lacked her own desire. There was that wedding ring on her finger that told her it was wrong. She was another man's wife! It didn't matter that the marriage was not what she had dreamed of. It was a marriage—of sorts. She had stopped Lyle, she had tried to explain that it wasn't right, but he had not understood. He had answered that it surely was not . . . too indiscreet . . . that it would be different next time. Next time? Did she want a next time? Oh, it was all too confusing!

Mary and Guy carried the conversation—excited over the meet and its accomplishments, and Cassie felt an overwhelming relief when they spotted the hotel at last. She needed time to think and that was impossible with those two expounding ideals around her head.

She and Mary Beth were escorted by the gentlemen into the lobby, beneath the appraisal of the viscount, and he saw all too well the look that passed between Lyle Stanton and his wife.

Mary Beth turned and shooed both men away. "Quickly, Auntie will be searching me out . . . and, oh, Guy, I don't want her to see you . . ."

"Cassie, can you meet me tonight?" whispered Lyle.

She saw Kirkby coming purposely their way. "No, now go."

"When then?"

"I don't know . . . Guy will get back to you . . ." she answered hurriedly.

"But why should I go?" asked Guy. "My room is here." However, he was taken firmly by the arm and led away by a jesting Lyle.

The viscount had by then reached his wife's side. "Good-afternoon, my lady," he said to Cassie, his voice a great deal quieter than he felt.

"My lord," acknowledged his wife. "Allow me to introduce you to Miss Mary Beth Osborne."

The amenities exchanged, Mary Beth made her escape on the excuse that her aunt would be looking for her, and Cassie was left to face her husband alone. "It is too bad Mr. Bamfield did not stay. I am eager to meet Lord Widdons's nephew."

"He had to go."

"With . . . your rusty-haired friend, no doubt," said the viscount, his voice underlining the pronoun, his lips forming a sneer.

"Yes, he and Lyle had some business or other," she stated lamely, looking away guiltily.

He was not about to create a scene with her in the hotel lobby. He hailed a passing lackey and requested him to send to the stables for his coach, whereupon he led his wife by the arm to the doors and outside to await their carriage.

"What? Where are you taking me?" she inquired in some surprise.

"To view our new home, madam," he answered curtly. He was annoyed with her, but it would have to wait until they were in private.

"My, you have been busy," she mused aloud. "So, that is where you vanished to this morning?"

He said nothing to this but looked sharply at her for a moment and then asked quietly, "Did you wonder for very long? I thought not when I saw you making merry with your . . . friends." There was a strange note in his voice.

"I wondered . . . for you were not thoughtful enough to leave word—as I did!" she snapped.

"You call that terse note leaving word?" he returned irritably.

"It was a sight more than you left!"

The carriage pulled up alongside the curbing, and he opened the door and helped his lady within. Jumping in, he dropped his hat and cloak on the seat before him and moved so that he was able to gaze at the woman beside him.

"You will no doubt tell me all about your excursion when you are ready." His voice had taken on a hard line.

"Oh?" said his wife, her chin up. She so detested such commands. "Is there no doubt?"

"None whatsoever," he answered at once, but he was already beginning to know her, and his anxiety to know her doings was greater at this passing than his determination to command, ". . . if you please, madam?"

She smiled at once. She was feeling an extraordinary amount of guilt for the kiss she had allowed Lyle. It soothed her somewhat to comply with his wishes. "As a matter of fact, I do please. I have had the oddest morning imaginable. It was fascinating, for we went to Lancaster Field to hear Sam Bamford!"

"No, really? I wasn't aware *he* had ventured up into this region. Thought he was still about with the Orator in London," said the viscount, interested. Then he frowned.

"I don't really like your getting involved in these open field meetings—they could be dangerous."

"Nonsense. In what way?"

"You don't understand the nature of a mob. Nor do their own leaders. The trouble is, the mobs are ignorant . . . the people themselves want reforming . . . Bamford himself admitted as much to me."

"You know Sam Bamford?" asked Cassie, momentarily diverted.

"He is one of my many acquaintances," smiled the viscount, amused at her awe.

"But, Kirby, do you mean to say *you* stand against them?"

"Not at all. But I have attended a meet or two—in Nottingham—and have had my pocket picked as well! No. The laws want reforming all right . . . but the meets won't achieve it. I very much fear they incite a repressive force from the ruling class, and I don't want you caught up in any such clash," he said gravely.

"Well . . . that is all very well, but I *am* involved. I am pledged to help with meet trainings, with donation collections . . . with . . ."

"Just a moment," he said sharply. "What do you mean 'donation collections'?"

"We must have some sort of fund to help the needy, to clothe their children, to feed them—at least some bread."

"I see. How do you propose to go about this?"

She blushed. "As Viscountess Welford . . ."

"I see entirely," he said drily.

"Do you prohibit the use of my name . . ."—she was looking downward unable to meet his eyes—". . . in order to achieve our goals?"

"As a matter of fact . . . no . . . my mother does much the same sort of work for the charities of her choice. No, I do not prohibit . . . but, Cassie, who was that man . . . you called him . . . Lyle?"

"He is Guy's friend. They share lodgings in Whitchurch . . . I met him there."

"He is a radical as well?"

"Yes." She was looking out the window now.

"Why are they in Liverpool?"

Cassie was able to face him for this and with a smile, "Guy is in love with Mary Beth. He is courting her, though her family does not approve . . . and Lyle is with him. I suppose they came, too, for the Lancaster meet today."

He took it in quietly and then just as quietly he put a request to her. "Cass . . . I have but one promise I would extract from you. Before you leave for any more gatherings . . . you will at least inform me of your intentions?"

"If it is your wish, my lord . . . I promise, and you will find that I never break one, once given," she answered softly.

He frowned again. "Indeed . . . do you also tell the truth . . . always?"

"Whenever possible," she answered evasively.

He cast her a doubtful look. "Then tell me more about Lyle."

"There is very little to tell."

"He cares for you?"

"I suppose he does in his way," she answered blandly. She looked out the window again. "He is . . . fun . . . to be with . . ."

It pricked, this last of hers, but the viscount held himself in check. Every inch of him raged with green blood, but he said nothing. He was a strong man, and in full control of himself. After a moment, he said, "Ah, here we are."

Cassie looked out on a three-story brick building of mellow lines. It was shielded from the walk by iron gratings and several tall, flowing willows. Flower beds blossomed amid squares of lawn, and the bowed windows gave off a handsome welcome. Cassie liked it at once.

The central hall was narrow and contained little furniture, though its wall table and mirror spoke of elegance and care. On the first floor was a drawing room, dining room and small ballroom. The long hall dipped into a kitchen and pantry. The second floor housed four bedrooms of considerable size, and the third was designed to accommodate the servants.

"Do you like it?" he asked, sounding much like a youth. She was surprised by it and turned round to find his eyes.

"Indeed . . . it is quite lovely. How long do we stay?"

"As long as it takes," he answered shortly.

"As long as what takes?" she asked at once.

"Never mind." He took her hand. "I don't care for mauve hangings in the drawing room. You may change them to your own taste."

"Oh, yes, I quite agree, they do look dreadful with this rug. I think brown velvet would suit the upholstery. But you said you were short of cash."

"And so I am. But I go to play picquet with Lord Widdons this afternoon and expect my finances to change."

"Oh, no! You would not hurt his lordship?" cried Cassie.

"You care so much?" he inquired, his eyes intense.

"I . . . I . . . he is such a good man . . ."

"He can afford to lose the little I intend to take from him," answered the viscount. "Now, afterward, Cass, what would you say to an early dinner and then the theater?"

"I should like that very much," she agreed. "Kirkby . . . thank you . . . you are being most kind to me."

"No, no, I am not. I am trying very hard to seduce you," with which he turned and opened the door, waiting for her to pass before him. She looked at him and felt a thrill of excitement rush through her and suddenly, all at once, the wench in the tavern seemed to fade from her memory. She tried to recall her, but she could see only herself kissing Lyle.

32

Dinner had been a soft time in space, a welcome interlude for the viscount and his lady. They heard no other voices, nor did they taste the food they ate. They were two alone —in Paradise.

Cassie linked her arm within her husband's as they strolled through the park and she gave no thought to any tavern wench. There was only this big strapping blade thrilling her soul, only this moment . . . only love. They passed the beadles patrolling the park, and the viscount detained one to inquire the source of the music. They were directed to the center of the park where they found a four-piece band playing in a gazebo.

It was perfect, and all through the concert, Cassie's green eyes lingered on her husband's profile. He was all she wanted. He was almost too handsome . . . too magnetically masculine, and she felt her blood warm. Suddenly she thought of their present relationship and wondered if tonight he would attempt to make love to her. The fancy bubbled within her, and she wondered if she would let him. Will you, Cassie . . . will you give in to him so soon after you told yourself you never would? She thought of *Don Juan* immediately, of the lines that had so made her chuckle: "A little still she strove, and much repented, And whispering 'I will ne'er consent'—consented!"

Was it always so when a woman was in love? Was she so weak? Cassie only knew she could hardly wait to return to their hotel room. She wanted to drop off her gown and stand naked before Kirkby Welford—to revel in his desire. It was true what Jack had once said to her . . . her body did burn, and she knew now it was for Kirkby . . . would always be for Kirkby Welford. She was in love with a profligate adventurer.

The viscount sat beside her in a quandary all his own. He sensed a change in Cassie, a softening. She seemed no longer reluctant to allow him near. She had brushed up against him this night in a way that had drained him of color, for he felt her body and went ill with aching. It had all started in the drawing room . . . back at the lodgings. Something had passed between them, and he felt it still. His every nerve was a-quiver. His awareness of her was driving him mad. His heart—traitorous organ—seemed unable to keep a steady flow of oxygen to his lungs, which in turn left him constantly breathless. His fingertips seemed to burn each time he touched her, and his vocal cords had gone numb. To be in such a state was not to his liking, and he felt almost a schoolboy on his first encounter with a female. But the constant thought that outweighed all others was, how would he get into her bed? He would have to go slowly for fear of frightening her off. Yet—devil fly away with this torture! A man can endure only so much! thought the viscount.

As a result of all these divergent reflections, neither spoke on their ride back to the hotel. Nor did they break the silence when they reached their hotel suite; still there seemed to be an affinity between them. Kirkby turned to Cassie and so close was she, so intoxicating was her sweet aroma that he backed away as though touched by fire. This, of course, confused the lady. He confused her further with a short, "Good-night, madam." He hesitated, and his voice came quietly though somewhat hoarsely.

"May your dreams be sweet, Cassie . . ." with which he nearly ran from her room.

She stood watching his retreating form, very much deflated. This is not what she had imagined. She had expected him to embrace her violently and cover her face with kisses. She had planned to put up some resistance, but not enough to deter him. What was he doing? Would he never again try to kiss her? What had she done wrong? She had flirted as much as she knew how . . . she could do no more without appearing to be forward. Yet *off he went!* She dropped off her bonnet and gloves, thinking herself very poorly treated. She threw off her stockings and then reached round for her buttons. Aha! Her buttons! Why had she not thought of them sooner? Really, there could be nothing forward in a wife's requesting her husband's assistance? A slow smile curved her cherry lips as she slowly moved toward their communicating door, and she stopped at its threshold. He was standing in his breeches, all other clothing having been thrown haphazardly to the floor. His broad back was to her and she gazed with hungry admiration a moment before calling his name. "Kirkby?"

He turned and she caught her breath at the light in his black eyes, but she managed, "Could . . . you . . . help me?"

He didn't speak but he went to her. Her long red hair was in his way, but he clutched it a moment as though stealing himself, before asking her to hold it up for him. He fumbled a few moments, cursing the pretty pearl things as "Devil's pieces." He threatened once or twice to tear the evil contraptions off and at last had the task completed. Again he bade her good-night and turned his back. His body was nearly trembling with the battle of will and desire. He couldn't look at her . . . wouldn't look at her.

Disappointed she moved away from him, but out of the corner of her eye she saw him drop to his cot, saw him staring at her, looking very much like a caged wild thing.

She didn't know how she could be so brazen, but the thought and the action came to her as one. She dropped her gown and stood naked before him!

Poor Kirkby, he stared at her luscious breasts in open agony. He put a hand to his wet brow and thought he could stand no more. He had vowed not to take her by force . . . to wait until *she* wanted him. But vows be damned if the chit continued to tease him.

For a man of his experience, he was not very quick-witted in this instance. Not for a moment did he realize that his bride no longer wanted to resist him. She wanted him to come to her, to take her. Oh, she would put up a bit of resistance—for the sake of her pride, but not very much . . .

In some pique she snuffed out the candles in her room and climbed into bed. Perhaps he would still come. Perhaps he was working up his courage . . . *but really Kirkby, you never needed courage before?* However, as these thoughts occupied her mind, the time ticked by and her bed remained cold. She knew all at once. He would not come. Perhaps she no longer interested him. Her caprices had wearied him. Oh no, that was dreadful! She wouldn't let him go . . . not like this! She loved him and she wanted him to love her. But how could he? He believed himself tricked into this marriage. He believed she and Jack had maneuvered him into her bed—a ready license proved this to him. She would go to him . . . she would tell him the license had been Tim's . . . she would explain.

She rose from her bed, she wore no nightdress, and when she entered his room, the moonlight from his open window cast its pale silver over her nakedness. His eyes devoured her as she came to him slowly, and all at once she knew . . . there would be no words of explanation . . . not yet . . . not *now*.

She approached him with a quiet grace, winding her spell around his throbbing heart, winning his soul. His hands went up to her waist, pulling her down to him, and his mouth covered hers voraciously, sucking in her breath, taking all she had to give. "Oh, Kirkby," she cried after a moment, "love me! Please, Kirkby . . . love me . . ." she begged at last.

"Love you? I adore you!" he whispered, hearing his words and realizing all at once how very true they were.

Her kisses covered his chest, his lean torso, went lower to his hard hungry rod. She held its firmness in her two hands, pressing her lips to it, lowering the pulsating muscle until it lay between her breasts.

He groaned with his wild heat, urging her, educating her to the exact mode of the act. "That's my love . . . come now—with me," he said, lowering his arm and lifting her onto the cot so that he held her thighs near his face.

She writhed beneath his ministrations uttering with a wild cry of pleasure as his finger explored her womanly sweetness.

He groaned and rose quickly to his feet. Their eyes locked as he reached down for her and lifted her in his arms. His voice was fierce with emotion, "You wild vixen . . . you are mine! I mean to make up for all those days you held yourself aloof!" And he carried her to their large four-poster bed.

She held him as he mounted her. She gazed up at his features wonderingly. God! how he moved her. Was there anything she would not do if he asked? His mouth was upon hers, his body was parting her thighs, already she felt his hardness demanding admittance, and her body thrilled. "Oh, please, Kirkby . . . don't think I tricked you," she pleaded. "I did not. It was Tim's license . . . he meant to marry Molly . . ."

He penetrated her at that moment and she heard his hoarse whisper in her ear. "Hush, wench . . . it doesn't matter . . . only . . . this . . . matters . . ." with each word the staccato of his plunge increased. Her nails raked his shoulders, her body moved in perfect rhythm to match his thrusts. They were one at last in heart as well as body—and Eden bloomed once more.

Afterward, she lay in his arms, her back was pressed

336

into his chest. He held a breast in one hand, her thigh in another. Again she tried explaining. She told him how Molly had run off, leaving Tim with a useless document. She told him how she had dived off the *Sweet Mary* and rushed to change at the cottage and take up that same license. She told him how she had used it to aid Jack's escape and why she thought Jack Rattenbury had used it to force marriage upon him. "You see, he knew I was . . . a maid. He can't be blamed for wanting to protect me . . . you do understand, Kirkby . . . don't you?"

"I do. But at this moment . . . it doesn't matter," he answered, bringing his head over her shoulder to kiss her mouth.

It would serve for the moment, for he was blotting out all memory of Peter's letters. He would not allow them to come between him and this enchantress . . . not now!

The next week was filled with activity. They had moved into their summer lodgings. He had met several times with the Asbatols. Cassie had captivated Liverpool's *haut ton*. She had taken up his list and proceeded to invite Society's leading ladies to tea. Not long after she began collecting donations for the "poor march" as she termed it. Not all these women agreed that it was a worthy cause, but they found her too dynamic, too animated, too lovable to refuse, and before long she had a tidy sum to deliver to Guy.

They had an appointment to meet in the Grotto. However, when she entered the coffee house it was to find Lyle Stanton waiting for her,

"Well now, lass, I've been longing to see you this past week. I'm that thankful to Guy that he couldn't make it today."

She was a bit nervous. She didn't want to be alone with him, she wanted nothing to spoil what she now shared with her husband.

"Why . . . why couldn't Guy make it?"

"Lady trouble . . . but he tells me you've collected quite a sum."

337

"Yes," she said, taking out a leather pouch. "You will deposit it immediately?"

"Aye, don't you trust me?"

"If I didn't, I wouldn't give it to you, silly," she smiled, unsure whether or not she spoke the truth.

"Ah, Cass," he said, putting the pouch away in a leather case of his own. "I've missed you, love. Do you come tonight?"

"Yes, Guy said he would come for me about eight—though my husband is not at all happy about it," she answered.

"No, and who is to blame him. You going off into the night with another man. I wouldn't like it myself if you were mine."

"Yes, well . . . I had better go . . ."

He stopped her, holding her gloved hand. "Cassie . . ."

"Yes, Lyle?"

He smiled for he could see something was different about her. "Never mind . . . we'll talk more tonight."

The viscount went through his day disturbed by what was happening to him. Several times he attempted to bring himself about. Guilt and remorse met him at every turn. Had he not his brother's letters? Peter was dead because of the Asbatols . . . and Cassie . . . what part had she played? His poor brother . . . not in blood . . . yet much more so. He would see her working patiently with her little tiger, Tommy, he would note her gentle command over the servants they had hired and feel his own heart swelling with love and pride—and his guilt and remorse would be beaten down. When Cassie's bewitching eyes laughed and begged him to join in her mirth, when she lay sleeping in his arms . . . oh! then she became a cherished madness.

Cassie's problem was not so complicated. She knew they were in Liverpool for some nefarious reason—probably to fleece some poor soul—it was the way he gained his money. But that did not matter! She only knew she loved

338

him. She saw his compassion, his tolerance when Tommy mishandled the reins, or neglected to carry out some trifling errand. She saw his soul and it seemed to her as handsome as his face. Her meeting with Lyle Stanton today confirmed her feelings. There was no one for her but the viscount. Lyle attracted her . . . she supposed it had something to do with his sauciness. It reminded her of Jack . . . but that was all. The Asbatols never crossed her mind.

"I do not see why we should not be invited!" pouted Leila Asbatol with a shake of her yellow curls.

"It would not be wise . . . we are not quality, my dear. It would look odd if the viscount were to single us out to mix with the *ton*. And besides . . . we had best stay out of that end of it." He was all too aware of his wife's attraction to the viscount—all too aware of their private little interviews when he was away from the house. He was sick of wondering how far these had gone. "And what's more . . . I don't want you meeting with Welford when I am not present!"

"But why not?"

"Because . . . you may talk too much . . . give away more than I should like!" he answered harshly.

She sneered at him. "You needn't fear . . . he hasn't taken up any of my many offers!"

His hand left its imprint on her arm as he shook her. She infuriated him. He would not be cuckolded.

She glared at him but didn't move from her position. How she was learning to hate him. Yes, Kirkby Welford had paid her many visits. Each time he learned more about their extensive operation and usually his information was obtained without her even being aware that she gave it. She enjoyed boasting and more often than not a little leaked out here and there giving him another piece of the puzzle. His light flirtation with her left her panting and hungry for his company. He filled all her thoughts. "I still want an invitation to that party. Did he not mention that he would be inviting merchants?"

"Not to this first ball. At any rate it does not signify. You have amusements enough! Now, I should like to know how Nancy's visit with you went? Are the girls all settled in and ready to take on the new clients I send them?"

"Yes, though she did mention a problem with that new little Irish girl you took off the boat. Really, Nathan, do you not think twelve years a bit young?"

"Nonsense. The girl's family all starved to death. She had no wish to go that road. She would have if I had not put her with Nancy, and well she knows it. What sort of trouble is Nance having with her?"

"Oh, it seems that client you sent was a bit crude. He was the child's first . . . and well, she has been waking up screaming every night. It upsets the other girls."

"For God's sake!" exclaimed Nathan, "must I think of everything? Gin her up like all the other neophytes we've brought in."

"It appears the chit don't take to the hard stuff . . . it makes her ill, so Nancy thought she might use some opium in the girl's lemon juice. I told her to go ahead . . ."

"Very well. Mind now . . . I don't want the girl too dazed. My customers are particular about the young ones . . . they like them frisky!" He moved forward and placed his hand over his wife's small breast and fondled it through the material of her blue muslin. "You know, Leila . . . it has been a while since · you have let me . . . and I don't mean to wait any longer . . ."

"Nathan! For mercy's sake . . . not now! If you are in such heat, go toss one of your harlots . . . only let *me* be!"

"You *are* one of my harlots!" he sneered, forcing her backward onto the sofa. Jealousy drove him for he knew her mind was on the viscount.

And she, Leila Asbatol? How could she bear to let his ugly hands touch her when she could only think of Kirkby Welford? Her husband's mouth was already on her lips and, as his hands ripped at her gown, she felt sick in her captivity.

The viscount sat musing over his correspondence while his wife stood back, hands on ivory muslin-covered hips, and surveyed her handiwork. Cassie had been rearranging the furniture, perhaps for the third time in one hour. He glanced up and found her thus, her expression somewhat displeased, and he was moved to laughter.

She pouted and gave her long hair a toss with her hand. "Really, you odious man! I have been exhausting myself trying to get the furniture just so for your dreadful ball, and you have the audacity to laugh at me!"

She looked a beauty and his heart leaped at the sight.

"Come here, madam," he said softly.

"Make me!" she bantered, her eyes twinkling.

"Vixen!" he called as he jumped to his feet.

She screeched and took off, laughing all the while. He made a hasty lunge for her. She evaded him and stood, keeping the length of the sofa between them. Again he lunged but landed himself into the cushions of the sofa. Undeterred, he was nimbly, swiftly over its back and chasing her round a chair. However, this time his lady made a strategical error by thinking he cared for such elegant things as Queen Anne chairs. He knocked the thing away without a second thought, ignored her protests of "unfair," jumped over the hapless thing, and caught his wife in a strong embrace where she struggled vainly.

"Now, madam, for making me work when I had leisure in mind . . . you shall pay a high tax!" he said, kissing the back of her neck.

She struggled and felt his hardness against her hips. This excited him further, and his hands went to her breasts, diving beneath her bodice for a better, more enjoyable hold.

"Release me, fiend!" she demanded dramatically.

"My toll . . . then you may go . . ." he compromised.

"No, beast! If I hadn't run . . . what would you have taken?"

"A kiss . . . or two . . ." he teased.

"Then have them now, and be done," retorted the lady.

"Ah, but no . . . I'll have three, four . . . and more —much more. It occurs to me that I have not yet taken you on the floor . . . and the thought drives me to it . . ."

"Kirkby!" exclaimed the lady, somewhat shocked and thrilled at the same time.

He had already eased her onto her knees while one free hand unbuttoned his breeches, releasing his hungry passion. Her well shaped derrière fanned against him, and he hastened to pull up her skirt pressing her forward onto her forearms. And there, he had her in post, on knees and arms, her breasts dangling for his grasp.

"What . . . are you doing?" she asked half in curiosity, half in doubt.

"I'm going to have you, sweetings . . . now," he said pressing his manhood between her thighs as though to prove his words.

" 'Tis but the middle of the afternoon," she objected, wondering how he meant to have her when he still had to turn her about.

"I know, and the light of day teaches me just what a beauty I have for my own. Lord! Cassie! Your butt is gloriously shaped, you have no idea what you do to me . . ."

"Kirk . . . the door! It is not locked . . . the servants . . ."

"Will get a considerable eyeful if they dare to disobey my orders and disturb us," he said grinning broadly, his hands moving sensuously about her form.

"But . . ."

"Cassie, do not say me nay, love. I want to wrap myself around you and love you and go on loving you . . ." he whispered as he positioned the tip of his extremity at her sweet opening and pressed for admission.

"But . . . this is all wrong . . ." she tried to explain and then suddenly, swiftly he had penetrated, proving her statement incorrect.

He groaned with exultant pleasure, finding this new station wondrously delightful, and he began deftly, sedulously, to bring his bride to the same opinion. She felt his deep plunges as he leaned over her back and fondled her breasts. His hands moved lower, pressing her flat belly before going lower to caress her adorable secrets. Then he was straightening to his knees, drawing her into him by her waist and she groaned with wanton abandon. "Oh, Kirkby . . . I love you . . . yes, Kirk . . . yes . . . it is so good . . ." she said, pushing herself back hard into his thrust.

33

It was an unusual meet, thought Cassie, watching the men drill beneath the open sky. Only a few torches had been lit for there was fear among them. They had heard rumors that a special force of constables had been appointed to search out their liberty meets and usher the radicals home. In Tynside that very day some of the radical leaders had been arrested for preaching treason.

Cassie smiled to see Guy in charge, for he was behaving as though he were a lightbob sergeant shaping his division. But she was herself too busy to watch him for long. She had arranged for coffee and biscuits to be brought to this meet, and she had to recruit some women capable of handling the job to help serve. In addition to that, she had to make the rounds to some of the ladies of quality who had decided to attend the meet and see where their subscriptions had gone.

She excited them, introducing them to Lyle, watching Lyle charm away their doubts. She incited them to compassion by pointing out some of the urchins and calling attention to their bare feet and gaunt cheeks. Oh, yes! here was power indeed, for although women of the time had no authority or place in government, their men did, and there was no accounting what influence females had at home.

Cassie was elated with the response. The leading dowagers and hostesses of Liverpool had come and, before they left, they had promised further donations to the cause. They declared the conditions of these honest workers to be intolerable. So it was with some irritation that she heard a few moments later Lyle's disdainful remarks.

"Sheep!" he muttered at Cassie's side, "the lot of 'em! Look at 'em march up and down to Guy's bleating! Makes a man sick, it does!"

"And you, sir . . . what would you have them do?"

"I'd have them hold barking irons in their hands. I'd have them learn how to use the things, I'd have . . ."

"Them arrested before the night was out! Lyle, be sensible. What good would it do to teach them such ways? It is hard enough for them without making them turn on the very government they need to aid them!"

He looked at her calculatingly a moment as though he would speak further but changed his mind. His smile all at once took over and nearly disarmed her. "Never mind all that now," he said suddenly, slipping his arm round her waist, "you and I have more important things to do than spend our time worrying over such as they."

She didn't like the sound of that. "Lyle . . ." she objected.

"Hush, lass. 'Tis a beautiful night . . . come walk with me yonder . . ."

"I can't, Lyle . . . I am a married woman," she said, blushing hotly beneath his appraisal.

"So you were the first time I kissed you, love . . . nothing has changed . . ."

"Oh, but it has, Lyle. Stop it now . . . here comes Guy . . ."

"Did you see, Cass?" exclaimed Guy jubilantly. "No mob, my hundred, are they?"

"No, indeed. You shall have them all in shape, come August, there is no doubt of it," she applauded him.

"Lyle, you'll have to take over for me now. I promised the viscount to have his lady home by ten, and 'tis nearly that now," said Guy, then turning an apologetic eye to Cassie, "Sorry, m'girl, didn't realize the time was getting on . . . don't think he will bludgeon me to death do you?" grinning wide.

"Perhaps you'll have to sustain a blow or two, but not to the death . . ." she bantered.

"A blow or two! Good Lord, Cass . . ." he ejaculated, ". . . one blow would do the job!"

"Sounds a bruiser of a man," said Lyle who had never met the viscount.

"A bruiser indeed!" said Guy, spreading his arms wide descriptively.

"Guy exaggerates," laughed Cassie.

"Does he?" said Lyle, gazing at Cassie's face, "I think I understand the situation now." He raised Cassie's chin. "Is he jealous, love? Yes, I can see that he would be. Are you afraid for me?"

She blushed hotly, for Guy was looking rather angrily at his friend. Hastily, before he had an opportunity to open his mouth and utter one of his blunt and usually ill-timed remarks, she said,

"Well then, Guy, shall we go . . . or do you mean to take a chance with your life?"

He chuckled and led her away while Lyle watched them thoughtfully. A moment later Lyle was turning to the men in the field. Marching . . . ha! He had far different ideas, and so he would let them know . . . and what was more . . . they now had the money to implement his plans!

Cassie and Guy reached her front door to have it swung wide before them, and there on his way out was Lord Eric Widdons. His blue eyes opened wide, and his hat went off nearly at once. "Lady Welford," said he with something of

346

deep feeling. "How good it is to see you again . . . I had hoped I might."

"My lord, I did not know you would be here tonight."

"Uncle," smiled Guy, mildly surprised, "you here?"

His uncle scarcely acknowledged him for his eyes were on Cassie as she entered the hall and glided up to her waiting husband. He was a stiff figure for he had not wanted her to go out tonight, and the fact that she was late only further irritated him.

"What have the two of you been up to, Kirkby?" inquired his wife, noting his mood and bracing herself for what was to come.

"Your husband has been fleecing me," smiled Widdons, catching the viscount's eye. Kirkby had told him that Cassie was not to know what they were about. She was to know only that her husband was a penniless adventurer using his title to gain him the fortunes of others, and Widdons rather liked going along with this.

Cassie frowned. "I see," she said quietly. "If you will excuse me, gentlemen . . ." She nodded good-night to them all and left them for her own chambers.

Some moments later, having dismissed her maid, she sat still fully clothed before a small fire. She looked up as her husband entered, marveling at the powerful sensations his presence always aroused in her. But she was angry with him. Lord Widdons was someone she was fond of, and Kirkby was using him. She returned her gaze to the fire.

He was but peeved with her. She had insisted on going to the liberty meet with Guy that evening. He was in no way jealous of Guy, for he had been quick to see that his wife and the young man had a close but unromantic relationship. But he did not like her to go out at night; then she had promised to be home before ten, and it was now near eleven!

He approached her and after a moment of moodily observing her, knelt beside her, and took her hands. "Madam, you were late . . . would you mind telling me why?"

She turned spitfire eyes upon him. "Never mind that now!" she snapped. "How dare you take advantage of Lord Widdons!"

This further annoyed her husband. Must she take up the cudgels in defense of another man against her own husband?

"Madam, I told you once before—his lordship can afford to lose the little I take from him!" and then because he could not resist it, "If he were a better player, I should not be able to accomplish it, so do not blame me—blame his lack of skill!"

"Oh! That is an intolerable answer! If that is the way you think, there is just no speaking to you!"

"Very well," he answered, taking her chin in his hand and turning her face to his, "but *why* were you late?"

"It was a busy night . . . we didn't realize the time," she said curtly.

"And this Lyle Stanton . . . was he there?" he asked, watching her eyes.

"Yes, Why do you ask?" She turned away on this, unable to meet his gaze and he did not miss it.

It infuriated him. "I see. Cassie, I don't want you attending any more of these meets."

"Ah, and if I say that I will continue to go . . . that you cannot stop me—what then?" She was in a rage and the words flowed into his startled ears, for his was still but a request and one that came from his heart. "What, my lord? Will you issue threats? Am I ever to humble myself at your threats! You must go to Liverpool with me, Cassie, or else I shall turn your people out into the cold. You must, or I shall sell your childhood home. You must or . . . or . . ." she turned from him for tears were running down her cheek.

Had she waved a sabre before his face, he could not have been more shocked. He had believed she loved him . . . all these days he had thought . . . but he had been a fool! This was his first reaction. She had come with him . . . true . . . because of his threat . . . and then afterwards in his arms . . . but that did signify love . . .

only pleasure. She was with him still because of his threats . . . her fears . . . because . . . what else could she do? Where else could she go? And it hurt to the very core of his being.

He grabbed her arm and pulled her roughly against his chest. "And will you say I forced you to this?" he demanded, his mouth taking her own in a brutal kiss that bruised her lips and astonished her out of her tears.

She hadn't expected this. She was but releasing her feelings, perhaps hoping for understanding, tenderness . . . forgetting what such release might evoke from him. She pulled out of his grasp.

"You're hurting me . . ." she said, leaning away from him.

"Hurting you?" he snarled. "Was I? But then . . . what else can you expect from such as I?" He stood up and paced a moment before going to the door. He opened it wide, turned, and gave her a mocking smile, and a "Goodnight, madam," before slamming it at his back.

She sat there before the fire, staring at the door, waiting for the inevitable slamming of the front door. The house shook from the impact, and Cassie dissolved in tears.

The crack in their domestic harmony did not end with this squabble. Theirs were passionate natures, and the break had yet to be settled. Cassie lay in her shift upon the covers, allowing the low fire to dwindle with the hours. She could not sleep. How could she when every minute was wasted wondering where he was, what he was doing, and with whom he was doing it. She had a long wait, for it was not until some minutes before three that Viscount Welford found his way to his bedroom.

He stood there swaying ever so slightly in the large frame of their door, allowing the candlelight to glow over his wife's form. There she was, her titian hair in sensuous disorder, her provocative curves shadowed in alluring lines just within his grasp.

"Well, well . . . playing the dutiful bride, waiting up

349

for your lord and master?" he sneered, his words only slightly slurred.

She would not admit it. "Don't be nonsensical . . . I was . . thirsty . . ."

For some odd reason this made him chuckle. "Thirsty? Aye . . . so was I," whereupon he began a roar of laughter.

She opened her eyes wide, understanding all at once that her husband was in his cups. She had never seen him this way before and wondered what next to expect. All at once he began yanking off his clothes. Wearing only breeches and boots, his black eyes glistening, he made his way toward her. She backed away, and it angered him.

"What? Is it the smell of brandy that frightens you, pet? No, for I'll swear you were used to it on board the *Sweet Mary* . . ." He had already caught her up in his arms, but this time unlike so many others, there was little tenderness in his touch. Indeed, it was more like cruelty.

"Stop it!" she hissed at him.

"Ah! Do you forbid me the marriage bed?" he mocked. "Shall I seek out a chambermaid to see to my needs?"

It stung her and she answered him with her hand. There they stood, glaring at one another, and then all at once as though he had dropped his defenses, his black eyes grew soft, and his voice came almost a plea. "Oh, Cass . . . Cass . . ." and his mouth came down upon hers and she did not refuse him.

So it went, for they loved but yet were caught up in a web of fallacious deeds. They were bombarded with morning visistors, anxious to further their acquaintance. Cassie often entertained Mary Beth and Mrs. Osborne, and on two separate occasions Guy escorted Cassie and Mary Beth to a local liberty meet. Each time the viscount had frowned upon her going, for he did not like it. But he had made up his mind not to interfere in this obsession of hers. The cause was coming along nicely, for one of the dowagers had donated the material needed to make the banners for the Great Meet being held by the Orator in August.

Sometimes Cassie would come back from these meetings much agitated.

"My lord, I know not what to do. There is a mean streak in the mob that one must deplore. They cry because they are hungry and indeed, I must cry for them . . . but, I had more than once to protect Tommy from their taunts! He suffers for his malformed body. He is one of them for he comes from the streets . . . and yet, they think nothing of kicking at him as though he were some poor beast! I am much out of patience, yet the Corn Laws must be done away with. I know not what else to do."

"I would spare you, darling. But you will not let me. The mobs behind the movement leaders lack discipline, and the way they have been forced to live has expelled all sense of compassion. They know only that *they* suffer! If you are committed to the cause, you must not forget that."

"Forget it? How can I? But . . . it is so frustrating . . . and sometimes I think Lyle is right . . ."

He frowned. Lyle's name had a way of forever creeping up into these discussions. "Right about what?"

She eyed him a moment. It wouldn't do to tell him that Lyle wanted to arm the mob, so she hedged. "Oh, he thinks the people too sheeplike, he doesn't trust petitions to do the job."

"He may be right in that," said the viscount grudgingly. "I fear Orator Hunt and his like will meet with disappointment if they continue these open field meetings. I have another letter from Sidmouth, and there is a hint of something I cannot like." He sighed and reached for her hand. "Look, Cass, could you not refrain from attending these meetings . . . just for a time?"

She eyed him, her chin up. "I am sorry, my lord . . . but . . ."

"Cassie, don't think it is because I don't care—I do. But they will not achieve their ends in this manner. They alienate Tory and Whig alike. The government and the leading aristocracy mean to put it down with force. Promise me you will not attend any more meetings."

"No, I cannot promise that. I am a part of it . . . I

351

don't go to cheer. I am directly involved," she said gravely.

He locked her in his embrace. "Obstinate vixen, you will break my heart yet."

"Heart? I did not know you had one," she teased.

He pinched her cheek, but his tone was serious. "I had one love, but now it's yours . . ."

34

The ball was finally upon them. The marbled floor of the ballroom had been cleared for dancing. Windsor chairs lined the wall, allowing the dowagers to sit and gossip. Flowers filled the air with their perfume, and music drifted through the open doors as sedan chairs, carriages, and elegant coaches pulled up before the Welford house.

Cassie stood in the hall beside her husband, and they made quite a pair as they greeted their guests. Her red curls were banded with lustrous pearls, while others adorned her ears and throat. Her white organza gown had leaves of seed pearls embroidered at the low, heart-shaped neckline which displayed her cleavage to perfection (in a way that made her husband stand courtly by her side). Strings of pearls hung in swags over her bare arms just below the shoulder line. She looked like an angel painted by Titian.

The viscount had not seen her while she dressed, for he had been with the Asbatols. He arrived just in time to change into his superbly cut clothes, and he looked the epitome of fashion with scarcely an effort. His black long-tailed coat was molded to his perfect body, as were his tight black breeches. His neckcloth was properly starched, and his white silk waistcoat was finely stitched with black thread. His ebony hair dipped over his forehead, and his thick brows accentuated his black eyes. Several lovely women cast looks of appreciation as they greeted him.

Finally, the host and hostess were able to leave their posts near the front door and go into the ballroom to mingle with their guests. His lordship was required to dance with as many ladies as possible. Thus Cassie found herself in the arms of one gentleman after another. It was not altogether a bother, for they flattered and flirted, and she was well able to see that her husband's eyes followed her.

She felt a pang of jealousy each time his selection gave him an especially lovely partner, and at times like these she would turn a radiant smile upon her own companion. However, the viscount and his bride had learned much about each other in the past three weeks, and they knew that none of these interlopers meant a brace of snaps to either of them.

Cassie winked at her husband as he waltzed with a dowager who had the uncomfortable habit of taking the lead. Noting this, Cassie giggled, but then something else caught her eye. Mary Beth, looking very pretty in a frothy pink gown, was pushing Guy who looked very stiff in his full dress, and rushing away from him.

Cassie excused herself from her elderly partner and went to the rescue. She found Mary Beth in the garden behind a yew tree. "Mary, what has occurred to overset you?"

"Oh, Cassie, he . . . has insulted me. I thought he loved me . . ."

"Insulted you? Nonsense. He adores you and well you know it!" snapped Cassie, never patient with stupidity.

"No . . . he does not," sobbed the girl. "He thinks my family are parasites . . . he thinks my loyalty an act. He thinks I have trifled with him!"

"Oh, for pity's sake! Stay here and compose yourself!" said Cassie, going back into the ballroom. She discovered

354

Guy taking a long gulp of wine. She removed the glass from his gloved hand, ignored his objection, and led him to the dance floor—all beneath the frown of her husband who wondered what was afoot.

"Guy, what is this nonsense? You have made poor Mary Beth cry! Do you want her to cry?"

"No! Her tears rip through me like a knife! How can you think I wish to distress her?" said Guy, much overset himself.

"What has happened then?"

"I . . . I asked her to marry me," he said sullenly.

"And?"

"Damn it! Excuse me . . . she refused."

"But . . . I cannot credit that. Refused? But why? She loves you!"

"Says she owes it to her family to marry Mr. Freigate. He has asked her to marry him . . . and she says she must!"

"That is dreadful. She does not love him . . . she loves you."

"That is what I thought until tonight. I believe the lady is nothing but a mercenary jade!" he said bitterly. "Yet—I love her still!"

"Oh, stop it, you young fool! She loves you. I will not allow this to go on. Go home now! It will do her good to think she has lost you. Tomorrow, attend me at ten . . . no, make it eleven. She will be there, without her aunt, for I mean to fetch her and bring her back with me. We will settle this matter! See if we don't!"

The waltz had ended but Guy stood still in position with Cassie.

"Indeed, Cassie . . . do you really think so?"

"Of course, I do, noddy. Now then, go on," she said smiling into his cherubic countenance.

"Yes, do go on . . ." said a familiar voice at her ear.

She turned to find Lyle Stanton ready to take her up for the next waltz. She had forgotten that she had issued him an invitation.

"Why, Lyle . . ." she muttered, dimly aware of a pair of black eyes watching from the other side of the room. He led her into a waltz, and she felt herself blush beneath his look. It was so intent, and she was sure Kirkby was watching still. "Lyle, please . . ."

"Please what?" he asked quietly.

"Don't stare at me so."

"I cannot help it. Do you know how lovely you are?"

"Indeed . . . my husband often tells me."

"Stop it, Cass!" he ordered. "Don't . . . for I don't want to know what *he* tells you." He looked around. "I have to be alone with you."

"You must stop it, Lyle. That afternoon with you . . . it was a mistake . . . I was lonely . . . upset . . . the kiss meant nothing . . ." she apologized.

"Then we shall have to make the next different . . ." he sallied, and there was a light in his eye that forced her to smile.

"You are a rogue!" she returned.

The dance was ended, and as they turned they found themselves facing a fury of a man. The viscount, arrogant, rugged, spoke in a cold voice. "I don't believe, madam, that I have the favor of this gentleman's acquaintance."

"Indeed—and so you should for you have often heard me mention his name," said Cassie, proceeding to make the necessary introductions.

The viscount sized up his man quickly and left him with an ominous glare before adroitly taking his wife by the arm. "My lady . . . I need a word with you in private . . ." he said, turning to Lyle, "You will excuse us?"

Lyle had little choice, for the viscount was already sweeping her away. Through the crowd they pressed, smiling, jesting with their company as they passed into the hall and across it to the small tea room. It was empty, and he gently pushed her before him.

As he closed the door at his back, she rounded on him, her green eyes sparkling militantly. What did he mean treating her like this? "Just what do you think you are doing?" she asked.

"I?" said he. "What am *I* doing? What the deuce are *you* doing flirting with that brazen gallant?"

All at once she realized what notions her husband had entertained, and she burst out laughing. She adored him for caring and went to him, putting her arms around his neck and attempting to draw his face to hers. He remained rigid. "I will have my explanation, madam!"

"Will you, my lord?" she teased. "But you have so much more . . ." she said, taking his hand and putting it to her heart, then as she lowered the bodice of her gown exposing one full delectable breast, she guided his hand in a caress while her lips pursed invitingly.

His mouth came down on hers fiercely, possessively. She was his heaven and earth—and his hell! His fingers stroked the firm flesh, and his mouth traced a line down her throat before returning to her mouth and then biting, just a shade too savagely. She pulled away giving him a reproachful look. "Devil . . ."

"Now tell me, enchantress, what *is* he to you?"

"Oh, Kirkby, nought. Though to be honest, I let him kiss me once . . . but it was very, very long ago . . . at a time when you were very cruel to me . . . and things were not as they are now . . ."

Again he stiffened, but she touched his cheek. "Do not mind it, 'twas but a little kiss . . . nothing to yours . . ." she was smiling most enticingly.

"I won't have it!" he commanded.

"No, you shouldn't," she agreed. "You *needn't*, for I have no heart, no fire, for anyone but you."

He looked at her a moment. "And what were you and Guy up to earlier?"

"He and Mary Beth had a spat of sorts . . . I am playing Cupid, you see."

"Oh, my God!" he groaned.

"But what harm can come of it?" she protested sweetly.

"A great deal," he said tweaking her pert nose.

"But they need help."

"And you think yourself experienced enough to give it?" he teased, his eyes lighting up.

She moved seductively, putting her arms about him and pressing against the hardness of his body, "Don't *you?*"

His hand went to her naked breast and fondled a moment before he sighed and pulled up the bodice of her gown to cover her nudity. But then her mouth met his, and he felt a stronger urge. His arms tightened around her, his hand went to the firm roundness of her backside, and he grabbed hard. "Blister it, woman, you've got up my appetite . . . and you'll have to appease it before I let you leave this room."

He excited her. Every inch of her wanted him, but it was not the time or the place. She enjoyed arousing him. She enjoyed having this power, but she rushed out of his grasp and made a show of mock terror. "Nay, Kirkby Welford . . . our *guests!*"

He made a snarling sound as he reached out and caught her wrist. He pulled her firmly against him, and his mouth was close to her own as he breathed, "Now, my fair charmer, you asked for it and, sweetings . . . you are going to . . ."

The door opened at his back, and he released her at once. She cast him a look of triumph and said casually, "Ah . . . shall we go see to our guests?"

The viscount cast a cold, but polite look at the intruders, a young couple standing doubtfully in the doorway, but he waved them inside before giving his wife his arm and whispering to her, "You'll pay for this later, my beauty! Depend upon it."

"My lord, I do depend upon it," she said, casting him a saucy look before going out of the room.

He watched the sway of her well-shaped hips as she walked in front of him, and he thought of the ballroom full with people. He would have to see them all out before he could take her upstairs . . . and he groaned.

"Your rout went well?" asked Leila, her hand sliding

from the viscount's broad shoulder down the length of his arm.

"Very well, thank you. Where is Nathan?" he asked. "I received a note from him specifically requesting me to come by at this hour."

" 'Twas not from him . . . ." she said, giving him a sly look.

"I see." said the viscount slowly. He would have to be careful. He knew Leila for a hellcat; if she felt herself scorned, she could turn on him and ruin the entire operation. He smiled warmly at her. "That is . . . most interesting, my pretty . . ." he was moving his finger over her lips, "now perhaps you will tell me what this is all about?"

"I wanted to see you. I was most vexed with you, darling. Why were we not invited?"

"Because our connection at this stage should be carefully concealed," he answered more briskly.

"Why?" she pouted.

He looked at her a long moment and the only thought that occupied his mind was, Cassie had nought to do with this woman . . . could not have . . . Peter was wrong. He answered Leila, pacing some distance from her. "Because I have Widdons in my pocket and should like to keep him there. He might raise a brow should he discover that I keep company with Nathan Asbatol."

"Really? Why?" she asked, somewhat surprised by this.

"Because, through Lord Widdons it has come to my attention that the business of abduction does not solely occupy your husband's time. He has been engaging in dealings which, while not specifically defined as illegal, are most certainly . . . shall we say . . . indelicate."

She frowned up at him. "Surely you don't mean our . . . well our connection with Madame Nancina's? How could he possibly know about that? It has been in operation but a few weeks . . . ."

"Madame Nancina's?" repeated the viscount. "No, he did not speak of a brothel . . . but of a certain shipping arrangement you have brought with you from Bristol."

"Shipping? The Irish servants you mean?" said she, raising a brow. "But, how could he know?"

"Nathan was a bit sloppy in his last dealing. He singled out a young man who caught on to his scheme and threatened to expose him."

"Why, that two-faced, double-dealing cove!" screeched Lelia in a temper. "He promised to keep mum if we paid him off—and we did—handsomely!"

"Exactly why I don't want to be openly connected with Nathan. He should have disposed of him. The young Irishman eventually got employment in Lord Widdons's service, and the story came out. I am afraid his lordship is much disturbed that you should be selling indentured servants to people in the United States."

"It is done all the time," she said.

"It is white slavery, my dear and, as I said, I do not want the stench to interfere with our present operation. We will keep our connection *private*."

She moved up close to him, a smile on her lips, but the aura of wickedness repulsed him. Her hand slithered up his chest. "But, darling . . . I do so want to see more of you . . ."

"Later, love . . . I believe I hear your husband coming in . . ." said the viscount with a sense of relief as the door opened at his back.

"My lord?" said Nathan, casting an ugly look at his wife, "I was not expecting you."

"No. I came by to advise you that all goes well with Widdons," said the viscount easily. "His son will be returning from Scotland some time in August. That gives us about twenty days to prepare."

"You know the route he will be taking?" inquired Nathan.

"No, not yet, but I shall." He nodded at Leila and started for the door. "And, Nathan, we will get a sizeable sum—no less than thirty thousand pounds . . . more than you have had in the past!"

Nathan's eyes lit up. "He has that much cash?"

"He does. I shall let you know about the details as soon

as I have them. Until then . . . I don't think we should meet, do you?"

"No," agreed Nathan, at once glancing at his wife, "I don't."

The viscount smiled as he departed. The noose was drawing tighter, and in a very short time he would have them.

At the Welford home Cassie stood in their comfortable drawing room looking her best, for she was in love. What was more, she was having a hand in arranging the lives of the people she liked best. She tossed a wayward strand of hair over her shoulder, put her hands on her blue muslin-covered hips, and snapped impatiently, "Mary Beth, you are not making any sense. Lord, girl, I have seen and spoken to your dreadful Mr. Freigate and must tell you that the poor fellow is as insipid as a glass of milk. How can you compare him to Guy?"

"I can't . . . and do not," cried the young woman in much agitation. "But, oh, Cassie, I was persuaded *you* would understand. Mr. Freigate is sickeningly rich—and stands to inherit a title as well . . . and oh, Cassie . . ."

"But does he love you? Do you love him?" demanded Cassie relentlessly.

"Love? It has nought to do with it. Pray, what does it matter, when there is my family to consider?" said Mary Beth, sinking onto a chair and burying her face in her hands.

"But, Mary, you share no feelings with Mr. Freigate. You can't mean to marry a man you don't love . . . to further your family's needs!" retorted Cassie vehemently. "It wouldn't be fair to Mr. Freigate!"

"But what then of my family?" asked Mary Beth stubbornly.

"To Hades with them!" cried Cassie impatiently. "You don't mean to make martyrs of both Mr. Freigate and yourself on such a plea? Or perhaps I don't know you and it is really for yourself that you want this match?"

"Indeed, Mary Beth!" exclaimed Guy Bamfield from

the drawing room doors. He had already taken a step into the room before she could speak, and the slamming of the door in the poor butler's face drowned out her reply. He looked an angry young man as he stalked down his beloved, throwing his top hat to a stool in passing. His complexion was pale, but his eyes glittered with emotion.

Mary Beth went to him putting one hand upon his blue coat as though to still his wrath, while Cassie stepped back, a slow smile covering her mouth. She had timed everything perfectly. She had fetched Mary Beth early this morning from the Grand Hotel, scarcely giving the girl time to don her yellow frock. And now, she could have kissed Guy for his timely entrance. It was just the sort of romantic encounter Mary Beth needed to convince her that she could never marry anyone else!

"Guy . . . dearest . . . you must understand," pleaded Mary Beth.

He took her arms in a firm grasp and his intense gaze scalded her face. "Understand? How can I? Explain it to me! If you can!"

"My parents are not wealthy. They have spent a great deal of their savings to set me in society, buy me pretty gowns—all in order that I make a good match . . ."

"Am I then a match to be scorned?" spat her lover. "My family name cannot be spurned, I do assure you, and my independence, though not a fortune would allow me to give you a comfortable life."

"But there are my sisters to be launched," she cried.

"And will you think of them each and every time Freigate puts his clammy hands on you? Will you think of them when his lips touch yours? Tell me, Mary Beth, what will you wish for your family then?"

"Stop it!" she cried, pounding on his chest. "Oh, do stop it, Guy!"

He pressed her to him and kissed her forehead, before setting her from him again. "How can I? Know all, my love, for he will exact his marriage toll . . . and will you then dream of me . . . ?"

"No, no, I couldn't . . . it has been only you . . . I could take no other . . ." sobbed the girl, her tears flowing freely.

"Nor I, Mary Beth," he whispered, holding her close to him.

Bravo! thought Cassie, much enjoying herself in spite of the girl's distress. Guy was saying just what he should . . . exactly the right words.

Much moved by her lover's soft passion, Mary Beth gave herself up to his embrace, and they forgot Cassie in their pledge to one another.

Cassie sighed for them and then cleared her throat, reminding them of her presence. "Well then," she said on a final note, "I am glad *that* is settled. We have but to set a date, arrange for the license and the minister, and manage things right and tight!"

"But oh, Cassie, my aunt will turn upon you to answer for it. I cannot allow you to involve yourself further," said Mary, much concerned.

"But that is nonsense. You will need a witness, and my title should help to carry the thing off since you are not yet of age, Mary. As to your aunt, I am quite capable of handling her when it comes. You cannot sell yourself to the highest bidder, and so I shall be pleased to tell them. Why —one would think we lived in the Middle Ages. These are modern times, and things have changed!"

"I still feel guilty about my sisters . . . they are depending on me . . ."

"Pooh! Guy can manage to sponsor one of them. And when she is married, she can take on the next. Am I not right, Guy?"

"Of course. Lord, Mary, I am no pauper . . . though I have nothing to Freigate—blister the fellow's eyes!" he added, remembering the way the man had cast out lures to Mary Beth.

The door of the drawing room opened quietly, and the viscount stood on the threshold taking in the sight of Mary Beth still wrapped in her beloved's embrace. He then glanced at his wife, raised his brows quizzically at her, and managed a droll smile before saying blandly, "Good-morning!"

Both Mary Beth and her young man blushed profusely and moved apart beneath the viscount's scrutiny. Not certain to his temper, they knew not what to expect. He suppressed a quivering lip—they could not meet his eyes and thus missed their twinkling—and further distressed the hapless couple by next saying, "Good Lord! Never say I have interrupted a *tête-à-tête* . . . ! How clumsy of me! But, I say, allow me only to remove my wife . . . and then, carry on, you two!"

Mary Beth nearly fainted and her beloved most certainly fought a convulsion of some considerable size. His voice squeaked, "No, no, we were just about to depart . . ." He turned to his betrothed and drew her arm through his before bowing to Cassie. It was almost more than the viscount could do to control his mirth as the young man bowed to him and pulled at Mary Beth, scarcely giving her time to pick up her shawl and bonnet as they made good their escape.

As soon as the door closed at their backs, the viscount roared with laughter and turned, his eyes brimming with mirth, to find his wife glaring at him. She shook an admonishing finger though she too was amused. "You horrid thing! You frightened them nearly to death! I do believe you are a devil . . . really, Kirk—how could you?"

"How could I not?" he said coming forward and scooping her up into his embrace as he placed a kiss on her nose. "They were very much in the way, my love. You may play Cupid to your heart's content. However, I want no hand in the business. What I want a hand in is . . ." he said, proceeding to show her.

35

The fragrance of summer days swept through July and brought the month to an end. August sweltered before them, and Cassie knew as well as any that things would not, could not remain the same. Though her will knew no bounds, though she was determined to ignore unfounded threats . . . still there were ghosts lurking about!

She sat sewing amid yards and yards of dazzling white cloth. Tommy sat some feet away from her, cutting patterns of triangles. The viscount too, not far from her side, looked up from his pile of papers, as he had intermittently throughout the morning. There was a tranquillity in watching her, an overwhelming sense of bliss in his heart. She had become everything to him, and he had pushed aside all earlier suspicions.

"Oh, confound it, Guy Bamfield! How can I possibly finish all this by next week?" she asked of the absent young man.

The viscount glanced up from his papers. Guy's name always had the power to catch his interest. Cassie's deep involvement in the movement was a source of displeasure to him, and it had a dampening effect on his mood. "What is it you are sewing, vixen?" he asked, frowning over the yards of cloth. He had assumed it was some gown or other. Now he could see it was no such thing.

"Liberty banners! We mean to wave them rather than shout, for Guy says the Orator wants everyone orderly. How does one keep a crowd of some seventy thousand people orderly?"

"My God! You don't mean to tell me now that *you* have decided to attend that affair?" he exploded. "I won't have you going all the way to Manchester with no one but Guy to attend you."

"*You* could take me," she said wistfully.

He frowned. It would be cutting it too close. He had to hold himself in readiness. "No, no, Cass, there are reasons why I cannot plan on it. Now really, love . . . do promise me you won't go."

She frowned also. "I told you, Kirkby, I would think about it. Don't make me promise now."

"But surely there is no need for you to be there . . . not with such a crowd?" he persisted.

"No, you are right there. But I do so want to see the Orator."

"I shall be happy to introduce you to him when we go to London," he retorted somewhat sardonically.

She pulled a face, but rose from her position and went to him. Bending her arms, she encircled his neck, and her lips brushed his cheeks. "I don't think I'll attend this one. Does it please you, love?" It was a soft whisper.

He sighed with some relief. "You are wise not to."

" 'Tis not wisdom that keeps me from it . . . but a regard for your wishes," she said, kissing his ear.

She had the power, this woman. She could make or destroy his day. He reached for her, but she jumped quickly away and cast him a naughty look, indicating Tommy's blushing presence. He sighed but allowed her to return to her sewing, which she did without relish.

366

"Drat these things! I'm tired of them . . . but they must be done."

"Leave 'em be if ye wish, m'lady," said Thomas shyly. "I be that pleased to do the lot of 'em fer ye . . ."

It was said with some pride, for a few weeks ago Cassie had discovered that Thomas was skillful with his hands. She had been repairing a long tear in one of the hangings when she had pricked herself. Going off to wash the small trickle of blood, she returned to find that Thomas had repaired the tear, and with some intricacy. She praised him highly for it, and blushingly he had advised her that he had learned the knack with a needle when he had spent a few years in the parish orphange.

"Oh, thank you, Thomas, but I must do my share. You may help me though whenever you complete those cuttings, for it is but one week we have to get these distributed, and then another week before the meet."

Just then the drawing room door was opened by their butler, and all heads went up at the announcement. "The dowager Lady Welford!"

A tall woman of uncertain age entered. She was thin and encased in a traveling habit of pale camel silk. A fashionable bonnet was affixed to what Cassie thought at first were rolls upon rolls of white cotton. However, a closer look discovered this to be the woman's hair. Thin lines played about her watery blue eyes and thin, pursed lips, but it was evident she had been a beauty in her day.

She gave Cassie a long look, the pale blue eyes lighting upon the girl's cinnamon-gold tresses with some distaste, and Cassie, ever sensitive, felt it! Here now was the wedge she knew would come. She would have to deal with the viscount's relatives and their prejudices . . . and there were bound to be both!

The dowager ignored Cassie after her first perusal and went directly towards the viscount who was already out of his seat. He kissed the thin fingers through their light gloves, and his black eyes twinkled at his stepmother. She had filled a void for him when he was young enough to need a mother, without being jealous for the one he had lost, and he was still quite fond of her. "Mother! How the deuce did you find me?" he asked in some amusement.

"You dreadful man, what sort of greeting is that! You cannot disappear and think I shall write you off! I still have my wits about me even though my youth has done! I applied to Siddy, and he gave over finally."

"Never say Lord Sidmouth gave you my address? Why, we had settled it between us that it would be given to no one!"

"Siddy was never able to refuse me anything, darling, and I was much distressed, you know, for I had a letter from Constance Berkley . . ." she allowed her eyes to stray meaningfully toward Cassie.

Cassie had risen and straightened out her simple gown of dotted blue muslin, allowing mother and stepson to greet one another. She felt some ire, for the woman seemed purposely rude, but she had allowed this to pass. A militant sparkle entered her green eyes at the dowager's offhand remark, and she was about to slash through with something cutting when the viscount's hand reached out, and he smiled warmly. "Love . . . come, it is time you met my stepmother."

In spite of her initial feelings, Cassie smiled and came forward, secure now on her husband's arm, and the introductions were made. However, the dowager was barely condescending and not the least bit interested in furthering their relationship. She turned her face once again to her stepson and in so doing incurred his displeasure. His brow went up, but she ignored it and pursued,

"Now, darling, let us allow your wife to return to her . . . sewing, or whatever it was she was doing on the floor, for I dearly wish to speak with you in private!" There was an unpleasant underlining to her voice.

The viscount felt himself in a damnable position. He was all too aware that his stepmother was doing her utmost to be rude to Cassie, and this he could neither like or allow. His pride and his growing devotion to his wife precluded her being held apart from him. However, the devil was in it that there was no telling what his irate stepmother would say . . . She had not come all this distance to keep silent. She too had read Peter's letters.

He underestimated Cassie if he thought he would have to beg her pardon, for she rushed to the fore most gracious. "Please, Kirkby, do take your stepmama into the gardens. I think you may enjoy a pleasant privacy there . . . I shall go have the servants prepare a room."

He smiled tenderly at Cassie. "Thank you, love," he said softly.

The dowager pulled a face at this and took his arm. She waited until the house was at their backs before rounding on the viscount. "Now, Kirkby, will you kindly explain to me how all this has come about?" She did not allow him to answer but hastened on in her austere manner. "I knew the moment I read Constance's letter that you had somehow tricked that creature into believing herself your wife —while in fact, she is but your mistress. Is that not so? It is all part of your scheme to avenge your brother's . . ."

"No!" his harshness halted her. "Cassie *is* my wife. She had nothing to do with Peter's death, and I won't hear a word against her. You know nothing of the matter!"

"I . . . I know nothing . . .? Are you mad? Did I not read his letters? Is she not the Cassandra Farrington he spoke of? Did she not betray him . . . plot against him . . . turn him in to the jackals?"

"No, she had no part in it," he said quietly. "You will respect me by accepting that."

"She has bewitched you! My God! The doxy has dazzled you as she did your poor brother! Oh, my dearest Kirk! How can you so carelessly stroll over his memory?"

"I am not doing that! Peter was mistaken about Cassandra," he said, gritting his teeth against the old suspicions.

"Mistaken? Peter? No! A thousand times no! He would not so malign another—as well you know! He would not have written such things about her without honest cause!" snapped the dowager.

It was true, hauntingly true. Yet the viscount had come to know Cassie, and knowing her, he loved her wholly, truly—but what of his brother's truths? Would he ever know the truth?

"Nevertheless," he answered after a dark pause, "Peter was mistaken with regard to Cassie, and *you* must return to London!"

"Must I?" said the dowager on a sardonic note. "No doubt so that you may carry on this fantasy you have created with that . . . that . . ."

"Mother!" he snapped immediately. "She is my wife!"

"So you have said. Well, I shan't go to London until you have been extricated from this marriage! I have but one son left to me . . ." She reached for his face but in his anger he pulled away. "Oh, darling . . . do not turn a deaf ear to me. You were not of my blood, but I have always felt you were mine. I want you happy, and know you can never be so with that dreadful woman . . ."

"Mother, you tread dangerous ground. Your wiles, though strong, have no force to cause a break between Cassie and myself. And I have not worked and planned to bring about the end of this ring I have pursued simply to have you come and wipe it all away with your foolishness. Your connection to Peter will surely come out if you remain, and that would then tie *me* to Peter!"

"Do you mean to pack me off then before I have dined?" she returned coldly.

"Don't be nonsensical, you know well you may remain the night . . . but I want you off as soon as you have rested."

"Really? Well, unless you mean to transport me willy-nilly to London, you shan't manage it, for I intend to stay."

"That is impossible. We will discuss it in the morning . . . and, Mother, I am not above packing you off . . . willy-nilly!"

"Fie on you! Horrid creature! Whatever would your father say if he could hear you?"

"In all probability he would applaud me, dearest. Now . . . do let us not spend the evening in argument. Cassie will have arranged for an extra setting at dinner, and I am certain you will want a bit of a rest first."

"Yes, but I shan't join you for dinner. I will require a tray sent to me in my room. I am absolutely devastated after that hideous journey and *your* ill usage!"

"As you like, madam," agreed his lordship, his eyes twinkling.

They returned to the drawing room to find Cassie in the midst of cloth. The dowager repeated her wishes coldly to the viscount's bride before leaving them to each other, and Cassie knew that the catalyst had arrived to challenge her peace.

Cassie tossed beside the viscount. He had been quiet that evening and had not joined her in bed until very late. She had awaited him anxiously, and his arrival did little to dispel her concern. In his preoccupation he had undressed in silence and but bestowed a peck on her forehead before giving her his back.

Really! thought Cassie now. It was quite enough to have endured his stepmother's rudeness, but then to be ignored by him as well . . . that was the outside of enough. She made a fist and landed him a shoulder blow that brought him round sharply. "What the devil?" he ejaculated in some surprise.

"Oh?" she said sweetly. "Then I *do* exist?"

"What in Heaven's name are you talking about?" he asked with some impatience. "Have you lost your mind?"

"Indeed, I was concerned with that very question. Have I lost my mind? Was it imagination that gave me a warm loving husband earlier today? Has he somehow been transformed into a stranger . . . or am I indeed befuddled?"

He gave her a long look. He had turned his back, but he had not slept. Emotion had worn him down, but he had felt her softness and wanted to hold her. His mother had opened a wound, she had drawn blood, and with it doubts had surfaced once again. But Cassie had the power, the magic over his soul, and suddenly he smiled and reached for her. Ah, but she was in a temper and drew away. "Nay, my lord! You have scorned me this night, and must now live with it . . . or sleep with it, as it happens!"

"You think so?" he asked huskily as he caught her round the waist.

She kicked his probing knee and bit down hard on his near shoulder. As he yelped in some surprise, she jumped out of bed, snatching a pillow to cover her transparent nightdress. "Now, my lord, you may continue your sleep alone, since that was what you wanted."

"But, Cassie, 'tis not my wish! Come now, vixen," he soothed, rubbing his shoulder as he spoke.

Some of her fury had subsided, but her green eyes glittered in the darkness, and he was taken with their lights. Fascinated, he watched in awe as she spat at him, "Aye, you want a bit of a toss, do you, husband? Well, it suits me not! Good-night!" she said, giving him *her* back and making toward their dressing room.

He jumped up immediately and barred the way, an imposing figure in his bold nakedness, "Prithee, wife, I call thee to duty!" he teased, his black eyes shining.

"Duty?" she ejaculated, her own eyes flashing. But gathering her senses, she retaliated at once by dropping the pillow, and spreading wide her arms. "Yea, then, lord and master, how shall I perform it? Shall I lie for you and allow you your pleasure? Aye then my lord . . . you shall have your duty and be forewarned . . . still *you will have none of me!*"

He was not angered but amused, enchanted, aroused. He drew her into him, arching her back, and his lips whispered into her ear, "Think you not I can bring you down, vixen? Think you that you will lie still beneath me without pleasure? Shall we see?"

Suddenly she pushed hard against his chest for she could already feel the hot blood racing through her veins. She would not be seduced now! Not in her anger. She would teach him never to shut her out again! "Release me, fiend! I'll have none of you!"

"No? But you just said you would perform your duty. Are you about to renege?" he said, taking her breast in his hand and thumbing the nipple. "Tut, tut, sweetings . . . are you not a lady of your word? Think you can offer and not give? Come, I'll teach you better manners!" he said, suddenly heaving her over his shoulder and giving her butt a resounding slap.

She objected most strenuously but found herself roughly flung upon the bed. "Oh! You brute!" she cried and then gasped beneath his sudden weight.

"Brute, am I? Know you the ways of a brute, love? Shall I teach you that as well?" he said, forcing her wrists above her head, bringing his lips to her white shoulders, tracing a pattern to the scoop of her neckline. "Ah! This cloth hinders my way. A husband would remove it gently, but a *brute* . . . now a brute would . . ." he said mockingly, as he ripped the gown off her body.

Again she gasped and opened her eyes wide, as a wild pleasurable sensation engulfed her. She fought it and him, wriggling in alluring contortions beneath him. "Will you use strength to gain your way? Is that not beneath you?"

"Beneath me?" he retorted amicably. "But . . . you have named me a brute—and a fiend!"

"Nay, then . . . I retract it—if you will but leave me be!" she returned.

He sighed long, but his smile was soft, meaningful. "Retract it not, my vixen, for I mean to have you whether you will or no!" His lips took hers, and she felt his passion sweep over her. Her resistance retreated before her own rising desire, and her arms drew him still closer as her body arched to meet him. But still she recalled her purpose. "Kirkby, promise me . . . you must promise me never to hold me aloof again . . ." It was a plea.

"Aye, love, but not because your body tantalizes me into frenzy. I would have you know that! 'Tis because I *love* you, Cassie . . . and loving you, I know the wonder of you. How then could I hold you from me?" and once again his mouth covered hers.

The dowager sent word next morning that she was with cold and would remain abed. The viscount had cause to raise his brow, but under the circumstances there was little he could do. There too he had not the time to fret over this, for several matters urgently needed his attention, and he was soon gone.

Cassie had seen her husband off, then retired to her room to don a riding habit of green silk with an exquisite top hat whose scarf of shaded greens adorned her cascading tresses. Thus attired she had every intention of taking Starfire for a run in the park. However, she was detained by the emergence of a small wiry woman in a mobcap who turned out to be Bertie, the dowager's personal maid. She approached Cassie quietly and somewhat diffidently, being shy by nature. "Please, mum . . . I see ye be goin' out, and I was wonderin' if ye would be so kind as to instruct the kitchen to see to m'lady's needs—as they seem doubtful of takin' orders from me . . ."

Cassie smiled and moved towards the hall bellrope as a loud banging on the front door brought the butler from his room at the rear of the hall. Guy Bamfield entered hastily, and Cassie noted at once that he was out of breath and in something of a sweat. "Guy!" she exclaimed. "What has. . ."

Ignoring the fact that two servants were hovering about, he exploded in his forthright way, "Cassie, thank God I have caught you before you went out. Are you promised anywhere . . . can you cancel?"

"No, I was but going to exercise Starfire . . ." she answered with the inflection of a question.

"Good, then you will not mind coming with me. That way you can still give him a run."

"But, whatever is wrong?"

"Do come . . . I can explain everything along the way," he said, suddenly aware of the servants' interest.

"Of course," said Cassie turning to her butler. "Oh . . . and Jenkins . . . kindly see to it that the staff adheres to all the dowager's wishes." She had little time to utter more for Mr. Bamfield had already taken her arm and was leading her out front where Thomas stood holding both Starfire and Mr. Bamfield's gelding.

"Will ye not be wanting me wit ye, m'lady?" asked Thomas hopefully.

Mr. Bamfield answered, "No, not today, Thomas, as we mean to ride swiftly. But have no fear, child, your mistress is safe with me."

"Aye, then I'll be finishin' up those banners, m'lady," said the boy somewhat dourly, for he was jealous of anyone who took up Cassie's time. His adoration allowed admittance to only one other, and that was the viscount. All others he held in distrust.

Cassie wondered at Guy as he hoisted her up in the saddle, and her mind was busy with this new quirk of his but, as they were winding their way through heavy traffic, she was unable to question him.

At last Cassie saw the outskirts of Liverpool and sighed, but as Guy turned onto the Manchester road, she began to feel uneasy. "Guy! Wherever are you taking me?"

He released a weary sigh. "Bless you for an angel, Cassie . . . do forgive me . . . but I couldn't blurt out the whole of it with your servants about . . . and we couldn't very well discuss the thing in the middle of Liverpool. But if you are against it, I shall take you back directly!"

"Against what?" she said with a show of impatience.

" 'Tis the license, you see . . . had a bit of a time trying to get one because Mary Beth is under age. Though I did find an office in Liverpool willing to issue it for a sum . . . I felt it unethical to use bribery to obtain a document that would sanctify my marriage!"

"Oh," said Cassie. "Then . . . how *do* you mean to obtain it?"

"I was given to understand that a magistrate in Eccles —'tis a town just outside Manchester, you know—would be willing to issue the license provided I could produce a sponsor to sign the necessary documents. Well, after conferring with Mr. Drummond, the magistrate, we settled it between us that *your* signature on the papers would satisfy him . . . therefore . . ."

"Therefore, we are off to Eccles!" supplied Cassie. "How very diverting! I reiterate . . . you are a horrid boy!"

This did not at all banish his smile but instead rather broadened it. "There now, I have always told Mary Beth you were a right 'un!"

"Have you? She would have it that *she* has always told *you* just how marvelous I am!" teased Cassie, grinning naughtily.

He blushed but countered at once, "Well, you see, that proves it then, and you cannot deny it!"

"Far be it for me to dispute it, infant! Lead on!"

He neither took insult nor pointed out to her that he had some two years on her, but did what the lady commanded and some hours later found them in Eccles before the rather simple brick structure that was the magistrate's home.

There were several delays at Magistrate Drummond's, the first being Mr. Drummond's inability to locate his reading spectacles. As these were needed to draw up the necessary papers, quite a search began. An excellent housekeeper, whom Cassie soon learned to appreciate, righted the oversight by discovering the glasses atop an open book in the library. The magistrate gruffly gave her thanks and began compiling the documents. However, this was soon interrupted by the striking of the clock. It was half past three.

Cassie and Guy then were informed that Mr. Drummond always took his tea at that hour, and all paperwork was put away while several cups of the brew were consumed and a lecture given on the many blends of tea and their relative beneficial effects.

It was not until some time near the hour of five that Cassie put her signature on the license and breathed a weary sigh of relief, thinking they were on their way.

The magistrate puffed out his chest and tipped his spectacles to his lips as he removed them and queried thoughtfully, "Been to see our minister yet, Mr. Bamfield? I daresay he could perform the wedding for you just as you should like. Excellent fellow . . . young and newly appointed. A connection of mine, actually. If you like, I could put you in his way . . ."

Mr. Bamfield gave this his considered opinion and totally surprised Cassie by declaring that this was a splendid notion. Hence, some ten minutes later they arrived at the Reverend Drummond's, who was in fact the magistrate's cousin.

But Cassie was even further surprised when she heard Guy set the date for the sixteenth of August. She pulled him aside and whispered, "Guy, you cannot mean to skip the Orator's meeting?"

"Tush . . . what nonsense!" he exclaimed. "Skip *his* meet indeed! Mary Beth and I will be married and then continue on to the meeting. Manchester is not far from here!"

"I . . . see . . ." said Cassie, bemused, but there, it was no use trying to talk to a radical.

It was not quite dusk as they approached Prescott Moors just outside Liverpool. Cassie was admiring the purple stretch of heather when a movement caught her eye and a heavy thudding caught her ears. She put out her gloved hand and halted Guy without a word. He too had heard the sound but thought little of it. But Cassie felt a chill rush over her back.

"What is that?" she whispered.

"I don't know . . . why?" answered Guy, frowning.

"Are there any meetings scheduled in this sector, Guy?" she asked on a tense note, for she had long been suspicious of Lyle.

"No. We have but one meeting at the end of the week to distribute the liberty banners and caps . . . and reiterate our pledge to the Orator. But why?"

"Well, then, Mr. Bamfield, they have called a meet without our knowledge, and I can just guess who is behind it . . ." said Cassie on an angry note. She was pointing to the crest of a grassy slope and an armed man dressed in a collier's whites.

He stood, his pipe sticking out of his lips, a musket resting across one arm, and he was shouting something unintelligible to another in the distance. Whomever he spoke to was hidden by the landscape, but Cassie and Guy had seen enough.

"Blister it!" said Guy beneath his breath. "Damn the idiots if this is another one of their bloody trainings! And if Lyle is behind it . . . I'll have his head! Come on, Cass!"

36

Kirkby had come home that afternoon to find a message awaiting him from his stepmama—She required his presence in her room. He sighed, asked after his wife, was advised by the butler that she had gone out, and then proceeded to attend the dowager. There he found her looking very fit, though she was reclining in her bed. She sat up and brought her quizzing glass to bear upon him, and he laughed.

"You don't mean to intimidate *me* with that old trick, Mama? I am too well initiated into your habits to be affected!"

"Where have you been?" she snapped, for she was bored with being indoors, a trick she had had to resort to because of his stubbornness.

"Out. But thank the stars, you are looking well. Head cold all gone?" he teased.

"As a matter of fact . . . no! The hellish thing has lodged in my chest." She proceeded to prove this by a series of gentle coughs.

379

"Ah . . . too bad. I do hope you will find this room comfortable while you are confined here," he said sweetly, measuring his words well.

She glared at him. "Has *she* returned yet?"

"If you are referring to my wife, no, she has not, and how did you know she had left?"

"Oh, Bertie was with her when her young man called," said his stepmother, much like a fluffy cat purring over some choice morsel.

He frowned, he knew what she was about, but it irritated him all the same. "No doubt you mean to expand on the point . . . do proceed," he said, taking a chair and stretching his legs.

"I have no idea what you mean by taking on that tone with me. After all, 'twas not my doing that your bride rushed off on horseback with some young man . . . familiar enough with her to address her by her given name."

The viscount thought at once of Guy and, as a matter of course, next wondered what muddle that young man had plunged his wife into. He grinned broadly, "Oh, I expect they will return presently . . . so do not bother your head about it."

Much shocked and somewhat curious, his stepmother glared at him. "What? Have you been then turned into a lamb? Are you so much milk? Your bride flaunts some strange young man before your nose, and you say nought but . . . you will await her return?" and then as an added setdown, ". . . and do stop grinning at me like a . . . a bedlamite!"

" 'Tis an oaf of a noddy you've raised, love," he sallied as he got to his feet, ". . . with better things to clutter his mind than the honest doings of an honest wife." He bent to give her a kiss, but she waved him away in some disgust.

He laughed and went to the door, pausing there to throw over his broad shoulder, "Rest easy, love, all will turn out in the end."

His smile was as irresistible as ever, and though she huffed at him and crossed her arms to show herself unyielding, she knew well that she was won over by him. He had ever the knack to soften her. She had loved him from the very start . . . partly because of the manner in which he had taken to Peter . . . and partly because he had so needed her. In the end, she could not have been more a mother to him had she borne him herself. And now . . . now she had to do something to bring him to his senses! She would not, *could* not allow this red-haired minx to ruin his life.

Secure in his new way of life, secure in his faith in his bride, the viscount settled down to his papers. However, the hours ticked by, and the oncoming dusk made him uneasy. With something of a frown, he started for the door only to be intercepted by Lord Widdons.

"Why, Eric, what brings you here?" asked the viscount.

Widdons was looking concerned. "Your butler tells me that Cass . . . that Lady Welford has not yet returned?"

"No . . . but what has . . ."

"I am a little concerned, Kirkby. Earlier today as I was entering town I saw that young nephew of mine . . . and Cassie . . . they were on the Prescott Road."

"Go on," said the viscount, feeling a terrible sensation clutch at him.

"I didn't think anything of it at the time . . . but I have just come from my club. There was talk about a group of radicals that drill on the moors. They carry arms . . . and we have a set of special constables going there to put them down . . . to *arrest* them. I went first to Guy's lodgings . . . although he had assured me his division of upstarts does not carry arms. I thought it best to advise him. But neither he nor that Stanton fellow . . ."

His words had sent the viscount into action. Before his eyes, he saw the man issue orders to his servants and within minutes, he was following the viscount outdoors.

"Thank you, my lord," said the viscount, hurriedly packing his horse pistol, "and please do excuse me for ushering you out so hastily."

"Excuse you? You forget my nephew may be in danger as well . . . I go with you, Kirkby!"

"Then enough of words. Shall we ride, sir?"

The arrival of Cassie and Guy upon the scene sent a hush of silence over the male crowd. There was nothing to be seen of women and children. Only men . . . and *they* holding firearms.

Lyle was there, shouting orders, but he stopped to face the newcomers. "Well, then . . . you found me out, did you?"

"What are you doing, Lyle?" cried Cassie, jumping off her horse, her green eyes accusing.

He reached out and attempted to take hold of her chin, but she slapped his hand away, and he grinned ruefully, "Aye, but you are pretty when all puckered, lass."

"Answer me, what does it mean?"

"What should it mean?" said Guy in answer, his face flushed. "Where did you get the guns, Lyle . . . where?"

"Where else, fool? I didn't waste the money Cass collected on coffee and bread. I got them what they needed —and I'm not the only one. These drillings are taking place all over the North! We mean to be ready for revolution—for that's the only way!"

"You are talking treason!" shouted Guy. "That's not what we want. We are Englishmen all!" He turned to the men. "Is that not right? Are we not all Englishmen? Do you mean to aim those guns at fellow Englishmen?"

They lowered their heads and mumbled. It was much like what had happened in London just two years before when the mobs marched on Westminster and Carlton House.

Cassie turned on Lyle, "Don't you realize you could get yourself and these men arrested?"

"So, you would rather they go on learning Guy's minor military evolutions . . . march like good little boys in rank?" sneered Lyle.

The collier with the pipe had made his way to them, and at this point he defended Lyle. "Meanin' no disrespect, m'lady . . . but wot ye know of it? Ye be a woman . . . ye jest don't understand . . ."

382

"What is there that I can't understand? I am telling you that these drillings will take us out of reform into revolution! We are neither prepared nor equipped for such a start!" Then to Lyle, "Now tell your men to go home!"

But it was already too late. A gun report exploded in their ears and a plucky youth standing among them made the mistake of retaliating. His shot went astray, but it brought the line of mounted yeomen down upon them.

Everything happened so quickly that Cassie could only stare. She was not even aware that Starfire had reared and scattered the men as he charged off in fright. It semed almost as though a whole cavalry was charging down the hillside. All around her colliers, weavers, many she had often passed a pleasant word with were shouting out to one another desperately. She heard Guy trying to take command of the situation, and then all at once she felt herself dangling in mid air.

Twisting around to see her captor, she found Lyle astride his horse. "Let me go!" she shouted. He was fleeing —that was her first thought. He had incited all this, and now he was running away, leaving these poor devils to their fate. To her own safety she gave no thought at the moment.

"What, to face the yeomen? I'll not leave you to them, love." He laughed and spurred his horse, hoisting her in front of him.

"And *you* . . . you are running away!" she accused. "How *can* you?"

"There is nought I can do for them. But I can for myself . . . and it's myself I am obliged to—no other!"

"Oh, my God! I had not thought it of you, Lyle. I really believed you were more than that . . ." She was almost in tears. "Now let me go—*let me go!*"

He stopped his horse. They were on an open stretch of moor. In the distance dark shadows moved, cries echoed. "Come with me, lass. I want you . . . have wanted you. We could deal . . . so well together."

"Let me go! We could *never* deal together. *You are beneath contempt!*" She had already freed herself from his hold and was sliding down the horse's flank. He could have prevented her, but he had no time to fight with an unwilling wench. He gave her one of his roguish grins and tipped his hat. "Till another time, love . . . may it be soon!" She saw him ride off, and then she was running back to the very heart of the fracas. The confusion was unbelievable. Constables and rabble alike stood ominously facing one another, neither group wanting to turn the thing bloody. Cassie rushed into their midst like a comet, catching everyone's attention.

"Put down your guns—all of you . . !" she shouted at the liberty men.

They mumbled and shuffled but stood their ground. Guy came to her side, shouting much the same. But it needed more. She pleaded with them:

"Look at you! You stand there holding a gun! For what? Do you mean to blast your way through? Do you? This cannot help our petitions. We will be put down as rabble . . . as criminals. Do you think that will gain our ends?"

"You tell 'em to leave us be . . . we'll turn in the guns!" shouted a collier from the group.

A uniformed constable urged his horse forward, coming up beside Cassie. "Sorry, ma'am . . . they've got to put down their arms and come with us peaceable."

The group at Cassie's back shouted their answer to this, and it was not good. Tension was running high. They were dissatisfied. Their women and children were home—hungry. If they were taken in . . . those same women and children would die of starvation. It was to them a matter of life and death . . . better, thought some, to aim their guns and shoot their way to . . . to . . . to what?

Among the special constables were several young men. They were fidgety, proud of their newly appointed position, and sensitive to the antagonism of the men they were facing. It was a desperate situation and needed but one wrong move.

The viscount saw the horse coming. He came from over the moors—the Prescott Moors. Kirkby called to Lord

Widdons to slow down and tooled his own horse into the path of the oncoming stallion. Starfire saw his path blocked. He was frightened, the shouting and the waving hands had spooked him, but some of that had been run off. Here before him was an authoritative figure, somehow familiar. He slowed, stopping at some distance from the viscount.

Kirkby dismounted, he spoke softly for he knew the horse. Starfire was unmistakable. Yes, here was Starfire . . . but where was Cassandra? "There now, beauty," he cajoled, ". . . there . . ." he said, taking the reins, running his gloved hand over the horse's sweating flanks, down its legs and over the hocks. "You seem to be all right. But where's your mistress?"

Kirkby looked up at Widdons whose expression was grim, and then they heard it. It echoed in the night, and then another bringing sure knowledge to the two men. Once again the viscount was mounted and galloping over the moors at a pace far too dangerous for its unyielding ground.

The situation needed a hero and Kirkby was well able to fill the role. He knew no fear, only an overwhelming need to get to Cassie, to find her whole.

In the fray, Cassie and Guy stood arguing their case, when a fiery young man at their backs took umbrage at something that the constable said. He came forward angrily, but he tripped, his safety catch was undone, and his gun went off. At the same time a youngster at the constable's back heard the pounding of hooves and turned round to see a devil, waving a pistol and looking as though he were coming right at him.

The yeoman heard the shot, saw the rider, and his finger worked before his mind. It was at the same moment that Cassie looked up and saw the riders. The yeoman's bullet found its mark.

The viscount felt a searing propulsion ram his head. He saw the night blast into a myriad of colors, and knew no more as he slumped forward on his horse. Cassie screamed! She had not seen his face . . . he was too far away and it was too dark. But the set of his shoulders, the manner in which he sat his horse, something told her it was her husband.

She could not tell what took possession of her, but in the confusion she saw all clearly. She reached up and grabbed the constable's horse pistol. He never knew what happened for she behaved like a hellcat in a fury. *"Get down!* Down! None of you move, or he is a dead man! Tell them!" she ordered. Guy was at her side, begging her to regain her senses. But she hissed at him to get a gun and stand as her second. *"Senses?* Violence is the only thing they will understand!" Then to the constable, "Tell them! Tell them to lay down their arms! At once! Or you will never see the light of day!"

He obeyed her, and as the yeomanry dropped their weapons, a cheer from the liberty crew went up at her back. It was then she shoved the gun into Guy's hand.

"Have their guns gathered—and don't drop your guard —I depend upon you!" Then she ran to the viscount.

Widdons had jumped off his horse and lowered Kirkby to the ground. He was examining the wound and looked up to see Cassie's face. Until that moment, he had still cherished hopes with regard to Cassie, but one look at her face told him such hopes were in vain.

"Kirkby," she called as she dropped to her knees, "Kirkby!"

Her hand went to his forehead where the blood was pouring forth, and for a moment she thought she might swoon. Instead she reached for her muslin underskirt and tore off a piece of cloth. This she dabbed to the wound, exposing it and then she let out a long breath. The bullet had only grazed his forehead and, though she was certain he would wake with a colossal headache, she was also certain he would suffer nothing more serious. "Oh, Kirkby . . ."

His eyes flickered, and he looked up into her face. It took a moment to get her in focus, but that done, he grinned. "You are leading me a famous dance, vixen," he said at length.

She laughed tremulously. "Oh, Kirkby . . . can you stand?"

He nodded and saw Widdons aid him in this before planting a kiss to his cheek and rushing off. "Cassie!" he shouted after her. But she had no time to reply. She returned to Guy and found all the yeomanry's guns gathered in a pile. Her own men though had remained armed. "What's this?" she demanded of them. "Put your guns down and think of them no more! Go on!"

They lowered their eyes, but one by one they obeyed, shuffling among themselves, wondering what next would befall them. She sighed and turned to the constable. "There! Now . . . tell them, good sir, that they may return to their families!" She waited a moment and then more harshly, *"Tell them!"*

"You may go to your families . . . you are free to go," said the constable, glaring.

She watched the men turn and begin to vanish into the moors. Kirkby and Widdons had by this time reached her side.

"Cassie . . . what is all this?" asked Kirkby, throwing away the cloth he held to his forehead and turning to eye the constable Guy still held at bay. "What is the meaning of this, sir?"

"And who may you be?" asked the constable from beneath his bushy brows.

"Viscount Welford, and this is my lady . . ." replied the gentleman with dignity.

"Aye, well, yer lady has stood in the path of the law and shall have to answer to it!"

"And your men fired upon and wounded me—and shall have to answer to *that*!" thundered the viscount.

The constable seemed suddenly to have developed what appeared to be an unreachable itch. "That may be . . . but her ladyship has committed treason!"

Cassie jumped to the fore, preventing her husband from answering this slur. "I, sir, have done nothing but aided the government in its attempt to confiscate weapons intended for unlawful demonstration. Mr. Bamfield and I saw clearly that you and your men had bungled the affair, whereupon we stepped in and managed the thing for you!"

"And ye left the culprits to go free!" he shouted at her.

"Did I?" she said sweetly, "I distinctly heard *you* tell them they were free to go."

"At gunpoint!" he snapped.

Widdons stepped in at this juncture. "Constable, you have the guns—quite a feather in your cap, I might add. I am sure the government was not interested in hauling 150 men to prison. It would have been a difficult thing indeed. I expect the viscount and his lady will be ready to forgive all offenses . . ."

The constable eyed the pile of guns. It was true, it would be a feather. He could say the men were frightened off . . . scattered.

"Aye . . . I suppose . . . it might be the best way," he mumbled reluctantly.

"I think, sir, after a time you will come to understand that it is really the *only* way," said Widdons amiably. "Now, come . . . shall we see what prize you have managed to win this night?" He was leading the constable off and the yeomanry, finally at ease, followed. Guy watched them a moment before lowering his gun.

"Whew! Thought we were in for it! Well, I mean . . . caught red-handed, weren't we? Dash it, Cass! Thought *you'd gone daft* when you thundered at me . . . I mean, holding a gun to a constable."

The viscount rounded on him. "Do not for a moment think you are out of this muddle, young scamp! What the deuce did you have in mind whisking my wife off to such an unthinkable affair?"

"No, no, my lord, it was not like that," started Guy, much horrified.

"Indeed, my lord," put in Cassie, "Guy knew nought of what was toward. We weren't even aware a meet was to be held—and certainly had no notion that our division had obtained weapons."

"Then how. . ." he frowned.

She interrupted him, taking up his arm. "Kirkby, your

wound needs attention. Do let us go home . . . I shall explain everything on the road."

He frowned darkly in Guy's direction, and the young man gulped as he watched the two depart, glad to be out of it. However, he heard his name called by his uncle, and it was not spoken sweetly. He sighed and braced himself for the inevitable.

37

Leila took up a casual position on her dark brocade sofa. She watched the younger, more attractive woman pace leisurely before her and gave her own short yellow curls a pat. Nancy was a charmer, there was no gainsaying it. She had until this past year been the main attraction at the brothel in which they held joint interest. However, many months ago Nancy had announced that she would take no more men. She had saved a tidy sum, she had reached the age of seven and twenty, and she would suffer it no longer. She had never liked men . . .

"So, Nancy, darling . . . what is it that has brought you here?" drawled Leila.

Nancy fingered a Sèvres dish and turned her bright green eyes upon her hostess. " 'Taint nothing that I can't tell ye . . . but I'd rather wait on Nathan."

Leila's eyes swept the woman from the top of her flaming locks to the toes of her blue slippers. "Really? Do you think he will do aught without my word?"

"Och, now . . . don't be stepping high, didn't mean no

bobbery . . . jest thought there would be no sense in telling me notions twice!"

The parlor door opened wide and Nathan, his gray brow raised, stepped forward. "Why, Nancy . . . what brings you here?"

Nancy greeted him by sitting on his Oriental desktop and smiling widely. "Lord love ye . . . come in, Nathan, take up a seat with Leila there . . . and I'll be telling ye!"

Nathan turned to his wife, a question on his face, but Leila shrugged her thin shoulders. "I have no idea, Nathan, I suppose she will tell us whenever it suits her."

Nathan strode to the sofa, sat obediently and waited, one brown fist to his chin, his eyes intent on Nancy. It was not the first time his wife noted his interest in the lively redhead. Lord! she thought to herself. I wish Nancy would favor his indulgence just long enough to give me some freedom to pursue Kirkby Welford. But not Nancy. She has never cared a fig for a man . . . not even that pretty boy. No, it has never been men that move her . . .

"There now, Nathan, don't be in a fret . . . 'tis no more than a trifle that I want. You see, being Madame of Nancina's is all very well, but that ain't enough. No, I've been out of course thinking how I've been the very broth of a friend, I have. We Scots . . . we're loyal by nature . . . but 'tis time I was shown some appreciation!"

"But I don't understand. We gave you the charge of Nancina's. You handle all the receipts and keep a neat twenty percent of the returns while I pay all the drafts!" exploded Nathan.

"Now don't be cutting the wheedle with me, Nathan!" she snapped, her voice, suddenly hard. "You pay all the drafts! You carry the mortgage . . . and keep us supplied with pipe dreams. But who pays for the pretty frills . . . the late dinners . . . the red spangles for me dolls? I pays it, I does! But I ain't come to spoon ye such! No, I been waiting for a token of yer appreciation . . . and since it ain't come . . . I ain meself surprised but not beaten! I . . ."

"Appreciation . . . what in the name of all . . . what are you talking about?" demanded Leila, for her husband had gone silent, thoughtful.

"I be talking of that little deed I dun aboot two months back. Did I not put ye in the way of one that would spy on ye?" said the redhead, standing up and swaying across the room to glare at Nathan. "Did I not give over the pretty bairn who came courting ye with his falsehoods?"

Leila stood up, her face white. "You did that as much for yourself as for us!"

"Aw now, Leila . . ." said the redhead coming forward to stroke her white cheeks. "Don't be taking on so . . . Lordy now, ye would think I was asking for the world! I ain't . . ."

Leila slapped the woman's hand away angrily. "What are you asking for, Nancy!"

"I ain't trying to pyke ye . . . no . . . but jest look how ye live, all finnified here . . . the best clothes . . ." she said, glancing over Leila's gown. "Why, the ten pounds or so that comes me way each week, 'tain't hardly decent. I want a hundred!"

"You are mad!" declared Nathan, getting to his feet.

She sneered at him. "I won't be bargaining with ye, Nathan! I've had time to think this out. Lord, ye get more than three—four hundred on me brothel alone! 'Tis one hundred I want—and 'tis one hundred ye'll be giving me!"

His hand swiped her face bitingly, and she staggered sidewise beneath the blow, but she righted herself immediately and looked a veritable titan in her fury. "Damn your soul to hell! Never—do you hear me, Nathan Asbatol— never raise a hand to me again, or I swear I'll see you hanged! Think not I don't have the means. I have it, for that lad you put away . . . he was writing this letter the night ye sent me to lure him out. He never mailed it . . . no, coz little Nancy fingered it!" She released a wild triumphant laugh as she noted Nathan's expression. "That's right! He was spilling out all he knew . . . meant it for that Select group they got hunting ye down . . .

Well, Nancy's got it right and tight—and may the fiends help ye if ye force me to use it!"

Nathan resumed his seat. Leila's expression was wary, her mind sifting this latest piece of news. Could she be tied in with Peter Eaton's murder? Of course she could. She said slowly, cautiously, "*You* could be destroyed as well, Nancy!"

"Could I? No, as it happens, the young blade never mentioned me by name. No, I don't think I could be tied to it."

"They would wonder how such a letter came into *your* possession!" returned Leila.

"Would they? Bless ye, think I come this far by chance? No, coves of mine, I survives coz I learned the turn of it. Peter now, he made it all the easier, poor bairn that he was. Sad is to tell, but he was wild fevered on me. Sech a swell flash he was . . . wrote me some prime little love notes, he did . . . well, this one I be talking of wasn't writ to me . . . and it sure now had nought to do with love, but as it happens he visited with me ofttimes . . . and *this note* . . . well, it comes to my way of thinking that it slipped out of his pockets during his stay! Lordy, we did play in Bristol in those few days . . ." she said as though reminiscing, "My, my, how things do get misplaced when a mort be packing for a journey. The wayward thing must 'ave slipped into me bags without me noting it, until just recent . . . when lo! *there it be!*" she said, turning her suddenly hard jade eyes on them. "Now think a Bow Street cull won't take to that little tale?"

Nathan moved across the room in ponderous fashion. He did not like this. The strumpet could cause them quite a bit of the ready as well as unrest. She would have to be dealt with. "Tell me more, Nancy . . . this letter, was it addressed to anyone in particular?"

"No, but 'twas to a member of the Committee he worked for, though it had the sound of a friend. It weren't dated for one thing, and he started it with 'Greetings, you old dog!' Must have meant it for a chum of sorts," said Nancy unconcernedly.

"Hmmm . . . very well, Nancy, it seems we have little choice in the matter. One hundred it is, though I shall want to look at this letter of yours," returned Nathan.

"Och now, think me a fool of a girl? Ye'll jest have to trust me to give ye a copy . . . so as ye'll know what he was spilling."

"Trust you?" interpolated Leila furiously. "You have already shown just how much we can trust you!"

"Now, now, there ain't nothing I dun that give ye sech as that to claim!" snapped Nancy with a shake of her red hair. "I give ye time to douce me with a bonus after turning in the pretty boy to ye. Found out he was working for that London Committee, didn't I? Where would ye be if I hadn't come through? 'Tis I who can't trust ye to do the right thing by me!"

Leila folded her arms and turned her a frigid shoulder at the same time that Nancy brought up her hard chin. Life had made her a scrapper, and she knew well how to get by. "I'll bid thee good-day. Don't be taking on so, pretty Leila. I earns me blunt . . . and faith, I have a long night waiting on me. Or did ye think a madame does nought in her ken? Tis *I* that stands in the parlor and puts the young nervous lads at their ease and gets them that spends bigger than most to lay over their blunt with a smile . . . and settles it when a little doll ain't in the mood. Lordy, I do earns me hundred . . ." she cooed as she moved toward the hall door. Tying the ribbons of her blue-striped bonnet beneath her ear, she swept them a sunny smile. "Ta-ta, loves . . . ta-ta . . ."

Leila was seething, but she waited for the sound of the front door closing before rounding on her husband. "You are not going to let that little snirp get away with this latest rig of hers, are you?"

"Do you think that is my way?" he hissed. "I will finish her for this and in a way she will long rue. But first, my darling, we must get hold of that little piece of paper she dangles over our heads!"

"I don't understand why you just don't put her away.

If she meets the dust, Nathan, she won't be around to use the letter against us . . ."

"Fool! Really, Leila, for a cunning woman . . . and you are one, how can you not see? She may have told someone . . . one of her little trollops about it. We can't take the chance!" He paused for a long thoughtful moment. "Leila, you will have to pay our little brothel a visit . . . while Nancy goes on a shopping spree with her girls."

"Shopping spree?" ejaculated his wife.

"Of course, my bird. I want our little ladies arrayed in the finest Liverpool has to offer—for their particular occupation," he said, smiling wickedly.

His wife suddenly understood and returned his smile warmly. She went forward to put her hands upon his chest, and he brought his mouth down hard upon hers. She responded to his embrace and sighed as he lifted her to the sofa. "Why, Nathan . . . at times like these you inspire me to almost . . . want you . . ."

38

It was the morning of the sixteenth of August. It was a bright, cool, crisp day and gave much promise. The viscount had risen before his wife, for he had received word from Lord Widdons the night before. All was set, and he had but to meet with Nathan Asbatol this morning and pave the way for the future. He arrived, looking the stud in his summer cutaway of ivory superfine, and Leila licked her lips. She had to find her way into his bed . . . somehow.

The discussion with Nathan did not take long, the plan was set. "Do you fully understand, that I shall have no physical violence with regard to the boy?" said the viscount slowly.

"I do. I, in fact, have very little to do, other than taking my men to the point you have outlined on this map . . . and making certain they don't make a muddle of it. Regrettably, all these dolts have little sense, and one never knows what they might do if I weren't there to keep an eye on them," said Nathan with disgust.

"Very well then. I think we have nothing more at present to discuss. So I wish us good luck in this venture! Good-day, Nathan . . ." he turned to Leila and bowed, "Leila . . ."

"Kirkby . . . have you the coach today?" she asked suddenly.

"Ye–s . . ." he said slowly, warily.

"Excellent! Then you can drop me off at the corner of DeMott. I have an errand to do there this morning, and Nathan needs the coach." She turned to her husband. "There love, does not that work out pleasantly?"

"Indeed," he answered curtly. There was little he could do now, for he had said he wanted the use of the coach this day. Very well then, let the trollop go, he would teach her later to flaunt her ways before him.

The viscount sighed and led Leila Asbatol toward his waiting carriage. He saw her situated beside himself in the coach and controlled a strong desire to chastise the woman when she immediately threw herself upon his chest.

"Kirkby . . . I have so long been wanting to be alone with you . . ."

"Have you?" he said drily.

Cassie overslept the appointed hour but made up for it with the haste of her dressing. It was already past nine by the time the chambermaid her husband had recently hired had done up the buttons of her blue traveling habit, and it was well into the new hour when she arrived outside the Grand Hotel in a hired hack. Another five minutes and she was ushering a flustered Mary Beth into the hack and ordering the driver to the designated meeting place. However, as she began her ascent into the hack, a familiar-looking carriage rounded the bend in the road as it came her way. A smile lifted her mouth in greeting, when all at once her green eyes froze. Was that not her husband? And was there not some strange, yellow-haired female sitting on his lap?

Cassie blinked, for she believed in the love she shared

with Kirkby Welford. She believed, she trusted, she had faith . . . and suddenly her heart ached.

Her pride kept her silent. She did not wave to him. She did not call him to a halt. She would not demean herself before another woman. Had he not held Cassie only last night? Had he not assured her that his stepmother could not put a wedge between them? Had he not said, "Cassie, there is none like to thee?" Had he not filled her life with poetry? And was he not betraying all that?

She turned away in pain and confusion. She was insanely jealous and therefore no longer rational. She sat silently beside her companion and made her plans!

She had intended to bring Thomas along this day. She meant only to go to Eccles where she would leave the Bamfields after the wedding ceremony and return home. She made a quick reversal. He spent his days with yellow-haired creatures! Very well then! She was a radical. She belonged with her brothers and sisters at this meet, and so she would go!

She bade Mary Beth wait for her and dashed back into the hotel, took up quill and paper, and jotted off her thoughts! Folding the letter, she slipped it into a hotel envelope before rejoining Mary.

The hack drew up at the corner of the Westley Park entrance, and Mary Beth waved excitedly to Guy who was fidgeting beside the post chaise he had hired. Thomas stood wide-eyed beside him, his pony strings in hand, for Cassie had dispatched the boy to the park to assure Guy that she was on her way.

Mr. Bamfield, his cherubic faced flushed, helped the women alight, paid off their hack, and ushered them toward the carriage hurriedly. "We are already behind schedule. Do but hurry, darling," he said as Mary detained him to plant a kiss upon his cheek.

She took umbrage at once for her emotions were high and easily overturned. She gasped, "Guy Bamfield!"

He relented at once and assuaged her somewhat by giving her pouting lips a kiss. He raised his head and said softly, "There now . . . am I forgiven?"

She smiled tremulously and allowed herself to be situated. He turned to find Cassie placing a note in Thomas's hands. "There now, Thomas. See to it that the viscount receives this."

"But . . . m'lady . . . don't I come wit ye?" he objected.

"No, lad. I shall be accompanying Mr. Bamfield and Miss Mary Beth to the meet at St. Peter's Field, and that is no crowd for you," she said firmly.

"But, m'lady, m'lady! How will ye be gettin' home alone? The lord . . . he won't be likin' that," pleaded the boy.

"Mr. Bamfield and his wife will be returning this evening to Liverpool, so you need not fear. I will return with them. Now off with you!" she said in a tone that indicated she would allow no further discussion.

Guy came forward, his brows drawn in a frown. "How is this, Cassie? You know I had originally thought your presence among our Liverpool faction would be needed. They have come to look for you at the meets. But, after careful consideration, I was persuaded that you had better comply with your husband's wishes, and you did say he did not want you to attend a meet of this size!"

"Did I?" returned Cassie in a strange voice. "Well, I no longer care what the viscount wishes! Orator Hunt has organized this meeting with good intent. It would be wrong for me as a declared radical not to support him with my presence! Now do let us proceed." This was not the Cassie he had to come to know. But he was in a hurry and all too aware of her strength of will to try to change her mind at this particular stage. He would try again after his wedding. His wedding . . . in a short while, his Mary Beth would be his wife . . . and he sighed with the thought and climbed in after Cassie. So it was that Thomas mounted his pony and made for the Welford house, and a hired post chaise took to the Manchester Road.

Thomas reached home some few minutes later and found that the viscount had not yet returned. However, the boy was well met by the dowager. She stood in regal form, her white hair piled high, her silk of summer maize hanging elegantly, her jewels glittering. She brought up her quizzing glass to survey the boy servant before her.

"What have you there, child?" she inquired austerely. It was not that she lacked the ability to feel compassion, but that she felt it beneath her to display it.

" 'Tis a note . . . for the viscount. M'lady, she dun told me to deliver it to him . . ." stammered the boy.

"I see. Well, he is not in. You may, however, leave it with me. I shall see that he gets it. Now . . . off with you, child, I am certain you have other duties to perform."

"But m'lady said I was to give it to his *lordship*," said Thomas, his dark eyes wide with terror, his knees weak beneath the strain of standing up to the likes of her.

"My God!" breathed the dowager. "What is this? Back talk from a misshapen little brat of a servant! Really, it would *seem* your lady lacks the manageability of her servants. Now give the note over at once!"

"Ye–s, ma'am . . ." said Thomas. He had no choice in the matter. After all, this woman was his lordship's mama . . . yet it worried him not to carry out his lady's exact wishes, and he stood a moment afterward.

"Off with you, child," snapped the dowager, but she met his glance and something inside of her twinged. "There now . . . I shall see to it that your master gets it."

Thomas departed and made his way to the stables to await Chips who was still out with the viscount. He would put this before Chips . . . for he had come to depend on the groom's counsel.

His lady was well on her way to Eccles by now. It was a tedious journey, for her companions made little conversation, so engrossed were they with each other. She smiled, sighed, and took to watching the road. The traffic thickened as they neared Eccles. Hordes of people, on foot, on horseback, in cobbled wagons filled the road, and Guy became excited at the sight.

"My goodness, we are going to have something of a

400

Derby Day at Manchester," exclaimed Cassie. "Just look at all these people."

"Indeed, this is nought. Sam Bamford writes that six thousand will follow him into St. Peter's Field . . . and at least ten will come at the Orator's heels. The word is that we shall have near to sixty-seventy thousand before the day is done."

"Oh, my, but I do hope the ceremony does not put us on the road too late, or we shall have a hey time of it getting into Manchester!" remarked Cassie.

As it turned out, the magistrate's cousin was the sort who believed in efficiency. He was quite ready for them, scolded them briefly on *their* tardiness, and called for silence when they began to explain, saying that they had been delayed long enough and should proceed.

Cassie stood back and watched and for a long soft moment thought of Kirkby. However, she then remembered the first time she had seen him with another woman . . . and then she recalled the second. He had given her a reason for that first occasion. What would be his reason now?

She bit her lip and determined to lift her spirit. She would not be brought low by him. She would forget it all —she would concentrate instead on the issues for reform.

Then all at once, she had pen in hand. Papers were signed, and once again she was inside the coach alone with her thoughts as Mary Beth and Guy congratulated themselves on their marriage.

The crowds had thickened considerably in the hour they had been at the minister's home. Cassie's face was pressed to the window when she spied a woman dressed in a worn gray gown trimmed in red, her apron carried the stains of the coal mine. She was shoeless as was the child at her heels. Cassie called the coach to a stop and opened her door. "Please, madam, do accept a ride from us. We go to Manchester."

"Aye, thank ye kindly, good mistress . . . 'tis the Orator we go to hear," said the woman as she rushed to the coach and heaved her child to its top. She clambered after the boy and once again the coach started forward. Cassie turned to find both Guy and Mary Beth smiling at her, and she smiled in turn, before breaking out with one of their rally songs.

It was certainly true—more than seventy thousand people were converging on St. Peter's Field in Manchester. They came—the Irish weavers, the coal miners, the Yorkshire colliers—in their whites, grays and blues. They came to shout, sing, and wave their banners. They came to voice their hopes and hear a man of power tell them it was not in vain. They came to hear the Orator!

The carriage was dispatched to the stables, and Guy ushered his ladies through the clusters of radicals and their followers to a large open field only just beginning to fill with people. Here they were recognized by some of their local followers and joyously hailed. Cassie smiled and waved her gloved hand, startled by the deep emotion arising within her. It was a pleasing sensation. It was good to be one with these people . . . to understand their sufferings, to feel herself expunged of guilt because she was trying to help.

At the far end of the field stood the hustings. It was a temporary platform of fresh wood, topped with poles bearing revolutionary banners, and peaked with liberty caps. Everywhere people were jubilant. Surely now, in such numbers, those in power must see! Surely now, those in power would care . . .

The sound of drums and bugles brought Cassie's head round, and she exclaimed, "Guy . . . look there!"

The trainings that had taken place in the moors all over Yorkshire, and the riding county had not been in vain. For the radicals were marching. They formed columns of fives and moved in lock step to the tune of their songs and the beat of their drums. They waved their liberty banners for all to see, and they were followed en masse by the crowds.

They poured into St. Peter's Field from all parts of the town and were greeted enthusiastically by their suffering mates. Wild cheers filled the air. They were strangers all, caught in one common bond—need! A set of Irish weavers set up a song and were joined by the clusters at their back. The tune was picked up and carried along and Cassie smiled, for she looked at the face of hope, and it was good!

They came, unarmed, with their women and their children, and the sober aristocracy and respectable farmers stood back and watched in silent horror. There were those who recalled the French Reign of Terror back in '92. What was this? they cried to one another as they retreated to their windows and watched in fearful awe. They were terrified by the force, angered by their unconscious guilt, and this was an unholy seed. Cassie purchased an apple from a passing vendor shouting his offers to the crowds and was thus separated a fraction from her companions as a sudden shout rent the air.

It was for the *Orator Hunt!* He had at last appeared. He was a man of impressive proportion and elegant raiment. He held up his hands for silence and was obeyed almost instantly. It was eerie how the hush fell over the dense mass of life. All eyes, seemed suddenly to have but one object and that the Orator. Henry Hunt returned their gaze. He was a gentle man, beloved by his people, adored and respected by his friends, and he smiled warmly with all the exhilaration of a man who looks out on a crowd of seventy-eighty thousand and discovers there a mass of living, breathing beings, responsive and waiting on his words. They had come because they wanted a peaceful end to their hardships.

Suddenly the Orator's words were drowned out by the sound of horses, many, many horses. Cassie's surprised eyes looked round to find a cavalry of yeomanry bearing down upon the field—*with sabres drawn!*

39

The viscount entered his house some forty minutes after Thomas. He had dropped Leila off at her destination and then continued on to Lord Widdons. His mind was still busy with the plans they had made as he entered his library and found his stepmother there.

"Ah, Kirkby, there you are," she said, coming forward to allow him to kiss her soft pink cheek.

His eyes twinkled as he performed the necessary. "Mama, how nice to see you up and about and ready no doubt to return to London!"

"Horrid boy! Why must you feel so about me? I declare you have never before been so rude to me."

"I have never before had so much reason—most of it the result of your own actions," he returned at once, his eyes twinkling still.

He moved to his desk and found a letter posted from London and bearing Lord Sidmouth's seal. His brows rose as he took it up. Breaking the seal, he unfolded the paper, and held it in the daylight.

Kirkby,

You made mention in your last missive, that your wife, whom I look forward to meeting, has taken up the radicals' views. 'Tis not an uncommon thing among gentle hearts, though I cannot approve. However, you must expressly forbid her active participation in these dreadful meets they hold. We understand that Henry Hunt draws some seventy thousand to his campaign in Manchester on the 16th of this month.

With regard to this particular meet, I have authorized the local authorities to use whatever means at their disposal to disperse the force, including the Manchester regiment of Hussars!

Lord Widdons writes me that all is proceeding according to design, and I look to your immediate success in that particular matter.

With regard to your mama who no doubt is now with you, please forgive. She is a most persuasive woman, may the saints preserve her, for truth to tell, had your father not snapped her up . . . I would have!

> As ever,
> Siddy

The viscount smiled ruefully over this as he handed it to his mother. He took a chair to scan the remainder of his mail. The dowager read Sidmouth's letter before giving her son a long speculative look.

"Kirkby, will you be taking lunch with me? I should so like to go out somewhere festive. We could talk."

"I shall ask Cassie," he said briefly, giving her a smile before dropping his eyes to the bills on his table.

She felt the note in her pocket—Cassie's note—and knew she should give it over. She banished the twinge of guilt she felt. She wanted him to herself a bit longer. Her sojourn in bed had not given her the prize she sought. She had thought perhaps he would spend time with her in her room . . . where she might persuade him to see the error of his ways. She thought perhaps Cassie would show herself the unfeeling doxy she knew her to be. She thought . . . but then it was all for nothing.

"Kirby, could you not tear yourself away from those dreadful papers and pay me some mind. I declare you are as rude as that frightful child!"

He smiled and leaned back in his chair. "What frightful child?"

"That hunchback your wife keeps about her!" snapped his stepmother. "He wants manners."

"Thomas? Why I am amazed," said the viscount, truly surprised. He knew Thomas to be far too shy ever to approach the dowager without cause. "Whatever can have put him in your way?"

"Why do you say that? I came across him earlier and his response to my commands was doltish!" she said irritably, knowing sooner or later the note would come up. "I declare . . . 'tis but twenty minutes to noon . . . yet I am famished. If you won't take me out for a private luncheon—just we two—do let us have it together here."

"Fine, but I would prefer to wait until Cassie comes down," he said absently as he had returned to sorting his bills.

"Come down?" she scoffed. "You must be aware that she is not even here?"

"Is she not? Out shopping, I suppose." He smiled but shortly, for his mother's expression annoyed him. "All right, Mother . . . out with it! It all has something to do with Thomas, does it not?"

"I don't know what you are talking about. All I want is a cozy little meal with the only son left to me . . . is that too much to ask?"

"Yes, when your intent is to drive a wedge between the only son left to you and his only wife!" retorted the viscount amicably. "Really, dear, Cheltenham enactments simply won't do!"

"What more have you learned about those dreadful

people Peter wrote about?" she asked, suddenly changing the subject.

He frowned. He was too well acquainted with her ways not to realize there was a purpose to this sudden turnabout. He rose and moved towards the bellrope. She got to her feet.

"What are you doing, Kirkby?"

"I am going to bring in Jenkins and inquire after my wife," he said on a hard note.

"Really," she said in a partially shaky tone, "one would think from your manner that you half suspect me of having done her in."

"I have often wondered to what lengths you might go to do in someone you believed to be a threat!" he snapped as he rounded on her. "Now do I call in Jenkins . . . or do you tell me what all this mystery is about?"

"Oh, very well!" she said, pulling the notepaper from her pocket and handing it over to him. It was no longer sealed, and he put up a brow at her.

"You read this?" he said, his voice on an edge.

She nodded, turning away from him. He gazed long at her and before reading it inquired, "How long have you had this?"

"Thomas gave it over to me forty minutes before you arrived. How long he had it, I know not," she said on a quiet note.

He unfolded the ivory paper, and once again that morning he read about Manchester.

Kirkby,

I once asked you what you did when you were away from me. You said you pursued your trade! I now know what that means . . . Your blond wench seemed older than the tavern wench, but they both had the favor of your lap. I own no longer wishing to share!

I go to Manchester to listen to the Orator. I had promised, I know, not to, but as you hold your promises cheaply, I no longer feel encumbered by mine. From there I shall purchase a seat on the stagecoach and return to the Grange until I can find Jack and the clean life aboard a smuggler's sloop.

Good-bye,
Cassie

For a long moment he said nothing, thought nothing but that she was a little fool to run off in this heady fashion. Why, she gave him no chance to explain! Stupid little love! Then, all at once it hit him with a heavy thud. She was off to Manchester—and Sidmouth had said the crowds there would be repressed! "My God . . ." he breathed at last. "Oh, my God!" He rounded on his stepmother. "You knew . . . you read her letter and knew she was off to Manchester . . . you read Sidmouth's letter and knew . . . yet you still tried to keep it from me!"

"I thought she was going . . . good riddance to her . . . please, Kirkby . . . I meant only to shield you . . ." she cried.

"Hell and fire, Mother! Protect me, is it? May God protect me from *you* . . . for He knows from my enemies I can well protect myself!" He turned from her and left the room. There was precious little time. He had to get his arms, his horse, and make for Manchester. But he knew he would never get there before the meet. Not on horseback! Then quite suddenly, perhaps because of Cassie's referral to a smuggler's sloop, he remembered the canal! Of course! There was a canal of sorts connecting the port of Liverpool with the manufacturing center of Manchester.

He knew instinctively what he would do. It took less than ten minutes for him to collect his pistol, hat, and steed, and but another ten to reach the docks. There was a hefty business about the wharf for Liverpool thrived on its West Indian interest. Slave trade was now abolished, but it was England's chief port, and the canal carried loads of cotton to Manchester daily.

He scanned the wharf for the sort of vessel he would

need to take him and his horse, and at last he found it. It was a six-man galley equipped with a sail, just large and lean enough to do the job with the swiftness he needed. He found its captain, a tall, stout individual in a short, dark jacket and whites.

Hastily but with extreme precision, the viscount explained his need and was pleasantly surprised to find the captain an intelligent sort, disposed to be helpful. A price was agreed upon, and another fifteen minutes passed before the captain returned with his crew. All in all, discounting the viscount, they were but four men. Thus it was that Kirkby Welford took to the oars.

The wind was in their favor as was the tide when they set sail. Another half hour passed before the captain called a reprieve and passed round a jug of ale. However, this respite was of short duration and once again, happily for the viscount's anxious state of mind (regardless of his body), they were off once again. It was grueling hard work but with the aid of the friendly breeze the docks of Manchester were reached. The wharfs were edged with warehouses, many some eight or nine stories in height and yet, though it was the middle of the day and no sabbath . . . *they were quiet.*

Then suddenly, almost the sound of an explosion—but actually, the screeching, screaming, bolting sound of terror!

Cassie stood a moment in stunned rigidness while the people around her gave vent to their fears! Everywhere masses of men and women began to run. She turned to look for Guy and Mary Beth, but she was carried along with the mob. The thunder of human voices and movement prohibited rational thought. The earth beat violently beneath her feet as the density of human flesh pressed and ran in their efforts to escape the onslaught of horses and swords!

She called out Mary Beth's name, but knew it was useless as she was swept away by the avalanche of screaming beings. Everywhere local yeomanry in their scarlet uniforms were stampeding the crowds. What riveted Cassie's fascination was the swing of their sabres.

All she could think was, "Swords? Why? Why the swords? What is all this about? Why have they marched on us?"

A man beside her picked up his cap of liberty which caught the attention of one of the cavalry who rode up and demanded the thing. She heard the young man refuse to give it up and as the man stepped back two more cavalrymen joined the first.

"What's to do here?" asked one of the newly arrived yeomen.

"The devil won't give up the damned liberty cap," answered the first. "Revolutionaries . . . the lot of 'em!"

"Then cut him down, damn him!" replied the other.

The young man with the cap made a wild dash for the safety of a building, while the trooper on horseback followed and Cassie blinked in horror. These yeomen—they were mill owners' sons, farmers' sons. Had they no pity for those less fortunate?

Another rushing mass reached her just as she managed to maneuver her way out of the crowd, and once again she felt herself pushed and pulled with the tide of the mob. She had a strong inclination to burst into tears but controlled herself with a shake. "Easy now . . . easy . . . 'tis no time to be bawling—what a cake you would make of yourself!"

This was all too unreal. She was too stunned by the sudden turn of events to be truly frightened. She had seen the Orator dragged by the yeomen from the hustings. She had seen him beaten as he was pulled along by them. She had seen the crowd of unarmed people trampled, and oh, God! Blood was spattered all about. And then she stopped, for not ten feet from her a yeoman swung his sabre at a woman. She saw the woman fall in a heap on the cobbled ground and gazed stupefied at the blood pouring rapidly forth. Then in a wave of anger and indignation Cassie came to life. With all the spirit and fire that was a part of her nature, she rushed forward and dropped to her knees beside the injured woman. She tore off a length of her blue linen skirt and applied it to the woman's shoulder in an effort to stem the flow.

The woman, a hurrier, no more than twenty or so, who made her way through life by drawing a loaded wagon through the coal mine, opened her weary, pain-filled eyes and mumbled something incoherent. Cassie recognized that she must be calling for someone, for it was a name that she repeated.

"Hush, now . . . we must somehow get you off this street and to a doctor," said Cassie reassuringly.

"Please . . . it's m'Tom . . . I can't find m'Tom . . ." sobbed the woman distressfully.

"Never mind that now. He'll find you soon enough, be sure of it," said Cassie. "Can you stand up? Perhaps if you lean on me . . ."

"I can try . . ."

Just then their heads were brought round by a man's string of oaths. He cursed the yeomen, he cursed life . . . and God!

"M'darlin, m'own poor darlin' . . ." he cried as he knelt to take his wife in his arms. "What 'ave they dun to ye . . . ?"

"You must get her to a doctor as quickly as possible. Can you manage?" asked Cassie, thankful for his arrival.

"Aye, thank ye, miss," said the man as he picked up his wife.

Cassie took to the street again. It was clear now except for those who sat tending their wounds, and those whose wounds had left them lifeless. It had been a massacre! She had to find Guy and Mary Beth and be certain they were all right. But oh, God! everywhere there were women and children dragging themselves to safety, and Cassie grimaced over the sounds of pain.

Once again she postponed her search, for the sight of a small boy no more than eight or nine lying limp in his mother's arms brought Cassie to a halt. She stooped to inspect the whimpering lad and found that he was covered with bruises.

"Pray, woman, however did this happen to him?" asked Cassie, horrified.

"They . . . they just trampled him down . . . they saw him and didn't care. Are they born of the divil? Are they without heart?" cried the distressed mother.

Cassie ran a practiced hand gently over the boy's limbs and shook her head sadly. "The poor lad . . . he has a broken arm, and it must be set for the swelling has already started. I used to go about with my mother and often saw her set a limb or two. Would you be willing to put your trust in me?"

"Aye, mistress, that I would," said the woman vigorously.

Cassie got to her feet and looked about for a makeshift splint. She picked up a broken freedom banner and standing on half of it, brought it up sharply so that it split in two. Collecting a few thinner shanks of splintered wood, she returned to the child and went down on her knees. Once again she tore her skirt, handing the lengths to the boy's mother.

"Here now . . . see if you can make this into several ties," she said before turning to the boy. She stroked his head and smiled at him, "Well now . . . are you a brave lad?"

He nodded his head somewhat tremulously, and she smiled again. "I'm glad. I broke my arm, you know . . . when I was about ten or so. The doctor was away, and my mother had to set it for me. What she did was to place a piece of wood . . ." she held up the thin slat of wood, "just like this, right in my mouth and told me to bite down hard when it hurt. I bit clean through! Think you can?"

Again he nodded and opened his mouth to receive the offering. She gave over the splinter of wood, and Cassie then took up his arm in a firm grasp. With a swift hard motion she yanked it forward pulling the bone into place. The boy went white beneath the ordeal but made hardly a sound. She then flexed his wrist and with a quick motion

412

slid her hand up and around the arm, making certain the bone was in its proper quarter before setting the splint in position.

She rewarded the lad with a pat to his head and noted the pathetic tears he held back. "Well now, my gallant," she said, taking the splint of wood, "have a look at this! You bit clear through!"

His lips quivered as he smiled and reached for the wood with his good hand.

"That's it! 'Tis an excellent keepsake," said Cassie, smiling warmly at him. However, a harsh voice at Cassie's back brought her head round.

A burly, scarlet-coated yeoman on horseback ordered them to move out of the street, and Cassie got to her feet, her green eyes flashing. "How dare you! If it wasn't for the brutality exhibited here today by such as yourself, we would not now be doctoring in the streets!"

"That's enough out of the likes of you!" snapped the yeoman. He had taken in her appearance, for Cassie, her red hair wild, her gown dirty and torn, was certainly not recognizable as a viscountess. Added to this was the fact that he had just come from splitting the skulls of two unfortunate male radicals and was still caught up with the frenzy of sudden and unprecedented power.

"I shall report you, sir!" threatened Cassie, incensed. "Tell me . . . what do you do the rest of the year? That is, when you are not running women and children into the ground? Has this been an adventure for you? Is this what you call a deed well done, running down your neighbors, your fellow Englishmen? That is what you are doing! And on what orders, sir? I should like to see your orders, for you cannot make me believe that you have been commanded by your superiors to do this!"

His hand came down hard across Cassie's cheek, and she put up her own at the sting. She could not believe it! "You filthy toad!" she hissed, standing her ground, feeling at that moment that had she a knife, she would have lodged it in his fat belly.

The yeoman was off his horse and on her in a moment.

His one hand grabbed her shoulder, his other raised with every intention of repeating the action. His companion called him to a halt. "Nay . . . you have not been looking on her, now 'ave ye, friend?" said his crony, for he had been gazing full at Cassie's alluring form.

"I'll warrant ye we can find a better use for this spitfire than a beating post!" he continued as his friend licked his lips with expectation.

The fat yeoman holding Cassie began to chuckle. "Aye, she do be fine-looking at that." He pushed her forward. "Come on, then . . . it's with us ye'll be coming, wench!"

Cassie struck out with all her might. Breaking free of his grasp, she found a broken liberty pole and picked it up like a baton, holding it ominously, keeping the fat yeoman at bay. However, he took his chances and made a lunge for her, grabbing at her traveling habit and pulling at the blue linen so that much of it gave way, exposing her full breasts.

Cassie gasped and put her hand to cover her nakedness when a voice thundered at them, "Damn you, swine! What do you mean by this work?" demanded a Hussar officer glowering down from the heights of his stately horse.

Cassie blushed but there was something about his voice that brought up her eyes to his face. And she gasped again! Lyle, Lyle Stanton in full Hussar uniform! What could this mean?

"She was resisting arrest!" mumbled the fat yeoman.

"Arrest? You miserable excuse for scum! Move off and be warned, if you are again found taking advantage of this devilish situation we have here today, it will be Newgate for you!"

The two yeomen had no authority before a Hussar of the King's Cavalry. They scurried off as fast they could, and then Lyle Stanton was winking at Cassie. "Sure now, I did want our time to be soon . . . though I could have chosen better circumstances."

"But Lyle . . . how . . . ?"

He chuckled, "Come then, up with you, and I'll tell you all about it." He was reaching down for her hand. She hesitated but a moment. She could use his help to find

Guy and Mary Beth. She gave him her hand, put a foot in the stirrup and allowed him to situate her at his back.

"Hold tight to me, lass, and tell me where you might be wanting me to take you?"

"I need to find Guy and Mary first . . . and you can tell me now, if you please, if I am in greater danger traveling with a . . . spy . . . than I would be on my own?"

He chuckled deeply. "On your own? Well now, you've had a taste of that? Like it?"

She shuddered, "No, no!"

"I thought not, love. Spy? 'Tis a thought, but not a fact! I was set upon some distance back . . . didn't like beating my way out of it, so I used my head. Only way to make it safely out of the city was to parade the uniform of one that none would challenge!"

"And the man who originally wore it?" she asked, her brow up.

"He'll suffer no harm—I left him my own, you see—providing he wakes up in time to find it before someone comes along and snatches the things up!"

"You are . . ."

"Save it, lass. You wouldn't be wanting to call curses down on m'head. Why, I saved you, I did . . . and not a word of thanks have I had."

She blushed. "You don't deserve thanks. Not after that night!"

"Heard it all turned out right and tight though," he answered brightly. "No harm done!"

"No harm done! What of the money spent on guns the government confiscated. All that money! It could have gone for food . . . clothes . . ."

" 'Tis over, lass . . . don't be harping on it. Thought you were a woman of a different cut. Didn't expect you to be forever chattering on about a man's faults!" he answered glibly.

She stared at his back. He was impossible. He would never see himself in the wrong of it. There would always be a ready excuse. Well, it didn't matter to her. All she wanted was to be reunited with Guy and Mary and find them unharmed.

40

The viscount had taken to horse, his pistol tucked into his cumberbund, ready to hand. His hat had been discarded and his black locks were scattered by the breeze. He was unsure of his path, having never been to Manchester, and the sailors' directions were sketchy, but he found his way after some little delay and was met with the horrific sight of what would soon be called the Peterloo Massacre. The carnage of the indigent was without deference to sex or age or guilt, and the sound of laughter from the yeomanry sent a wave of fury through the viscount.

There too, he heard some Hussars in their attempt to stem the brutality of the local forces, but they were outnumbered and could not be everywhere at once. He stopped one of the King's men and demanded furiously, "Colonel . . . what the devil does this mean? Who in hell ordered this?"

"What can I say, sir? We got the orders to march on the Orator and disperse the crowds. But this bloodshed . . . 'tis the work of these locals. We've had the devil's own work chasing 'em down to keep them from the bloodletting."

Just then the viscount observed two yeomen on horseback corner a young man on foot. One of the yeoman's swords waved, and the viscount made his horse dash across at a reckless pace. Almost simultaneously his foot came up knocking the yeoman's sword away, and his voice thundered, "Fie! Fiend! You dare to raise your sabre against an unarmed man! Get you gone before I have you hauled into jail!"

The Hussar had ambled forward and added his orders to that of the viscount, and the yeoman grumbled but thought it wise not to put up an argument. Again the viscount turned to the Hussar. "The field is empty . . . where have all the people gone? I mean . . . seventy thousand people . . . where could they all go so quickly?"

"Those that were not run down took to the roads. Those that were hurt dragged themselves to whatever inns would take 'em. Faith! What can I tell you? They were there one minute, staying for that precious Orator of theirs . . . then the next they was watching him get beaten and dragged off. All at once some doltish locals started waving sabres in the crowd . . . they just fled . . ."

"I see," said the viscount, but then a man down the street caught his eye. He had the look of Guy Bamfield and like a bolt, the viscount was charging his horse his way. He reached him, and the man spun around in some surprise. However, it was not Guy. Streets and squares were passed and searched before he decided to start doing a tour of each and every hostelry in Manchester.

"Look, lass, we best be stopping at a posting house. Chances are you'll find them there . . . and if not, you'll be wanting a post chaise to take you home," said Lyle lightly.

"Home?" she said absently. "Oh, God!"

"What is it, love? Trouble in that quarter? Come to

think of it, didn't you tell me you weren't coming to this meet? What changed your mind?"

"Which question must I answer first?" she asked tartly.

He laughed. "Lord love you, no need to whip me with that tongue of yours. I could just leave you here . . . let you do whatever comes to your mind."

"No," she said hastily, "you wouldn't do that?"

"No, as it happens, I have a fondness for you, love. I told you once we could deal together."

"Oh, Lyle . . . I . . . I just don't want to think right now. Perhaps, we could stop at an inn . . . until I have figured out just what I am to do?"

"Your servant, ma'am," he answered at once.

She hated the notion of returning to Liverpool . . . not after Kirkby's infidelity . . . not to his gloating mother. There was nothing there for her, yet she longed for him, longed to accuse him . . . longed to hear him say it was some long-lost sister . . . a cousin—anything other than who it was. She wanted to forget the day's terrors, and she wanted to do it in her husband's arms. However, there was little chance of that.

They reached a posting inn, the Red Hart by name, and Cassie allowed Lyle to go in ahead of her. He said he would procure her a room, and she was too tired and too diffident of her ragged appearance to do so herself.

A few moments later, wreathed in soft smiles and gentle looks, Lyle returned and assisted her off her horse. He held her waist firmly and his tone had softened further as he advised her that a room awaited, and Cassie once again longed for the viscount.

Welford was by then a desperate man. He had done a tour of the streets and had searched no less than five inns in various parts of the town surrounding St. Peter's Field. He was both irritable and deadly concerned when he walked into yet another inn and discovered there Guy and Mary Beth Bamfield. His every thought had been for Cassie. He heaped on his head the recriminations of a lover who has kept a measure of himself aloof. If only, he thought, if only he had told her the whole story, she might not now be here. But where was here? A bloodbath . . . and God! let her be safe!

Thus, it was not surprising that his anger was turned on the two people before him. He strode forward, his drawn brows and dark lashes veiling his fury. "Bamfield! Where is Cassandra?" he demanded harshly.

"Oh, my word!" cried Mary Beth, falling into tears once again, "we don't know . . . we don't know."

Behind the viscount's harshness had been hope, and Mary Beth had just dashed it to the ground. "Damnation, girl! What in hell does that mean . . . you don't know?"

Bamfield's arm was in a sling, another bandage round his curly head showed a dark dry spot on the forehead, and he winced as he rose to his feet and stood in front of his wife. However, he was not insensible to the viscount's emotions and understood the man's distress. His voice came calmly, quietly, "I must ask you, my lord, to direct your harshness against me . . . not my wife!"

"Gladly!" shouted the viscount. "I would be pleased to direct my fist against you for this day's work. How dare you bring my wife here . . . and then abandon her!"

"Please, my lord, you misunderstand . . ." offered Mary Beth, fearing for her husband's life.

"Do I?" sneered the viscount. "Then perhaps you really know where Cassie is and mean to tell me?"

"My lord, Cassandra was with us near the hustings . . . she moved away to purchase an apple when suddenly the horses of the yeomanry were stampeding the people. The Orator was pulled off the dais and beaten before our eyes. The crowd broke before I could catch hold of Cassandra, for the yeomen had begun pressing and wounding those in their path. Women, girls and youths were indiscriminately sabred and trampled. Yet still we could see Cassie. Then suddenly she was swept away by the crowd. We have ourselves only just now come in from searching the streets," said Guy in much distress.

"Be ye looking for her ladyship?" asked a man suddenly from behind the viscount.

Kirkby whirled and all eyes went to an elderly, gray-haired fellow in the coal miner's white garb. He puffed on a pipe, and his slouch hat flapped about his ears.

"What do you know of Lady Welford?" demanded the viscount.

"I know of her . . . seen her at a field meeting or two . . . heard ye speaking now . . . thought I might help . . ."

"If you do, you will be well paid," said the viscount, reaching into his pocket.

"Aye, thought as much," nodded the old man. "Well now, saw her more 'n onct today. First time . . . was back some . . . she was 'elping some lad when two yeomen set upon her. Meant some dirty business by her. Was getting ready to risk me old head I was when a young blade of a Hussar stepped in and scurried 'em off. Took her up he did and saw none of her until a few moments ago."

"Well, come on, speak up, man?" snapped the viscount.

"The coin if ye please, m'lord . . . been twigged a time or two and thought ye might 'ave a mind to run off and forget . . ."

He was cut off as two gold coins dropped into his open palm, and the viscount thundered, "Now out with it!"

"Well . . . I was looking in on the Red Hart . . . after me own . . . but in walks her ladyship with this same Hussar."

The viscount waited for no more as he gave them his back and stalked into the street. The Red Hart was but a hundred yards away, and he sliced the road as he traversed its length. What did this mean? Why would she go into a posting inn with a Hussar? Had she been forced . . . or was she intending . . . No! Not Cassie! He knew her better than that! She hadn't turned in his brother Peter. She was no murderess, and she was no doxy.

Cassie turned at the chamber door of her room and gave Lyle her hand. "Thank you, Lyle . . . in spite of everything . . . you have treated me with kindness, and I do appreciate it."

"Do you now?" he asked pushing past her hand, kicking the door closed at his back. He ambled into the room and plopped on the bed, throwing his hussar hat to one side, unbuttoning the top of his red coat before Cassie's startled eyes.

"What do you think you are doing?" she demanded.

"Oh, lass, it's tired I am. And we've the price of one room between us . . . what with the wild prices they be charging below . . ."

She bit her lip. She hadn't thought to bring a fat purse and had but half a crown in her skirt pocket. "You . . . you . . . can't stay here . . . with me . . ."

"Does it worry you, love? No one will know," he said, getting up, going towards her, catching her waist in his hands.

"I will know," she said, frowning. "I shall have to contrive somehow to get another room." She was worried about appearances, for she was not afraid for herself. Not with Lyle . . . he was not the sort to . . . hurt her? And then she looked up into his face and her heart felt suddenly as though it needed help. The twinkle was gone from his eye, replaced by something hard, determined.

"You've put me aside once too often, love," he said, his voice low, "but no more . . ."

"Lyle, no . . . this is not like you! I can't believe you would . . ." but already his mouth silenced hers. She pushed ineffectually at his chest, and he suddenly released her a moment, holding her only by one arm as she struggled. "Lyle . . . never say you saved me from the jackals simply to have at me yourself?"

"And why not?" he sneered. "You are too much a woman for their like. Oh, love! They would not appreciate you as I would . . . don't fight me, Cass," he said, forcing her to him, kissing her neck fiercely. " 'Twould go so much easier for you if you wouldn't fight . . ."

"Don't you realize what you are doing?" cried Cassie,

still struggling against him. "My husband will have your neck!"

"If he can find me!" Again his mouth took hers harshly, savagely. His grip hurt, she felt repelled and sickened by his groping hands, and she beat furiously at his chest. In the struggle the remainder of her bodice gave way, exposing the fullness of her soft high breasts. He loosened his hold to get a better view, and an animal sound formed in his throat. She broke away and ran toward the door, but he jerked her back by her long hair, wrenching another cry from her, and the terror of her helplessness made her scream!

Already his mouth returned to press itself against hers and silence her panic, already his hands ravaged her satin skin and pulled her down to the hard wood floor. She sobbed when he allowed her breath, and she begged for release but his hand went over her mouth, and he whispered hoarsely, " 'Tis a fault with you, Cass, this chattering habit of yours. Aw, love, you're not a virgin child. You know this won't hurt. Why do you fight me?"

She bit his finger, and he jerked his hand away. "You knave! I've been made love to by a man! A real man! Think you any other could please me after him? I fight you because it is not my choice to have you!"

"Poor wench! But you'll change your tune . . . shortly . . ." he breathed heavily, his hands exploring her exquisite body.

She couldn't stand it! She thought she would go mad from his pawing! She kicked beneath him, her hand found his hair, and she yanked with all her might. He yelped, and she was able to throw him off balance. It was her moment. He had given her slack, and she used it to bring up her knees. With her new leverage she sent him flying backward. She scrambled to her feet and made for the door, but he threw himself forward catching her ankles and bringing her down. She landed with a heavy thud and felt a bolt of pain shoot through her, winding her. He mounted her, furious now, and his hand repaid her for the injury to his pride. His slap brought another scream from

422

her, but not just a scream of pain for she called for Kirkby! With all her heart, with all her strength she called for Kirkby!

And then suddenly the door came crashing in. It burst open as though taken by an explosion and Viscount Kirkby Welford filled the opening. He was a storm, a fury unleashed. He picked up Lyle bodily and set him up straight before his fist found the man's face and belly and began to pommel with unmerciful brutality. And Cassie, sobbing, saw her love, and she buried her face in her hands for a moment. She had to do something . . . Kirkby was going to kill him.

Lyle Stanton scarcely understood what was happening. He only knew excruciating pain as he felt his eyes blackened, his teeth loosened, and his nose broken! He had been but moments ago delighting in the violation of a woman he had long wanted, excusing it because he truly believed in the end she would enjoy the act as much as he. And now, suddenly, he was being beaten to death by a madman!

And the viscount? He had entered the inn to inquire after his wife, only to hear her voice calling his name! He had raced up the stairs and smashed open the door to find an animal assaulting her. The sight drove him nearly to insanity. It was as though a button had been pressed in his mind, shutting out all but the need to destroy the blackguard before him. Only Cassie's voice, only her plea kept him from it.

"Kirkby," she sobbed, "Kirby . . . please . . . just send him away . . . I only need to be with you . . ."

The viscount heard her but could not refrain from landing the fellow one final blow to his midsection. Lyle slumped to the floor with a groan and the viscount bent over his wife to take her into his arms. She was trembling all over, and he held her tenderly. His lips kissed her forehead as he placed her upon the bed and covered her with its quilt.

"My own sweetings, hush, there, love . . . hush . . ." he whispered in an effort to calm her fears and still her

423

sobs. However, his black hard eyes found Lyle and watched him as the man crawled towards the door. The veins in the viscount's neck stood out, and his eyes glittered, for Lyle was making good his escape. Kirkby moved toward him.

His wife's hands stayed him. "Nay, Kirkby, nay. Let him go, do . . . please . . . just stay with me . . . hold me . . ." she pleaded.

The viscount's lips were pressed thin and his fists itched to do more work, but his wife called him back, and his expression softened at last.

He went to her and held her, and she felt whole. Had this morning's torment really existed, she wondered? Had there really been another woman? For here he was . . . at no little effort to prove his love. He had come after her . . . he had found her . . . he was here loving her!

There were words then, all having to do with love. Nothing else mattered but that they were reunited and alive.

41

It was late. The undrawn drapes showed a sky alight with stars that twinkled at the lovers in their bed. Cassie lay on her back staring into the darkness, thinking, remembering, and remembering, her eyes clouded over. The crisis was past, and once again doubts haunted her. She moved and found the viscount perched on his elbow gazing down at her face. His hand reached, his fingers stroked, and he bent to kiss her lips, but she put up her hand, detaining him.

"No, Kirkby . . . there is *something* you must explain . . . I *need* to know," she said solemnly, fearfully. "The woman in the coach . . ." She dreaded his answer.

He sighed but sat up, and his hands stretched out and went behind his head as a pillow. "Yes, indeed. There is Leila . . . and Nathan . . . and my brother . . . all should be, must be explained."

She turned round on him, and her lovely nipples brushed his chest. She felt him quiver and his hands came down to touch. She slapped them away. "Leila? Was that her name? What has Nathan to do with it . . . and your brother . . . you never mentioned you have a brother . . ."

"And I shan't be able to explain it all now, if you don't keep yourself at bay, little love . . ." he teased.

She blushed happily and pulled the covers round herself. He sighed as he watched her, but smiled and began his lengthy tale, starting at the beginning. He told her of Peter Eaton. He told her of their closeness and Peter's enlisting in the Select Committee, and he told her how he came to Farrington Grange. She interrupted him now and then, especially over her name in Peter's letter, and afterward she sat silent a long while before exclaiming with much dissatisfaction.

"But *I* was never in Bristol . . . and that last letter he wrote you had to come from Bristol. I don't understand . . . and how could he think me evil? 'Tis ridiculous—we scarcely knew one another? And goodness! That explains why the dowager loathes the sight of me . . . but . . ."

"But what, darling?" he asked for she suddenly looked as though she had had an inspiration.

"Well, of course! Why did you not think of it? There must be another woman with my hair coloring . . . he must have met *her* in Bristol!"

"I have thought of that, but if there was, she has never appeared before me, and I have met with the Asbatols several times. Why would Peter have been introduced to her, and I not be accorded the same privilege? He certainly could not have meant Leila!"

"Leila . . . yes! What of Leila? You have told all, but that does not explain why she was in your lap!"

"Good lord! You don't think it was on invitation, my girl, do you?"

"Well, I couldn't know as I was not there at the outset. So kindly tell me what she was doing there if not by invitation!"

He laughed. "I believe the woman thinks me attractive."

She pinched his bare arm, and he caught her hand and

put it to his lips. "Careful, vixen! Don't show your claws to me or you might find them clipped. Now come here . . ." he said, lifting her into his arms. His mouth found hers, and she felt herself slipping into *their world* once again—a bright full world where every touch was joy, every sense alive, and all else forgotten.

Suddenly it was morning. A bleak, gray dawn, but Cassie thought it beautiful for her beloved's face was nuzzled against her shoulder. A knock sounded at the door and a man's voice called out loudly, "Eh . . . in there! There be a couple calls themselves Bamfield anxious in knowing of ye."

Cassie started to open her mouth when the viscount's voice boomed over hers, "Tell Mr. Bamfield to go . . ."

". . . with his bride to Liverpool. I shall be calling on them when I reach home with the viscount," answered Cassie, hastily cutting off her husband. She pulled a face at him and said, "You horrid thing, they only wanted to be sure I was all right. After the way you ranted at them . . . 'tis no wonder. They probably thought you came in search of me simply to administer a beating!" The viscount had related all his doings, including his meeting with Guy and Mary Beth.

"Own it that you deserved one," grinned her husband.

"I shall not! Beast! Get up at once and arrange for our breakfast. You have this lamentable habit of seducing me and forgetting to feed me. We went without dinner last night, you know!"

"Ah, but I understand you consumed an apple?" teased the viscount.

"Oh, Kirk, 'tis not funny . . . all those people . . ." said Cassie, her face clouding over. "It was . . . awful . . . I still cannot believe it."

"Nor I," agreed the viscount as he got out of bed.

She appraised him as he moved about the room, donning his clothes. She scanned the ripple of his hard muscles, the slimness of his waist, loving every move he made. He was her everything, and the thought made her sigh. He heard her and turned round, giving her a scampish grin.

"This time, my vixen—stay put—please! No more adventures." He flicked her nose. "I'm off to get you something decent to wear, and I'll be back as soon as may be, for I'll have to hire a post chaise for our journey to Liverpool."

She blew him a kiss but started up as he reached the door, and the covers fell away from her naked body. His eyes swept her and their blackness was filled with glinting lights as he warmed over.

"Kirkby . . ." she called, ". . . a hairbrush—for your comb will never do—and a toothbrush as well . . . and the red tooth powder if you please . . . and have a girl bring up some fresh washwater for you have soiled what little there was . . . and . . ."

"And that is quite enough, vixen! My God! I have a cockatrice for wife," he smiled broadly.

"But never say you mean to starve me. Aren't *you* hungry? I certainly am," she pursued.

He laughed. "We'll breakfast upon my return." But as he reached the door, he turned to her again and called softly, "Cassie . . . I love you . . ." He was gone.

Much time passed before they were in a dark brown coach on their way to Liverpool. Cassie, now suitably attired in an ivory muslin gown with puff sleeves and a modest neckline, gazed quizzically over herself and then at her husband. "Dearest Kirkby . . . this . . ." she said sweeping a gloved hand over her frock, "is quite different from the gowns you bought me at the outset of our marriage."

"Hmmm," said her husband noncommittally.

"I like it not," she returned sweetly.

"I do," said he. "But never mind it, Cassie. Have a look at this article in the *Morning Register,*" he said giving the paper a slap and handing it over to her. She read aloud:

"The following account was taken from the Vicar of Alderley, who saw the entire proceedings of yesterday's horror from a near-by window overlooking St. Peter's Field. He told this reporter that it all started as the cavalry approached the dense crowds who in turn used their utmost efforts to escape. But so closely were they pressed in opposite directions by the soldiers, the special constables, the position of the hustings, and their own immense numbers, that immediate escape was impossible. The rapid course of the troops was, of course, impeded when it came in contact with the mob, but a passage was forced in less than a minute. On their arrival at the hustings, a scene of dreadful confusion ensued. The Orators fell or were forced off the scaffold in quick succession. During the whole of this confusion, heightened by the rattle of some artillery crossing the square, shrieks were heard in all directions, and as the crowd of people dispersed, the effects of the conflict became visible. Some were seen bleeding on the ground and unable to rise, others, less seriously injured but faint from the loss of blood, were retiring slowly or leaning upon others for support. The whole of this extraordinary scene was the work of a few minutes!

"No resistance, no stone-throwing was enacted against the yeomanry, yet they pressed on with their weapons. This reporter would like to conclude by adding that some six hundred people, of whom no less than one hundred were women, have been seriously injured and that the death toll stands at this time at eleven."

Cassie laid the paper in her lap and gazed at her husband. "But Kirkby, why? It doesn't say why?"

"Parliament fears political agitators, the locals feared this meeting, and I can only assume that the local magistrates having had the word to proceed with caution, quaked and gave panic-stricken orders. However, Sidmouth's letter indicates to me that he had in mind such as this might occur!"

"It may just bring on that revolution the government bothers their head about. The people are bound to react," said Cassie with feeling.

"That may be, but I doubt it. They have the Orator and

Sam Bamford locked up, and I doubt those poor fellows will get out for some time."

"On what charges? 'Tis unthinkable!" cried Cassie.

"They will find charges enough. But Cassie, let us not think of it now. Come . . . I want to hold you," he said drawing her into his arms. The article in the newspaper had drummed up all the fear that had enveloped him yesterday. And he wanted her in his arms, safe, happy . . .

Thus Liverpool and the Welford house were reached. They entered the hall laughing over some jest, coming up short and silent when faced with the drawn countenance of the dowager.

She moved towards the viscount, her aged hands trembling.

"Kirkby . . . I have been so worried. The papers . . . they are all of St. Peter's Field . . . they're calling it *Peterloo*. . ."

"They should be!" snapped the viscount for he was still incensed with her. "Now if you will excuse us, ma'am, my wife has been through an ordeal, and I should like to see her comfortably situated in our room."

She found that her lip quivered in spite of her resolution. So he would take this creature's part over her? Very well then, so be it. "Of course," she said with some dignity.

Cassie gave her a long thoughtful look, but there was little she could do or say. The woman believed that she was involved with the Asbatols, and until Kirkby entrapped them and got to the bottom of it, nothing would change the dowager's mind.

The viscount saw his wife to their room, ordered her bath prepared, and went to her. He took her hand and put it to his lips. "I have to go out, darling . . . to Lord Widdons. You see . . . all is set for the morrow. Asbatol will be riding out with his men to capture a coach with the Widdons heir . . . only, they will have a surprise in store for them. I must assure myself that nothing has changed since last we met."

Cassie held him for a long moment before whispering, "Come back soon . . ."

His kiss was sweet and tender, his voice was a balm. "How could I not, with you waiting . . ."

Cassie awoke in a darkened room. It was morning, she knew it had to be morning, but every limb ached, and then memory flooded her. "Kirkby . . ." but even as she reached out for him, she knew he was gone. "Oh, Kirkby!"

She jumped out of bed and pulled the drapes open, blinking at the brightness of the sun. She scanned the room and then the dressing room, and just as she was about to ring for her maid, a knock sounded softly at the door.

"Come in," she called hopefully.

A mobcapped chambermaid appeared. She was a youthful, lanky sort with freckles covering her shiny face, and she bobbed a curtsy. Cassie indicated that she might lay the tray of coffee and biscuits on the table and then charged right in with her questions. "Has his lordship gone out?"

"Yes, m'lady . . . he did. Said to tell you he won't be back till dinner . . . and not to fret it," smiled the girl.

"Oh, I see. Very well, thank you," she said dismissing her.

"Will ye be needing me to help ye with yer buttons and sech?" asked the girl.

"No, oh, perhaps later . . . I'll ring," said Cassie absently. She was worried. He had said he would be in no danger . . . but she was worried all the same. These were a desperate lot . . . Oh, she would go noddy if she didn't keep herself busy!

She would take Starfire for an outing. He needed some lengthy exercise. She gulped down her coffee and threw on her riding habit of blue linen without assistance. Brushing out her long hair, she piled it high and pinned on her top hat with its flowing blue organza scarf. Then she was off to the stables. There she discovered that Chips was with the viscount, and her poor Thomas down with a toothache.

"How long has it been paining you, lad?" asked Cassie with much concern.

"Off 'n on, m'lady . . . but it hurts something fierce today," sobbed the boy.

"Then off to the dentist you go. Tell him Lady Welford wants you to get the best of . . . never mind, I shall see you there myself. Can you manage to saddle our horses?"

"Aye, that I can . . . and anything else you may wish, m'lady . . . anything . . ." said the boy bravely.

"That will do nicely . . . now do but bring the horses round for I am returning to the house to inquire after a dentist," said Cassie going off.

Some two hours later saw the wretched boy's tooth drawn. However, the doctor had allowed him a brace of whisky to set off the pain, and Cassie saw him headed home in somewhat better spirits. She sighed as she watched him take his pony and mounted her own steed, dropping a coin into the link boy's hand and thanking him for caring for the horse while she was occupied.

"Tell me . . . where may I get a bit of a ride and perhaps do some shopping from here?" asked Cassie after a thought.

The link boy scratched the top of his dirty head. "Don't really . . . eh now, mayhap ye'd like to take yerself over to the wharf . . . like it meself . . . they got hot apple pie there now . . ."

She smiled. "In which direction would that be?"

He pointed, and she smiled at him before heading that way. However, as she progressed, it became more and more apparent to her that this was not the sort of neighborhood for her to traverse alone. She attempted to turn her horse about but found the traffic too congested and took instead a side street, thinking to head down another avenue towards the main pike to her house. However, this proved to be an error in judgment. She tried to retrace her path when suddenly she saw something that startled her. She stared hard at the back of a woman, a young woman, noting every line, every detail to the top of the woman's cinnamon-gold hair. Then the woman turned, and Cassie saw that while they had similar forms they were actually quite different. Her double was not really so, for she was some six or seven years older. Her cheekbones were wider . . . her lips thinner . . . but never mind, these were but minor details. This must be Peter's evil angel . . . she *had* to be! She had moved to Liverpool with the Asbatols of course! Cassie made a snap decision and urged Starfire forward. She had to stop the woman and speak with her, but already the redhead was rounding the corner.

Cassie kept her in sight until the redhead entered a shambles of a building. Cassie dismounted and searched round for someone to watch her steed. At last she found a youth, shoeless and in some rags, and placed the reins of her horse in his hands.

"My name is Lady Welford . . . take care of my horse, and there shall be a large fee for you."

He smiled up at her and nodded his head. She was pretty and he liked her smile. He'd be happy to watch her horse, but he only nodded.

A moment later Cassie was inside the building. She felt an instant wave of revulsion pass over her, for the stench was almost unbearable. She could scarcely see in the dim corridor, but she heard a sound and followed it down a long narrow hall to another. There . . . thank God, she thought as she spied the redhead knocking upon a door. She was about to proceed but she stopped for she could just make out the form of a man concealed from the redhead but in open view to her where he crouched behind a pile of rubbish. Cassie could see him inching out and she knew instinctively he meant some harm to the woman. She called out harshly from her fear, "Look out!"

Nancy spun round immediately and saw her attacker. She flung her reticule at him full in the face, stunning him a moment, just enough to get past him, and she grabbed hold of Cassie's hand. "Come on, dearie . . . he do mean to follow!" she snapped.

Cassie gave her no argument but ran down the hall with her full speed. However, neither had reckoned on the man's having an accomplice at the other end.

42

A dark brown, gold crested coach rumbled over the rutted road. It had one driver and one postilion garbed in blue livery. Its occupant appeared to be one youth dressed in superbly cut velvet. However, the brow that was steeped behind his low-crowned, feathered hat was that of a man well seasoned. Beneath the open book positioned in his lap, lay a very deadly pistol. He was not the fourteen-year-old son of Lord Widdons, but a Bow Street runner.

The road they took was a lonely one in much disrepair. It was flanked with stretches of deep dark woods and thickets. Asbatol sat his horse some distance away from the roadside, his men, two burly, rough individuals, horse pistols in hand, faces well-covered with their belcher scarfs, sat astride their horses a few feet before him. This had been the designated spot, just before the posting house. The armed postilion would be expecting no trouble here.

Asbatol caught sight of the coach as it took the bend in the road and he motioned his men into action. They came out in a rush at the coach, and one of them aimed a shot in the air as warning. "Stand . . . stand, I say!" shouted one of Asbatol's men. They waited only long enough for the coach to brake before aiming their pistols. "Now drops yer irons, m'friends, and mayhap ye'll be gettin' to drink yer ale!"

Their orders were complied with. Asbatol came out slowly, his own face covered with his neckcloth. It was almost too easy. "Get the boy out!" he thundered at his men. "Come on you sluggish fools!"

It happened in a flash. A gun went off from within the confines of the carriage and the first of Asbatol's men fell backward off his horse. There he lay, immobile and unconscious from the wound to his shoulder and the force of his fall. The other turned his horse sharply intending to make his escape, but found his path blocked by a sturdy rider pointing an ominous pistol at his head.

"Hold there, covey!" said Chips grimly.

Asbatol witnessed this before his heels pounded his horse's flanks, and he was off. However, the viscount was not so easily lost. Asbatol heard him at his back and fired aimlessly, hoping to slow his pursuer but again he knew not his man. Kirkby Welford would have his prize. They took the road at a reckless pace, but Asbatol's horse was no match for that of the viscount's. Within moments the viscount was riding abreast, reaching out, catching Asbatol's reins, slowing him down. Up went Asbatol's gun, but the viscount was ready for this too. His own finger never hesitated—and gone was Asbatol's pistol as the blood poured from his right hand.

They were at a complete stop now, and Nathan Asbatol was livid with desperation and fury. "A trap . . . it was all a trap?"

"Peter Eaton was my stepbrother," was the only answer he received, and then with something akin to a snarl, "Now get down!"

"Very well . . ." Nathan answered slowly raising his leg, bringing himself over and imperceptibly taking a small pistol from his saddle pocket as he touched the ground. It was his last chance, his only chance. He had no clear sight of the viscount but the viscount's horse.

His shot went off! The air echoed with the cry of agony and a proud steed went down. Kirkby's attention was wrenched from him for one unthinking moment. It was, of course, his mistake, for in that moment, Nathan Asbatol heaved himself halfway onto his horse and was away. The viscount looked up and quickly aimed his gun, but it was too late for Asbatol was out of range.

It had taken some moments for the viscount to requisition another horse from the prisoners, taking the better of the two animals. He was off for Liverpool, certain that he would get there in time, knowing he would have to get there in time if he was not to lose his prey. The runner had sourly said he didn't think Asbatol would return to his lodgings, but the viscount was counting on it. After all, he would have to get cash, and he would have to get his wife.

Asbatol was a cunning man. He did not go near his lodgings. Instead he sent a brief note to his wife instructing her to collect their money and meet him at the docks. She did not understand what had gone wrong, but she was no fool and knew better than to tarry. She hated this, all this slinking and running. Nathan was a thorn to her now. He was failing too often. Sooner or later she would have to find a way of escaping him.

Nancy and Cassie had not escaped the heavy-set brute at the end of the dark corridor. He had blocked their path, and it seemed to Cassie for one horrid moment that all was at an end in this world. His cheeks were red from drink, and his eyes glowed much like the rats that squealed across the hall. They were trapped! They found themselves shoved roughly into a dark windowless chamber no more than ten square feet in size. There they stood, too frightened of what they might find if they were to relax their limbs upon the floor.

It was Cassie who spoke first. "What is your name?"

she asked after a sigh, "and why are those men keeping us here?"

"Me name be Nancy. You be here coz ye had no mind and kept not to yeself!"

"Very well, Nancy . . . you may be as disagreeable as you like, but I promise you, it won't serve! I have a host of questions, but I shall start with the one that made me follow you to this dreadful place. Were you acquainted with a young man by the name of Peter Eaton?"

"Och now! Peter is it? Why do ye ask?" returned Nancy suspiciously.

"So then you did know him!" said Cassie triumphantly. "Now, for my second question. Why have those men locked us here—and don't start on my stupidity again! Once we know why, we might, between us, devise our escape."

"Listen to the lovely now! I don't see hows it got anything to do, one with the other . . . nor how ye come to know of me and Peter but . . . thing is . . . well, ye might as well know. It would seem me little plan to get me pockets lined backfired. The filthy swine has decided to put me away . . . but not till he gets the letter . . . no, he'll be trying after the letter he will . . ."

"What letter?" asked Cassie.

Nancy gave her a long appraising look. "Ye ain't told me who ye be . . ."

"I am Cassandra . . . Lady Welford," she said openly.

"Och! Never say so . . ." with which she burst out laughing. At length she dried her eyes. " 'Tis the viscount then that be yer ever-lovin' mate?"

"Yes . . ." and then Cassie realized that Nancy was, of course, connected with the Asbatols. Well . . . what could her knowing that she was married to the viscount do? Nought . . . it could do nought to hurt Kirkby. "Why do you find it amusing?"

"Well now, Nathan, he won't find it so easy to dispose of ye, will he? No, not wit the viscount taking over things as he been doing."

"No, that is a plus in our favor . . . but tell me,

437

Nancy. This letter . . . would it be for sale? Perhaps my husband would be interested in its contents . . . why not tell me about it?"

Nancy put a finger to her lips. "Hmm . . . well now . . . that do sound good. So then I'll tell ye why we be here. I'll tell ye all about Peter Eaton's letter!"

The viscount reached Asbatol's house just a moment too late. Leila had already received the message from Nathan to collect what cash they had stored away and to proceed to their tryst, for they had but one small piece of unfinished business to conclude before they would depart Liverpool.

The viscount stood a long moment at the Asbatols' doorstep, for he was at a loss as to what to do, where to go, and then he remembered the brothel. Just perhaps Leila made a stop there? He made for his horse and once again was tooling down the busy avenue.

Nathan Asbatol reached the dilapidated building Nancy and Cassie had entered some time ago. He lit a tallow candle and made his way to the room holding the women. At the door were slumped the two men he had hired to do the job, and he gave them a kick that brought them out of their slumbers.

"Dolts! Wake up! You gin-noddled fools!" he cursed.

One of the men rose hurriedly, rubbing his eyes. Shoving the empty gin bottle out of sight with his heel, he said, "Look, guv . . . we dun wot ye told us, but there be another mort in wit that Nancy! She come up out of nowhere, she did, and there was nought for it but to lock 'em both up!"

"What?" ejaculated Nathan. "Damn idiots! All right, move aside!"

Cassie and Nancy had been deep in conversation. Nancy had informed her ladyship all about Peter Eaton's connection to her and to the Asbatols.

"But what I don't understand is why Asbatol sent you to Peter in the first place?" said Cassie doubtfully.

"Lord love ye, girl. He and Leila were up to something when Peter arrived in Bristol. They couldn't get out of it and they didn't want to insult the new man Charles had brought along, thinking he'd be useful. So, they sent me along to *entertain* him. He was sweet . . . he didn't realize what me . . . er . . . occupation was. Thought he had seduced me, ye see, poor boy. 'Twas in his sleep he said a few things that made me suspicious . . ."

"I see," said Cassie thoughtfully. "How could you have been so thick-headed as to come to *this* place? I mean, really, Nancy . . . you must have realized it was a trap!"

"Lord love ye, didn't think on that end of it. Ye see, I had me a girl, a bonnie lass . . . Irish child she was. Took to her right off for the wee bairn was frightened of the men. Well, never mind it . . . two days ago, Leila comes for her saying as Nathan sold her to some lord for a week's fooling. It happens in our line, but . . . well, then I got this note from her saying how this lord wasn't satisfied with her and left her here with no means. I was sure it was her writing. Mayhap they made her write it. I jest couldn't leave the doll . . . now could I?

Cassie looked at her rather dubiously. " 'Tis rather heartwarming for a woman who turned in a young man to his death!"

"Lookee 'ere! I didn't know they was going to kill the lad. Thought when I took him out that night, they was but going to give him a beating, to scare him off . . . Ye see, I saw him writing things down one evening—knew he was a pound-dealer—had to tell the Asbatols. But I swear I didn't know they would kill the lad—they never let on they would put him out!" returned Nancy.

"It's true, she didn't know, but may I inquire what such tales matter to you, madam?" demanded Nathan as he entered the room.

Cassie spun round to stare at Nathan Asbatol for the first time. She was instantly repelled by his dark, beady eyes. His wicked soul permeated his being and gave off a shock, and Cassie was sensitive to it at once. He had no pity, this man, no honor—there would be no mercy.

"Now, madam, kindly tell me your name and what you are doing here," said Nathan as neither woman had chosen to speak after his entrance.

"I am here because your henchmen chose to put me here. Perhaps *you* can answer why," said Cassie.

"Your name, please!" snapped Nathan.

"Go on, little bird, give it to him . . . it should set him on his ears!" laughed Nancy. "Eh, Nathan, ye'll have a bit of explaining to do to that partner ye took on . . . this 'ere is his lady!"

Cassie had no way of stopping her. Something was wrong. She had known the moment Nathan walked in that Kirkby's plan must have gone awry. According to the design of things Nathan should now have been in custody. Where then was Kirkby? Oh God, was Kirkby all right?

Nathan looked astonished for but a fraction of a moment before he let out a long laugh. "Well, well, Lady Welford! 'Tis an honor!" with which he gave over to mirth once again.

The viscount had after some effort located Nancina's. It was richly furnished in red velvet and gold spangles, and he had but a few minutes' wait before a young woman came out to greet him. She was scantily garbed in blue silk, and her light brown curls cascaded over white shoulders. She was certainly no more than sixteen, but she had the look of twenty-five.

"Well now, m'fine blade, what may we be doing fer ye?"

"Some information, if you please. I should like to find Nathan Asbatol."

The girl grinned broadly. "Lord love ye . . . he won't please ye the way we could, but if that's what ye want, sure now I'd be that delighted to tell ye what I know . . . but, we don't *give* nought away here."

He smiled. "Of course not," taking out a coin, "But I already have his home address. What I want is another place he might go to when it is not convenient for him to stay at home."

The girl frowned. "Aw now, only Nancy would know that . . . and she has gone out!"

"Has she?" said the viscount, one expressive brow going up. He found this particularly interesting. Perhaps this Nancy had gone to meet the Asbatols. He slid the gold coin toward the girl's hand and she took it up eagerly. "Where has she gone, this Nancy?"

"She didn't say . . . but I did hear her complaining how she hated going down to the west docks . . . sorry, that's all I know."

He tipped his hat to her and as he left, she sighed and called out. "Lookee now, if ye have it in mind fer me to earn this coin, come on back and I'd be happy to . . ."

But he had no time to muse over this, he was already on his horse and making for the docks. It was an almost impossible gamble, for the docks held scores of buildings. He couldn't possibly go through all of them to find Nathan, but he would have to try.

Leila, her nose hidden behind a scented handkerchief, entered the room and raised her brow to find her husband laughing. Then she turned and saw Cassie. "Who the deuce is this mort?"

"Why, Leila . . . the viscount not only betrayed us, he allowed me to get the better of him in more ways than one. He has sent us his bride to hold hostage over his head!"

Cassie gasped. "Kirkby . . . what have you done to Kirkby?"

Leila felt an overwhelming sense of irrational jealousy as she gazed at Cassandra, and she spat at her, "Shut up!"

Her husband was more affable. "Unfortunately, very little. He has by now recovered and will be searching Liverpool for us. Therefore, we will have no choice but to let you accompany us . . . after we dispose of Nancy here."

"You don't mean to harm her? I am witness to it if you do!" returned Cassie at once.

"Really? You think it matters. We hold you hostage, yes, but the viscount will never see you again, nor will you

441

live to tell what you saw," returned Leila, moving toward Cassie and giving her a yank of her hair.

Cassie let go her hand, landing the woman a resounding slap across the cheek that sent Leila reeling sidewise. "Why, you little doxy! I'll make certain you suffer for that!" cried Leila.

"Go to the devil!" said Cassie far more bravely than she felt. "Kirkby will see you there himself . . . and before this day is out!"

"Leila, never mind her," snapped her husband. He turned to Nancy who was watching all this, a calculating glint in her eyes. "Are you prepared to hand over that letter of Eaton's."

"No, ye get that . . . and away wit me. I'm not daft, Nathan."

"Very well, you leave me no choice," he sighed. "I have made arrangements for you to take a little trip to South Africa. I am told they pay very high prices for white women with fair hair . . ."

"You wouldn't dare!" screeched Nancy.

"By the time your girls, that is, if they have the letter, think to use it . . . Leila and I will be in a new land . . . quite out of reach."

"You are both despicable! But it will never work. You don't really think you can ship off a woman with no one the wiser?" gasped Cassie.

"I think I can ship off *two* women with no one the wiser!" retorted Nathan. "Do you think this is a first with me? *Do you?* I am well acquainted in the white slave trade. I expect no trouble."

The street urchin walked Starfire up and down the street wearily. He rested at intervals, but he was getting restless and wondering why the pretty lady had not come out of that old building. He had seen an ugly man, followed by a yellow-haired mort go in, but no one was coming out, and he found the entire thing most strange. However, he was a street child and had long ago learned to keep things to himself and not to get involved in things that did not concern him. He held onto the reins and sighed.

The viscount arrived at the west docks and began a systematic search. He inquired of the corner beggars after Nathan, after Leila, giving out their descriptions, and was receiving negatives one after the other until he looked up and saw Starfire. He frowned a moment, wondering if he could be mistaken . . . and then began making strides toward the horse. His heart beat furiously, what did this mean? Why was Cassie's horse here? What had occurred? He reached the boy and brought out a coin, but he felt his hand begin to tremble. "Tell me, lad . . . who gave you this horse to walk?"

"A lady . . . said her name was Welford. Over two hours ago it was. Promised me a handsome fee if I was to care for her horse, but she never come out . . . nor did those others that went after."

"Which building was it, boy?" snapped the viscount impatiently.

He pointed to the building in question. "Dunno why anyone that fine would go in there."

"Never mind that now. Listen to me, lad. You are to go fetch the constable. Ride this horse to him and tell him Lord Welford requests his presence immediately! Do you understand?" said the viscount, placing the coin in the boy's hand. "You will be amply rewarded upon your return with the constable."

"Aye," said the boy, well pleased.

"Now hurry!" said the viscount, already on his way toward the two-story structure. Cassie . . . in there . . . ? Why? The wood planking creaked beneath his steps as he stalked the long corridor, and the two men slumped against the wall at its end looked up. The viscount thought quickly, for even in the dimness of the light, he could tell these were but street beggars. He pulled out his leather purse and dangled it. The men looked at each other and then at him before one of them leered. They meandered down the hall towards the viscount. "This is for you, there is well over a hundred pounds . . . the constables will soon be here . . . I think it best if you were to take it and disappear." The two men glanced at one another and found the viscount's suggestion met with their definite approbation. The "guv" they had recently been taking orders from had been both harsh and stingy. They grabbed for the purse, argued between themselves who should hold it, and were gone from the viscount's vision.

Kirkby stood a moment at the door, listening. His pistol was held well and cocked. He heard Cassie's voice. Somehow they had tricked her here. He heard Nathan's hard tones, and knew himself correct in his assumptions. He stepped back and gave his heel to the weak-hinged door in a strong wild thrust. It went flying open and he stepped in, his gun aimed at Nathan's head.

Cassie shrieked with happiness but just as she rushed to the viscount's side, Leila grabbed hold of her arm and shoved a small lady's pistol into her waist. Nathan made for his own concealed weapon, but the viscount was upon him, shoving him into the wall hard as he drew out Nathan's gun and flung it out of reach. There they stood all at bay.

"Leila, let my wife go . . . it will run the worse for you if you do anything foolish!" said the viscount slowly, cautiously. He felt his heart in his throat.

Nancy watched speculatively, wondering how best to save herself.

Leila hissed, her eyes hard beads. "One move from you, my fancy lord, one move—and your little doxy is dead!"

Cassie had an idea, but she would have to be careful, unobtrusive. Quietly, she slipped off a shoe, slowly, precisely she aligned it just so. She would have to wait for the right moment, but her heart beat so wickedly hard, she was sure Asbatol would hear, would guess her intentions.

"Good girl!" called Nathan, "Tell this double-dealing bastard to release me, and we'll . . ."

"No, Nathan. You are going nowhere with my wife!" snapped the viscount. "I believe if you consider the situation you will find that your Leila cares very little whether or not *you* escape. She cares only for her own neck—

which would have a much greater chance without you!" He saw Nathan make a threatening move toward Cassie, and his voice came wildly. "Bend your knee and you are a dead man! I promise you! Leila wouldn't give a fig, and she wouldn't retaliate at this juncture, for she is smart enough to realize it would seal her fate!"

"He is right, you know," agreed Leila. "I can't afford to go on with you, Nathan. I have just enough cash to set myself up, and I don't mean to take any more chances. The viscount can do what he likes with you," she said, starting to inch round, pulling Cassie along backward with her. But Cassie had maneuvered her half-boot just so, and when Leila stepped back toward her, she stumbled and was thrown off balance for just a moment. However, it was enough for Cassie to tear away. Cassie went forward and down simultaneously. Nancy ran toward the door, and Leila's gun went off . . .

Epilogue

A month later, the tryst at St. Peter's Field was hailed by most of the aristocracy as just the sort of action the devil agitators needed to set them back on their heels. The Prince Regent was commended for the cavalry action, and Lord Sidmouth was inclined to feel pleased with himself. As to the people, they had lost both the Orator Hunt and Sam Bamford to prison where these two peaceable reformers were to serve the next two years. Such were the times. Still, the rabble went on with their meets, still they drilled on the moors at night, and there were rumors and reports that the purchase of pistols had gone up considerably.

Nancy recovered from her wound, and appeared as a witness for the Crown in their case against Leila and Nathan Asbatol. For Nancy's cooperation in the matter, she was allowed to proceed on her way. Nathan was deemed a very bad fellow and sentenced to hang. His wife appeared to the all-male jury a woman much put upon, and although the judges heard testimony from Viscount Welford declaring this to be a very inaccurate picture, it was their considered opinion she had little to do with her husband's dealings, other than keeping silent—and really, they asked one another, what could a wife do but protect her mate? She was tried and found not guilty.

Of Mary Beth and Guy Bamfield? Unfortunately, her family disowned her for her waywardness. Guy felt this to be no great loss and proceeded to keep his wife busy with such things as babies, while he continued to fight for the causes of humanity!

Of Lyle Stanton? An opportunist ever, he went into the streets that fateful night, bleeding, broken, and nearly defeated when he caught the eye of a lady. He felt her watching him from her carriage across the street. He looked up and managed one of his smiles. It was all that was needed. She was out of her coach in a trice and at his side. Poor soldier, cried she! As it turned out, she was a lonely widow, about to depart for the United States where her husband had died building up a shipping empire. She needed a man's protection . . .

The dowager Welford? She became quickly cognizant of the facts relating to her son's death. It was not very difficult for her to admit her mistake and welcome her daughter-in-law. Cassie held no grudge, and soon all London opened its bright arms to Cassandra, Viscountess Welford. It was a fascinating life, but after a while she began to long for the peace and loveliness of Farrington Grange. With the knowledge she had gained regarding her husband's activities, she learned of his comfortable wealth and persuaded him that the Grange was a worthy cause. It would, she reasoned, pay for itself once it was set back in order. He chuckled, for there was little he could refuse her and off they went to the country.

Scooping his wife into his arms, he carried her up the staircase before the bright eyes of her servants (who were heard to sigh contentedly) and into their bedroom. However, upon entering this chamber, they discovered there a large weathered tub. It was, of course, a brandy tub and one that had never seen a customs house. Resting on its top was a folded notepaper, somewhat soiled and smelling of salt. Cassie took it up and read aloud:

M' darlin's!
It came to me mind that I never bumped ye with a wedding gift, and I hear tell, 'tis in order, seein' as the thing took! So here it be, with all me good wishes. And Cassie lass, if ever it do turn sour . . . and ye itch for a ride on a smuggler's sloop . . . jest give me a holler!

Jack Rattenbury

The viscount grinned over her shoulder as he read this, but he turned his wife to him and held her waist in his large, strong hands. She laughed happily, pressing herself against his solid frame and gazing into his burning, black eyes. Her voice was almost fierce with its intensity. "It will never, *never* go sour! I promise you, Kirkby Welford!"

"That's the truth. Now kiss me, vixen, for I love you," he whispered, softly folding her deep into his embrace.